THE QUEEN OF THE PLATFORM

A NOVEL OF WOMEN'S RIGHTS ACTIVIST ERNESTINE ROSE

SUSAN HIGGINBOTHAM

ONSLOW PRESS

A Note on Usage

Ernestine Rose and her fellow activists generally used the term "woman's rights" where we would use "women's rights." As they got there first, I have followed their lead.

CONTENTS

Prologue

January 1892

When there is little to do but wait for one's death, one might as well write of one's life.

Age and infirmity have sunk their teeth into me, and although it is not in my nature to give in, I must concede they have the better of the fight, now that I am in my eighties (I need not dwell on how far). These days, my principal activity is my daily excursion in my Bath chair. A strong man pushes me patiently about Kensington Gardens so that I can admire its beauties, watch the people passing through, and, if truth must be told, fall into a pleasant doze. Then we head back to my lodgings on St. Petersburgh Place in Bayswater, where I can read the day's newspapers—an increasingly depressing task, not so much for the state of the news but for the probability that I will see yet another death notice of a dear friend. After that, I might read a book from the circulating library. And then there is my attendant Miss Byrne's pretty caged bird to watch. I have taught it to eat from my palm, for I am not in my dotage and I understand perfectly well that Miss Byrne bought it not for herself, as she claimed, but for me.

So those are my days. If I live to see the summer, which I rather hope I will not, I will fill them in much the same manner, except that I will be wheeled about Brighton to admire the sea. No one looking at me, a frail old lady in a Bath chair, would guess that in my prime, I traveled from country to country, across the Channel and across the Atlantic, in all seasons and in all terrains, by sleigh and by train, by boat and by coach.

But in my decline I need some occupation, so I have decided to write my story. I will probably burn it, as it really is no one's business but my own, but whatever the irksome state of my body, my mind is still sharp and clear (if prone to the occasional slip), so I may as well exert it. It will allow me the opportunity for reflection, which is generally agreed to be a good thing, and perhaps I will recall some things that have blurred over time. Miss Byrne has bought me a lovely stack of paper, a good pen, and a quantity of ink, so there is nothing left to do but to seat myself at the secretary, beneath the painting of my dear one, and begin to write. No doubt I will make mistakes; though I have been speaking and writing English for well over half a century, the language is still not a reliable friend to me and will trip me up on occasion. Yet it has been years since I have spoken, much less written, the languages of my youth—Yiddish and Polish—and I doubt I could manage either. I have not had the opportunity to use them in a very long time.

If Miss Byrne peeks, so be it. But I don't think she will. Still, I may drop into German here and there in recounting the more foolish moments of my history. An old woman has her pride.

So where to start? I ponder it, but not for long, for there seems to be only one logical place: in Piotrków Trybunalski, Poland, then—and now—under the heel of the Russian czar.

1

MAY 1813

Everyone in my family was angry with one another, and it was my fault.

I had not meant to upset anyone. I had only asked Mama whether she might have another baby, because I thought that would make her feel better about little Jacob. Why, our neighbor had lost a child a while back, and Mama herself had remarked just a few weeks before how she was almost her old gossipy self now that she had a new baby. Mama had caught me listening and told me not to tell anyone what I had heard. I had promised her, although the wink Mama had given me told me that she was not all that put out with me. Mama loved to laugh, and the follies of our neighbors amused her.

But that was when little Jacob was alive. My question had made Mama cry, and Aunt Rachel, who was Papa's widowed sister, had boxed my ears. That had made Mama and Papa angry at Aunt Rachel, who said that they spoiled me and that she had come all the way from Warsaw to help and that she had a good mind to go back. Sosia, my older sister, who was Aunt Rachel's favorite, had started crying at that. Finally, Papa had taken me into another room and told me that he knew I meant no harm, but the midwife had told Mama when Jacob was born that it would be dangerous to have another baby and that I must not ever bring up the subject again. Then he had told me to go outside and play with my friends. But I had not really felt like playing, so instead I decided to have a little adventure—to go to Piotrków's market square and look around. It was not far away at all.

I had been as sad as anyone else when Jacob died, even though I had been a little jealous of him while he lived. What fuss there had been at his birth! No girl baby in Piotrków ever prompted that sort of celebration, though I had surmised that the circumcision could not have been pleasant from the way he squalled. But having been the youngest for many years, I enjoyed the novelty of having a baby around the house and loved to tickle his fat little feet and make him giggle. I had looked forward to helping him with the Torah, and thought that if he studied the Talmud perhaps I could study with him. Aunt Rachel, who had been on one of her visits when he was born, had rolled her eyes when I said that. "How far are you going to let that nonsense go, Nathan?" she asked my father. "What man wants to come home to a wife with her nose in the Talmud?"

"What can I do? She reads everything she finds. At least she's reading the Torah instead of some silly novel."

Knowing that Aunt Rachel liked the occasional novel—indeed, when she was in good humor, she had been known to let me peek at hers—I smiled at the memory. My walk was already improving my spirits.

I passed by the town's old castle—really just a tower, and hardly impressive compared to the fortresses I would later see—and after crossing the bridge over the Strawa River soon arrived at the town square. It was not a market day. Had it been, my adventure would have probably ended quickly, as someone from the Jewish quarter would likely have spotted me straightaway. In truth, to an adult, the town must have looked quite shabby, and even I noticed some boarded-up shops and a few beggars, some of whom were quite young men and were missing eyes, arms, and legs. For the past few years, our part of Poland, known as the Duchy of Warsaw, had been under French control, but the upheaval of the previous year, occasioned by Napoleon's disastrous invasion of Russia and his ensuing retreat (it was a point of pride in the Jewish quarter that Napoleon had somehow found the time to visit our very pretty synagogue), had left the Russians in charge and Piotrków's economy in shambles. But I had been in this part of town only a couple of times, and always with an adult, so there was plenty to interest me even if the city was a little tattered.

For a while, I ambled about, admiring the stately buildings and stopping once at a confectioner's to spend the little pocket money I carried. The man behind the counter looked at me peculiarly, but he sold me my little cake, which I took outside to nibble. My walking and munching took me to Piotrków's Bernardine church, a magnificent edifice attached to a monastery. I was walking around it, daring myself to go inside and explore, when I saw the painting on the wall.

No one could have missed it. It was in lurid colors—it must have been touched up regularly—and showed a pretty blond boy in old-fashioned clothing having his throat slit by a bearded man, whom I quickly recognized as a rabbi, as my father dressed similarly. Surrounding the rabbi and his prey were a crowd of men, although their features were so grotesque they hardly looked human.

As I stared at the painting, trying to figure out what it all meant, I felt myself being stared at. I turned to see a woman standing beside me. She was holding a broom; presumably she either swept the nearby streets or was employed as a char-woman at the church. "What is this?" I asked politely.

"Don't you know?"

"If I did, I wouldn't ask." Sometimes I thought that the intelligence of adults was overrated.

"You're from the Jew quarter. Aren't you?" When I nodded, thinking this was a rather rude way to put it, she continued. "Your people killed Christ, and they killed this boy to drink his blood on Passover. Or to use in their bread. That's what this is."

I reviewed my family's Passovers—a great deal of baking and cleaning, with which I had to help, followed by a feast, but no Christian blood and certainly no slitting of throats. "We don't do anything like that. We have wine. I got a sip this year."

"Are you calling me a liar, girl?"

"It is a lie! We don't do that!"

The woman brandished her broom. "Away with you!"

Having decided that the woman was crazy, I obeyed and hastened in the direction of the square. My adventure had lost its allure, and I sat down wearily on a bench in the market area with the notion of resting a little before heading back to the Jewish quarter and the comfort of home. But I had scarcely sat down when someone cried, "There she is!"

A group of boys, wearing school uniforms, stood by me. "You there!"

"Good day," I said, and began to walk away, but the boys, who were probably about two or three years older than me—I was seven—planted themselves in my path.

"Where do you think you're going?"

"Home."

"You're not going anywhere." A boy grabbed my arm, twisting it so that I yelped in pain. "Why don't we slit your throat, Yid, and drink your blood, like you people do?"

"Throw her in the well!"

"Or the river."

"To the river!"

With all my strength, I wrenched myself free and started to run, but I was surrounded. What could I do? Aside from being outnumbered and outsized, I had not the faintest idea of how to fight, my education having been sadly deficient on that score. I looked around for something with which to defend myself and could only find a chunk of stone. Just as I was about to hurl it, someone seized my hand. "Off, you louts! Picking on a little girl. You ought to be ashamed of yourselves."

"We weren't going to hurt her."

"She was going to hurt us!"

"We only wanted to scare her. She's just a Yid."

My rescuer stared at them with the contempt they deserved. "Off with you, you brats!" My knowledge of Polish did not encompass what he said after that, but it made an impression upon the boys, who scurried off, whimpering.

The man looked down at me as I released the stone. "What's your name, little miss?"

"Esther—Esther Züssmund," I stammered. Suddenly, it all became too much for me—the nasty woman, the taunting boys, the knowledge that I was probably in trouble at home, the gentleness with which I was being questioned now. "I want to go home!" I wailed, and started bawling.

"No doubt. What does your father do?"

"He's—he's the rabbi."

"Oh, I've seen him about. He should be easy to find." The man patted my shoulder. "Come with me. I'll lock up my shop, and then I'll take you back to your people."

I obeyed and followed the man into his shop. He handed me a handkerchief and disappeared into the back as I struggled to compose myself. Finally, I wiped the last of my tears away, and for the first time took note of my surroundings.

What paradise had I stumbled into? Everywhere around me were books, mainly in Polish but a few in Russian, reflecting our current overlords. We had a bookstore in the Jewish quarter, of course, but it had only a handful of Polish-language books, and certainly not the book that caught my eye now. "George Washington!" I breathed.

As I reached for the book, a set of keys jangled, and my rescuer, wearing a hat now, reappeared. "What about George Washington, missy?"

"*The Life of George Washington* by Parson Weems. Oh, I would love to read that!"

The bookseller squinted at me. "You can read Polish, little missy?"

"Yes."

"And you know who George Washington was?"

"He is my favorite American patriot."

"Well." The bookseller plucked the book off the shelf. "Tell you what, missy. If your father approves, you can have the book."

"Oh, thank you! But everyone at home is probably angry at me."

"More worried than angry, I imagine." The bookseller ushered me out the door and locked up. "What made you wander off?"

"I shouldn't have, but it's been so lonely at home, and I just wanted to get away." I dabbed at my eye. "My brother died a couple of weeks ago. We've sat *shiva*, but everyone's still so sad. He was the only boy in the family." I brightened. "Maybe no one's even noticed I've gone."

"I very much doubt that. But tell me about the American patriots."

I obliged as we headed toward the Jewish quarter, my troubles almost forgotten as I recited everything I knew about George Washington and (for good measure) Thomas Jefferson, which admittedly was not much. I was expounding on the Declaration of Independence when I heard a familiar voice cry, "Esther!"

"Mama!"

My mother, who usually moved at a stately pace, dashed toward me as fast as I dashed toward her. She scooped me up and covered me with kisses and tears. "Where were you, my darling?"

"Looking around."

Mama released me, and I saw that she was at the forefront of a group of women, some smiling, some glaring at me, some looking with trepidation at the bookseller. He advanced and doffed his hat. "Your little girl wandered into the market square, madam, so I took it upon myself to see her safely home."

"I thank you." For the first time since our reunion, Mama frowned at me. "The entire quarter is searching for you, Esther. We will have a little talk about this when we get home. I am sorry to have caused you trouble, sir."

"No trouble. We had quite a nice chat about George Washington."

"And Thomas Jefferson," I added.

"I have to tell you that she was being harassed by a group of boys when I came across her. They are quite capable of being vicious to Jewish people, as you probably know. I wish it were not still true, but it is."

"I well know it." Mama shook her head. "That is something else we must talk about, Esther."

The man held out the book. "This caught your daughter's eye. I told her that if your husband approved—or you—she might have it."

"That is very kind of you. George Washington? Ah, yes, the child is mad for America." Mama nodded down at me. "You may have the book, Esther."

I needed no prompting from Mama to thank the bookseller profusely.

"I heard from your daughter that you had lost a son. Please accept my condolences."

Mama sighed. "At least I don't have two to bury now." She scowled at me, but I was too engrossed in examining my new book to care.

We said goodbye to my kind friend and soon met up with the other search parties, including two led by my father and Aunt Rachel, the latter of whom dissolved into tears upon seeing me safe. Everyone agreed that I was due for a scolding, but that it could wait. But my questions could not. As I sat snuggled between Mama and Papa that evening, I asked, "What does that painting mean? The one on the church with the little boy?"

"That vile thing," Aunt Rachel muttered.

My father sighed. "I do not want to have to tell you this at your age, but you must know. It is called the blood libel. Jews have been accused for centuries of killing Christian children and using their blood for our rituals, such as baking our Passover bread. Sometimes we are accused of poisoning wells, too."

"All lies," Mama put in. She stroked my black curls.

"All lies. But people believe them, and the churches sometimes encourage them. As the church here does with that painting. The Prussians took it down when they controlled

Poland, and the French kept it down, but when the French left, the painting came right back up. We have asked the church to remove it, but to no avail. It is not only untrue, it is dangerous. People have been killed by mobs because of these lies. If a Christian child goes missing—"

"As you did," Sosia put in.

"Sorry," I mumbled.

"If a Christian child goes missing, suspicion falls first on us, even if there are half a dozen more logical explanations. And if the child is found dead . . ."

I shuddered.

"I don't want to scare you; it does not happen often. But that is what the painting means. And that is why you should not go outside the Jewish quarter alone. There are people who believe everything they are told about us."

I frowned. "But shouldn't people think for themselves, instead of believing what someone tells them to?"

"They should. But it is easier for some people not to. Particularly if they are unhappy or oppressed and need someone to blame their troubles on."

"So instead of blaming the men who made war and made them poor, they can blame us."

My father stared at me, as did Aunt Rachel. "The child's no fool, I'll give her that," she said after a moment or two. "You could do worse than let her study with you, I suppose."

"Much worse." Papa patted my head. "But come, it is time for bed."

Though I was normally wont to put up a protest, I felt that I had caused enough ruckus for the day and obeyed. I had said nothing about the woman or the boys, as my nature was to keep things to myself, but Mama knew me better than anyone in the world. "Would you like me to sleep with you tonight, Esther?"

"Yes."

With my new book in my hand, I curled up next to Mama as Sosia, relegated to the truckle bed that was usually mine, pulled it out with a great clatter. Thus comfortably situated, I could think about my eventful day with only a twinge of sadness. Instead, I made a vow as I drifted off to sleep. I would never accept blindly what I was told; that was the path of fools like the ones I had encountered today.

I would question everything.

2

SEPTEMBER 1822
TO JANUARY 1823

"I haven't seen you in my store in a while, Miss Züssmund."

My kind friend the bookseller had gray hair, and I had grown womanly, but otherwise his store looked much the same as it had nine years before. "I was visiting my married sister in Breslau. She had a little girl a few months ago."

"Ah, I thought you might have gotten married yourself. Aren't Jewish girls of your age generally betrothed by now?"

"Some, but not me." I gave an airy shrug. "I am more than happy to wait. Marriage would interfere with my studies."

"I see your studies are in German now."

"Yes. I improved my spoken German in Breslau, and now I must learn to read it better."

The bookseller handed me my purchase—*The Sorrows of Young Werther*—and I set off for home. Having passed through Christendom safely, I found my father waiting for me. "Once you put away your things, come to the study. We must talk."

I wondered why the parlor would not do, but I quickly obeyed. I moved to sit in my usual seat—where my father's pupils sat, and where I had sat as well before my heretical opinions disqualified me. "No, sit here." He indicated an upholstered chair that usually had a pile of books stacked upon it. Clearly, their removal signaled a momentous occasion.

The chair was even more comfortable than it looked. As I settled into it, Papa cleared his throat. "Esther, you will be seventeen in January."

"The thirteenth," I said. Papa hardly needed reminding of the date, but if he was going to state the obvious, I supposed I could too.

"More than old enough to marry. I have contracted a marriage for you."

"Marriage? I was not looking to marry."

"I am surprised you do not ask about the man. You know him, of course. Saul Levinsky." Not receiving any response, he added, "The furrier."

"I know who he is."

"Most young women would be pleased with such a husband. He is pious, successful, and if I may be a judge, handsome."

"All those things may be true, Papa, but I will not marry him."

"And why not?" My father peered over his spectacles. "He is only in his twenties. I could see your opposition if he were an older man, or a widower with children, but that is not the case."

"He can be old or young, with no children or a pack of them. I will not marry him."

"I do not understand this. He has an unblemished character, and everyone speaks well of him. He has a good temper; I would not match you with someone I did not think would treat you kindly. I may add that he is eager for the match, and was not at all unreasonable about your dowry."

My father frowned. "You do not fancy yourself in love with someone, do you?"

"No. This has nothing to do with anyone else, not even Mr. Levinsky. It is simply that I refuse to be the object of a bargain. If I marry, it will be to a man of my own choosing, on my own terms."

"What on earth have you been reading, girl?"

"Many things, but I do not need to read to know what injustice is. It is unjust for women to be traded like cattle. We are rational human beings and should be treated as such."

"Traded like cattle! You are intelligent, Esther, but in some ways you are a silly child. I am marrying you to a good man who will treat you well and keep you in comfort. It is what every father should do for his daughter. Surely you do not expect to be a spinster."

"I would prefer that to marrying a man I do not love."

"Love." For the first time, my father smiled. "My dear, love is something married people grow into. You know I loved your mother dearly, but I hardly knew her before we married. If that is your chief objection, you have nothing to fear. You are a charming young woman, and I have no doubt that Mr. Levinsky will cherish you. And you will come to love him."

"No, because I would always resent being pushed into a marriage I did not want. Would Mr. Levinsky enter into such a contract against his will? I think not. It should be no different for me." I leaned forward in my chair. "You said it was your duty to make a good marriage for me. I disagree. You have done your duty. You gave me a good education, you taught me to think and to question. Through that you gave me the means to support myself, if it ever becomes necessary. That is all you owe to me."

"Yet you owe a duty to me, daughter. The duty of obedience."

"I do not defy you for the sake of defiance, Papa. Surely you know that. I have been obedient to you in most things."

"*Most* things."

No doubt this was an allusion to my recent refusal to attend synagogue. I had pointed out that since we women were required to sit apart from men, out of their view, so as not to distract them from their prayer, my not being in the building at all would be even more conducive to their prayers, but this perfectly logical argument had not been well received. This, however, was not the time to renew it.

"I will continue to be obedient in most things. But I cannot give in on this point. I think this custom of arranging marriages outworn and cruel, and I will not be a part of it. If you turn me out on my ear, so be it, but I will not marry any man who is not my own choice. And does not the Talmud require that both parties to a marriage enter into the contract of their own free will? I admit that it is somewhat inconsistent for me to rely on it, but it must be mentioned."

My father sat in silence. To avoid staring at him, I fixed my eyes on the mantle clock. Finally, he said, "I suppose I should have known this would not be easy, even though for nearly any other girl in the town, it would have been a simple thing. You do not accept the religion of our fathers; why should I have thought you would accept marriage? What shall I do with you?"

"You don't need to do anything with me. Just let me stay as I am, keeping your house. You know I do it well."

My father stared at the wall gloomily as I patiently sat back in my chair, my hands folded.

I did not fear my father, which is not to say I did not respect him. He had never been harsh to me; I could not remember him ever striking me. It was because I respected him, and loved him, that I dared to oppose him. Had I feared him, I would have agreed to this marriage, then packed my belongings and slipped away in the night.

"I will break the contract," he said finally. "You are a foolish girl, but I will not force you into marriage. It is true about the Talmud, but more so, it would have distressed your dear mother. She indulged you a great deal. A great deal too much, I fear."

It was humbling to think that all my pleadings had probably not swayed my father—only his love for my late mother, who had died the year before. How I missed her! I doubted this conversation would have taken place had she been alive, for she understood me like no one else did and would have never arranged a marriage behind my back. I leaned over and kissed my father's cheek. "Thank you, Papa."

My father grumbled something, and I hurried off to set the table for supper. It was a somewhat silent one, and I was feeling guilty enough about my refusal that I wanted to lighten the atmosphere. "I will be writing to Sophie tomorrow," I said, referring to my older sister, who after marrying and moving to Breslau had adopted this German name. Too late, I reflected that Sophie had happily accepted the husband who had been picked for her (a rabbi, at that, and old enough to be her father and then some). "Is there anything you want me to mention to her?"

"Only that her sister is a foolish girl. I do not expect Mr. Levinsky to give up easily."

"I'm sure he will be reasonable," I said sunnily. "There are several other girls in Piotrków he would like. Like Liba." She was the prettiest young woman in Piotrków, and her father, a merchant, the most successful man. I thought she was silly, but my own observations, combined with my novel reading, had informed me that this was not necessarily something men minded. "I'm surprised he didn't try her first. Perhaps her father is aiming higher, maybe even for a man from Warsaw."

"It is unbecoming to speculate in this manner."

"I'm sorry, Papa." Clearly, my father had had enough of my charming conversation. It was altogether a relief when he retired to his study, and I—having helped our servant, Mina, clear the table—to my little chamber.

I should not, of course, have been surprised that I had been the subject of an offer. As even my Christian bookseller friend knew, it was the custom then, and most likely still is in Polish towns like ours, for Jewish fathers to arrange their daughters' marriages, and why should I have thought that things would go any differently with me? I was not too young to be married off, and as the daughter of a respected rabbi, with a little money of my own and what I was told was a pretty face, I was only too eligible. But I had thought I would be able to discern that an offer was being made for me, and it was disconcerting to realize that all of the negotiations behind my back had taken me unawares. Nonetheless, custom had not shaken the resolve I had formed some time ago, from my reading and my own consideration of the subject: that my husband, if I was to have one, must be of my own choosing. Perhaps I should have made this clear to my father earlier.

I was sorry to have disappointed him, of course, but what else could be done? In any case, what would he do without me making certain, as my mother had, that he had a well-run household so he could study in peace? Mina would have disturbed his books on many an occasion had I not promised her to see to the dusting of his study myself. He would soon realize that my refusal was perfectly sensible and the best for all parties concerned. Having resolved all this to my satisfaction, I settled at my desk with my book and my German dictionary.

~ ~ ~

What my father said to Mr. Levinsky I do not know, for my father did not speak of the matter, and I did not ask. I had feared my rejection of him would be noised about—not so much for my own sake as my father's, for I recognized that my rebellion put him in a difficult position—but Mr. Levinsky appeared to have kept quiet on the subject. No doubt he had a matchmaker looking for a more suitable bride. All had ended quite nicely, in my opinion.

A few weeks later, I came home from teaching some poor children their letters—an activity of which my father wholeheartedly approved, and which I enjoyed—to find my father in the parlor. "You are being taken to court by Mr. Levinsky. In Kalisz."

I stopped in the act of removing my bonnet. "Me?"

"I offered him a reasonable sum for breaking your marriage contract, but he was not satisfied with that. He wants your inheritance, and as all of it is in your name, he must take you to court."

"What does my inheritance have to do with this?"

"It was to be part of your dowry."

I sank down onto the sofa.

My maternal grandfather had been a wealthy man, and a very worldly one. It was to offset any displeasure his God might feel with him for this that he had chosen my father, of modest means but a promising young scholar, as a husband for his only daughter and supported him while he studied for the rabbinate. But while my mother had come to her marriage with a fine dowry, things had been arranged so that when she died, my sister and I each came into money of our own—not enough to make us rich, but certainly enough to keep us from want.

That is, unless it was given to our husbands.

"You promised him my inheritance?"

"He agreed to let you have a portion of it for yourself."

"How reasonable of him. And now he is suing for it?"

"In lieu of your marriage, yes. Of course, if you changed your mind—"

There were all sorts of things I wished to say to my father, but I decided against saying them. "I'm going to see Mr. Levinsky. Now." Before he could remonstrate, I was out the door.

I had been avoiding the street where Mr. Levinsky's shop was located, at considerable inconvenience to myself, as it was next to the bookstore I frequented when I didn't feel the need to cross to the Christian part of town. A friend or two tried to accost me, but I stomped on by and into Mr. Levinsky's store, where I rang the bell furiously until Mr. Levinsky appeared. His frown turned into a smile when he saw me. "Miss Züssmund."

"What on earth do you mean by taking me to court?"

"What on earth do you mean by refusing my perfectly reasonable offer for you?"

"I don't want to marry you. I don't want to marry anyone."

Mr. Levinsky stepped out from behind his counter. As Papa had said, he was a good-looking man, and not terribly old for me. I had been in his shop several times and liked him well enough, but that did not make me wish to be his wife. "Your muff looks as nice and fluffy as it did when I first sold it to you."

"It has held up very well. But—"

"Think of all the pretty things you'd have if you married me." He studied my pelisse. "My fur trimming, isn't it?"

"Mr. Levinsky, I am quite happy to pay you for your goods without the necessity of your having to marry me."

My would-be husband looked at me benevolently. "It's natural for you to be nervous about marriage. I don't blame you a bit."

"I am not nervous about marriage, sir. It is not a trip to the dentist. I simply do not wish to be married. I may someday, but not now, and I reserve the right to choose my own husband. My father meant well, I know, and I am sure you will make someone a fine husband, but you must look elsewhere."

"I don't want to look elsewhere. You were my first choice, and frankly, you were my only choice. If I can't have you, then I must have the benefit of my bargain. But all this unpleasantness could be avoided if you would see reason. What will you do if you don't marry?"

"There are any number of things a single woman with a little money of her own can do."

"But I will have your money, my dear."

"No, you shan't." I raised my chin. "I will see you in court, Mr. Levinsky."

~ ~ ~

In the normal course of things, this matter would have never reached the Polish courts; it would have been settled by a rabbinical council. Mr. Levinsky, however, had evidently felt such a tribunal would be biased in favor of my father, and because I thought it might be biased against me, I could not argue with his choice.

We were not due in court until the winter term, which started after the New Year. This was fortunate, because I needed to educate myself on the law as best I could. The proceeding would be conducted without lawyers on either side, but because Mr. Levinsky was in business, he had more legal knowledge than I. As for my father, he was of no use whatsoever in this dispute. He made it clear that he felt that Mr. Levinsky was in the right, and besides, he seemed strangely preoccupied. I thought it might be his health—in his younger days he had fasted a great deal, which had dismayed me when I saw him so pale and gaunt and our cupboard so full of good food—but he said he was perfectly fine. So I found a battered copy of the Napoleonic Code— although Napoleon no longer ruled Poland, his code still held sway—and made it my nightly reading. I soon reached two dismal conclusions, the first being that I did not have much of a case, and the second being that as a married woman, I would have only a few more rights than the cow in the dairyman's stall. Even if I had to impoverish myself in the process, I was determined to avoid this fate. But I would rather not impoverish myself, so I grimly studied on.

Since my sixteenth birthday, I had been receiving the interest of my inheritance, and as I had nothing to spend it on except for books and finery, I had sufficient funds at my disposal to get to Kalisz, about a hundred miles from Piotrków, and to lodge myself while my case pended.

I would be making the trip alone. "Although you won't accompany me, I hope you will give me your blessing," I said to Papa as the driver and his sleigh pulled into view.

"I wish you a safe journey and good health."

"No victory?"

"I believe the judge will see this as everyone else does. Child, has this not gone far enough? Agree to marry Mr. Levinsky, and you will be the mistress of his house, and a cherished one. He has even told me that he will not interfere with your reading. What more could you ask for?"

"A husband of my own choosing, whom I dearly love. I will settle for nothing less." With Mina's help, I gathered up my baggage and furs—all of Mr. Levinsky's supplying, which I admit was ironic, but it was freezing cold—and headed outside. "I will write you when I arrive there safely."

~ ~ ~

Anyone who takes pleasure in riding in a sleigh, I must say, has never traveled in such a conveyance out of necessity. Between the bitter cold, the howling wind, the occasional blinding snow, and the indifferent roads, our journey took several days. We often had to stop and change the horse, and I too needed to thaw out beside a fire. At night, I variously found myself squeezed in bed with my plump landlady, a mother and her two kicking little daughters, and a grumpy old widow. Everyone, of course, was curious as to my journey, as it was not then common for a girl of my age to be traveling alone. I simply stated that I was going to visit my sister, which was true insofar as I did have a sister.

Although I had allowed for ample time to get to the opening day of court—or so I thought—I had not reckoned on a particularly brutal snowstorm, which stranded us just a few miles outside of Kalisz. It cleared, however, the afternoon before court was to begin, and I had every hope of getting to the city in time to find a room for the night.

Then, as we were gliding along in the dusk, I heard a peculiar sound. Before I could form a word, the sleigh tilted crazily to one side, then to another, before somehow righting itself and coming to a dead stop.

My driver muttered a few Yiddish words with which I was not familiar, despite it being my first language, and then, having ascertained that I was unhurt, clambered out of the sleigh and began an inspection. It soon emerged that we were missing a few nails, which had caused some difficulty with the runner that could not simply be fixed with the application of a hammer. "We'll have to wait until the morning, miss. I'll need help."

"Please! Can't you get help now? I have to be at Kalisz at ten o'clock. Everything depends upon it."

"Miss—"

"I'll pay you for an extra day. An extra two days! Please! If I don't get there by ten, this entire journey will have been for nothing. I'll be penniless, or married. Or maybe both."

I had never acquainted my driver with the purpose of my journey—being from the countryside outside of Piotrków, he had not been privy to the gossip that had begun to swirl after Mr. Levinsky filed his lawsuit—but the money I pulled from my reticule, and perhaps the prospect of spending the evening listening to the wailings of a seventeen-year-old girl, convinced him to go in search of help. As I was ill-clad for riding the horse he unhitched and had never ridden one to begin with, he left me to wait in the sleigh, but first he handed me a pistol. "Robbers?" I asked, trying to keep the quaver out of my voice.

"Wolves."

And sure enough, soon I heard their howling. I have been in desolate places since then, but never have I felt so cold, so forlorn, and—yes—so terrified. I huddled under my furs and asked myself whether this was truly worth all of the trouble I was taking. Was there anything so terrible about being Mrs. Levinsky? I must confess that if my would-be husband had come upon me in his own sleigh, and had flashed his charming smile and offered me the seat next to his, I probably would not have refused, and might well have agreed to marry him out of sheer gratitude.

But the wolves kept their distance, and so did Mr. Levinsky and any other eligible Jewish men. Instead, my driver and another man appeared in the small hours of the morning, and I had to choke back a sob of relief when I caught sight of the pair. The latter took out his tools and quickly, if grumpily, repaired our sleigh while the driver helped and I held the lantern. In due time, we were on our way, and soon the sweet sight of Kalisz appeared.

Kalisz, the capital of our district of the Kingdom of Poland, was an ancient city, dating from Roman times. It sat near the Prussian border, and as a result was enjoying a period of prosperity, which showed in its new buildings. Among them was the courthouse, which looked both elegant and intimidating. There were some inns nearby, and bidding my driver farewell and paying him handsomely, I hastened to procure lodgings in one and make myself as seemly as I could with the hour of ten fast approaching. That being accomplished, I hurried into the courthouse and quickly discovered I had no earthly idea of where I was supposed to be, and none of the people bustling around had the slightest inclination to help me. After threading through a maze of corridors, I landed at the proper room, only to hear my name being intoned in Polish as I pushed on the heavy door. "Miss Esther Züssmund. Is Miss Esther Züssmund in the courtroom?"

"I am!" Lest the judges miss my presence, I waved my hand as I came through the door. Few, I am sure, have entered a courtroom with such exuberance.

The oldest of the judges frowned, but whether at my lateness or my gesture (or both) I did not know. Meekly, I took my place alongside a group of gloomy-looking people, whom I rightly supposed were also parties to cases. It was then that I spotted Mr. Levinsky. Evidently he had arrived with plenty of time to spare, for he looked well rested and self-satisfied, which was rather his usual state. He gave me a friendly nod, which I confusedly returned as one native of Piotrków to another.

I have no idea what dire consequences would have resulted had I not been present when I was called, but having satisfied itself of my existence, the court then was content to forget the great cause of *Levinsky v. Züssmund* for a week or so. Mr. Levinsky looked in each morning to see if our case was on the calendar, but I, terrified that something might transpire in my absence, attended the entire session each day. I did not consider the time spent in court unprofitable, for I observed closely the arguments that were presented, the reactions of the judges, and the demeanor of the litigants. Those who did best, I saw, were those who remained polite and respectful to the judges while not debasing themselves with cringing humility. It was something I would have to remember, as I had a tendency toward sharpness. When not in court, I studied my friend the Napoleonic Code, but I also took advantage of the well-stocked bookshop. It had a much better selection of German books than Piotrków, which was seeming more and more provincial every day.

At last, our case was called.

Mr. Levinsky, as the plaintiff, was called to the stand first. To my annoyance, he made a most sympathetic witness.

He had bargained with my father in the best of faith, and had had no reason to believe that I (here he turned his sad eyes upon me, then to the tribunal) would have any objections. He knew himself to be eligible, having had other men offer their daughters in marriage to him, but he had long had his heart set upon me. My father had been similarly pleased with the match, stipulating only that I reach the age of seventeen so as to guard against the dangers of early childbirth. (Here I was grateful to be sitting down, lest the court engage in a contemplation of my hips.) If I would only consent to the match, Mr. Levinsky said plaintively (or should I say plaintiffly?), he would dismiss the suit this very instant, and the whole affair would be an amusing story to tell our grandchildren.

So now we had grandchildren.

The judges proceeded to read the marriage contract, which they found unexceptionable. I had seen it only briefly, as my father kept it locked with his private papers and I had not been able to find the key. (I had certainly tried hard enough, mounting a full-on search when my father was at synagogue.) Something in its language made me frown, but before I could ponder the matter further I was called to the stand.

Having promised to tell the truth, I stated my name and age and confirmed that I was indeed my mother's co-heir. The preliminaries being over, the head judge said, "Is it true, Miss Züssmund, that you have refused to marry Mr. Levinsky?"

"It is. I was not consulted about this arrangement, and I cannot agree to it."

"Why? Is there something objectionable about Mr. Levinsky?"

"No. I know nothing ill of him; indeed, I am certain he will make some woman a good husband. But his not being objectionable is no reason to marry him. I could say the same about nine of ten men in Piotrków, I suppose, and yet I would not want to marry any of them. Well, maybe seven or eight out of ten."

The judge frowned at me over his spectacles. "Clarify something for me, miss. Is it not the custom of your people to arrange for their daughters' marriage, with a suitable dowry? It is the custom of many of us Poles as well, at least of the better classes."

"It is, Your Honor."

"So why should your case be any different?"

"To me, the worst argument that can be made is, 'This is how things have always been.' Custom should not be a chain upon us. With all due respect to the court," I added.

"Are you opposed to marriage?"

"No, Your Honor. Most people marry sooner or later, and I do not fancy myself different than most people. I simply want to choose the person whom I marry."

"Are you in love with someone?" He frowned at me. "A Christian man, perhaps?"

I had observed before that everyone thought Christian men were irresistible to womankind, at least to Jewish womankind. "No, Your Honor. Certainly not. I have not had sufficient acquaintance with any young man to fall in love with him."

The youngest of the judges smiled benevolently upon me. "Might you be a bit skittish of marriage, Miss Züssmund?"

"Horses are skittish, sir. With due respect to the court, I am not a horse."

"The court will take notice that Miss Züssmund is not a horse," the third judge said. Not unkindly, he asked, "Don't you trust your father to choose well for you? He is a rabbi, a learned man, is he not?"

"He is."

"Don't you think he has your best interests at heart? It is natural for a father to want to see his daughter married."

"I do."

"Has he ever been cruel to you? You are nicely dressed, and appear to have been far better educated than most girls your age. You do not have the manner of a girl who fears her father."

"He has not been cruel to me, and I do not fear him. I love him and respect both him and his judgment. In most matters, I would dutifully submit to his will. But I cannot concede to him the right to choose my husband for me."

"Even if it means the forfeiture of your inheritance? It is a considerable one."

"Even if it means the forfeiture of my inheritance. But it should not, because that would be unjust. The contract was made without my knowledge, and I have not consented to it. May I read the contract, Your Honor?"

"You may."

I read it once, twice. My memory of it had not been mistaken. "Your Honors, the Code tells us that even if a daughter has property in her own right—as I do—the dowry should be taken from the property of the settlers, which I understand to be the parents, unless it is stipulated otherwise. Am I correct?"

"You are."

"Then, Your Honors, this contract makes no such stipulation. It states the amount of my dowry, but it does not say its source. As I read it, my father was obligated to pay it out of his own funds. Everyone may have assumed that the money was from my inheritance, but this does not stipulate that it was."

"It is our intention that counts," Mr. Levinsky said. "We clearly intended that it come out of Miss Züssmund's inheritance."

"We will retire to consider this matter," the head judge said. "Would you like to be heard before we do?"

"I would, Your Honors." I rose. "Even if this contract was not inadequate—and it is—what satisfaction can Mr. Levinsky gain from possession of my dowry? He has said time and time again that if I agree to marry him, he will drop this case. It is me he wants. Is that not true, sir?"

"It is," Mr. Levinsky snapped. He waved his hand. "Well, look at her."

The court, thus bidden, looked at me, as did the spectators. Under these circumstances, honesty impels me to admit that at seventeen, I was a pleasing sight. Today I am wrinkled and skinny, with a dowager's hump that would, if I were supplied with two nephews, permit me to play the wicked Richard III on stage—but then my eyes were bright and alert, my features regular and smooth. The fashion of the day, molded closely to the body, proclaimed that my figure was well developed. My glossy black hair cascaded around my face in ringlets, of which I was quite vain; indeed, even today, as Miss Byrne would tell you if placed in the dock, I am still quite vain of my white ringlets, and will not take my chair ride unless they are just so.

"And if I may make another point, Mr. Levinsky has an opportunity to mitigate his damages. Although he cannot have me, he can find a bride with an equal or larger dowry, I am sure, if he looks afield. He cannot have two wives at a time. Should he be allowed to have two dowries at a time, then—and his bride as well? I think that would be most unjust."

"Anything else, Miss Züssmund?"

"Why, yes," I said. "There is the matter of equity. Equity, I believe, is a feature of the English common law, but the Civil Code gives it a slight nod. I did not consent to this contract. I did not even know of it until it had been signed. Should I pay, with what my dear mother left me, for something that was done entirely behind my back? And I will pay either way, if Your Honors uphold this contract, because if I do not marry Mr. Levinsky, all that is mine will be his, and if I do marry him, all that is mine will still be his. It would be most unjust."

"Anything *else*, miss?"

"No, sir. I believe I have covered my points."

"Then we will recess until two o'clock."

This was enough time for the court to decide our case and enjoy a pleasant meal, and enough time for me to return to my inn and take my own meal, which I could hardly taste for worry. Had my journey here been futile? How humiliating it would be to return to my father's house, defeated and penniless.

But I would at least not be tied to a man I did not love. With this bracing thought in mind, I trudged back through the slush to the court.

The courtroom was full, and as I pushed my way toward my defendant's seat, there was a murmur. Was it I, then, who was the attraction here? I folded my hands demurely and awaited the entry of the judges.

"Rise," a clerk called, and I obeyed. Despite my best efforts, I was trembling.

"The court has considered this case carefully," the head judge said. "While we believe that Mr. Levinsky has some cause for complaint, we cannot award him what he seeks, which is the young lady's hand. Nor is it just to force Miss Züssmund to forfeit her property for a contract to which she never consented. The young lady made a good argument for herself; it is almost a pity that she was not born a man. We find for the defendant. Case dismissed."

More stunned than elated, for the moment, I gathered my things together as Mr. Levinsky came forward and shook my hand. "I bear no grudge, miss. You were worth the fight. In all honesty, I don't think I could have taken your money if I'd won anyway."

"I wish the best for you, sir, and hope you will be happy."

"Oh, there's more fish in the sea. Have a safe journey home, Miss Züssmund."

He trotted off jauntily. As I shall not have another occasion to mention him, I may say that some years later, in Cincinnati, Ohio, I saw a shop sign reading *SAUL LEVINSKY & SON, FINE FURS* and could not resist the temptation to peek inside. There, behind the counter, stood a young man, clearly the son, while in a corner, a plumper, older version of my erstwhile suitor whistled as he pieced some pelts together. A handsome lady of my own age brushed a pelerine. "Think this will suit Mrs. Longworth? She's so fussy."

"It's beautiful, darling!" Although Mrs. Levinsky plainly hailed from the United States, Mr. Levinsky clearly was a child of Poland.

I smiled and walked away.

~ ~ ~

Made warmer by the satisfaction of my victory, my journey home was uneventful. Still, I was grateful when my sleigh pulled up before my house, one of the more substantial ones in our section of Piotrków. From the smoke rising from the chimney to the new curtains that graced the windows, all looked cozy and inviting.

New curtains? What had been wrong with our old ones? Mama had had them made shortly before she died. And what had gotten into Papa to replace them anyway? He liked a clean house, but I could have put up black curtains and he would not have noticed.

And who was playing our piano? It had been my mother's as a girl, and she had been adamant about taking it to her marriage, and about having my sister and I taught to play. I was but an indifferent player, but Sophie was fairly accomplished. Could she be visiting? Surely she would have told me?

As these thoughts whirled through my head, the piano ceased to play and Mina opened the door. "Welcome home, miss," she said somewhat hesitantly. Behind her stood my father—and Liba. She wore a *sheytl*—the wig that satisfied the requirement that a Jewish married woman cover her hair.

"You and Papa are—"

"Married," Papa said, kissing me on the cheek. "A week ago."

"*Mazel tov*," was all I could say.

3

JANUARY 1823 TO APRIL 1828

For someone who had scoffed at my desire to marry for love, my father was certainly besotted with his little bride. He still attended faithfully to his rabbinical duties, and he taught pupils, but instead of shutting himself up in his study in the evening, he sat in the parlor listening to Liba play and sing.

Even if Liba and I had been of temperaments to suit, and even if Papa had done me the courtesy of informing me of his intent to marry beforehand, our situation would have been difficult, but as it was, it was well-nigh unbearable to my seventeen-year-old self. Liba had her own recipes, her own ways of managing the house, her own tastes in furnishings—none of which I shared. Everything that could be repainted was repainted; everything that could be replaced with something newer was replaced. Only the furniture in my room was spared, and only because I raised a considerable fuss about the matter. Even our meals, though of course impeccably kosher, assumed a rather pretentious air. Only on one occasion when Liba was indisposed did I reintroduce one of my mother's recipes, previously my father's favorite, and Liba grumbled so much about it that I gave up and stowed my mother's receipt book away with all of my other precious things.

Then there was Liba's family—a large one, always coming in and out of our house now. Civility demanded that I be polite to them, and Liba demanded that I help entertain them. My only occupation, now that my reign as housekeeper was over, was my studies, and I could no longer pursue them in peace.

I realize now that I should not have begrudged my father his happiness. He was only fifty, not an age when a healthy man—or a healthy woman, I must say—wants to live a celibate life. Besides that, he sincerely grieved for my mother, and living with only the company of Mina and a rebellious daughter could not have been the most pleasant of existences. And, of course, there was the importance to the male heart of having a son and heir; although my mother had done her best, poor little Jacob had been the only result. Soon, it became clear that Liba might remedy this situation, or at least produce a more biddable daughter.

With all this in mind, I began to contemplate my future. There was no one in Piotrków I wanted to marry, and even if there had been, my successful foray into the law appeared to have scared off any potential suitors. Aunt Rachel in Warsaw would have taken me in, albeit grudgingly, but she had died soon after Mama. There seemed but one solution, with which I presented my father one evening when Liba was at her parents'. "Papa, I have a request. I would like to visit Sophie." She and her family had recently left Breslau for Berlin.

"For how long?"

"For as long as she wishes me to stay."

"Has she invited you?"

"Not in so many words, but I believe she would be pleased to have me there. She said as much in her last letter home. I can help her with her child if she wishes."

"You could help Liba."

"I would be more of a hindrance than a help, Papa, and you know it. Besides, she has her mother." (That was a bit of an understatement. Since Liba's pregnancy had become obvious, Liba's mother had spent more time at our house than her own.)

"Yes. Well, I see no harm in it, as there seems nothing that suits you here. You may go, if Sophie is willing."

"Thank you. I will wait until Liba is safely delivered, of course. I would like to see my new brother or sister."

This seemed to gratify my father.

Liba, needless to say, was even more gratified by my decision, which meant that the next few weeks passed relatively pleasantly. Finally, late in 1823, ten months to the day after my father's marriage, Liba was delivered of a healthy boy, David. Not since Jacob was born had I seen such a fuss made over such a small being, beginning from when the midwife held him up, continuing to when he was circumcised and named eight days later, and ending three weeks later when Liba triumphantly exited the house to take her ritual bath. It was all pleasant enough, though, and I played my appointed part in all the celebrations, which for us women mainly consisted of cooking, eating, and gossiping. Meanwhile, Sophie had issued an invitation for me to stay indefinitely, so I kept myself busy with packing.

What to take? Although no one had said it, I knew that I might never return. Distance aside, Piotrków was not the sort of place one came back to after Berlin. So I packed every material thing that was precious, or simply useful, to me— my mother's receipt book, her pearl necklace, the diary in which I'd recorded much juvenile foolishness, my German dictionary—plus clothing for all seasons.

When at last the day of my departure arrived, I waited in the parlor for the wagon that would take me to Piotrków's coaching inn. As I began to strap my trunk, Papa hurried in. "Wait. I have something for you." He held a beautifully carved casket. I had no reason to ask what it was; for as long as I could remember, it had sat on Mama's dressing table. "Your mother's jewels. They were to go to you upon your marriage, but—" He gave an eloquent shrug.

So Papa too suspected I was going forever. I held the casket tenderly. "Thank you, Papa."

"I hope that recent events have not made you feel unwelcome here, my child. You have a home here as long as you wish—your home and your own room. There is no need for you to leave."

"No, Papa. As the book says, 'To every thing there is a season, and a time to every purpose under the heaven.' It is my time to see the wider world. And besides, what is there for a single woman to do if I stay? I do not think I would fare well as the village matchmaker."

My father smiled reluctantly. "True. God be with you, my child."

He embraced me, the first time since our quarrel over my refusal of Mr. Levinsky. I couldn't even complain about the blessing.

Liba was busy nursing a very appreciative David. I chucked my brother's chin, kissed him on the forehead, and lightly kissed Liba on the cheek. "May both of you thrive," I said, and I meant it.

~ ~ ~

In those days, Berlin was sort of a promised land to Polish Jews of a liberal stamp. To say that sounds peculiar, for it was not exactly welcoming to us—indeed, Prussia, or rather its French occupiers, had granted Jews full citizenship only within my lifetime, in 1812, and since the French had left Prussia there had been a certain amount of backsliding on the part of the government as to what we could and could not do. Many had simply given in and converted to Christianity. But despite these drawbacks, Berlin was the center of enlightened Judaism, and even though I had largely rejected the religion (and any other), I had long yearned to go there, especially after my sister's husband decided to leave his native Breslau for Berlin. As the mail coach jounced closer to our destination, I fairly bounced in my seat—as well as I could bounce crushed next to a family whose baby had spent the last hour bawling.

Berlin in those days was surrounded by a wall, not to keep out an invading enemy as in days of yore, but to collect customs from merchants passing in and out of the city. The wall had another purpose, however, as I soon discovered when our carriage pulled up at one of the city's many gates and the guard began questioning everyone inside the coach. I was last. "Name, miss?"

"Ernestine Luisa Süssmund." Polish Jews who came to Berlin, at least those who wanted to blend in quickly, liked to equip themselves with German names, and I thought that this one had a fine Teutonic ring. It did not appear to be impressing this guard, however.

"Citizen of Prussia?"

"Poland."

This won me a glare. "What is your business in Berlin?"

"I am visiting my sister and her family," I said in German, which I had made a point of speaking at inns and taverns since leaving Poland. My accent, I knew, left a lot to be desired, but

I had made myself understood. Anticipating the next question, I added, "Sophie, married to Samuel Morgenstern."

"What does he do?"

"He is a rabbi."

There was no mistaking the frown this time. "How long do you intend to stay?"

I looked at my large trunk, which had been lifted from the carriage during this conversation and sat waiting for me to join it. "As long as they wish."

"Indefinitely, then."

"Indefinitely."

"You'll need a permit, then, miss. Any Polish Jew needs a permit if he—or she—intends to stay in Berlin for more than three days. You must post three bonds for your good behavior or get permission from the king."

"Good behavior? That is foolish. If I behave badly, it is my own fault and should not lie on others. But I certainly have no intention of behaving badly. I simply wish to help my sister and to attain knowledge."

"It's the bonds or the king, miss. Make up your mind."

I had no reason to believe that I could not get the necessary bonds. My brother-in-law had sufficient means to post one, and no doubt as a rabbi he could prevail on two other householders to do the same. But that seemed a poor way to start out my visit, by inconveniencing so many, and besides, the law struck me as irksome and foolish. "The king."

"Then I'll take you to the palace. If he's not receiving petitioners, there's a hostel outside the city wall where you can stay for the time being." He surveyed me, not unkindly. "Some rough characters there, miss. Not really your kind of place. Sure you don't want to post bonds?"

"I will take my chance with the king."

Leaving my trunk at the customs office, I was then driven to the palace, at the terminus of Berlin's finest boulevard, Unter den Linden (which, true to its name, bristled with linden trees). Despite my fears—what if the king would not see me? what if he did not like me?—I looked around admiringly at the well-dressed people strolling and riding by, the Opera House, the university, and finally, the Palace Bridge over the River Spree that brought us to our destination.

After a series of conferences between various officials, I was informed, to my vast relief, that the king would see me, although I would have to wait a while. I was ushered to an anteroom, where for want of any other occupation, I mentally rehearsed the reasons why the king should allow me to stay in Berlin. At last, a man stepped into the room and beckoned me. "The king will see you. This way, miss."

Having halfway expected to be led into a throne room, I was somewhat disappointed to find myself in front of a man in his fifties, sitting behind a desk and wearing neither ermine nor a crown. I kicked a curtsy. "Sire," I said.

King Frederick William III said, "You may sit, Miss—"

"Ernestine Luisa Süssmund."

"You are a Polish Jewess, I understand, and wish to stay in Berlin. Why?"

"My sister and her husband live here, and I want to pay her a prolonged visit. And I have always wanted to live in Berlin. It is a fine city."

"You are quite young."

"I am nearly eighteen."

"I am surprised you are not married. Are you looking for a husband? Is that why you are here?"

"No. I am in no hurry to marry."

"Then how will you live, if you do not marry? Are you expecting your sister and her husband to support you?"

"I have a small inheritance of my own, which will keep me for years if I am prudent. And if some misfortune should befall me, I can work as a governess, I suppose."

"Most Jews in this city are poor. There is not much call for governesses among them."

"Then I shall be very prudent."

"Your brother-in-law is a rabbi. I am told by my men that he bears a good reputation and is a man of some substance. Why, then, will you not post a bond?"

"Because, sire, the law is both unfair and arbitrary. Must a Christian stranger coming into town post bonds? I am no more likely, no less likely, to do wrong than him or her. And besides, if I do wrong, I, and no one else, should be made to suffer for it. But I have no intention of doing wrong. I simply wish to live here, and will trouble no one."

"I will say that I believe you. I also must say that you do speak German fairly well, for a Pole, and no doubt will improve quickly," the king said. He eyed me closely. "And you already look quite the German in your dress. Tell me, Miss Süssmund, are you attached to the Jewish faith?"

I had to choose my words carefully, for I knew that the king was a religious man. "I find much to value in it, sir, but I am a doubter."

"Then why not convert to Christianity? You may live undisturbed while you take the necessary lessons. I will be happy to serve as your godfather. It can be accomplished with very little delay, and then you will have little difficulty finding employment as a governess in a Christian household, I expect." He smiled. "Or finding a Christian husband, I daresay."

Had I been a man, I would have had to give deep consideration to this offer, which I had no doubt was kindly meant, despite this unwelcome comment about marriage. A Jew in Prussia could only follow certain professions; absurdly, one could study law, but not teach or practice it. The civil service was closed to us altogether. It was that, and not any attachment to the teachings of Jesus, that drove so many Berlin Jews into the Christian faith. But of course, as a woman, all professions were closed to me, be I Jew, Christian, or Hindu. "I thank you, sire, but I have not abandoned the trunk in order to attach myself to the branches. If my reason prevents me from being Jewish, it cannot allow me to become Christian." Lest the king find this too impertinent, I added, "Besides, it would shame my father, who is also a rabbi, and I would not dishonor him—or my brother-in-law—in such a manner."

The king gazed at an inkwell. Finally, he said, "I see no harm in letting you stay for as long as you wish; you are honest, at least, and rather refreshingly so. I will have a clerk draw up the paper, and I shall sign it."

I thanked the king and soon was back at the customs gate, presenting my paper and claiming my trunk in triumph. I was practically a Berliner!

~ ~ ~

My sister and her husband lived, as you might expect, in Berlin's Jewish quarter—not a required residence anymore, but still the heart of the Jewish community. Their house, not at all grand but much taller than any residence in Piotrków, impressed me immensely. I settled into a little room on the third floor, and helped with their little girl—another Ernestine, in fact. Though my brother-in-law was observant, of course, he had fallen into some Berlin ways, a state of affairs which no doubt would have distressed my father but was far more congenial to me. All would have been very pleasant, then, except for one thing, which any fool should have anticipated but I had not. Nature abhors a vacuum, and the presence in the rabbi's house of a reasonably pretty female of marriageable age, with some money of her own, was a vacuum many sought to fill.

For a while, at least, Sophie and Samuel kept the suitors at bay, but soon even Sophie began to take the side of the matchmakers. "I can see not wanting to marry when you were stuck in Piotrków, but there are so many nice men here to choose from. You'll be an old maid if you don't let someone marry you, and what an unpleasant life that would be!"

To give the Jewish men of Berlin their due credit, most of the prospects were, in fact, quite presentable. Had I met any one of these men in the ordinary course of events and gradually improved his acquaintance, it is entirely possible that I might have come to love him, and to gladly accept his proposal. But I had not endured that freezing sleigh ride to Kalisz just to be the subject of another bargain, Berliner or no Berliner. So in early 1827, having turned one and twenty, I set off on my own. It took longer than I had anticipated—several landlords assumed that a young, unmarried woman could only have one reason for living alone, while others did not wish to rent to an unconverted Jew—but finally, the king's letter opened a door (literally) to me, and I was the proud possessor of my own room in a building close enough to the heart of the city to be pleasant but far enough away to be affordable. It was a humble abode—a bed, a table that doubled as a writing desk, a washstand, and a chest of drawers—but it had a view of the street, rather than the alley, and for the first time in my life I was accountable to absolutely nobody, save of course to the city authorities for my good behavior. Every young person, male or female, should have the experience of living alone and free; it is a disagreeable thing when one is old.

Soon, though, I realized that life in an apartment building had a distinct liability: the smell of cooking, not just mine (which I found agreeable enough) but everyone else's. I could crack a window, but of course then I shivered with the cold, for I had moved in the depths of winter. Sighing, I soaked a handkerchief with cologne, which I had made myself from my mother's formula, and pressed it to my nose.

Something tugged at my memory. My mother had burned a little strip of perfumed paper from time to time that filled the room with a delicious vanilla scent. It had been of her own making, created from a recipe that had been passed down for generations. But had she passed it on to my generation? I pulled her receipt book out of my trunk and lovingly thumbed through it. Finally, I found what I wanted. It was a little vague—rather inconsiderate of my ancestors, and Mama as well—and most irritatingly of all did not inform me what type of paper would smolder gradually instead of bursting into flames. I would have to experiment. But I certainly had time to spare.

Had the authorities been watching me—and this being Prussia, no doubt they were—they must have wondered as I went from little shop to little shop and then, laden with paper, spices, and oils, trudged back to my apartment. Thus supplied, I began my foray into scented-paper-making. Thanks to my mother's family, it did not take too long to produce a scent that delighted my nose, but it took much, much longer to find a paper that burned properly. One attempt involved so much smoke that I am amazed the neighbors did not complain, and another came very near to catching my little apartment on fire. But I persevered, and after a couple of weeks was rewarded with a lovely smell wafting through the room as my paper, folded in the style of an accordion, gently burned to bits. This success was followed by another, and another, so that I had to share my triumph with someone. I hurried over to Sophie's, where I was met with delight by my little namesake. "Tell me that you don't want one of your own," Sophie said after I had spent a good hour making merry with my niece.

"I do, but I am in no hurry."

"You may not be in a hurry, but men are. By the time you decide to get off your high horse and marry, you'll be on the shelf."

"I'll take my chances." I set one of my papers on a saucer and put a match to it. "Smell!"

Sophie, briefly distracted from her lecture, sniffed. "Why, it reminds me of Mama."

"It's her recipe. I re-created it. My apartment stank, and I—"

"You wouldn't have to live in a smelly apartment if you'd stayed here. Or if you would get married."

"Who knows? He might live in a smelly apartment too. Maybe even smellier. But the paper makes it so much better."

"It is pleasant," Sophie said grudgingly.

"I'll leave some with you then. I was thinking of selling them."

"What, peddling them from door to door?"

"No. Consigning them to a druggist's, or a fancy goods shop. Very respectable. I thought I'd stitch a dozen together and put a cover on with some made-up name. *Madame Hortense's Aromatic Papers*, or something like that. Or maybe I should use a German name instead. *Frau Blum's Aromatic Papers.*"

"You could make yourself a Frau in reality, you know."

I should have known my sister couldn't have resisted that opportunity. Having taken it, though, Sophie said, "It does seem a good idea, though. I know some of our friends would buy them, and I'm sure they'd do well with those who live in those blocks of apartments that are being built. It wouldn't hurt for you to have some more income, especially since you insisted on leaving most of your inheritance with Papa and his silly wife."

"I was afraid it might make me a useless creature and corrupt me. Besides, it helps keep off the suitors."

"Really, child, you are hopeless." My sister shook her head. "Now let us find a good name for your papers. I would go for the French. It has more snob appeal."

~ ~ ~

Madame Sylvie's Aromatic Papers, as Sophie and I settled on, did not make me rich, but they did give me a modest income, sufficient to avoid depleting my inheritance. With this as my profession, so to speak, I settled into a routine. In the mornings, I would read the newspapers in one of the coffeehouses where respectable women were welcome. Returning home, I would prepare a batch of my scented papers for consignment, then read, followed by a walk. Then I would fix myself a meal. Besides Sophie, I gradually made a few lady friends, and on occasion I might go to the opera or to a concert with one of them.

Then, one fateful day (for I can only call it that), I walked into a bookstore. It styled itself an antiquarian bookstore, but in reality many of the volumes were only a few years old, which suited me fine, since I had read enough dusty old tomes at my father's. As I hunted through the disorderly shelves, I squealed when I happened upon German translations of Thomas Paine's *The Rights of Man* and Mary Wollstonecraft's *A Vindication of the Rights of Woman*, both of which I knew of but had not found in German up until now.

A rather good-looking man of about thirty stood behind the counter. I had the impression that he had been watching me closely, but I had been too caught up in my browsing to care. "I would like these."

"Certainly. Shall I wrap them?"

"No, it would be a waste. I intend to read them straightaway."

The man nodded and wrote out a receipt. "If you don't mind my asking, miss, are you from outside Berlin?"

"Poland."

"Warsaw?"

"No. Piotrków Trybunalski. You've probably never heard of it."

"I have, in fact. I am from Ujazd. Not far away at all, except that my town is under Prussian control. My family is Polish. It's a pretty place, but I wanted to see more of the world, so I moved here. It does have a rather nice castle, though, or what's left of one. But I prefer the modern world, despite my occupation."

"So do I."

"I don't imagine many young ladies in Piotrków know of Mary Wollstonecraft. I think I have a translation of another of her books here, if you'd like me to unearth it for you for your next visit." He smiled and waved his hand. "It doesn't look organized, but I know where things are."

"That would be lovely.

"Do you have family here in Berlin?"

"My sister and her husband. He is a rabbi."

"Ah. I thought you might be Jewish. So am I. Or are you a convert to Christianity?"

"I am Jewish by birth, but I profess no religion. I am not a believer."

"Did your family cast you off for that?"

"By no means. I see my sister regularly. I came here of my own choosing. I wished to live independently."

"Are you enjoying it?"

"Very much. I think it is good for a woman to live on her own."

"You don't find it lonely?"

"No. I have much to occupy my time. I read nothing but old books with my father, and now I am discovering the new."

"That must be very exciting for you."

"It is." I sighed. "I wish I could have come here during the days of the great salons. Or that I could attend the university. I thought once of dressing up as a man and enrolling, but I wasn't sure I'd be convincing."

"Not at all." The bookseller appeared to smile. He glanced toward the door as a bell announced the arrival of another customer. "I hope you will come back to give me your opinion of what you have read, miss. May I ask your name?"

"Ernestine Süssmund."

"Marcus Kaufmann. I will have that book ready for you, Miss Süssmund"

I left in high spirits. Mr. Kaufmann wanted to hear my opinion—mine! And did he not look a little like Lord Byron? Like any self-respecting young lady in Europe in the 1820s, I had developed an infatuation with the English poet, despite not having read a word of his poems at the time. At age fifteen, after giving the matter a great deal of thought, I had decided that I would be duty-bound to run away with the lord should he appear in Piotrków and ask me to do so; his death in 1823 had greatly saddened me, because I knew perfectly well that it would not have happened if I had been in command of his affections and positioned to nurse him back to health. Mr. Kaufmann possessed a decidedly Byronic chin, and he wore his cravat similarly. These things could not be ignored.

Soon I was visiting Mr. Kaufmann's bookstore regularly —at first during the early afternoon, when other customers might be there, but later just before closing, when we would not be disturbed. By and by, Mr. Kaufmann, hearing me confess that my written German was not all it could be, offered to give me lessons after he closed his shop for the day. He had taught before to supplement his income. Since his coming to my lodgings might occasion unpleasant speculation, he suggested that the lessons take place in the room behind his shop where he took his meals and handled his accounts.

I was not a complete dunce. The thought occurred to me that Marcus, as I now called him, might want to take me to bed—and I longed for it. Healthy young women have as many desires as young men, as much as society tries to pretend otherwise. Mine, which had hitherto not troubled me much, were becoming most intrusive. Even when I was mixing the ingredients for my papers, my head was full of Marcus and what we might do together.

So with my consent obtained, our private lessons began. To Marcus's credit, he did teach, and to mine, I did learn. We would work in earnest for about an hour, and then Marcus might read me poetry—some of the German poets, some of his own. At other times we would speak of whatever subject took our fancy. Though not a nonbeliever like myself, Marcus had a healthy skepticism about religion and no longer kept the Sabbath, which endeared him to me even further.

My sister, of course, had no idea of these private lessons; had she done so, she most certainly would have hog-tied me and hauled me kicking and screaming back to my father's house. I continued to visit her regularly, smiling demurely in her parlor and all the while thinking of the day I would lie in Marcus's arms. It was coming soon, I knew. Each day, Marcus bent a little closer to me as he read over my lesson. Each lesson, my heart beat a little faster as he did so. I longed to speed things along, but my instinct told me otherwise.

Then, one fine day in April, Marcus read my essay—which I considered my best to date—on political economy, a subject for which I'd had to consult several books. He looked up. "Tell me, Ernestine, what are your thoughts on free love? What do you understand it to be?"

Though this was far off the topic of political economy, I had encountered it in my reading, not entirely coincidentally with the advent of Marcus. "That men and women should be free to satisfy their desires. That sexual congress should not be limited to procreation, but for pleasure. That marriage is an oppressive institution. That—"

"Do you agree with this philosophy?"

"I do."

"Then love me, little one. Let us have pleasure together."

Marcus led me to an extremely conveniently placed sofa (it had been in my thoughts for some time), where after a great deal of kissing and caressing and a corresponding removal of clothing I let him guide me onto my back. "But how was my essay?" I asked with a virgin tremor in my voice as his hand began to move up my thigh.

Marcus nuzzled my neck as his roaming hand made me gasp. "Your best yet."

4

APRIL 1828 TO DECEMBER 1830

In 1830 a young man by the name of Robert Dale Owen, whose dear father I shall have occasion to mention later, published a little book in which he offered advice on how one could avoid conception. A couple of similar books, published in England, had preceded his by several years. But Mr. Owen's came too late, and the others, if they were ever translated into German, had eluded me. So without any of these texts to guide me, I serenely relied on the belief that as long as a woman abstained from sexual congress for three days after her monthly course, and had frequent intercourse at other times, she would not get with child.

In truth, though, I did not concern myself much about the matter, for I was superbly happy. Marcus and I soon started spending all of our nights together, although having been admitted to his bedchamber, I found it rather disordered and insisted on tidying before I became a regular occupant there. We continued to work on my German writing, but it was eclipsed by our new pastime.

My courses had always been irregular, so I thought little of it when June, and then July, passed with no need to resort to the rags I kept for their arrival. Besides, I had been with Liba when she was with child, and she had been wretchedly miserable in her first months, puking at the slightest provocation. I, on the contrary, had never been in better health, and Marcus was always complimenting me on my fine bloom. But when August came and went with nothing to show for it but a drawerful of pristine rags and somewhat less give in my stays, I had no choice but to face reality.

It was my habit to call on my sister at least every other day, usually at a time when I could play with her little girl, but on this grim occasion I chose a time when my niece would be napping. My face must have been a perfect map of my misery, for I had hardly entered the parlor when Sophie asked, "My God, what's wrong?"

"I'm with child. At least, I think I am."

"Whose?"

"Marcus Kaufmann's."

"Who on earth is he?"

"A bookseller."

"Jewish?"

"Yes."

Sophie indicated the sofa. "Sit. Tell me about it."

I told my tale, minus the caressing of thighs and whatnot. When I had done, Sophie asked, "Do you love him?"

It was not a question I could answer readily. I loved lying in his arms, and I enjoyed his company. But I had not contemplated spending the rest of my life with him. "I don't know."

"Then you probably don't. You foolish, foolish girl." Sophie gently stroked my hair as I huddled against her. "How far along are you?"

"I think four months."

"There is a woman I could take you to, but I doubt she could help you when you're this far along. I wouldn't risk it. Does his store do well?"

"I don't think so," I admitted. "I don't think he has much of a talent for business."

"No, I imagine his talents lie elsewhere." My sister sat up straighter, the better to contemplate my situation. "It's clear that he is going to have to marry you, assuming he's a man of honor—"

"He is. At least, I think he is."

"If he's not, we will see to it that he marries you anyway."

"But I don't know if I want to marry. Not like this."

My sister ignored me. "And although I will never admit to having said this, it is also clear that he must convert if he is to support a wife and child in any comfort whatsoever. And that means that you must convert as well." Sophie shook her head. "You foolish, foolish girl."

We sat in silence, tears running down my cheeks, and jointly contemplated my folly. Finally, I asked, "Will you tell Papa what has happened?"

"No. I believe we can wait on imparting this pleasant news to him. Besides, I have to blame myself as well for letting you out on your own." As I prepared for another round of tears, Sophie handed me a handkerchief. "Come, dry your eyes. All of this bawling is bad for the baby."

~ ~ ~

I trudged back to my lodgings. The thought occurred to me that if I had obeyed my father's wishes and married Mr. Levinsky, I would not be in this situation.

It was the time of day when I usually prepared my papers, but I did not have the heart for it. Besides, for the first time, I began to feel the weight of my pregnancy. Instead, I stretched out on my bed and stayed there until it was time to walk to the bookstore. There, as soon as Marcus locked his door, I said dully, for the second time in hours, "I'm with child."

"Oh." Marcus put his arms around me. "I'm sorry. I should have been more careful."

"*We* should have been more careful."

"Don't fret, sweetheart. Of course I'll take care of you. The best thing to do is to marry as soon as possible, don't you think?"

I should have been pleased, I suppose, that Marcus was indeed a man of honor. Yet I almost would have preferred some Byronic caddishness rather than this rush to matrimony. "Perhaps we should—"

"I think we should seriously consider converting. Neither of us is observant, after all. If we do that, I'm bound to get something that will allow me to better support a family." He looked around ruefully. "As you may have guessed, this does not pay well."

"I'm not sure I want to marry, Marcus."

"Why not? Surely you don't want to be treated as an outcast."

"Why is it that a woman who bears an illegitimate child is an outcast, and the man who fathers it is—just a man? How is that fair?"

Marcus shrugged. "It's not, I suppose. But it's the way of the world."

"I hate those words. Something that is unjust should be changed, always."

Marcus's expression was the equivalent of a pat on the head. "Go home and rest, my dear. I know this has upset you. But—"

"—not resting would be bad for the baby."

"Precisely. We must take good care of you."

~ ~ ~

Two days later, Sophie and Samuel convened an awkward meeting at their house, with Marcus and I as the subject.

The first few minutes were devoted to castigating Marcus. Having received a rabbinical scolding from Samuel, followed by a sisterly scolding from Sophie (the latter far more vigorous than the first), he behaved with admirable dignity. He should not have given way to temptation, he acknowledged, and he took all responsibility upon himself. He knew his duty, as he had already told me, and was fully prepared to carry it out at any time my family named. Although he had gathered I had some money of my own, he was quite willing to forfeit any right to it.

The conversation then turned to Marcus's prospects. He admitted that he was struggling to keep the store afloat, although as long as he just had himself to support it had not been something that concerned him. His father was a merchant, but was not well off and had exhausted his means in educating Marcus, who had attended the university in Berlin. Marcus had, in fact, no interest in commerce; he had started selling books because it was at least something he enjoyed. What he would like to do was to work for the government, but that of course was closed to unconverted Jews.

My brother-in-law sighed and shook his head. He could not advise Marcus to do what everyone knew he would have to do: convert.

I sat in silence, inwardly cursing my stupidity. I should have been making myself useful to my sister all this time, not causing her heartache. "We could emigrate," I suggested.

"The United States has none of these silly laws, not that I know of. Marcus could find work easily."

"The United States, dear?" Marcus said. "It's really always struck me as a vile place. So pushing. So—democratic."

"I quite agree with Mr. Kaufmann," Sophie said.

Had Sophie, who was clearly the guiding force here, shown the slightest enthusiasm for America, I am quite certain that Marcus would have allowed himself to be persuaded. But as it was, my suggestion sank like a ship lost in the vast Atlantic, never to be heard of again.

(I am rather proud of this metaphor, and will not scratch it out.)

Having satisfied themselves that Marcus was not going to run, however, my sister and brother-in-law were content for the time being, and after a scolding by husband and wife together, directed at both of us this time, they let us go. "So do you think we must convert?" I asked as we made our delinquent way to the bookstore.

"It seems to be the best thing. I know a man who belongs to the missionary society—"

"No." If I, a nonbeliever, was going to go through this sham conversion, it was not going to be at the hands of a missionary. "I believe I know someone who can help us. Let me try him first."

"If you wish." Marcus smiled at me in a rather irritating manner. Probably he thought it wise not to argue with a pregnant woman, and it was true that over the past few days I had been rather cranky, though I assumed this was from my situation and not from any changes the baby might be causing to my constitution. "Who is he?"

"The king."

"Really?"

"Really. I had an audience with him once."

This time Marcus's smile appeared unforced. "You do amaze me, darling."

~ ~ ~

That evening, I composed a letter to the king. I did not tell him my exact circumstances, but I did tell him that Marcus and I wished to marry. I could not bring myself to say that I had experienced a change of heart, but I did say that we had decided to convert and that to spare our families' feelings, we would like to do it discreetly. Since both of us were reading people, might we be allowed to guide our own studies?

A few days later, a parcel arrived for me. It contained a gracious note from the king, informing me that he remembered me well and was delighted to learn of my decision and would be happy to make the necessary arrangements, including suitable godfathers. (I winced.) Enclosed was a nicely bound Bible, inscribed from the king, with a list of passages with which we were to familiarize ourselves.

The late Abraham Lincoln, whom I did not appreciate fully during his lifetime, had a saying: "If you make a bad bargain, hug it all the tighter." It was in that spirit that I grimly set to learning what Christians call the New Testament. It was not altogether an unpleasant task, for at last I learned the source of the stories Christians were always referencing. So that was the water-turned-into-wine business! So that was the miracle of the fishes! I smirked at the contradictions I found amongst the Four Gospels, each of which we were nonetheless expected to take as the unvarnished truth. And then, of course, there was the most irritating line in the whole book: *Wives, submit to your own husbands, as to the Lord.* How much evil and cruelty had that single sentence caused, I wondered? Not for the first time, I considered calling off the whole thing and rearing my child alone.

But I could not. Even if I was willing to face down the scorn of the world, I could not subject my sister, whom next to my father I loved more than anyone in the world, to more humiliation than I already had. And Marcus deserved the opportunity to know his child. He'd even bought a pretty silver rattle, which he could not afford.

So I sighed and plodded on with the New Testament, and reviewed it with Marcus. When the minister whom the king had appointed to receive us into the church, Pastor Hetzel, quizzed us, he was duly impressed. And I must say that nothing goes to waste in life, for in years to come, when someone with whom I shared a platform thought to get the better of me by quoting the Lord and Savior, I could quote him right back.

Pastor Hetzel having pronounced us as Christianized as we were likely to get, the king took over. I had assumed that he might get some minor officials to serve as godparents, but I had sadly underestimated the enthusiasm of the king for this project. His idea of suitable godparents for Marcus turned out to be Karl Wilhelm Salamon Semler, a member of his privy council, and Professor Bethmann Hollweg, a professor of law at Berlin's university who was also serving as its rector at the time. Seeing me to the altar of Christianity were Friedrich von Motz, the minister of finance, and Carl Friedrich Heinrich Graf von Wylich und Lottum, the general of the infantry, who had negotiated with Napoleon years before and could no doubt be trusted with this matter. Naturally no one expected these men to travel to Pastor Hetzel's church in Charlottenburg, nor to my little apartment or Marcus's cluttered bookstore, so a room in the palace was called into requisition. This, of course, meant that the king could pop in. I could only hope that Prussia did not experience a crisis while all these important people saw to the safe conversion of a foolish girl from Poland who had gotten herself in the family way.

As a rabbi, my brother-in-law could not be expected to make an appearance, but he was kind enough to let Sophie attend, for what other opportunity was she likely to get to see the palace, much less the king? So in October 1828, we all gathered at the palace in a room that held a portrait of the lovely Queen Louise, the inspiration for my middle name. My ringlets twined around my face perfectly, my gigot sleeves (which I note are returning to fashion, proving that everything comes around) puffed grandly, and there was enough of a chill in the air that I did not have to remove my pelisse and risk revealing my condition. I wore a fashionable arrow ornament in my hair, which pointed sideways and thus had the additional merit of directing the eye away from my midsection.

It was an absurd occasion, but I was mindful of the king's real kindness and did nothing to make him regret it. It helped, too, that while the godfathers and the king were all believers, they were also realists, and they knew as well as anyone that Marcus was converting only to improve his prospects, so they did not smother us with piety. There was some sprinkling of water upon us, which flattened my pretty ringlets, some Father-Son-and-Holy-Ghosting, some amen-ing, and then cake and lemonade were handed all about. Because I was in the ravenous stage of pregnancy, I appreciated these at least. There was pleasant talk afterward, during which I discovered that Herr Semler was interested in prison reform and schools. I talked law with Professor Betham-Hollweg, finance with the minister of finance, and Napoleon with the general. Indeed, I talked more than Marcus, who seemed somewhat dazed by the occasion. I worried that I was out-talking the king, but he simply smiled at my sister and said, "What a charming young lady Miss Süssmund is."

"She can certainly talk," my sister agreed.

~ ~ ~

"You were rather forward during our baptism," Marcus said to me the next day in what I did not think was a particularly Christian spirit.

"Forward? I was simply being polite. Although I did find the conversation interesting. I did not realize prisons here were in such sad shape."

"When we marry you must be more cautious. Your open manner could be misconstrued."

"You had no complaints about my open manner when you took me to bed."

"But it did end in my taking you to bed. Now, dear! Don't look so cross. It's just that men generally prefer not to hear so many opinions from women, especially women they barely know."

"We should be seen and not heard, then."

"Well, I wouldn't put it quite like that, but—"

I'd spent the last few months studying with Marcus, and I'd felt free to express any opinion I wanted. He'd never complained; he'd seemed to enjoy it. Had it been a ruse? Was it only my face and body that attracted him?

My father had told me that little girls shouldn't ask so many questions, each time I'd questioned something in the Torah. But in the end he had answered my questions, although his answers had been less and less satisfactory to me as the years went by. He'd never told me that I could not express my opinions, although I suppose he would have been happier if I'd had different ones. "I can't do this."

"Do what?"

"Marry you."

"But the baby—"

"I'll take my chances," I said. I turned and walked out of the bookstore.

~ ~ ~

"You're absolutely mad," Sophie said later that afternoon. She was slightly out of breath from climbing the stairs to my lodging. Marcus had told her the news. "Do you have any idea what life will be like for you as an unmarried mother?"

"No one has to know. I'll go away and have the baby in secret. Call myself a widow."

"And what will you tell the child when it wants to see its father's grave? And do you think Marcus will simply give up his child? Think, Ernestine. You're no fool. He could take it from you."

"He wants a ninny. I'm not going to be his ninny."

"Lie down. You look exhausted."

Sulkily, I obeyed, laying my hand on my belly as I sank back against the pillows. Sophie saw my faint smile. "You felt the baby move?"

"Yes. The second time today. I was going to tell Marcus."

"Ernestine, men are men. He doesn't seem a bad one, considering, but they have their vanities. Here is what I am proposing. Come live with us, and have the baby there. No one shall bother you until after it's born—not Marcus or anyone else. Getting married is a huge change for a woman. Getting with child is another. I think you need to deal with one at a time. After the baby is born, you and Marcus can reach some sort of arrangement."

"All right."

Sophie stroked my forehead. "You must be worn out, poor thing. I've never seen you agree with something so quickly in your life." She tucked a coverlet over me. "Sleep. When you wake up I'll take you to my house. And then the pampering will begin."

~ ~ ~

True to her word, Sophie moved me out that very day. I looked at my room regretfully as the man she had hired carried out the last of my things. It had been a good room to me; it wasn't its fault I had acted foolishly.

Samuel, I am sure, could not have been entirely happy about my returning to live with them under the circumstances —unmarried, pregnant, and Christian to boot—but he treated me kindly, as he always had, telling me that I had a home with him and Sophie as long as I liked. In January 1829, with my confinement approaching, it was he who I asked to write to my father, a task that I had been dreading but knew could not be put off any longer in case I died in childbirth. "Perhaps it will be best coming from another rabbi," I said. "I mean, I could hardly have Pastor Hetzel write to him, could I?"

A few weeks later, my father's reply came from Praszka, the border town to which he and his young family had moved during my sojourn in Berlin. "I don't dare even to read it," I said softly. "Just tell me what it says."

Samuel nodded and scanned the letter. "He is very sad and disappointed in you. He thought you had better sense.

He is also very disappointed in us for not supervising you properly, and in himself for letting you go off to Berlin in the first place. He is praying every day that you will come safely through your ordeal, and he loves you very much."

"Thank you, Samuel."

"He also is hurt that you did not write to him yourself."

"Then I shall do so now."

I wrote a letter to my father—not the best composition of mine by any means, but one in which I thanked him for his kindness and assured him of my love. It was good I wrote it when I did, for the next morning, a snowy day in February 1829, I went into labor.

Having been cocooned in Sophie and Samuel's house for the visible part of my pregnancy, save for walks in the privacy of their little garden, I had been spared the censorious remarks of the neighborhood, though Sophie's close friends knew of my situation. But I knew full well that in the eyes of some, it would have been better if both myself and my child perished, and it was the anger I felt at this knowledge that gave me the strength to fight through what proved to be a labor of nearly twenty-four hours. Today, of course, a laboring woman can get a soothing whiff of chloroform, but all I had was Sophie's hand, which I thought I was going to wrench off. By now, it was clear that she was with child herself (I had told her it was catching), but she and the midwife pulled me safely through and at last placed a darling little girl in my arms at about five thirty in the morning. She looked like me, everyone said, but I could not deny the resemblance to Marcus either. "Has he asked about me?"

"Every hour. Will you see him?"

I stroked my baby's hair. "Yes."

That afternoon, after I had rested, Marcus came in and took our child into his arms. "She's beautiful," he said softly, then carefully handed her back to me. "I am sorry we quarreled. I only want to do the best for you and our daughter. Will you marry me?"

"Yes." Now that our child was a reality, I could not let the world fling the word "bastard" at her.

But within a day or two of giving birth, I fell into a state of depressed spirits that was nothing like I had ever experienced before or since. What was wrong with me? I had a beautiful daughter, Marcus was more loving than ever, my sister and brother-in-law were supportive and kind. I told myself all of this, and everyone else told me this as well, to no avail. At last the midwife was called in. "This happens with many a new mother," she said sympathetically as I listlessly nursed my baby. "It will pass, but it takes time."

"Do you think it would help if we were married?" Marcus asked.

The midwife shook her head. "Best just to keep her here."

You may get an idea of the depths of my depression from the fact that I did not even object to being spoken about as if I were not present.

But the midwife was right; I did slowly recover. In a month, I was able to be present when our child, who we named Amalia Charlotte, was baptized (though I would have dispensed with such a ceremony, Marcus was troubled by her not officially bearing his surname and carried the point over my feeble objections). In two months, I was able to walk in the Tiergarten with Amalia and Marcus and to show our baby all the pretty sights. And in three months, in June, I at last stood at an altar and married Marcus. "Just wait a little longer, sweetie," I hissed to Amalia, who chose the moment we exchanged vows to start nuzzling around for my breast. "We must make you into a proper little lady first."

For all this progress, my spirits were still somewhat fragile, and I had been slow to regain my physical health after childbirth. For that reason, Marcus and my sister decided that we should travel instead of settling down in Berlin straightaway. We could well afford it, as Papa, relieved that our marriage was to go forward and no doubt concerned by the reports he had from Sophie, had sent a draft for part of the inheritance I had left with him. So having married in the morning, we set off in the afternoon on our travels, making a leisurely progress through Prussia and some of the other Germanic states, Holland, and Belgium before finally making our way to Paris, where we found life so pleasant we decided to stay for a while. Marcus, who had been feeling somewhat awkward for living on my inheritance, began selling French books to customers in Berlin, and he also picked up work teaching German, having quickly acquired a good command of French. Through an unspoken agreement, he confined himself to teaching commercial travelers and schoolboys, thereby avoiding any young ladies who might become enamored of his Byronic chin. As for me, I had Amalia to keep me quite busy. I was not burdened, however, because at my sister's insistence, and to my secret relief, we had engaged a nursemaid, Elke, to travel with us. She was a mature woman, a friend of Sophie's own nursemaid, and she soon became more of a friend than a servant to me as I adjusted to the married state.

As for Marcus and I, we rubbed along well enough. We both enjoyed traveling, which helped, and we both loved Amalia, which helped even more. With my health so much improved, we resumed our marital relations, although Marcus did not seem as intent on pleasing me as he had when I was his lover. Still, there was one source of tension: When we went out in company, which happened more and more as we gained fluency in French, I could not help but voice my opinion when matters of import were debated. Marcus said nothing, but I could feel his disapproval, especially on the occasions when other men actually listened to what I said and agreed with it. But what else could I do? I could not simply stand there mute, and I had never been one for empty chatter. It was not as if I were behaving coquettishly, as some of my new friends did. Nothing I did or said could be misconstrued as faithlessness to Marcus.

Besides, in that summer of 1830, there was plenty to talk about.

After the downfall of Napoleon, the Bourbon dynasty had been restored to the throne, so the two brothers of the guillotined Louis XVI had ascended the throne in turn as Louis XVIII (Louis XVII, the poor boy, having died in prison during the Reign of Terror) and Charles X. Having been a mere child when Louis XVIII was crowned, I had paid little attention to his reign, but when his death brought Charles X to power, I was fourteen and more disposed to take an interest in such matters. It soon became apparent even to my young self that Charles X would be no enlightened ruler, but if given his way would gladly take the country back to the absolute monarchy and the wretched inequalities that had led to the French Revolution. But the Chamber of Deputies, the legislature, had not proven as docile as he had hoped. The previous summer, the king's supporters had lost their majority in the chamber. The elections in June had gone even worse for Charles, who in hopes of distracting the people had started a foolish war in Algeria. There was a general feeling that the king had something else up his sleeve, but no one was certain what.

On this July day, Marcus was with a pupil. Having spent the morning playing with Amalia, who was toddling around quite nicely, I put her down for her nap and decided to take a stroll to the Palais-Royal, which aside from the Louvre was my favorite place in Paris.

Having been to Paris several times—it saddens me to realize that given my present state of decrepitude, I shall not see it again—I have become a little jaded about the Palais-Royal, but in 1830 it was a wondrous place. Even well-traveled, sophisticated men marveled at it, so you can only imagine what it was like for a young woman from a provincial city in Poland. In its arcades were restaurants, cafés, and food stalls to suit every taste and every pocketbook, shops where one could buy things that one would never have thought one needed. Though my tastes were rather simple and my possessions few, I loved to peek in the shop windows. Who would buy the elegant pistols that shot perfume instead of bullets? What was the point in wearing stockings so sheer? Just sipping coffee or lemonade in the garden or at my favorite café was equally entertaining. Having grown more particular in such matters since my arrival, I silently critiqued the fashions of the English tourists and expatriates who filled Paris in those years of peace following the Napoleonic Wars. With fascination, I watched as the prostitutes, who abounded at the Palais-Royal, sidled up to likely-looking men and purred, *"Monsieur, me voulez-vous?"* Sometimes I was solitary, sometimes I came with Marcus, and at other times I found a lady friend with whom to while away an hour or two before returning to Amalia.

Today I found Marie, a widow of about thirty who made her living teaching music. She barely greeted me when I sat beside her, but thrust a newspaper at me so hard that it slapped me in the eye. "Read!"

I obeyed her tapping finger, but Marie's conversation was faster than my ability to read French. "The king is suspending the liberty of press. Any paper that wants to publish will have to get royal permission, and that will last for only three months."

"And I suppose only papers friendly to the king will get permission?"

"No doubt. But there's more. He's declaring the election results invalid, and he's changing the qualifications to vote, depending on the type of taxes paid. There's to be a new election in September."

As Marie fumed, I read the paper for myself. The king had issued these proclamations in the form of four ordinances. The restrictions against newspapers, he claimed, were necessary because the periodical press was merely an instrument of disorder and sedition. Among its sins were encouraging defiance of the king, attacking the church and religion in general, and confusing the populace. There was little said about the provisions regarding elections, and what in fact could be said? It was clearly a naked grab for power, meant to disenfranchise the professional classes in the city, especially business owners and lawyers, in favor of more conservative country landowners.

"Does the king think the people are simply going to accept this?"

"He's a fool if he does. For one thing, this is going to throw hundreds of printers and journalists out of work. Like my brother, who's a father of two."

"It's going to hurt us too," said the waiter, handing me my coffee. "People come here to read as much as anything else. What are they going to read, if all we can hand them is the government rag?"

Around us, similar conversations were buzzing. Some of the patrons were fretting over the possible effect on the

Bourse, others about the loss of jobs in a city that had just suffered through a hard winter and had finally seemed to be on the mend. Others were upset simply about the censorship itself. What would follow, if the king got his way? Jailing—or worse—of all his political opponents?

At length, Marie and I decided to walk to the offices of the *National,* where her brother was employed and where Marcus and I had acquaintances as well. We could not get inside, but the man who barred the door knew us. "The office is full of journalists from all the papers, discussing the ordinances."

"Are they going to resist them?" I asked.

"Oh, yes. They're drawing up a protest now. The ordinances are completely contrary to the letter and spirit of the Charter of 1814."

At length, men, perspiring from the heat of their close quarters, began to stream outside. Marie embraced her brother. "Save that for after I return from prison," he said, grinning. "That's where we're likely to be after we publish tomorrow."

Having spent more time away from Amalia than was my wont, I somewhat reluctantly headed home. "Papa!" Amalia squealed when Marcus appeared a few hours later.

"Marcus, have you heard the news?"

My husband scooped up Amalia and kissed her, then kissed me. "Yes, and I believe there will be unrest. I must see a client tomorrow, so I shall be away, but you must be very careful of yourself."

"Of course."

The next morning, Marcus left our lodgings immediately after breakfast, which as we paid for board and lodging was brought to us. But I had not promised Marcus that I would stay home—not in so many words—so after changing out of my dressing gown I left Amalia in the capable hands of Elke and hurried to the Palais-Royal. Sure enough, men from four newspapers, including the *National*, were handing out free copies, all of which gave prominence to the protest drawn up the day before. For the benefit of those who could not obtain their own copies—quite a few, with the crowd thickening by the minute—young men hopped upon tables and chairs and read the papers aloud.

A crowd of yet more young men, wearing printers' aprons, joined the throng. "Our livelihoods are being destroyed by this law. Yours may be next. Will you join us?"

There were cheers in response, and a few cries of "Down with the king!" but they were scattered. Still, my heart thrilled. Was I to witness a revolution?

But I was soon to learn that even a revolution involved a certain amount of aimless milling about. People came and went, but no one had anything much of interest to report, until around noon the news arrived that the government had seized the presses of the *National* and another paper. With this, the crowd grew louder, and some men began to chalk remarks on the wall about the king that were none too complimentary, and in several instances obscene. Shopkeepers began to close up, some joining the crowd, others scurrying off. Other business owners stayed long enough to paint over any references to "royal" or the royal arms on their signs and shopfronts.

Soon a group of police arrived to force everyone out of the Palais-Royal and lock the gates. One yelled at me—for there were few women around by now, even the prostitutes having concluded that this was a bad time to conduct business—"Go home, miss! It's going to get ugly."

I did not. And it did.

Dispersed, the crowd fanned in various directions, but I stayed with the portion of it that was squeezed in the Place du Palais-Royal and the streets surrounding it. As troops from the Royal Guard arrived and pushed the crowd back, the people began to hurl anything at hand at them. Some yanked up the paving stones to serve as missiles; others, standing on balconies or rooftops, showered them with roofing tiles and flower pots. I could not bring myself to do this, but nor could I bring myself to leave. So I shook my fist and shouted, "Down with the king!" until I was hoarse.

Then shots cracked through the air, and men began to fall.

Someone shoved me into a doorway, out of harm's way. There, as I watched, trembling, two men lifted their motionless comrade above their heads. "Death to the king's ministers!"

I would like to say that I played a heroine's part at this juncture, but I had never seen bloodshed before, and besides, this turn of events raised my fears for Amalia. So as fast as I could, I made my way to our lodgings, which were only a few streets away. It was no easy matter. The streets were overflowing with people, and young men with sticks and canes were smashing the streetlamps that were suspended across the streets. There was no looting, though—save for an armaments store that I passed, which was stripped of all of its goods.

When I at last reached my street, I found it too in ferment. Young men were running about, calling out for others to join them. One of them, whose father kept the bakery over which we lodged, waylaid me as I started up the stairs. "Madame Kaufmann. Can you help make bullets for us in Father's oven, once you've seen to your girl?"

"Of course," I said, and hastened upstairs.

Elke had closed the windows, although it was a hot, sunny day. Amalia, stacking her alphabet blocks, frowned at me. "Mama out," she said sternly.

"I know, darling. But I came home just in time to read you your story. 'Puss in Boots'?"

Amalia nodded and snuggled against me as I read from Charles Perrault's book of fairy tales, in French, because Marcus and I had decided it would be good for Amalia to be brought up to speak that as well as German.

Having read Amalia her story, plus the second one she demanded, I put her down for her nap. When I returned to the little parlor, Elke said, "Mr. Kaufmann stopped in earlier. He was a bit upset to find you gone."

"Well, I wasn't to know that there would be so much of a stir. And I returned as soon as things started looking bad." That was not strictly true, I reflected, but it was true that I had scurried home when the shooting started. "And I now I must make bullets, it seems. I will be downstairs if you need me."

Anne, the baker's daughter, was in charge of the bullet operation, which soon was in full production. I had been at it for several hours, and fancied that I was developing quite a system, when I looked up from my work to find Marcus glaring at me. "What on earth are you doing?"

"Making bullets. Would you like to help?"

"For which side?"

"For the people's side, of course."

"Have you forgotten our child?"

"Of course not. Elke knows where I am—she sent you here, did she not?—and I know that Amalia is perfectly safe with her. But as it happens, I will come up to put her to bed, and then if I am needed here, I will come back. If not, I will stay upstairs."

Marcus turned on his heel and stalked out. I looked after him for a moment, then returned to my work. Did he really expect me to do nothing to help my fellow man?

But as promised, I came upstairs in plenty of time to tuck Amalia into bed, and as Anne had released me from my duties for the evening, I stayed in the parlor and tried to coax Marcus into a better humor. "Aren't you just a little bit stirred by what is happening? The king has been oppressing his subjects for too long. You must admit that."

"I don't see why a lady has to be making bullets."

"What if I help make provisions for the men tomorrow, then? Would that sort of baking suit you better?"

"What about just staying here with our child? She needs a mother."

"And she has one. You know perfectly well that I do not neglect her or anything else. This has been a most unusual couple of days." I rose and began to massage Marcus's shoulders, which usually made him come as close to a purr as a man could and quite often ended up with us in bed—or, on one memorable day when Elke was away, on the parlor floor. But this day, Marcus was determined to be angry with me, and finally I gave up and settled into a book. But it was hard to concentrate with the sounds of shots in the distance.

Finally, though, the night grew quiet. Marcus and I made our silent way to bed. It was a warm, muggy night. I did not sleep well, and neither did Marcus, although Amalia, who had long since reached that blessed stage of sleeping through the night, snored peacefully in the anteroom she shared with Elke. Lying in silence, I wondered if I did not understand men, or if I just did not understand Marcus. Or perhaps it was the other way around.

Having fallen asleep just before dawn, I woke to the sound of gunfire, more intense than the day before. Even if Marcus had not been in our apartment to stop me, I doubt I would have ventured outside, for there was fighting in nearly every street, and I simply could not hazard myself in that manner—not with Amalia to think of. It was even dangerous to step outside on the balcony, as one poor Englishman found out when he opened his shutters and got a bullet in the head. So I kept as far away from the balcony and windows as possible and with Marcus passed a weary day of explaining to Amalia that no, she could not go out for a walk; no, she could not go to the bakery; and yes, Papa would be happy to give her another horsey ride. Meanwhile, outside, bands of workmen, veterans, and students battled the royal forces in the streets, while from the balconies above ours and all around ours, the people threw everything they could lay their hands on—bottles, rocks, paving stones, crockery—down upon the king's men. I dislike violence and take no pleasure in harming another human being, and yet I could not help but silently cheer them on.

When the streets at last grew silent, Marcus and I, leaving Amalia inside with Elke, dared to step outside. Nearly all the paving stones were gone from the street, which was beginning to sprout a barricade at either end. As we walked over to take a closer look at one of the barricades—a mélange of miscellaneous objects—a lady well into her fifties straggled by, burdened with paving stones, and laid them in place. I tugged at Marcus's hand. "At least let me help with the barricades tonight. I can't just sit here."

Marcus just shook his head. But later that night, when I kissed Amalia good night and slipped out the door, he did not stop me. All night, I labored with others, some who had spent the day fighting, others like me who could help only in this small way. By dawn on Thursday, July 29, Paris bristled with barricades.

That was the day of victory. In the morning, the people took the Louvre—in those days, still a royal palace as well as a gallery—and a few hours later, the tricolor flag, not flown in fifteen years, waved proudly over the Tuileries. The royal forces had abandoned the city for the royal chateau of Saint-Cloud, where the king and his family were holed up. General Lafayette, the hero of the American Revolution, came out of retirement to reconstitute the National Guard and proceeded to the Hôtel de Ville, where the victors were trying to figure out who would govern France, and in what form. A republic, as I hoped? Or a constitutional monarchy, with a chastened Charles X? With the king's grandson, a mere boy? With Louis-Philippe, the Duc d'Orléans? It was a given that any holder of that title stood ready to assume the throne at a moment's notice. As the sun sank with no answers to my questions, I sat on the balcony, Amalia playing by my side, and sewed tricolor cockades, the provisional government having invited the women to do so. Even Marcus couldn't find fault with this eminently ladylike activity.

Although rumors circulated of the royal troops rallying to attack the city, no such thing happened. Wearing my cockade and handing out the others I had made, I strolled in company with Marcus and Amalia along streets that were peaceful but denuded of paving stones and still barricaded. Someone had been busy: the walls blossomed with placards urging the people to accept Orléans as their leader. The Louvre, all of its windows smashed, was a pitiful sight, but it was ringed by guards protecting its precious art. No one would be walking around toting the *Mona Lisa* under his arm—not that any Frenchman or Frenchwoman would have been so barbaric as to try.

Marcus gazed around. "Are you proud of all this?"

"It could have been so much worse. There was no destruction for the sake of destruction. No killing of the innocent—not on our side, anyway."

"I'd like to get out of this place for a while. The seaside, perhaps."

"That would be lovely." I smiled. "Amalia will love the sand. Shall I make the arrangements?"

"No, I will."

Probably Marcus thought I was going to find a revolutionary beach. But having never seen the sea myself, I was excited enough about the prospect of our trip not to be put off by his ill humor, and when I squeezed his hand, he surprised me by putting his arm around me.

The next day, Marcus having gone to teach a lesson, I once again left Amalia in Elke's care and joined the crowd that had gathered around the Hôtel de Ville in the general expectation of seeing something of importance happen. Sure enough, Orléans, riding a mare—which had to be lifted above the throngs of people and the barricades at points, an endeavor which the creature bore graciously—came into view. He was greeted with cries of "*Vive la République!*" and "*Vive Lafayette!*" I was not the only one who wanted to see the monarchy consigned to the past.

But Orléans made it safely to the entrance and the waiting General Lafayette, and presently the pair, holding a huge tricolor flag, appeared on the balcony overlooking the Place de Grève, to more shouts of "*Vive Lafayette!*" As the cheers subsided, the general stepped forward and gave Orléans what I can only describe as a resounding kiss, followed by an embrace.

"*Vive le duc d'Orléans!*"

So a monarchy it was to be. I shook my head in disgust. "He may have cause someday to wish himself off the throne," I muttered to myself.

But it had been a revolution nonetheless, and there was reason to hope that Orléans as King Louis-Philippe might be an improvement over his predecessor. If he was not, the people would find it out in time, for as I was to learn, sometimes it took years for people to discover what was best for them.

~ ~ ~

Over sixty years have passed, and yet I can hardly bear to write what comes next. Yet I must, or give up on this project of mine altogether.

After Orléans made his appearance, I returned home to find Marcus waiting for me. "Our daughter is sick," he said. "While you were out gallivanting and playing the revolutionary, she fell ill."

I did not even stop to defend myself. I ran to Amalia's bedside and found her burning with fever.

We called in the best physician we could find in Paris, the best nurse—everyone. We never left her bedside. But nothing we did, nothing the physician or the nurse did, availed. Four days after she had fallen ill, our darling died in our arms.

I pass over each of us rending our garments in our anguish—a Jewish custom it turned out neither of us had left behind—and the bleak little funeral and our wordless return home to our lodgings. Our neighbor the baker had sent up some food, which neither the two of us nor Elke could touch.

"I suppose I shall write Sophie and my father," I said finally, though I hardly felt up to lifting a pen.

"Will you tell them that you shamefully neglected our child?"

"Shamefully neglected? What on earth do you mean?"

"You know full well what I mean. You were hardly here in her last days."

"Hardly here! I sat with her day and night, just as you did. Marcus, have you gone mad?"

"I mean before she fell ill. You came home long enough to shove a meal in her face and to put her in bed. Out of sight, out of mind. Well, she's gone now, and you can be as carefree as you like. Are you happy now?"

"Marcus, why are you saying these horrible things?" I looked at Elke, who had come into the room and laid a hand protectively on my shoulder. She was a much larger, heavier woman than I, and to this day I believe her presence may have saved my life. I stepped forward. "Perhaps you should lie down. You're exhausted." It was true; I doubt he had slept in days. "Let me take you—?"

"Admit it! Just admit it! All you've ever cared for is your own foolishness. You cared nothing for our child."

"It's not true. Please—just go rest." I took his hand. "Please, let me take you—"

With an oath, Marcus flung me off, so violently I nearly fell backward. "Damn you, you little whore! I wish I'd never met you."

He turned and slammed the door behind him as I collapsed sobbing into Elke's arms.

Two days later, the baker came upstairs, leading Marcus. My father had allowed himself an extra glass or two of wine on Purim, but had never reached more than an amicable state of tipsiness before yawning and heading off to bed. There was no way to describe Marcus other than stinking drunk. The baker dragged him to our bed, flung him down like a sack, and then without a word extended a hand to Elke and I and led us downstairs. Wine was not the only thing that reeked: underneath the liquor I caught the unmistakable odor of perfume.

I fully expected some disaster to happen—Marcus setting the place on fire, or even spontaneously combusting as Dickens's Mr. Krook would do so grandly a quarter-century later—but the baker, perhaps expecting the same result, took it upon himself to sit watch upstairs, and all was quiet. Finally, about twelve hours after making this memorable return home, Marcus appeared at the baker's. He had clearly been to the bathhouse, for he no longer reeked, and he had been to the barber as well. "I am sorry, Ernestine. Very sorry."

"I think you had better be."

"I have secured places for the three of us on the diligence to Dieppe. Will you go? I think it would be good for us all."

Three of us? For a moment I thought he was still half-mad and meant us and Amalia, but then I realized that Elke was the third person. I nodded curtly and allowed Marcus to lead me upstairs, but that night I slept beside Elke.

In the morning we set off for Dieppe. It was a resort that had become fashionable five years before, although nothing in the aspect of our miserable little party suggested that we were on a holiday. Marcus would sometimes weep into his hands if we were alone in the coach, and all that kept me from doing the same was that I had done all of my weeping. But he was gentle, sober, and attentive for the entirety of our journey. I could not believe this was the same man who had called me a whore.

At last, we arrived in Dieppe, where our little Amalia should have romped around and collected shells. It was on our second day there that Marcus said, as we gazed mournfully out to sea, "I am very sorry, my love. I cannot express how sorry I am for my conduct. I was a beast."

"You hurt me to the very bone."

"I was half-mad—perhaps more than half—with grief. You must not think for a moment I meant any of those terrible things I said. I love you dearly."

It was actually the first time he had said this. Etiquette demanded I tell him that I loved him in return, but I could not force the words to my lips. Marcus did not press me, but said, "I think we should go back to our lodging. The sun is very strong this time of day."

I nodded and followed him inside.

We spent the rest of August at the sea. It was on our last night there, as we lay in bed, that Marcus turned to me and took me into his arms. "Love me, little one, as you did that first time, so sweetly and trustingly. We can make a fresh start."

A fresh start; a second child. A child that, if it were conceived, would prevent me from what I had been contemplating for the past month. I sat up, knowing that what I was about to say would either be the worst decision of my life—although admittedly there had been a lot of competition over the past two years—or the best. "No, Marcus. This must end."

"What do you mean?"

"Us. We must end." I steeled myself to stop talking gibberish. "I want a divorce."

"I was cruel on that one day, and unfaithful during that debauched night after, as you probably guessed. But as I said, I was half-mad with grief. Her sweet little face, so still and pale—it shattered me. Can you not forgive me?"

"I can, and I do. But what if something happens to our next child? Will I be blamed for that?" I stopped him from speaking. "Perhaps that is not fair, but this is not fair either: that I make myself into a creature I don't recognize to please you. I will always fall short. I will talk too much, care too much about politics, support the cause you do not support. We had best go our separate ways now, before we come to hate each other."

"I could never hate you. Are you truly that unhappy?"

"Yes. It could be overlooked while our Amalia was alive—she made up for it all. But now that she is gone, I can bear this no longer. You are a good man, a kind man—the fault lies with me, I am sure of it. I simply must be allowed to be myself."

"What a strange little creature you are. But I would not see you miserable. If you want me to go, I'll go. I should be returning to Berlin anyway. Once there, I'll see to the divorce."

"Thank you."

"You don't expect me to leave tonight? It's late."

"No. You can stay where you are." I rose. "I'll sleep with Elke."

Poor Elke. She had not signed up to be my bedmate.

The next morning, we left for Paris—an odd journey in which we made stilted talk about the state of the world and the weather. Once we were back in our apartment, Marcus gathered his clothing and books together and placed them neatly in his trunk. "I suppose this is all of it." His voice softened. "Are you sure you'll be all right by yourself here?"

"Yes."

"I don't doubt it. You're well set for money?"

"We've been living off my inheritance all this time," I snapped.

"Touché." Marcus gave a slight smile, which I did not return. He touched my cheek. "I'll be off, then. I'll keep in touch about the divorce. Is there a particular ground you prefer? Mutual consent would be the most accurate, I think, but you might enjoy the one for giving up the Christian religion."

"I do."

"I thought you might. Then it's goodbye. Take care of yourself."

I managed some sort of farewell as Marcus followed the boy who was bearing his trunk downstairs. With a certain sense of relief, I sank onto the sofa. For better or worse, I was my own woman, or as close to it as I could be until Marcus filed for the divorce.

And yet I must tell the truth here. Though I could not say I loved Marcus, I did feel affection for him, and probably would have even if we had not shared a child. It would not have taken very much for him to have won me back. And once or twice, I had had my own doubts. I would be lying if I said that as I sat alone in our—my—lodgings, I did not shed tears. I had not married Marcus with the intent of later parting from him.

But now we *had* parted, and I knew that we would never see each other again. Henceforth, my life was in my own hands. It was up to me to decide what to make of it.

~ ~ ~

Revolution is catching. Although 1830 was no 1848, one uprising followed the next that year, and in November 1830, the spark of rebellion took fire in Poland—my Poland—when a group of officers from the military academy in Warsaw rose against our Russian overlords. I could not sip my coffee in Paris while Poland's fate hung in the balance, and with Amalia dead, what did I have to lose by going? So, having helped Elke find a good position with a wealthy family, I packed my belongings and traveled through France to the Rhine Province.

There, at the fair city of Koblenz, my journey was brought to a dead halt.

"But I am a Pole," I protested. "What harm is there in allowing me to travel to my homeland?"

"Revolution, that's the harm. You could be a spy, for all I know," said the guard. "We're not letting anyone bound for Poland into Prussia unless they have a good reason."

"Isn't seeing my family a good reason?"

The man studied my passport. "You've been gallivanting around Europe, and you just happen to want to visit your family during a revolution. After being in Paris for *their* revolution."

I shrugged, probably too French a shrug. "It is a beautiful city."

"Then I suggest you go back there." He drew my passport closer to his chest. "Or if you like, you can sit and think about it in the blockhouse. But you're not getting any farther than that."

What to do? Even if locking me up was an idle threat—and I was not sure that it was—I could be putting Sophie and her family in Berlin in danger if I continued to raise a fuss. Perhaps even Papa and the rest in Poland might be at risk. "I will go back."

"A wise choice. And there happens to be a diligence headed back the way you came that will leave in an hour." He snorted and slapped my passport back into my hand. "A pretty head like yours shouldn't be troubled with politics anyway."

Had I done to the guard what I wanted to just then, I would not be writing this now.

Under the eye of another guard, I took a meal while awaiting the departure of the diligence. I had said my goodbyes to my friends in Paris, given up my apartment. Should I return there? Despite the sorrow I had suffered there, I loved the city and its people, but I felt foolish returning in defeat—or not even that, since I hadn't even made it to Poland—after letting it be known that I wanted to help my homeland. "I talk too much," I muttered to my plate.

But there was a place I had yet to see: London, the greatest city in the Western world. It was high time I took a look at it. Perhaps there I could lose myself—or find myself.

5

JANUARY 1831 TO MAY 1836

From the moment I set foot in London in early 1831, I was overwhelmed. So many people! So much riches! So much poverty! I spent the first two days there with my mouth perpetually agape, except when I was dodging the conveyances that careened around the corners, seemingly with the intention of mowing down anyone in their path. When not doing that, I was busy looking out for anyone who might kidnap me and sell me into prostitution. Having been told by several passengers on the steamer that the streets teemed with procuresses, I had determined to fight to the death anyone who might accost me, but either I looked too worldly-wise or the wedding ring I prudently wore discouraged them, for I was never bothered in that manner. Of course, it is also possible that I simply could not understand my would-be abductors, for I had arrived in England knowing scarcely a word of its language.

I had learned German with relative ease, as Yiddish derived in part from it, and French had not given me much trouble. But the English language! It tied me in knots. There were the words that sounded just alike, yet had entirely different meanings. There were the words that were pronounced nothing like they were spelled. There were the words that had multiple pronunciations, such as "read" or "lead." Every time I thought I was close to getting a good grasp on it, something new came to trip me up.

Yet I did my best. I attended the theater, although on my first evening I chose a Shakespeare play, which confused me even more, especially because I had always understood *King Lear* to be a tragedy, and this version ended in glorious happiness, with Edgar and Cordelia marrying and the king cheerfully relinquishing his throne and its attendant cares to the younger generation. I spoke the language each time I bought something to eat, although in the first weeks I often ended up with some very odd meals. Finally, having decided to revive Madame Sylvie in order not to deplete my inheritance further, I went from shop to shop with my perfumed papers when I felt that I could at least carry on a semblance of a conversation. I kept a dog-eared dictionary in my hand to use as a last resort. "I make these," I informed shopkeeper after shopkeeper. "They make you smell better. Shall you like to sell them?"

Usually, some haggling over the shopkeeper's share of the profits ensued, with me invariably coming out the loser, although it would be some time before I realized this. Others, of course, simply turned me away, though whether it was lack of interest or my unintended insult about their olfactory state, I do not know. One creature invited me to his back room, but I fortunately surmised that his interest was not in my papers and fled, learning several new English words in the process as he yelled imprecations after my retreating self. Gradually, though, I found some modest success, and as my command of the language got somewhat more assured, I was able to rid myself of the shopkeepers who had cheated me.

I had not gone to London for lack of anywhere else to go. After Amalia's death, I received the kindest possible letters from Papa and Sophie, both of whom spent some time commiserating with my loss, which each could understand, having suffered the death of a child. Both said essentially the same thing: I should return to Berlin, where I could quietly await my divorce from Marcus ("the vile seducer" in Papa's parlance, "that man" in Sophie's) and start over again. Divorce was not uncommon there, and there was no reason why, in time, I could not be happily and respectably settled, the center of my own loving family.

I did not toss these kindnesses aside lightly. Women who had done far less than I had, and with far better excuses, had suffered much worse. Had my lot been different, I could have been walking the streets. But I had been a mother and a wife, and I could not return to my girlhood as if those things had not happened. It was best that I remained on my own and put my energies to some good use, so that someday my family would speak of me with pride again. So I peddled my papers, and inspired by Marcus's example, I put out some circulars and gradually obtained work teaching German to girls— having been given leave to name my godfathers in Berlin as my references. I found my way to doing charitable work as well. Thus, after a year or so in London, I could give a satisfactory report of myself. I was working hard, I was doing some good, my English was improving, and I had avoided romantic entanglements. The latter was easy enough, because I called myself "Mrs. Kaufmann," which of course I was, and most people assumed that I was a young widow whose heart lay in her husband's grave.

Yet I must say, I was lonely during those first months in London, and more often than I care to remember cried myself to sleep. More than anything, of course, I grieved for Amalia, but I also missed my visits to my sister—those days where I could simply walk over and sit in her parlor. I even missed Marcus in a way, and often wondered whether I had done the right thing in separating from him. It was true that he had not understood me, but was any man likely to? Having learned to enjoy a man's touch, I missed it keenly. At five and twenty, it was a hard thing to realize that I might spend the rest of my life alone.

But for the most part, I avoided wallowing in self-pity by keeping myself as busy as possible. Now that English no longer sounded like gibberish to me, I began attending lectures. One of the first was by Mr. Robert Owen..

I had read what I could find about Mr. Owen in translation, but it was not until I came to London and acquired sufficient English that I came to appreciate fully his great humanity. At the turn of the century, Robert Owen, in case you have forgotten that wonderful man, had found a place managing the huge textile plant in New Lanark in Scotland. Infuriated at the harsh treatment of the workers there, he had made conditions there humane—and profitable as well. He had even opened schools for the workers' children. Encouraged by the results, he had established similar communities in England and in the United States, where he had traveled and lectured. His New Harmony settlement in Indiana had foundered, but he had returned to England as full of the breath of reform as ever. His premises in London served not only as a lecture hall, social center, and headquarters but as a labor exchange where workers, using a currency based on hours expended, could trade their own goods.

One foggy Sunday evening in the autumn of 1832, then, I walked to the lecture hall and found that I had arrived with little time to spare. As I looked with some difficulty for a seat, a young man rose and gestured to the chair beside him. "Here, madam."

"Thank you."

As I settled into place with the young man's assistance, Robert Owen appeared on the platform. In his early sixties, he was not handsome, and indeed his features could be called somewhat odd-looking, but that hardly mattered when he began to speak. He spoke of the lure to the poor of gin-palaces, blazing with gaslight and warmth—indeed, the first time I had seen one on a damp, cold day, I had been tempted to peek inside. He spoke of the irrationality of the Sunday laws, under which museums and other institutions were shut up on the Christian Sabbath, the one day of the week when working people had their leisure. He spoke of how so much evil and injustice could be remedied through simple means such as free education and jobs that paid good wages. He spoke of how marriage turned cheerful, lively young women into drudges, old before their time, and criticized marriage without love as little better than legalized prostitution.

When Mr. Owen had done, he invited others to comment, and a couple of men held forth; by the expression on my neighbor's face, there was nothing novel about them speaking and nothing new about what they said. Once they said their part, Mr. Owen began to walk away from the platform.

But there was so much goodness and truthfulness, not to mention good common sense, in what had been said, I could not let it all pass by. I stood. "Excuse me, sir," I faltered. "I agree with all you said. But there is one thing that I would like to add, if I may. It is the effect of the Bible on women, and thus on marriage. It states that woman was created only because it was not good for man to be alone. From that flows all of woman's wrongs. She may be a drudge or a plaything, but never an equal companion, never a rational helpmate. She is only an appendage—a toy to be picked up or a tool to be used."

As I spoke these words, the realization came to me that people were listening—not simply tolerating me, but nodding in response to my points. With this encouragement, I continued in this vein for longer than I had intended. "Thank you for hearing me out," I said finally, and sank down in my seat, only to hear applause, the most vigorous coming from the young man who sat next to me.

"You spoke beautifully," he whispered.

"Thank you," I said dazedly.

"Shall I fetch you some tea? There's usually a scramble for it."

"That would be lovely."

The young man hurried away. Though he was rather slight in build, he must have been adept at getting through crowds, because he returned in triumph in a remarkably short time bearing not only a steaming cup of tea, but an accompanying bun. I had barely got out the words to thank him when I saw a figure coming toward us—Robert Owen himself. After nodding at the young man, who evidently was a regular at these meetings, he bowed as he approached. "To whom do I have the pleasure of speaking?"

"Mrs. Ernestine Kaufmann."

"I wanted to say, madam, that I enjoyed your little talk. I gather you are not from England."

"I was born in Poland, but I have lived in Berlin and Paris."

"I see. I hope you will come to future meetings."

"Certainly. I was very impressed."

"It is our habit for me to take the Sunday night lectures, and one of several others to take the Sunday morning lectures, but I hope you might consider speaking at some of our other meetings."

Was I really being invited to speak by Robert Owen? "I would be delighted," I stammered.

"Good. We shall arrange something, then. Now I must see a gentleman over there before he leaves. But I must ask, do you have someone to escort you home—your husband, perhaps?"

"I am separated from my husband. Divorced, actually." I seldom mentioned this, because unlike in Prussia, hardly anyone in England was divorced. In those days, an English divorce required proof of adultery and a private Act of Parliament, and almost every case was brought by a husband. Not surprisingly, then, English people had a rather low opinion of divorced women. Mr. Owen, however, was better traveled than most and had criticized England's illiberal divorce laws, so I doubted that he would mind. Indeed, he merely nodded and turned to the young man next to me. "Will you see Mrs. Kaufmann home, then?"

"Of course."

"Good. Mrs. Kaufmann, Mr. William Rose knows London like the back of his hand. He'll get you anywhere you need safely."

I turned to Mr. Rose after Mr. Owen had left. "Truly, sir, I don't want to put you to any trouble—"

"It's my pleasure, madam. Mr. Owen is right. There are some rough characters out this time of night, and you're practically a stranger to London."

"I've been here for nearly two years."

"Practically a stranger."

Not wanting to keep Mr. Rose longer than necessary, I quickly finished my tea, and Mr. Rose put on his hat and coat. I gave him my address, a pleasant but rather obscure little court which even some hackney drivers had trouble finding, but Mr. Rose was unfazed and began walking in the right direction. As he guided me expertly past our fellow pedestrians, many of whom were the worse for drink, I cleared my throat, it being my practice to take the opportunity to converse in English whenever I could. "Mr. Rose, I do not mean to be what I think they call a Pry Paul, but do you have family here in London?"

"Paul Pry, if you don't mind a little correction. My mother and my sisters, and some uncles."

"Do they attend these meetings too?"

"No. They don't share my views."

"I have had that experience. They differ with you about Mr. Owen's ideas?"

"Yes, but more so about religion. The truth is, I don't believe in God."

"Really? Neither do I."

"I thought as much when you gave your speech."

"There are so few of us. But it must be lonely for you. It has been at times for me."

He nodded as I impulsively pressed his hand. "Yes, but Mr. Owen has been very kind to me. And my master and his family treat me well."

"You are an apprentice, then? What trade do you follow?"

"I'm a silversmith." He tapped the top of his cane, which bore a dog's head in silver. "I made this mount. The sporting gents like them."

"It's lovely. When will your apprenticeship be over?"

"Just another two years. Then I'll be one and twenty."

Goodness, this was a *young* man. At twenty-five I felt positively ancient walking beside him. "Do you think Mr. Owen meant what he said about my speaking in public? I know my English is far from perfect."

"Mr. Owen never says anything he doesn't mean. You sound just fine to me." He cleared his throat. "But if you like, you can come by my shop and try out a speech. My master pretty much leaves the shop to me these days, and I can listen and work at the same time."

"I would like that." We had arrived at my lodgings; Mr. Rose had led me some way I had never gone myself. "You do know London."

"No credit to me; I'm what they call a Cockney. Born and bred here. Stop by my master's shop any time. It's on Shoe Lane."

"Ah, yes. I expected to see shoes on sale there, but there was not a single one. Why do they call it Shoe Lane if there are no shoes?"

Mr. Rose look at me pityingly. "That's just the way it is, Mrs. Kaufmann."

~ ~ ~

What to talk about? I had saved some of the papers I had written for Marcus, and though the early ones sounded rather jejune now, the later ones would do, although I had to translate them from German into English. This being done, I practiced speaking them aloud—for I was determined not to read from notes—and when I was satisfied, I went over to shoeless Shoe Lane and found the shop that employed Mr. Rose.

Mr. Rose was working behind the counter. He wore a shop coat that I thought suited him better than the frock coat he'd worn to Mr. Owen's meeting. "Mrs. Kaufmann. I was thinking you wouldn't take me up on my offer."

"But I have turned up, like a bad shilling."

"Bad penny."

"A bad shilling is worse, is it not?"

Mr. Rose chuckled. "Let's hear it."

I began declaiming, to find that Mr. Rose was a very exacting audience. He stopped me when I began to speak too quickly, made a chopping motion when I began to ramble, and said, "Get to the point, madam," when I went off on a flight of fancy. But none of his criticisms was undeserved.

At last, Mr. Rose—who true to his word had been working the entire time—pronounced me satisfactory. Knowing that the most sacred hour in the English day— teatime—had arrived, I offered to make some, to which Mr. Rose somewhat reluctantly assented. "I'll be happy to make it," he said.

"By no means, Mr. Rose. I have been monopolizing you shamefully, so I will take the work of tea upon myself."

To this day, I cannot forget the expression on Mr. Rose's face when he took his first sip. He tried to conceal it, the dear boy, but it was clear that I had blundered. "Does it not taste good?"

"Well." Mr. Rose heroically took another sip. "There's an English way of making tea, and there's—another way of making tea. Yours is not the English way, I guess."

"I won't be offended if you make it more to your liking."

"Well, if you don't mind." Mr. Rose's face was so relieved that I could not help but smile.

As Mr. Rose worked his magic with the tea kettle, I took the opportunity to look around the shop. "Is this all your work?" I said when he returned with a cup of tea.

"Most of it is."

"I must say I do prefer your tea to mine. You do fine work—I mean, with silver. Will you be joining the business in time?"

"I don't know. I have no complaints about my master, but I think now and then of going to America. You know that the Reform Act was passed, I'm sure, but most working men still can't vote here."

"And no women, of course."

"Very true. Anyway, I sometimes think I'd do better in America. But I don't know. I have to serve out my articles before I can make plans in that direction."

"I have sometimes thought of going there too."

"Who knows? Perhaps we both will." Mr. Rose cleared his throat. "So are you going to tell Mr. Owen you're ready to do a talk?"

"If you think I won't make a fool of myself."

"No. Tell him."

~ ~ ~

My maiden speech took place on a Wednesday. I knew not to expect a large crowd; it was the Sunday evening lectures that drew the multitudes.

I had continued to practice the lecture I delivered to Mr. Rose, but the more I rehearsed it, the less I liked it; it just did not seem to fit a London audience. Then I thought of what Mr. Rose had said about the Reform Act. It had been in the papers for months; the radicals said it did too little, the conservatives that it did too much. But it had not done a thing for women; in fact, it specifically limited the franchise to men, something that had always been assumed but never spelled out in cold black and white. So what better subject did I need?

There were multiple speakers scheduled. I was the third, and the only woman. I would not be the first lady to speak before a London audience, though; several had done so already, with varying degrees of success. As I tapped my foot nervously, awaiting my turn, I was glad that Mr. Rose was there; already I thought of him as a friend, and a lucky friend at that.

Mrs. Kaufmann was announced. Mr. Rose gave me a friendly squeeze of the hand as I rose and stepped up on the platform. This room was by no means as large as that in which Mr. Owen lectured, and the platform barely deserved that appellation, but even the foot or two it put me above the audience was daunting. Fifty pairs of eyes stared at me as I stood there, willing myself to start talking, which up until now had never been a problem.

Well. These people hadn't come here to see me standing on a platform like a lay figure. "We all know of the Reform Bill," I said, and Mr. Rose gave me a puzzled look. "Let me say now: it is an advance. Men can vote who could not do so before, and who can argue with that? But it does not allow women to vote—in fact, it specifically prevents them from voting. I suppose since we were not all explicitly prevented from voting before, we ladies should have taken our opportunity while we could!"

Mr. Rose, his face relaxing, chuckled. So did two other people.

"There is always talk of the royal succession. I do not follow it much; I am too much of a republican at heart, although I keep living in monarchies despite myself. But it seems safe to say that when the present king is no longer with us—I believe it is rude to say 'dies' of such an august personage—he will be succeeded by the Princess Victoria. Is that not absurd? The country will be ruled by a woman—at least in name—but that same woman could not cast a ballot at the meanest little shire in the land!"

There was outright laughter this time. I had my audience.

For ten more minutes—I did not want to overstay my welcome—I spoke, then sat down to a round of applause. "I did it!" I hissed to Mr. Rose.

"You certainly did." He smiled. "And did you see Mr. Owen come in? He heard almost every word."

I sat grinning foolishly as the next two speakers took their turns—they might as well have been speaking in Latin, for I did not attend to anything they said. The speeches over, it was time for tea, at which Mr. Owen approached me. "Well done, Mrs. Kaufmann. I trust we shall be hearing from you again."

"I thank you very much for the opportunity. And Mr. Rose for giving me good advice."

"He's a most sensible young man, you'll find."

Mr. Rose blushed.

A couple of people congratulated me on my speech, and then it was time to leave, it being taken for granted that Mr. Rose would escort me. "I hope you don't mind that I altered my speech."

"Not at all. It was an improvement. Did you practice?"

"Only a little in my head."

"I could never do that."

"I did try to follow your advice about not rambling too much."

"I noticed." After some hesitation, Mr. Rose asked, "What got you interested in the rights of women, if you don't mind me asking? Was your husband cruel?"

"No."

My answer must have sounded as brusque as it looks on paper, for Mr. Rose said, "I am sorry, Mrs. Kaufmann. I didn't mean to overstep."

"You didn't." I hoped my next words fell more softly. "In truth, I can hardly answer your question, because it seems that as soon as I learned to think, I could not understand why little boys could ask all the questions they wanted, while little girls were supposed to sit and be quiet. I could not understand why everyone made a fuss when a boy was born, but only shrugged at a girl. It struck me as injustice, and I cannot remember a time when injustice did not make me angry."

"Well, I think that you can do a lot to change people's minds. If they listen."

"Thank you, Mr. Rose."

"Would you like to try out your next speech on me?"

"I would be delighted to."

In that manner, I got into the habit of going to Mr. Rose's place of employment every week or so, and in giving a speech every few weeks. I do not want to give the idea that I was a lioness, drawing multitudes; I spoke at the smaller gatherings, first on Wednesday nights and then later at the women's meetings held on Friday nights. Mr. Owen drew the crowds; I was but a mere sideshow. Moreover, my Polish accent, with the overlay of German it had acquired in Berlin, was still strong, although it was improving; Mr. Rose, at my insistence, stomped his foot on the floor when it began to thicken, as it often did when I grew excited or weary.

Meanwhile, Mr. Owen, having found that I was quite alone in England, treated me almost as a daughter. He encouraged me to mingle more with like-minded young people, and so as a result I began to attend not only the lectures of Mr. Owen's group, but its dances.

Mr. Rose also became a regular fixture at these gatherings, although it soon emerged that he was a novice at the terpsichorean art. Having learned the popular dances while I was in Berlin and Paris, including the waltz, I undertook to instruct him, after his work was done for the day, and found him an excellent pupil. "I think you shall soon surpass me," I said after a particularly vigorous waltz. "The ladies will be fighting each other to have you as a partner."

"I have a very good teacher. You will dance with me, won't you, next week?"

"Of course," I said. "But you must not let any of the young ladies go without a partner. It is a gentleman's duty to see to it that no lady is forlorn. And who knows? You might meet your true love." Though I had not been bold enough to inquire, I did wonder from time to time why Mr. Rose, who aside from his other fine qualities was rather good-looking, had no sweetheart, at least as far as I could tell. Perhaps he was waiting until he had served out his apprenticeship, though I wondered how long the ladies would allow him to go on in this condition.

Mr. Rose made his dancing debut, as it were, a few days later. As I had predicted, he was much in demand, and even the few wallflowers went home well satisfied. I danced with Mr. Rose twice (including a waltz), as well as with Mr. Owen and a few others, and went home tired but content. I could feel myself growing younger.

So I settled into a comfortable routine of speaking, teaching, making my perfumed papers, and dancing, but one February evening in 1834 found me in low spirits, which Mr. Rose, to whom I was paying my usual visit, soon noticed. "You seem a little sad today, Mrs. Kaufmann."

I stepped down from the imaginary podium I had mounted. "Yes. I should not have inflicted myself upon you today. The truth is, it is a sad day for me."

"Why?"

I hesitated, but Mr. Rose was a dear friend—my best, in fact—and I found myself wanting to tell him everything. "I had a child with my husband—she was the reason we married, as a matter of fact." I wondered how Mr. Rose would receive that revelation, but his face registered no disapproval. "She died when she was quite a little thing. Today she would have been five."

"I am so sorry." Mr. Rose awkwardly touched my shoulder. "Why did you never tell me this? I thought we were good friends."

"It is something I dislike to speak about. Anyway, although I have never ceased to grieve for her, it is only two days a year—the anniversary of her birth and that of her death—that are hard for me now."

"What was her name?"

"Amalia Charlotte Kaufmann."

"A pretty name. Did she look like you?"

"I thought she did, but my husband thought she favored him. I suppose we both were right. I wish I'd had a miniature done of her, but of course I always assumed that there would be time."

It was the time when Mr. Rose closed the shop for the day. As was my habit when I was there at that hour, I helped him tidy up and closed the shutters. "I must admit, Mr. Rose, for some reason her death is weighing heavier on me this year than usual. Perhaps it is because she would have been starting to read and write by now; it is something I looked forward to teaching her. It would help if I did not have to go home to an empty room. Would you like to come over and share my evening meal? There is a little sitting area, so all will be quite respectable, and my fellow lodgers aren't scandalmongers. Most are in the theater."

"I would be honored."

We shut up the shop and walked to my lodgings, where we dined on some fish we'd bought on the street. With Mr. Rose's encouragement, I told him the story I have recounted here—the first time I had told it in full to anyone. I told it not without a few tears, but the telling of it gave me an immense comfort. "You have been a kind friend to me," I said as Mr. Rose began to collect his things. "I feel much better than before. Perhaps we can have another such evening, without the weeping on my part."

"I would like that." Mr. Rose hesitated. "Actually, there was something I'd like to ask you. I'll be turning twenty-one in a few weeks. My apprenticeship will end."

"I believe a celebration is in order, then."

"Well, my fellow apprentices have a night out planned, but there's something else I have in mind. I'd like to go to Greenwich. It's a Cockney thing, really. You go there by steamer, see the lions—I mean, see the sights like the observatory—have a good meal, and then take the steamer home."

"It sounds lovely."

"I was thinking I'd like to go with you. You've never been, I think, and, well—I like spending time with you better than with anyone else."

How could I say no after that? Not, in fact, that it ever entered my mind to do so. Indeed, I found myself looking forward more and more to our journey as the days passed. Mr. Rose was an excellent companion, and I had never been to Greenwich, so why should I not anticipate it with pleasure? The occasion rated my prettiest dress, on which Mr. Rose had complimented me (bashfully) several weeks before. It happened to be his favorite, he'd said.

On a beautiful Saturday in early May—Mr. Rose had been given leave—we went on our excursion. Boats have never agreed with me—my crossing to England had been a thoroughly miserable experience—but I managed the steamer nicely enough, especially with Mr. Rose pointing out the sights as we glided down the Thames. Once on land, a gratifying experience in itself, we enjoyed all the pleasures Greenwich had to offer, which included nodding at the pensioners at the Royal Marine Hospital who were enjoying the fine day, admiring the Painted Hall, watching the ball drop from the mast of the Royal Observatory to mark one o'clock, giggling at the young swains chasing their sweethearts down the hill on which the observatory perched, and strolling in the park. Finally, we sat down to dine on whitebait, a London delicacy that Mr. Rose took very seriously. I was worried that the tiny fish (no one ate just one) might not be prepared to his standards, but he pronounced them delicious, and then taught me how to pepper and lemon them properly. "You'll make a good Londoner yet," he said as I handed one to him in triumph.

At nightfall, we boarded our steamer. "It's been a perfect day," I said as we stood watching the lights of London twinkling at us as the steamer made its way upriver. It was hard to believe that this was the grimy city we'd left that morning.

"Yes. I hope what I am going to say won't spoil it, but I must say it." Mr. Rose turned his gaze from the riverbank to me, not quite meeting my eyes. "I love you. I've loved you since the night I met you."

He bent his head and put his hand upon the railing, as if bracing for my rebuff. I had to brace as well because of the wave of sheer happiness that was rolling through my body.

How could I have been so blind to his feelings—and mine? I was utterly content in this man's company. He was the kindest person I'd ever met. I trusted him absolutely. I'd told him of my folly, and he had offered only sympathy and understanding. And though he'd been a somewhat gawky youth when I had met him two years before, that was no longer the case. He had a fine form, and I could only too easily imagine it pressed against my own. Admittedly, he was six years my junior, but there was no good reason other than tradition that a man should be older than the woman he loved, and now that I considered it this seemed a particularly silly tradition. Evidently Mr. Rose didn't seem to mind.

Why, I'd even worn his favorite dress for this outing.

"Look at me—William."

He obeyed.

"I love you too."

"Really?"

"Really. How could I have not realized it?"

William pressed his lips to mine, rather to the delight of some boys standing near us, who called, "Kiss her again!" To avoid such interruptions, we strolled to a secluded part of the steamer to kiss some more (the boys' injunction being a perfectly reasonable one), and we continued to kiss and caress in the hackney coach we took from the dock to my lodgings, William seeing me safely inside my room. As he turned to leave, I said, "Stay the night."

"You mean—?"

"Yes. What is the point in playing the blushing virgin?" I shrugged and smiled. "That cow has already escaped through the barn door."

"Horse," William said. Then he embraced me, and on my narrow bed, with William's finely attuned fingers exploring my body, we found that we had the last ingredient for a loving relationship—passion—in abundance.

I will say nothing else except that William exercised the appropriate precaution against getting me with child, that at some point I remembered to wish him a happy birthday, and that the flexibility of youth is astonishing. My old bones ache just to think about it.

~ ~ ~

"Wake up, sleepyhead. I've made you tea."

Quite naked, I raised myself up to find William, wearing trousers and a shirt, standing over me. "Is it late?"

"Nine. You looked so content, I didn't want to wake you. But you might want to put something on in case the tea spills."

I shrugged on the shift William offered me before he handed me a cup of steaming tea. "I am content. I haven't slept so well in years."

"And I was admiring you as well. You're so lovely and lush. Not too plump, but not skin and bones either. You're—"

"*Zaftig*," I offered. "It's Yiddish."

"My *zaftig* Ernestine. Do you have any regrets?"

"Only that we didn't become lovers earlier." As I nestled against him and sipped my tea, I glanced in the mirror and winced. "And that you have no doubt discovered my ringlets require a bit of maintenance."

We exchanged some more sweet nothings and kisses. Then William asked, "What are we to do now? Live together? Keep company as we are now? Or marry? You know that here, it is a Church of England wedding or nothing, unless we marry as Jews or Quakers."

I shook my head. "I love you dearly, but I will not submit to another church wedding, and as you don't believe in God, the Jewish people aren't going to want you. I doubt they'd even want *me* back." I did not add that I sometimes thought my marriage to Marcus might have been more successful had it had not begun with the farce of our conversions to Christianity.

"I don't want a religious ceremony either, but if we live together and don't marry, I fear that people will be unkind to you. The woman always bears the brunt of such things, you know, and with you speaking in public as you do, you will be more of a target than most women. If anyone insulted you, I could not control myself."

I noted with interest that the possibility of my giving up speaking had not seemed to enter William's thoughts. "Then we must live apart and be discreet. It will be easy enough as long as I do not get with child." I took his hand. "And yet I would dearly love to bear your child."

"I still think of going to America, you know. But only if you want to go as well. There we could marry before a justice of the peace. And then we can have that child."

"I do want to go. The only thing that has kept me from going before is that I could not make up my mind to go there completely alone. Not very brave of me, I suppose." I smiled up at William. "And perhaps something was telling me that I did not want to leave you behind."

"Then I shall start saving." He anticipated what I was about to say. "You may have enough to get both of us there, but I don't want to use your money. The law gives me your property when we marry, but I do not intend to be bound by that law. I have learned from you how unjust that is."

How had I not loved William from the very start?

~ ~ ~

We did conduct ourselves discreetly, at least for the first year or so, with William visiting me in my room once or twice a week, or maybe two or three times. Or was it three or four times? Perhaps we weren't that discreet at all, but thanks to our precautions, I never got with child.

As our plan to emigrate grew nearer to fruition, William said one day, "I think I should introduce you to my mother and sisters. I have broken the news that I will be leaving the country, and I have also told them that I am not going alone."

"A divorced Polish-Jewish atheist who is six years older than you? I'm sure they'll love me."

William grinned. "They had better. I must warn you, Ma says what she thinks. And you will find my sister Mary Ann a bit odd. She may not even speak to you."

This sounded as if it was going to be a delightful visit.

But on the appointed Sunday, I put on my most demure, least divorced-shameless-hussy gown and proceeded with William to Ship Yard, where his family lived. "It's seen better days," William warned me. "Some of these houses were standing before the Great Fire of 1666, and they're beginning to show their age."

"Fancy that."

"And don't expect anything nautical about the area. It's named as it is because there was a tavern named the Ship back around the time of Charles II."

"Oh, I learned my lesson with Shoe Lane."

Ship Yard, hard by Temple Bar, was a narrow street nestled in a rabbit's warren of alleys, courts, and crooked streets, each dirtier and dingier than the last. I supposed it must have been a fine place back in Charles II's day, and some decades afterward, but it had declined severely over the past fifty years. The King William IV public house, however, had not received word of the neighborhood's decay; it sparkled and shone.

Most of the houses, once belonging to prosperous families, had long since been carved out into apartments, and the building to which William led me was no exception. We went up a dingy staircase, which must have been grand a century before; I fancied some dandy staggering up it after a night of dissipation or someone's bejeweled mistress listening for her lover's footsteps.

Having reached the second floor, William knocked on the first of several doors, and a pretty young girl of sixteen ushered us in. "William!" she said. "This must be your—"

"The lady of my heart," William said.

I had learned from William that his father had been a tailor, and that his mother and his sisters were needlewomen. The small parlor, which was well kept, testified to their trade: a dress form stood in a corner, and a table was covered with cloth, tape, and shears. An older woman, who could have been no one other than Mrs. Rose, sat on a sofa next to a young woman who was apparently the older of the daughters. All bore a resemblance to William. "Ma, this is Mrs. Kaufmann—Ernestine. Ernestine, this is my mother, and these are my sisters, Mary Ann and Hannah."

Hannah, the younger sister, waved us to two chairs and perched on a stool as Mrs. Rose and Mary Ann studied me. "So you're the woman who's dragging my son off to America."

"Ma, no one is dragging me to America. You know I've wanted to go for years. I wouldn't go if Ernestine didn't want to go, but as she does, we're going together."

"So you might be staying if you had met someone else."

"Maybe, but she's the lady I love."

I studied the courtyard outside the window. As it was not a pleasing sight—I suspected that this neighborhood had not fared well during the cholera epidemic of a few years before—I turned my eyes to a sampler that hung on the wall. It was beautifully worked, and clearly dated from the last century. "Did you work that?" I asked.

"I did." Mrs. Rose did not unthaw even for that.

Hannah, now busying herself with the teapot, said, "William says that you have traveled around, Mrs. Kaufmann."

"I have. I enjoy seeing new places."

"And now you're heading off across the Atlantic," Mrs. Rose said. "But they do say the Jews wander around." She looked at William. "She's not even your religion."

"I don't have a religion, Ma. I don't believe in God."

"At least you could have found a Christian girl who doesn't believe in God."

I fixed my gaze back on the sampler as Hannah, sounding rather desperate, asked, "Will you take a cup, Mrs. Kaufmann?"

"Yes, please."

I suspected that Mrs. Rose could have gone on grumbling forever, but under the influence of tea, she mellowed and asked William a few questions about his employment—he was working as a journeyman, saving both for his passage and for a good set of tools. Encouraged by this change in atmosphere, I admired the dress on the form—it really was quite well done—and we talked for a while about the tailoring trade, which was becoming less lucrative these days.

We were getting ready to congratulate ourselves upon a reasonably successful visit when Mary Ann, who had scarcely spoken, said, "William, you are being deceived."

"How?"

"By her pretty looks and sweet smile. She will treat you like her first husband, bedding any man who takes her fancy."

"Mary Ann!" William rose.

"Not in front of your little sister!" Mrs. Rose protested.

I set down my teacup carefully. "No doubt you assume that I am an adulteress because I am divorced?"

"Why else would you be divorced?"

"I was divorced under Prussian law, which does not require adultery for a man to divorce his wife. I was faithful to my husband. We parted for other reasons—chiefly, an incompatibility of habit and opinion."

Mary Ann scowled, but said nothing more. Poor Hannah looked mortified as only a sixteen-year-old girl could look, so I said, "William tells me you enjoy going to the theater, Hannah. What plays have you seen lately?"

It was a fortunate change of subject. Hannah kept a scrapbook of the plays she had attended—mostly penny shows—and was most happy to show it to me.

"Well," I told William as we finally emerged into Ship Yard, "I think one of them likes me. That's one more than I expected."

"I'm sorry Ma and Mary Ann acted as they did—especially Mary Ann. I should have stood up for you more."

"It would have probably made things worse, at least with your sister. Anyway, you need not tell your mother I said this, but I do admire her. It couldn't have been easy for her, raising three young children on her own after your father died."

"It wasn't. Nor was it easy for her to get the premium for my apprenticeship, especially as I could have gone into other trades at much less expense. But I was fascinated when I first saw a silversmith at his work, and I begged to be allowed to go into that trade. She fussed about it, and then she worked and worked to cobble together the payment."

"Ah, now I cannot dislike her at all."

William nodded. "Perhaps it was her example that makes me like a certain type of woman. One who can take care of herself." He cleared his throat as we passed onto Fleet Street. "Have you told your father about us—that we intend to marry?"

I winced. "I am going to tell him at the same time I tell him we are going to America. I may as well give him all the news at once."

"You're not ashamed of me, are you?"

"Why on earth would I be ashamed of you?"

William looked away. "I'm not an educated man, and I work with my hands. Not with my brain."

"Your brain is as good as any, and I rather like the way you work with your hands—double meaning fully intended. You create beautiful things; no fool can do that. I will be proud to call you my husband." I squeezed his hand. "I have not told Papa for only one reason: he may not be able to reconcile himself to a son-in-law who is not Jewish. Of course, Marcus converted, but he at least was born a Jew."

"He would cast you off?"

"I hope not, because he is very dear to me. But it happens. If it does, though, there is no question of where my loyalties must lie. With you."

William kissed me, right in the middle of Fleet Street, and after that we had no more nonsense about my being ashamed of him.

Had William and I been the only persons concerned, we would have emigrated straightaway, but we had decided to journey to America with a group of followers of Robert

Owen, with a rather vague plan to form a communal settlement of the sort Mr. Owen had founded in New Harmony, Indiana, in the previous decade. It was true that the New Harmony venture had lasted only a few years, although a coterie of reformers remained in the area, but what were mistakes but to be learned from? Many of our fellow emigrants had yet to get their affairs in order, which slowed our progress considerably, although at least it gave William more time to save.

As we waited, we more and more disliked our state of living apart, so at last William and I declared ourselves married in fact if not in law—a moral marriage, as our friends Richard Carlile and Eliza Sharples, who were impeded by his inability to divorce his estranged wife, called their union. We felt a little ceremony was in order, however, so we summoned a baffled notary to my room to witness our vows. "Is this even legal?" he asked as William and I promised to love, cherish, and be faithful to one another, that if those things no longer held true, we would part without rancor, and that if we should part, I would have no claim to his support and he would have no claim to my inheritance.

"It is in the new moral world that we wish to create," William said solemnly.

I do believe that the notary muttered "Bedlam" under his breath, but it was too faint for us to take umbrage.

Knowing that William's family would disapprove of a ceremony not sanctioned by the church or the law, we had not invited them, but Mr. Owen and a few other of our friends were present. There being no reason why a moral marriage could not encompass cake, we had ordered a delicious one for our guests to enjoy. Even the notary mellowed under its influence. "You really must attend one of

Mr. Owen's meetings," I said as I offered him a second piece. "They are very informative."

"Well, I might just do that, madam."

Because the Greenwich steamer was where we had declared our love, we journeyed by water to Greenwich after our guests had left. There we took a room at a good inn, dined on fish, and celebrated our marriage in a sumptuous bed. Afterward, we lay side by side and talked of the future. "You don't think you'll get homesick for London?" I asked.

"Time will tell. But you are dearest to me of all the world—and you are going with me. Where you will go, I will go; that will be my home."

"That sounds depressingly biblical, but I can't argue with the sentiment."

"What about you? Won't you miss your family?"

"I do, but it's not as if I can see Papa anyway." The Polish uprising I had tried to join years before had been crushed, and since then, the Russian government had exercised an iron hand over Poland. Thousands with liberal views had emigrated; on some London streets I heard so much Polish that I could have imagined myself back in my native land were it not for the Cockney street vendors crying out their wares. Papa had warned me not to return even for a short visit, and I doubted I would be allowed into the country even if I tried.

But with William and I as married as we were going to be until we could find a justice of the peace in America, it was time to write to Papa and Sophie. Without going into the troublesome detail of the nature of our marriage ceremony, I simply informed Papa that I had married William, leaving him to deduce for himself that my Cockney husband was not Jewish, though with Sophie I was somewhat more confiding. With both, I made a point of mentioning that there was no necessity for marriage this time, purely love.

A few weeks later, their replies arrived. William bent over me as I read the letters, Papa's in his spiky Hebrew, Sophie's in her elegant German script. "Papa is not casting me off. I do not think that he is particularly pleased at our marriage, but he seems to bear it philosophically enough. I suppose I really cannot shock him now. He actually seems to like the idea that we are going to America; he says that he will encourage his sons to leave Poland when the time comes. Sophie, on the other hand, is worried that I am going to be scalped by red Indians, or die of an ague, unless we get shipwrecked first. She does think you will be good protection against the Indians, though, and she thinks you sound like a lovely man, even though you are a fellow infidel."

William grinned at me. "Then we're all set."

~ ~ ~

A rag doll, followed by a ball, grazed my cheek as I bent over the basin into which I had already deposited most of my latest meal. I raised my head. "Miss Smithson! Master Smithson! Can't you let me puke in peace?"

"Sorry, ma'am." Master Smithson moved a foot away from me and resumed battle with his sister.

There was an endless supply of young Smithsons in steerage—evidently born in rapid succession, from which I inferred that Mr. Smithson had seldom been required to travel from home. They were immune to seasickness, and it seemed that this held true for gravity as well, because no matter how the ship *Napier* tossed and turned, the Smithson children remained upright, sprightly, and bored out of their minds— hence the missiles that flew in steerage on a daily basis.

One other person in steerage was immune to seasickness —my dear William—and if I had not loved him I would have found this quite irksome. As I wiped my face with a grimy cloth, he bounded down the stairs that led from the deck. Even the captain had complimented him upon his sea legs; all he needed was a sailor's cap to make him the jolliest of tars. "Come on up! It's fine out today. The fresh air will do you good."

I sighed and took his hand. "I suppose it can't do any harm."

"That's the spirit." He glanced at the Smithson children, who were staring at him wistfully. "We'll watch out for them, Mrs. Smithson, if you want to let them join us."

Pied Piper-like, most of the young Smithsons followed us to the deck as Mrs. Smithson feebly called her thanks.

With the younger Smithsons safely by our side and the rest in no imminent danger of going overboard, William and I gazed out at the ocean. It was calm, which I perversely found rather dull despite the misery that the sea inflicted upon me when it was more lively. "Are we any closer?"

"Captain says a week or so." William pointed. "Look, I think that's a dolphin!"

"It's a dolphin, all right," called a sailor. "A school of them, in fact."

The Smithson children—and I—squealed appreciatively as the dolphins sprang out and into the water as if for our express amusement. "I'm glad you had me come up," I said as we lost sight of our friends. "I feel much better."

"I'm glad you do, because there's something I think we need to talk about. Our colony."

We were traveling with about thirty-five other followers of Mr. Owen. "What of it?"

"We've made no plans, except to head to New Harmony. Shouldn't we be trying to set some rules for ourselves? Figure out how we are to divide our labor? I'm willing to do whatever hard work needs to be done, but I also want to practice my trade. I've worked too long and too hard at it to give it up to plow the fields. What are you to do? I know you don't want to cook and do laundry all day long, not when you could teach or lecture. And where do we even want to settle? These are things we could be talking about while we're at sea, but no one seems to want to talk about them."

"You're right. We should have a meeting this very night, assuming the sea is not like the night before." I had not even bothered climbing into our berth, but had huddled with William in a corner as the ship did various acrobatics, always righting itself just when I was convinced that we would come to rest at the bottom of the Atlantic. One of our fellow freethinkers had even been heard to pray, though William and I had stood firm in that respect at least. I had taken some comfort in the thought that he and I would perish together, and that perhaps our bones would be found in a tender embrace.

"But who is to call it?"

"Who better than you? Think of how much help you've given to Mr. Owen over the past few years, organizing his events."

"Well, I'll give it a try."

That very evening, William did convene an Owenite meeting, which took place amid the baggage with William seated on a barrel. It attracted a number of spectators from the non-Owenite contingent, some of whom had a number of misconceptions about us, the chief being that we had no respect for marital bonds and that the ladies among us were shared freely among the men. I suspect these people were rather disappointed to see us all seated with the same partners with whom we had boarded.

"In a few days we'll be in America," William said, to general cheers. "I think we need to start making some plans, so we won't quarrel among ourselves once we get there. Of course, I'm sure we will quarrel about some things anyway. It's only human na—"

"Like her baby keeping us up all night."

"It's a baby! What do you expect?"

"I'm sure that won't be a problem once we get off this ship," William said. "I was thinking about the bigger problems, really. How are we to divide our labor? How are we to settle our disputes? What work are women to do? There is no reason they should be confined to domestic chores."

"Not that there is any dishonor in such work," I put in.

"All these decisions can wait," said one man. "Why fret over them when we haven't even found a place to settle?"

"That's something else we could talk about," William said. "Settle near New Harmony, or somewhere else? I think we should start to narrow it down. I'm sure no one wants to live in a slave state, but that still leaves a lot of places to choose—"

"We could live in a slave state," another man said. "We wouldn't have to own slaves ourselves."

"But we would become corrupted by the slave system," I said. "What if we had to hire someone to do something for us, and he sent his slave to do the work?"

"Surely, Mrs. Rose, we could find someone without slaves to do our work."

"True," I said, not so much to concede the argument as to rescue poor William, who was looking miserable on his barrel.

A clap of thunder ended our discussion. Soon we were all in our accustomed state of misery, and even William confessed to feeling queasy.

We tried the next morning to further our discussion with our fellow Owenites, but to no avail. "No one wants to think beyond the present moment," I told William later as we took a turn (or in my case a wobble) on the deck. "Don't look so glum, darling. You tried your best, but they are simply not prepared for communal life."

"No." William stared out at the horizon. "And to be honest, I don't think I am either. I really just want to make a life with you, without worrying about others."

"Why did you not tell me this before?"

"I know you are fond of Mr. Owen, and enthusiastic about this community. I didn't want to disappoint you."

"It is best to find out these things now, instead of somewhere in Indiana. Which, truth be told, I do not think I could find on a map were it not labeled."

"So we will break off from the others?"

"Yes." I squeezed William's hand. "We can carry out Mr. Owen's principles in other ways. I must admit that I am a little relieved myself. And I imagine the others will not miss our nagging them. But where shall we settle, then?"

"Not in a slave state, we know." William smiled at me. "Why not New York? It's right there when we step off the ship, and I can open my own shop or find employment with someone else."

"Then New York it is."

Our fellow travelers took the news of our defection calmly, as I had predicted, and the last we saw of them they were standing on the dock, quarreling over how best to get to Indiana from New York. Later, I learned that they did get there; after that, they scattered in various directions, and our planned colony was never heard of again. But I had no thought for them as William and I stood hand in hand on the steamer that transported us from the ship into New York Harbor. All of our worldly goods—our clothing and bedding, William's tools, my mother's receipt book and jewelry casket, the Perrault from which I'd read to Amalia, and a dozen or so other books—stood in trunks around our feet. In front of us stood a new world of possibilities.

6

December 1836 to July 1841

"We ladies have all the rights we need."

"But we really don't—"

The lady of the house shut the door firmly in my face. "Not very neighborly," I muttered to myself.

Just days after William and I arrived in New York, Judge Thomas Herttell, a member of the state legislature, had proposed the subject of protecting the property rights of married women, with the goal of introducing a bill to that effect. It was an issue in which I now had a more than theoretical interest, because William and I, now that we were in a nation where we could marry without a religious ceremony, had gone before a justice of the peace and legalized our union. I knew that William, my darling, could be trusted with what I had brought to the marriage—but I also knew that other women were not so lucky, that what they could call their own could be dissipated at the racetrack, in the gambling dens, on ill-advised business ventures, or even on well-intentioned causes. A few months afterward, we met Judge Herttell in person, for he was a fellow freethinker and had the additional merit of having been able to call Thomas Paine, the American I most admired, a friend. Impressed by the venerable judge and his cause, I had promised to help him as best I could by circulating a petition supporting his proposal, which had not attracted much support despite its making so much sense.

Neither had my petition.

I banged into the little shop on Grand Street where William plied his trade and over which we lodged. Usually, I would look around admiringly at it, because William and I had set it up together; anticipating that it would take a while for William to gain a reputation as a silversmith, we had decided to offer an array of fancy goods for sale, along with my contribution of cologne waters and, of course, Madame Sylvie's papers. With Christmas and New Year's around the corner, we'd worked hard to make everything as appealing as possible. "Our neighbors are fools," I announced. "And I'm freezing."

William looked up from the hair receiver he was crafting. "No signatures yet?"

"Not a single one."

"Come warm up, dear."

I crouched before the stove that warmed the tiny shop. "The men are bad enough, but the women are worse. They say, 'I don't need this. My husband knows what's best for us.' Or my favorite, 'We have plenty of rights already, what do we need with more?' What rights, I ask? They never tell me."

"Perhaps it's the wrong time of year. Ladies are preparing for the holidays."

"They should be thinking of their future." I sighed as my chilled hands began to thaw. "I'll go back out tomorrow. I did get one lady to promise that she would buy a silver knife from you for her daughter."

William grinned at me. "See, your powers of persuasion do work."

~ ~ ~

The next day, picking the time that was usually quietest in William's shop—he had no assistant, so I usually did the honors—I set out on my mission once more, starting where I'd left off the day before. In the belief that married women would be the most sympathetic to my petition, I looked for houses that appeared to be occupied by families instead of single lodgers.

I knocked on a likely-looking door, which was opened by a servant girl—an Irish servant girl, as her brogue quickly revealed. "Good afternoon. Is the lady of the house at home? My name is Mrs. Rose, and I am circulating a petition, which I would like to speak to her about." I had learned that it was best to state my business up front, as some might assume I was selling needles or suchlike, others that I was passing out religious tracts. Even with this preamble, a servant the other day had tried to interest me in buying the household's old clothes.

"A petition about what?"

"The rights of women to own their own property."

"Who is that person, Maggie?" The lady of the house, for in her neat cap she could be no one else, appeared behind the servant. "I'll deal with her."

Maggie retreated. "I will not take up your time unnecessarily, madam," I said. "I am circulating a—"

"Where are you from?"

"My husband and I live a few blocks away on Grand Street."

"You're not from this country. Where are you from?"

"Poland, originally."

"You look Jewish. Are you?"

"By birth, yes."

"Then get yourself off."

"Madam?"

"Are you deaf? I said, get yourself off. I can spot a Jew a mile away, and I won't have one in my house. You dirty Jews are nothing but troublemakers. You—"

I whirled around before hearing exactly what trouble we caused. The door slammed behind me.

I could not help the tears that came into my eyes. I'd been reminded of that long-ago day in Piotrków when the woman and the boys had hounded me; I had expected better of America. But I wasn't going to help my cause by weeping, or let another stupid woman dissuade me, so I brushed away my freezing tears and knocked at the next suitable house. It was substantial and well kept, exactly the sort of place that might contain a lady who had brought property to her marriage.

This time, a black servant opened the door. In the hallway stood a massive, ornate coat rack, fitted with a looking glass. A couple of chairs with plump cushions stood on either side. More unnerved from my last encounter than I knew, I said only, "Is the lady of the house at home?"

"That will be Mrs. Turner. Your name?"

"Mrs. Ernestine Rose."

The servant disappeared down the hall. I heard her saying, "A foreign lady here to see you, ma'am."

Mrs. Turner, middle-aged and stylishly dressed, appeared soon thereafter. "If you're the French girl who's been sending those letters badgering me for a place here, it's no use. My girls don't want a Frenchwoman here. Their minds are made up, and there's no changing them. Pity, because you are rather pretty, though no one would take you for twenty years of age, my dear."

Oh my. Flushing, I said, "I am not looking for a place, madam."

"If you're here to scold your husband, you'll have to do that when he gets home. Some men just need variety, you know. Nothing personal."

"My husband is accounted for. I should have stated my business earlier. I have a petition—?"

"I hope you're not one of those do-gooders. I mind my business. Let them mind theirs."

"I try to do good, but I am not a do-gooder. This concerns women in general—their right to hold property. I gather you have been married?"

"I have. The scoundrel ran off with everything I owned and ran through it all before he had the decency to drink himself to death. So I took up this line of work."

"My petition is exactly about that. It is to prevent married women from being deprived of their property. May I show it to you?"

"I suppose. Come into the parlor."

I followed her into that room, which featured more mirrors and amply cushioned chairs, although the color scheme was pale yellow, not the scarlet I had naturally expected. A young woman looked up from her study of the latest *Godey's Magazine* to frown at me. "You sound French. You're not the Frenchwoman, are you?"

"No, I have other business here. And I am Polish, actually." Not letting my back touch the chair, I took a seat.

The young lady chuckled at my primness. "Nothing goes on in this room but talk. Talk and some very good games of cards."

"I see." Settling in my chair more comfortably, I turned toward Mrs. Turner, who was looking at me somewhat impatiently. Having never gained entry to a house with my petition, and certainly not to a house of this nature, I was at a loss at first. "One of our representatives in the state legislature, Judge Thomas Herttell, plans to introduce a bill to allow married women to keep the property they bring to their marriage. At present, when a woman marries, her husband gains control of everything she owns—even her clothing. Even if she has to support the family, he can lay claim to all her wages. He can do whatever he pleases with them, for good or for ill, and there is nothing she can do about it."

"That I know."

"I am circulating this petition to help Judge Herttell— to show the legislature that this is an injustice, and one that women care about. I am circulating it to women for that reason. If we can make ourselves heard, we can change this foolish law. And if we change that, who knows what we could do next?"

"Well, it makes good sense to me. Can't hurt. I'll sign."

I produced pen and ink, very quickly lest Mrs. Turner change her mind, and watched in awe as my petition acquired its first signature. "Thank you so much."

"I can sign," the young lady offered. "Who knows? I might get married."

Mrs. Turner shook her head. "Better not. Wouldn't help the lady's cause to have it signed by all you girls. Would it?"

"Probably not," I said reluctantly. "The legislature might get the wrong impression. With no women there to set them straight, that is an easy thing to do."

Mrs. Turner chuckled and invited me to have tea, assuring me that few clients came this time of day and that she would ensure that I did not encounter them if they did. That being the only objection I had to staying, I agreed, for I was curious as to what led an intelligent woman to this sort of life and hoped that she would broach the subject. She did not disappoint: She came of a respectable family but after her parents' deaths had made an ill-advised marriage at a young age to a man who had proved to be a gambler and a drinker as well as a philanderer. Left destitute, with her children having died young, she had taken in sewing but had met a woman who had offered her a place in her house. "I never went hungry or cold, I went to the theater regularly, and I wasn't working myself blind night after night." Having saved her money, she had opened her own house when her mistress died and had made a success of it. "Now ask me who has it better, my girls or those poor creatures you see wearing themselves out with the needle."

I could not argue with her, though I could not help but think that if girls were trained up to professions or trades as their brothers were, there would be no need to choose between ill-paid drudgery and selling their bodies. Mrs. Turner then got me to give her my own (quite abbreviated) life story. "Twenty-three," she said, referring to William's age. "You'll want to make sure he stays satisfied."

"I think we manage that nicely."

"Everyone can do a little better, dear. Just let me give you a few tips. Trust me, he'll like the results—and so will you."

Blushing, I listened as Mrs. Turner dispensed her advice, which I promised to put into practice that very evening. We parted with mutual good wishes, and I emerged back into respectable society, ignoring the glances that came my way as I sallied forth. I had a signature! Resisting my urge to rush home and share the good news with William, I went up a block or two and knocked on another door—and obtained a second signature, this one from a widow. Perhaps the most likely signers were those without husbands around to tell them how many rights they had, I reflected.

It had been a glorious day, notwithstanding the hateful woman I'd encountered at the outset. And it turned out to be a glorious night, because I put one of Mrs. Turner's tips into practice. William was most appreciative, and as predicted, I enjoyed myself as well.

And yes, I have written the preceding few paragraphs all in Yiddish, not without considerable trouble on my part. If you have managed to read them, I commend you for your own effort.

~ ~ ~

In the end, I obtained five signatures on my petition and consoled myself that it was five more than I would have obtained had I done nothing. It was perhaps not the best time to be circulating petitions about property, because the economy, which had been booming when William and I arrived, was teetering, and in the spring of 1837, it crashed. Thousands were thrown out of work.

William had to resort to repairing jewelry to keep us afloat, and I had to help out more in his shop, which along with our lodgings was now on Frankfort Street, not far from where the Brooklyn Bridge is today (so I am told; it was under construction when I last saw New York). On fine evenings, William and I liked to walk over to Battery Park, where we could stroll around and admire the vessels going to and fro. We also liked to attend the meetings at Tammany Hall, just a short walk away, although it has since moved. (I never met people so little inclined to stay in one place as New Yorkers.) The Society of Moral Philanthropists rented the hall on Sundays, holding lectures in the morning and evening and debates in the afternoon. William and I seldom missed a Sunday there.

Shortly after our move to Frankfort Street, we came to Tammany Hall on a Sunday afternoon to find Mr. Benjamin Offen, an English-born shoemaker who led the Society, with no one to debate because his scheduled opponent had fallen ill. "I could speak by myself," he was telling Mr. Gilbert Vale, the editor of the *Beacon*, a freethought newspaper with strong links to the Society, "but the people are expecting a debate, and besides, I will be speaking tonight. I suppose we shall have to refund their money."

I knew that things were rather tight for the Society these days, and it needed any penny it could get. "I can debate you."

Mr. Offen turned to me. "You, madam?"

"I have spoken in public before, in London, and I disagree with you about Mr. Owen's ideas, which I support and you do not. So why not debate?" I smiled. "I can give you a perfectly good argument."

Mr. Offen looked at William, as if seeking his permission. "My wife is an excellent speaker," was all he said.

"Well, then we shall give it a try. Something must be done, after all."

Having lived with an Englishman for some time now, I knew this meant that Mr. Offen was in the depths of despair.

William helped me up onto the platform, and Mr. Offen introduced me as "Mrs. Rose, a Polish lady," presumably to explain my accent and perhaps to win me some sympathy, Americans being rather well disposed to Poles thanks to General Ko?ciuszko's exploits during the Revolution. Then we began our debate, which concerned whether Mr. Owen's socialist beliefs were conducive to happiness. I of course took the Owenite side.

I had never formally debated, but despite his grumblings about little girls asking questions, Papa had always been willing to enter into discussions with me, which frequently turned into friendly disputes—at least until I abandoned religion altogether. Mr. Offen was old enough to be my father and then some. So I could almost imagine myself back in Poland, if my father had been a raging freethinker instead of a pious rabbi, and as a result felt quite at ease despite having not spoken in public since I'd left London. Mr. Offen, who had taken the stage with such gloomy courtesy, soon began to brighten as he made the happy realization that I was not making a fool of myself, or of him for sharing the platform with me. The audience, which had clearly shared his apprehension, began to study us, and not their shoes, and to laugh when I wanted them to laugh and nod when I wanted them to nod. When we went over our time, no one bothered to tell us.

At last, however, we tired, and the audience gave us a round of applause. Mr. Offen smiled at me as he helped me off the platform. "I think that went very nicely, Mrs. Rose. I will be seeing you here again, I imagine."

It was more of a command than a question.

Thus, I became a regular feature of Sundays at Tammany Hall. At first my appearances were confined to the debates, but by the fall, I had moved to the coveted Sunday evening spots. The *Beacon*, of course, made note of this, but to my surprise, the *New York Sun*, one of the large dailies, did as well. William kept a scrapbook of all these notices, and I could not resist sending clippings, with translations, to Papa and Sophie. Sophie was full of questions: Were the men in the audience respectful? Was I frightened? How did a woman dress for the podium? Papa expounded at length upon his opinions of Robert Owen's philosophy, which I found he had taken some time and what must have been considerable trouble to read up on. (His opinions, of course, did not match my own.) Then he informed me that his brilliant daughter was the talk of Praszka, and our former residence of Piotrków as well. He supposed he might be doing a great deal of the talking.

When I read that, I knew that I had finally redeemed myself for my foolishness of a decade before. I must also say that I cried.

~ ~ ~

In December, William and I attended a meeting to address the topic of common schools. It was a topic that interested us greatly, for there could be no better means of addressing the inequalities in society than by affording every girl and boy a free, excellent education. We hoped that someday our interest might become more personal, because we were still wishing for children, although nothing yet had occurred to raise our hopes in that direction. It was ironic, I reflected, that having fallen pregnant so quickly when I was unwed, I could not manage this feat now that I basked in married respectability.

But I digress. The meeting was held at the Broadway Tabernacle, which had been built to accommodate a popular preacher. Because of its size (it held thousands), it was a popular meeting place, and William and I were encouraged to see it packed on this particular night, even though it meant we had to sit in the gallery.

The first couple of speakers were quite sensible, and the next speaker, who was introduced as the Reverend Mr. Breckinridge, formerly of Kentucky, started out that way. Then he launched into a diatribe in which he called for a moral crusade against infidels, which nonbelievers were called in those days, and which some of us were quite happy to call ourselves. He ranted about Thomas Paine, decried the Sunday speakers at Tammany Hall (we had a certain reputation by now), alluded daintily to free love, and summed up with his vision of how the common schools could be used to give children a religious education. Which religion? I wondered. Obviously it would be Christianity, but which of its infinite varieties would suit the good cleric? I couldn't see the Protestants happily learning to pray the rosary, or the Catholics putting up with married priests. "Perhaps the Mormons could run the schools," I suggested to William, probably not in the lowest voice I could have used.

Mr. Breckinridge, meanwhile, was heading toward his grand conclusion. "If we allow the infidels to prevail, we shall perish—and we shall deserve it. But never fear, because we will not. I am ready to fight the infidels with their own weapons!"

"And what would those be?" William hissed to me. "Logic?"

As Mr. Breckinridge sat and quaffed something from a glass—I assume it was water and not good Kentucky bourbon—ushers began to hand out cards for those who wished to put their names down for a subscription, whether for the benefit of Mr. Breckinridge or the schools I do not recall. I rose to my feet. "May I be permitted to ask a question of the chair?"

The chairman looked around, then upward. "You may."

"I do not wish to intrude upon the audience, for they came here to discuss the matter of education, which as a woman is dear to my heart. It is dear to my heart as a foreigner, too, because a great country should have a well-educated populace. But since the subject of infidelity has been raised, and since I know that the infidels, as you call them, only seek to propagate knowledge and truth without mystery and superstition—"

"Throw her out!" someone yelled.

"A Tammany Hall infidel!"

"Put her out!"

"Let the lady ask her question," said Mr. Breckinridge, rising.

The hissing turned to clapping, which went on for a ridiculous time before I finally could be heard. "Thank you, sir. I merely wish to ask, are you sincere in saying that you are ready to fight infidels with their own weapons? If so, may I ask which weapon you wish to choose?"

Downstairs, people were standing on their seats simply to stare at me—those who were not too busy stamping their feet and calling me an infidel, I should say. William had arisen and put a protective arm around me. If I had been near the railing, I might have feared for my safety, but as it was, I stood calmly as Mr. Breckinridge, who could no better be heard than anyone else at this point, tried to hush the crowd.

"It is a fair question from a fair opponent," Mr. Breckinridge said at last. "However, I have always been taught never to fight with a lady."

Cheers filled the building. One would think that the man had done something besides refuse to engage in a sensible argument.

There were still some hisses directed at me, however. Not wishing to distract from the more rational speakers who I hoped would follow Mr. Breckinridge, and not wishing to put William into a position where he might have to fight, I whispered to him, "I think we should go."

Amid some cackling, we made our way out of the gallery and downstairs, where William helped me arrange my shawl before we stepped out into the cold. Lo and behold, Mr. Breckinridge himself appeared, adjusting a muffler. "Why, it is you, madam. Allow me to say that you speak excellent English." He smiled. "And your voice carries quite well. Few ladies could make themselves heard from the gallery, I believe."

"Thank you. I have been practicing projecting it. It is essential for a speaker."

"You speak in public, madam?"

"Yes. Usually at Tammany Hall."

Mr. Breckinridge turned his attention to William. "Are you married to this lady, sir?"

"I have that honor."

"And you let her speak in public? In that viper's den of Tammany Hall? I am amazed."

"I don't command my wife, sir. She is my companion, not my inferior. But as it happens, I share her beliefs, and I am quite happy to have her speak. She does so beautifully, I think. You ought to come hear her. Perhaps you might even find something in our viper's den to agree with."

"And I would be quite willing to debate you there—or anywhere." I took William's arm. "Good evening, sir."

A couple of days later, the *New York Herald*—which made a great show of despising us Tammany Hall infidels, but also realized that we made good press—printed a piece about the meeting in which I, misidentified as a French lady, was duly mentioned. *The lady, who was calm and unmoved during all the excitement she had occasioned, left the gallery, and the reverend gentleman soon after was seen passing through the crowd to the door. We hope he had an interview with his fair opponent and converted her.* "What bosh!"

"Bollocks," William agreed, and got out his shears to add it to his scrapbook.

~ ~ ~

By 1839, the newspapers were in a perpetual state of indignation, for there were now a number of ladies speaking on public platforms. Besides me, there was Mrs. Mary Gove, who talked about the workings of the female body, the foolishness of tight-lacing, and what she called the Solitary Vice. (Although I found her admirable, on the whole, I did wonder whether the Solitary Vice was worth all her time and trouble.) There were the Grimké sisters, the Quakeress Mrs. Lucretia Mott, and Miss Abby Kelley, who spoke against slavery. By and by, I met most of them. But no one was more prominent, or more adept at raising journalistic ire, than Madame Frances Wright D'Arusmont, a Scottish heiress better known as Fanny Wright.

Madame D'Arusmont, as she became known after marrying a Frenchman, had been a friend of General Lafayette in her youth, and she had visited Thomas Jefferson at Monticello while touring America. She had established a commune in Tennessee for slaves—slaves she had purchased herself for the express purpose of freeing. (Like New Harmony, which Miss Wright, as she was then, had also visited, the venture had failed miserably, and the slaves had been resettled in Haiti.) She was a good friend of Mr. Owen's son Robert Dale Owen, who was said to have been half in love with her, and the two had started a newspaper together. But she had capped all of this by taking to the platform, speaking on the rights of women and freethought—subjects dear to my own heart. She drew crowds—some to listen, and many to jeer, for she was simply ahead of her time.

At this point, Madame D'Arusmont was particularly unpopular in New York, as she had supported Van Buren for president, and in the wake of the crashing economy, he was blamed for everything. Her lectures in 1838—William and I attended one—had been interrupted by louts who hooted and banged their feet throughout the proceedings. But she was still welcomed by the Society of Moral Philanthropists, and so in early 1839, I found myself sharing the platform with her. It was a benefit for old Mr. Offen, who had been hit particularly hard by the economic downturn.

Having known in advance that Madame D'Arusmont would be present, I had reverted to my habit of practicing in front of William, and this talk, on freedom of speech, went well, I thought; I even spotted the man scribbling in the front row, plainly a newspaper reporter, nodding in approval before he caught himself. Mr. Offen enlarged upon the theme I had set, and then Madame D'Arusmont, a tall woman in an elegant black silk dress, approached the podium to applause that took some time to die down. Somewhat to my disappointment, she spoke mainly in generalities, but they were pleasing to the crowd and earned even more applause.

At the reception afterward, I paid a quite sincere homage to Madame D'Arusmont, who smiled and nodded down at my five-foot, two-inch height from her superior vantage. "You speak quite well yourself, Mrs. Rose."

"Why, thank you."

"You are a native of Poland, I understand. Polish is your first language, then?"

"No. Yiddish."

"Ah." Madame D'Arusmont looked momentarily puzzled. Evidently there had been no Yiddish speakers in General Lafayette's entourage, or at Monticello. "I understand that you have been speaking here regularly. Have the press been harsh to you?"

"No, not particularly. But they have hardly noticed me."

"Oh, they will, my dear. Just you wait." Madame D'Arusmont put on her bonnet and shook my hand. "Don't let them scare you off when they do."

~ ~ ~

A New Fanny Wright, I read a few days later. *Tammany has found, in the person of a Mrs. Rose, who we understand is a Polish lady, reported to be divorced from an elderly gentleman of that unfortunate country, and now married to or living with a very good-looking young American, who attends her on her duties at the Hall.* The reporter proceeded to a description of myself—*Of good figure, rather embonpoint, and tastefully and neatly dressed*—followed by a summary of my speech, with every *th* being rendered as *d*. I looked up at William, who was drinking his morning coffee. "Do I really sound that bad?"

"Of course not. Am I really dat good-looking?"

I smacked him with the newspaper. "Of course you are."

I reread the opening sentence. The reporter had gotten some things wrong—Marcus had been by no means elderly, and if William had not been his usual quiet self, it would have been clear as soon as he opened his mouth that he was not American—but it was disconcerting how much he had gotten right.

"You don't think I told the reporter about your divorce, do you?" William took my hand. "It is nothing to be ashamed of, but I know you don't want such personal things bandied about."

"No, I know you better than that. But I wonder who did tell them all that."

"Perhaps someone who came over with us. Or maybe he just made it all up—or thought he did."

I sighed and fingered the little silver locket that William had made me. Inside was a strand of Amalia's hair, still in a perfect little black curl. "True. But I wonder what else he could find out."

A few days later, I received a note from Madame D'Arusmont inviting me to take tea with her at her lodgings on Canal Street. Naturally, I accepted, and found myself at a building so faded-looking that I was certain I must have misread the address. But all was quite right, and soon I stepped into a room that quite matched the building's unpromising exterior. "You must forgive me, Mrs. Rose. I keep no servant, and I was brought up to be perfectly useless, so I could not sweep a floor properly if my life depended upon it. The girl here is quite inefficient."

I itched to set the place to rights myself, which would not have taken much effort, as it was a small chamber, furnished very meagerly. The nicest thing about it was the carpet. "My husband sent that from France. He and our daughter will be joining me here shortly, and I trust we shall then move to more pleasant accommodations. But enough about this tiresome subject. I believe you have been christened the new me, and made a divorcée to boot."

"That part is true. My first husband divorced me under Prussian law, at my request."

"Really? You will pardon me for my inquisitiveness, I hope. Was he cruel to you?"

"No, he was a good man, but I was not in love with him. We had a child together—well, the child necessitated the marriage—and when she died, I could see no point in continuing it." I fiddled with my wedding ring. "I tell you this in confidence."

"And I will tell you in confidence, Mrs. Rose, that I married for precisely the same reason. It seems we have much in common. I am fortunate, though, in that our girl is flourishing, although our second daughter died quite young. My condolences on the loss of your child."

"Thank you. I still miss her."

"The press made you sound quite ridiculous, I thought. You have a pronounced accent, but you are quite intelligible. I hope you will not let that article, and ones like it, discourage you from speaking."

"No."

"I did not think it would." Madame D'Arusmont smiled. "So you are legally married to Mr. Rose?"

"We had a ceremony of sorts in London, which was quite enough for us, but we legally married here in New York."

"Ah. I would not have guessed it. He still looks at you as if you were a star fallen out of the sky, just for him."

We talked at length. Madame D'Arusmont had not been getting good audiences lately—she had been forced to hire a dingy hall, which attracted only a few curiosity-seekers—and she was planning to return to France in a few months. She spoke with affection about her daughter, and with politeness about her husband, who had taught children at New Harmony some years before. When I mentioned the subject of the Owen family, I soon regretted it, for she and Robert Dale Owen had fallen out over money, and she was quite bitter on the subject. Having made his acquaintance in London, I knew him to be an upright young man, scrupulous in his dealings, and I did not doubt that Madame D'Arusmont was honest as well. I was certain that there had been a dreadful misunderstanding between these two excellent people, but when I said as much, my companion only snorted. Despite this hiccup, though, I enjoyed my visit, and I later had Madame D'Arusmont over to our own lodgings before she left for France in June. "Don't let them silence you," she said before we parted for the last time.

I promised her—and myself—that I would not.

~ ~ ~

For years, freethinkers across the United States had commemorated the great patriot Thomas Paine on his birthday, January 27. Some groups held simple dinners, but others made the occasion a grand one, with the meal punctuated by toasts and speeches and followed by a ball. New York City's freethinkers naturally opted for the latter. But there was one problem: women were welcome at the ball—indeed, there would not have been much of one without us—but we were excluded from the dinner. "Why can't Mrs. Rose and the other ladies come?" William asked when Mr. Vale from the *Beacon* delivered his invitation for the 1840 celebration. "They already come to the Sunday meetings. Surely they would enjoy hearing the speeches— and in the case of Mrs. Rose, making them."

"We are always happy to see the ladies on Sundays, and of course at the ball. But the dinner is different."

"How? I know spirits are served, but I have never heard reports of any wild excesses."

"Well, there is tobacco—"

"Which surely you can go without for a short while," I put in, though William had been handling the matter quite nicely himself.

"It really comes down to it being a masculine affair," Mr. Vale said sheepishly.

"I see. Well, I am sorry, sir. I must decline. I cannot go where Mrs. Rose and others of her sex are not welcome."

"That was marvelous," I said when the door shut behind a chagrined Mr. Vale. "But I am sorry you will have to miss the dinner. I have heard they are quite entertaining."

"Who says we shall miss it? We'll host our own."

And so we did, with the help of several friends. I invited Miss Elizabeth Munn, a young Englishwoman who had approached me after one of my lectures, to give a toast, and our good friend Lewis Masquerier, a Kentuckian who also was an abolitionist, gave a stirring speech. I too spoke at length, and William even overcame his shyness to give a number of toasts. To encourage the attendance of the ladies in our circle, most of whom were temperance advocates, we substituted lemonade for wine and spirits. It flowed freely and refreshingly, so that everyone was quite fit to participate in the dance that followed.

William, who had become quite adept over the years, was much in demand despite his married status, though he saved the waltzes for me. I danced with Mr. Josiah Mendum, who worked for the *Boston Investigator*, the freethought paper in that fair city. "You must come lecture to us in Boston, Mrs. Rose. Boston can be stodgy, but it is changing."

"I would be honored."

I did take Mr. Mendum up on that offer in June of 1841 and met him and his dear friend Mr. Horace Seaver, who edited the *Investigator*. I was charmed by Boston, and indeed would have considered moving there except that after struggling for the past several years, William was now getting his business in New York on firm footing. He'd had to hire an errand boy to keep up with his new customers, and he had moved his store, and our residence, to Chatham Street, the better for fashionable gentlemen, and those aspiring to be fashionable gentlemen, to find him. But there was another reason to stay put as well. I had felt fatigued in Boston, and I was beginning to suspect that this was not due to sightseeing or travel. It was too soon to be certain, but I had missed two courses, which was most unusual. Since poor Amalia had been born, they had been quite regular.

When I missed a third course, I consulted a midwife. After our meeting, I hurried into the store where William bent over his work. "William! I'm with child! Oh—pardon me, Master Roberts. I did not see you."

William's errand boy stammered out some combination of congratulations and farewell and fled into the back room as a laughing William stepped from behind the counter and took me in his arms.

7

July 1841 to September 1842

Having started nicely enough, my pregnancy soon devolved into sheer misery. My ankles bulged, my legs ached, I became acutely sensitive to any sort of smell, and I snapped at my dear William morning, noon, and night. After a while, he started spending more time in his workshop than ever, and I cried in his absence, thinking he would never love me again. I could not lecture—the very smell of a slightly crowded hall made me acutely nauseous—and with my swollen ankles and my clumsiness I could not circulate my petitions, which made me feel quite useless. It was all I could do to heave myself around City Hall Park. "I feel like a cow put out to pasture," I muttered to William, dapper beside me, one day during my eighth month.

"You look beautiful."

"I most certainly do not," I retorted.

I really do not know how the man put up with me.

In January 1842, after what felt like eleven months of carrying my child, I finally felt the pangs of labor. All things considered, I had not had a terribly hard time delivering Amalia, for a first birth, and I had some hopes that this might be an easier process.

These hopes were entirely for naught.

My labor dragged on for hour upon hour, and I fainted twice from sheer pain and exhaustion, for nothing I was doing seemed to be speeding our child into the world. Before my second descent into unconsciousness, I cried out for William, and when I came to myself I found him holding my hand, which he retained for the rest of my travail, withstanding all of the attempts of the midwife and the physician to exile him to the parlor. He wiped my forehead, helped me walk around when my attendants thought it necessary, and comforted me.

All this while, our child was making almost no progress, and I was growing weak.

"She cannot go on like this for much longer," the physician said, and the midwife nodded, all of which I observed as if I were on another plane of existence. "I can use forceps, if you consent, sir. I am skilled at using them—but I cannot guarantee that your child will survive."

"Use them. Save my wife at all costs."

He did not ask my opinion—the only time in our marriage that he failed to do so. It was just as well, because everything was beginning to fade to darkness around me.

"He's a marvel with them," the midwife said cheerfully, as I slipped into oblivion once more.

I awoke to the sound of an infant's cry, and to William's tears of relief splashing against my cheek. After that, all was comparatively easy. I delivered the placenta with surprisingly little fuss—in my lucid moments, I had envisioned it being scraped out of me, as it had Mary Wollstonecraft and the tragic Princess Charlotte. After I had dozed a little and been placed in fresh linens, the midwife deemed me capable of holding our son, somewhat bruised by his ordeal but apparently healthy. "He's so beautiful," I said, cuddling him. I could almost forget the thirty hours of misery I had endured, not to mention over nine months of carrying him about.

"A wonder," William agreed. He had the look of a washrag that had been wrung too many times. Tentatively, he stroked our son's head. We'd decided to name a boy Joseph Thomas, after William's father and our hero Thomas Paine. I knew my father would not feel slighted; many Jews preferred not to name a child after a living relative.

Joseph investigated my breast with interest. "Like this," I told him as I guided him to my nipple, and he obligingly latched on. What a bright boy he was!

I smiled at William. "Thank you for staying by me. I hope this messy business has not scarred you permanently."

"I was so frightened of losing you." He swallowed. "The doctor thinks you should not bear another one."

"I do," the physician acknowledged as I looked at him inquiringly. "I think it would be unwise, given all the difficulties you had delivering this child. And you are, well, five and thirty."

"No need to harp on that," I grumbled. But the look on William's face could not be ignored. "You may well be right, though."

For the first time in many hours, William smiled. When Joseph had finished nursing, William asked to hold him, and my happiness was complete when I saw one beloved in the arms of another.

Although William continued to fret about me, I recovered from my ordeal fairly quickly, although I date the backaches that have plagued me for decades to Joseph's birth. I had dreaded a visitation by the black cloud of depression that descended upon me after Amalia's birth, but to my surprise, I only occasionally fell into low spirits. Joseph was what women call an easy baby, who was only mildly colicky and learned to sleep through the night with merciful ease. I delighted in showing him off to our friends, who indulged my motherly pride. When Joseph's feeding schedule became predictable, I even took him to a lecture. He slept through the entire thing, though whether that was a compliment or an insult to the speaker I cannot say.

What plans we made for little Joseph! We agreed, of course, that he should choose his future for himself, but that did not mean that he could not enjoy our guidance in making that decision. William's business was doing well, and it would be a pleasure for him to pass it on to Joseph, but both of us rather hoped he would become a professional man. I preferred the law, as it was something I thought I might have pursued myself had I been a man, but William, believing that the physician had saved me from dying in childbirth, leaned toward medicine. And perhaps he might even go to college? There was Columbia College, right here in New York, but both William and I had a predilection for Harvard. It was entirely possible that Joseph might confound us and choose Yale.

Meanwhile, I kept a little account of all of his baby doings—his sleeping through the night, his rolling over, his first tooth, his sitting up, his first crawling, and what I was quite sure was a distinct "Mama."

He had my chin and William's nose, and I could see a little of Amalia in him as well. It was our unbiased opinion that he was the prettiest baby in New York. We would have to make sure that the young ladies did not distract him from his studies.

And yes, I am stalling.

~ ~ ~

It was in September when I awoke to find Joseph feverish and fretful. By the time William fetched the physician, he had developed a rash.

Scarlet fever. There were few words more frightening to a parent, and I had especially good reason to dread them. I, along with Sophie and our brother Jacob, had had the disease back in Piotrków. We girls had had a mild case; Jacob had died. When Papa told us that God had chosen to spare us but not our brother, I was struck instantly by the illogic. After all, Jacob had been a perfectly nice baby.

But that arbitrariness was the last thing on my mind as William and I tended our poor Joseph. Every remedy that could be tried, we used. Everything that could be done to make him more comfortable, we did. We had the best physician we could find, and we had a second physician come to look at him, just in case. It was to no avail. Three days later, the second of my children died in my husband's arms and mine.

Elizabeth Munn was with us. I do not know what we would have done without her, for William was as shattered as I was. She called in our old friend James Thompson and his wife, Mary, who made the burial arrangements, and the two of them forced us to bed, for neither of us had slept for days. When we woke hours later, we found our flat immaculate and poor Joseph laid out beautifully in a little casket. "I have a suggestion," Mr. Thompson said hesitantly. "Perhaps you should have a daguerreotype made of your son. The photographer can come right here; I have heard of them doing such. It will be a great comfort to you in years to come, to always have his face before you."

Neither William nor I had submitted ourselves to the photographic art, which was still something of a novelty. But I remembered aching to have a miniature of Amalia. I looked at William, who nodded sadly. "Please have it done."

The photographer arrived soon after. Mr. Thompson carefully bore our boy to a sofa, where Mary and Elizabeth arranged him on a shawl with his favorite stuffed dog beside him. William roused himself enough to ask the daguerreotypist about the process, which he carefully explained. One day, he assured us, anyone would be able to take a photograph. My heart was too heavy to enter into the subject of this glorious invention, but I was indeed moved to tears when the photographer later handed us the finished daguerreotype. It was a wondrous thing, not having to trust to fickle memory to recall the features of our beautiful boy. I snipped two locks of hair from his head: one to place in my locket with Amalia's, the other to place in the case behind the daguerreotype.

Mr. Thompson had arranged for our boy to be buried. Mr. Offen said a few words as William and I wept beside Joseph's grave with the Thompsons supporting us and Elizabeth patting my hand. We came home to a good, nourishing meal, which we ate to please everyone else. Our friends stayed the evening. Mr. Thompson, who was a merchant but whose grand passion was chess, played a game with William, who even on a happy day would have lost, and did this dismal day as well. Mrs. Thompson and Elizabeth read aloud from *The Old Curiosity Shop*. But finally, they had to leave William and me alone.

Joseph's things had been neatly stored away, and everything was ready for us to go to bed. There was nothing for us to do but go there, and huddle in each other's arms and reflect upon how quiet and empty our flat seemed now. Just a few days before, we had been thinking it a little crowded.

"I suppose I should open the shop today," William said the next morning.

"Yes."

"Would you come and help me?"

Over the years, I had learned to repair watches and other jewelry. It had proved useful in the lean years when William could not afford an assistant, but it had been a long time since my services were necessary. But I knew he did not want to leave me alone in our flat, and I did not wish to be left alone. So I nodded and followed him down the stairs. There I worked diligently, even as I found that tears ran down my face.

After an hour or so, William told his real assistant that he would be out for the rest of the day, and asked me if I wanted to take a walk. Having received my assent, he put on his hat, which bore a black band. I too was in mourning: black silk and bonnet with a heavy veil. I'd resisted the crape the dressmaker had urged upon me; I was quite miserable as it was without adding that monstrous fabric to my wardrobe.

We aimlessly proceeded to the Battery. "Ernestine," William said quietly as we sank upon a bench. "I would prefer not to try for another child. First, I do not want to break my heart again. Second, the doctor advised against another childbearing, and I am afraid of losing you. So I suppose it comes down to the same thing. But if you feel we must—"

"No. I would as soon live."

"I miss him very, very much. I know from you and Amalia that we will never stop grieving for him."

"No."

"But at least we have each other. We have kind friends, too."

"We do." I pressed my hand to his. "We are fortunate in them, and in each other."

"I think I would like a change of scene. Just for a few days."

Traveling was the last thing I felt like doing, but it was preferable to sitting in a parlor listening for a baby's happy babbling that we would never hear again. "Where?"

"Niagara. I think it would do us good."

And so we traveled to Niagara, destined for the Cataract House, kept by General Parkhurst Whitney. It was the finest hotel there, indeed more than we could afford, but Mr. Thompson, whose business was flourishing, would hear of us going to no other place and pressed the money upon us. "Besides, I have a commission for you, which I know you will execute gladly. I would like you to give this to the headwaiter." He thrust some coins into William's hands. "Tell him it is from his friends in New York City. He will quite understand what it is for."

So with this mysterious commission—neither of us had the spirits to inquire further—we set off for Niagara. By agreement, William removed his black hatband and I confined my mourning to wearing a plain black silk dress with no veil; it was something of a relief not to have pitying glances cast our way. Most of the trip was made by railway, an innovation of which I thoroughly approved and usually enjoyed. Not this time. Staring out of the windows of the train in silence, William and I brought down the spirits of everyone on board, I fear, even without our mourning garb.

It was dark when we arrived in Niagara. Our hotel was but a short walk from the station, which was just as well because we could not see any of the scenery, although I thought I detected the sound of rushing water. At the desk we mentioned Mr. Thompson's name, which proved to have quite magical powers. The room we were sent to was immense, and the porter who carried our luggage promised us that we would have a fine view in the morning. He, like all the staff I had seen, was a black man. "I think you are from the South?"

"I am, ma'am. Most of us are. We can put together a little something if you'd like to get a bite downstairs, or we can bring it up, whatever suits."

"I think tonight my wife and I will eat in our room," William said. "Does that suit you, dear?"

I nodded wearily. "Very much so."

After an interval, a waiter arrived, bearing a tray from which a delicious aroma wafted. For the first time in days, I felt my appetite tempted. "Will the headwaiter be on duty tomorrow?" William asked.

"Fact is, sir, I'm the headwaiter. We're a little short-handed tonight."

"Then I have something from your friends in New York City to give you." William pulled out his coins.

"Do give them my best regards."

Thus our mysterious commission ended, with us no wiser than before. We sat down to our meal, which proved more than equal to its promising appearance. Then we settled to bed and fell into the deep sleep that follows a long train ride.

I woke in the morning to find William dressed suitably for a day of exploring. "You look like quite the woodsman," I said.

"All I need is an ax."

Could we be joking again? It seemed almost indecent, but I smiled nonetheless.

Mr. Thompson and our other friends had warned that good attire would be worthless for touring the falls, so I set aside my black silk and donned a faded dress that I had hemmed unfashionably short, topping off the effect with a pair of gumshoes. William complimented me on my high style, and we went down to breakfast, having vowed not to peep at any scenery beforehand. The headwaiter, busy with his duties, still found time to bestow a smile upon us.

After breakfast, guidebook in hand, we made our way the short distance to Prospect Point. And there we gasped in unison at the falls in all their glory.

I am not much for rhapsodizing. All I can say is that as I beheld that glorious rush of water, I felt very small and yet utterly alive, and that I understood why William, in all his wisdom, had decided to bring us here. "Thank you," I said as tears streamed down my eyes.

"I knew we needed to see something larger than ourselves."

Holding hands, we must have stood there a solid hour.

For the rest of the day, we toured the American side of the falls, admiring them from all possible angles, but nothing matched that first viewing for us. We returned to the hotel exhausted, and were quite content to lounge in the baths that it furnished and to enjoy the view of the rapids from the veranda. The next day, we took the ferry to the Canadian side, where we were provided with oilskin garments and assured that we would get completely drenched, a promise that was fulfilled multiple times. We finished up our excursion with a carriage ride and, as it was still somewhat warm, a dish of ice cream.

Our spirits were so much improved by these outings that on the veranda that evening, we joined several other couples for tea and conversation. Our companions included two visitors from Virginia, a merchant and his very pretty young wife. Like most Southerners I have met over the years, they were a charming pair. "I wish we could have brought the children with us," Mrs. Pendleton said after we had spoken at length about everyone's travels. "But I would have had to bring our servant Ginny with us too, and although she is quite a member of the family, I assure you, it simply wasn't worth the risk."

"Risk?" I asked.

"Oh, did you not hear? I suppose it was in the Southern papers, not so much the Northern ones. Last year, a couple brought their children's nursemaid with them to this place. They sent the girl to fetch some milk, and she never returned. The abolitionists ran her off to Canada." My companion lowered her voice. "The servants here were undoubtedly responsible. It's said that many of them are escaped slaves and that they have friends and relatives on the Canada side. General Whitney denies everything, but he would, wouldn't he? Still, he keeps a lovely establishment, but if Ginny comes next time, we will have to stay elsewhere."

I dared not look at William. It had surely dawned on him, as it had on me, why Mr. Thompson had given us the money for the headwaiter.

William and I bid good night to our Southern friends—thinking what lovely people they would be if they learned to do without their slaves—and were heading toward our room, and a well-earned sleep, when a trio of young women approached us. I had seen them looking my way earlier and had wondered what I had done to get their attention, but had attributed it to the natural urge to stare about that overtook some people when traveling. "Excuse me, madam. Are you Mrs. Rose, the lecturer from New York?"

"I am."

"I am Mrs. Jane Manchester. I heard you at Tammany Hall some time ago and enjoyed it immensely. I have been telling my friends about you. If it is not too troublesome, we would like to beg a favor of you."

"I will do my best to oblige."

"Would you be willing to speak here tomorrow? My friends are from out of state, and they are so eager to hear what you have to say. And I know there are many here who would come to hear you; this area attracts so many interesting people. I was so bold as to ask the proprietor if there would be a room available, and he said it would be no trouble, and you could charge if you pleased. I know it is such terribly short notice, and so very presumptuous, but—"

Even if I could be so cold-hearted as to disappoint these ladies, I had no desire to do so. I missed speaking, and had planned to return to the platform once I could do so without neglecting Joseph. I looked over at William, who nodded. "I will be happy to speak. I never charge. Is there a topic you would like?"

"Oh, any topic will do. Eight o'clock, then?"

Having settled everything with Mrs. Manchester, I resumed my walk to our room with William. "You truly don't mind?" I asked when our door was shut. "I mean no disrespect to our dear boy's memory."

"No. I wish he'd had a chance to hear you speak. But life goes on, and we must go on with it." He gave a half smile. "I must confess I have missed seeing you on the platform."

We spent the next day exploring some more, though all the while I was mulling over what to speak about. Religion, or the lack thereof, was too delicate a subject to spring upon a general audience unannounced; I did not wish to make trouble for General Whitney or Mrs. Manchester. Political economy was perhaps more than what people on holiday had bargained for. Abolition might put in danger what appeared to be a thriving stop on what people would soon be calling the Underground Railroad. I had strong opinions about how to raise children and had spoken about this in the past, but it was too painful now.

"You'll think of something," William said, patting me on the arm as I frowned at the rapids.

"I suppose I could always babble about nature."

Still mulling over the possibilities, we went to our room for tea (and a catnap), then dressed. I felt almost guilty for taking the care over my appearance that I did, but Mrs. Manchester would hardly be pleased if I took the platform looking like a wraith, so I added just a hint of color to my cheeks.

General Whitney, to my surprise, was waiting for us as we came down the staircase. He led us into a large room crammed with people, mostly women, although a number of men were standing against the walls. As Mrs. Manchester introduced me, I looked around the room and recognized Mrs. Pendleton among the guests. Even a chambermaid was there.

There was no doubt now about my topic.

"My friends. When I accepted the kind invitation of Mrs. Manchester and her friends to speak, only last night, I anticipated a dozen or so people—and now look at this room! It shows what a few women, working together, can accomplish. Now just think what *many* women, working together, can accomplish.

"You may have had your suspicions by now that I am not a native of this country, and I can inform you that your suspicions are quite right. I am a Pole, married to an Englishman. My husband and I arrived in America only a few years ago. But for some time now, I have been pursuing a purpose dear to me—the purpose of petitioning for a bill that would give married women in New York the right to control their own property. I have no complaints about my own husband—he is quite too good for me. But many women are not so fortunate. They bring property to their marriage, only to see it squandered foolishly. There is nothing radical about this bill; it simply allows women to keep what was theirs all along.

"There are those who say that women cannot be trusted to manage their own property. Yet we trust them absolutely with the upbringing of their children—surely more precious than property, would you not say?" My voice faltered, but only slightly. "And consider this: if a woman marries at age twenty, is widowed at age forty-five, and remarries at age fifty, we act as if she has forgotten all of the good sense she has acquired over those three decades and hand the management of her property over to her new husband."

For another thirty minutes, I went on in this vein. The ladies had been attending to me earnestly, but quietly; used to the sometimes boisterous crowds in New York, I could not tell whether this was a good sign or a bad one.

Then the applause began, interspersed with calls to sign my petition. Fortunately, I was in the habit of taking it with me, and William, early on in my speech, had thought to retrieve it from our room. New York ladies crowded around to sign it, and ladies from other states read it with the thought of putting forth ones of their own. Mrs. Manchester went so far as to pass hotel stationery around so that everyone could take notes, and I spotted Mrs. Pendleton scribbling away.

"You really must come lecture in Albany," a lady said. "And throughout the state. They're the ones who need to hear what you have to say, not just the big city folk."

"Very true," I said.

It quite astounded me that I had not thought of it before.

~ ~ ~

I left Niagara Falls with a bouquet of flowers, a pocket full of addresses where I could find hospitality if I chose to lecture in various towns, and a lovely purse. The latter had contained the proceeds of the collection taken up for me at my talk. Although I kept the pretty purse, I bundled the proceeds in a handkerchief and handed it to the headwaiter before I left. "Please add this to what your friends in New York City sent you."

Our apartment was still, and yes, a little sad, but the flowers along with some souvenirs we had brought from Niagara brightened it, and William and I were thinking of other means to brighten it as well. "So many young people at my talk," I said the next morning at breakfast. "I have been thinking that we might have sociables at our apartment for the young people in our circle. A place where they can have nice conversation, and perhaps some music if they are so inclined, without all the insipid card-playing so many young ladies engage in."

"I like that idea," William said. "Of course, I like most of your ideas, but I think this is a good one."

"*Most* of my ideas?"

William grinned mysteriously. "Perhaps you can do some matchmaking. Miss Munn, for instance."

"Oh, she is a little too young to marry just yet. But when the time comes, I think Mr. Mendum would make her a fine husband."

"Does he know this?"

"He'll find out in due time." I looked up at William as he rose to head downstairs to his shop. "Will you be quite well for the shop today?"

"Yes. I've got plans for some new canes, and some orders to catch up with too, no doubt. And you?"

"Yes. I have plenty to occupy myself with."

I kissed William goodbye as he went out the door. Then I picked up my petition, pen, and ink and left the apartment. It was time to get back to work.

8

January 1844 to January 1846

"Pardon me, madam." The representative from Buffalo expectorated into an adjacent spittoon, one of many that graced the halls of the New York legislature. It seemed that they were utterly necessary to good government. "What exactly do you women want?"

"To have the right to hold our own property," I said, making considerable effort to retain my patience. My opening remarks to this legislative committee had made our wants quite clear.

"No, what do you women want in general? To tear down the fabric of our society? To go out into the factories and toil like drudges while your husband stays home and cooks?"

"No one should be toiling like a drudge, male or female, and while I certainly believe that society could stand some improvements, I have no desire to tear down its fabric. But if a woman wants to go out into the world and work, without neglecting her family, why should she not have that pleasure?"

"Should a woman sit in these very halls?"

"Well, I am sitting here, and the halls appear to be bearing up quite well. But I suppose you mean as a legislator. I say—why not? We are subject to the same laws as men; why should we not have a say in making them?" I considered telling him that the first thing we ladies would do would be to remove the spittoons, but decided against it. Instead, I gave him a sweet smile. "We are not asking for anything today other than to own our own property. It is something that any loving parent of a daughter should want. A father works hard, sacrifices to give his child fine things, leaves her a tidy sum of money—only to have it fall into the hands of a wastrel and vanish when she marries."

"Well, women shouldn't marry wastrels."

"I am afraid they sometimes find out the truth too late. After all, no man tells his sweetheart that he intends to drink up or gamble away her fortune. He is on his best behavior."

The legislator grunted. A second man rose and said, "What you are seeking is simply unnatural. Women should trust their husbands to look after their interests, as most certainly will. The man is the head of the household. It is ordained by God."

"I was not aware that God was a member of the legislature, sir."

A silence fell over the room. I took it as a dismissal and rose. "Thank you, gentlemen, for allowing me to take up your time."

Someone escorted me out of the hallowed halls of the committee room into a public area, where I found Mrs. Paulina Wright and Mrs. Elizabeth Cady Stanton awaiting me. We'd met here at the legislature, where I had learned that unbeknownst to me, Mrs. Wright had been circulating petitions in the western part of New York for nearly as long as I had been plodding along with mine in New York City and elsewhere. Mrs. Stanton, from a prominent New York family, had moved to Boston with her husband but often returned to visit her parents in Albany, where she had taken an interest in the bill that dear Judge Herttell had introduced so many years before. He had since retired, but other legislators had taken up his cause. This year, the petition I had brought to Albany had contained hundreds of signatures—a far cry from the five I'd managed to get back in the winter of 1836–37.

"Well, how did it go?" Mrs. Stanton asked.

"Some asked good questions. Others acted like oafs."

"Isn't that the way of the world," Mrs. Wright muttered. "I met with a similar reception."

"Well, a few of the gentlemen I met showed themselves to be friends to our cause," Mrs. Stanton said. "But of course some would not even meet with me."

"Still, at least we are here," I said. "We have shown that we cannot be ignored any longer."

"True," Mrs. Stanton said. "Shall we go to my family's house for tea?" She patted her dress. "Baby is getting quite annoying."

We walked a few blocks and arrived at a pleasant house, where Mrs. Stanton escorted us into a parlor. As we awaited our tea, Mrs. Stanton introduced us to her child, a pretty boy of about two who toddled in, pulled at our gowns and my earrings, and then toddled off with his nurse. "Do you ladies have children?"

Mrs. Wright said she did not, and I echoed her. I saw no reason to darken the mood by going into further detail, especially since Mrs. Stanton had informed us that she expected her next child in March.

A servant soon arrived bearing tea. "My father took this house so my brothers-in-law could stay with him and Mother while they are establishing their legal practices," Mrs. Stanton said. "He would have done the same for me if I had gone into the law—provided, of course, that I had been a boy. And I sometimes wish I had been a boy, because I have always been interested in the law." She looked at me. "What would you have done, Mrs. Rose, had you been a boy?"

"I imagine I would have been destined for the rabbinate," I said. "I was a very pious child, and quite the budding Talmudist. I could argue its finer points for hours. Fortunately for my father, I was born a girl, so at least his plans were not wrecked when I declared myself an infidel. Perhaps if I were a boy I would never have questioned the existence of God, as religion coincides so nicely with what men want for themselves."

"You told your father outright you did not believe in God?"

"I did. Of course he was unhappy, but he thought it was a passing phase. It has not yet passed."

"I wanted to be a missionary in the Sandwich Islands," Mrs. Wright said. "My parents were dead, so there was no objection from them, of course, but my church said that an unmarried women could not be a missionary. I suppose it was too much like preaching for them, but I never received an explanation. In any case, I soon fell in love and married, and Mr. Wright and I decided that we could not countenance a church that would not condemn slavery. So we left the church."

"So the world lost a lawyer, a rabbi, and a missionary," Mrs. Stanton said. "And got us instead. Perhaps it might come to think it got the better of the bargain."

~ ~ ~

"It is so kind to take me to Boston with you," Elizabeth Munn said as we settled into the train bound for that city.

161

"Well, I have friends there I think you would like"—Mr. Mendum in particular—"and I have a selfish motive as well. I feel somewhat out of my element with this particular lecture, so the more friendly faces, the better. How does one follow Ralph Waldo Emerson and that clever young Mr. Thoreau?"

"You were invited, weren't you?"

"Yes. Still, I must say I do feel my lack of a Harvard education at such times."

"You have Hebrew as opposed to their Greek and Latin."

"True, and I doubt either can say a word in Yiddish or Polish." I smiled. "See, you are making me feel better already, and that is usually dear William's forte."

Elizabeth and I settled to our books and, occasionally, to watching the scenery. There was not yet much to watch; winter still had this area firmly in its grasp on this March day, and the snow that had fallen a few days before was dingy and melting.

Since Joseph's death, I had traveled all around New York State, giving my lectures and circulating my petitions. William, whose labor was funding all of this, stayed home and worked at his silversmithing and jewelry making. I missed him terribly, but he and I had agreed that my lecturing served a noble end. It also kept my mind occupied, for there were still times I fell into a deep depression thinking of Joseph and Amalia.

I must have been thinking of them just then, for Elizabeth slipped her hand into mine and squeezed it.

~ ~ ~

Although it was Sunday morning, Amory Hall was crammed with people waiting to hear me. As I lifted my green bonnet veil to survey them, I could at least take some satisfaction that none of them were in church.

I looked out at the hall that had held William Lloyd Garrison, Ralph Waldo Emerson, and Henry David Thoreau just weeks before. Then I straightened my shoulders and flicked back a stray ringlet. "The study of man—"

The audience looked at me as I faltered, and I realized that I had as much right to be here as my predecessors. Had I not been invited, as Elizabeth had pointed out? It was time to give these people what they had come for. I lifted my head higher. "The study of man, as an individual, together with his relation to his race, was universally allowed by the wisest of the ancients."

~ ~ ~

"A little bird—that being Mr. Seaver—told me that you did quite well yesterday," Mr. Mendum said, showing Elizabeth and me into his office at the *Boston Investigator*, which he now operated with Mr. Seaver. I hoped Elizabeth was not overly finicky about neatness, as Mr. Mendum's office was full of dangerously teetering heaps of paper.

"Well, the audience seemed quite receptive, and I have been invited to speak elsewhere here. It was a relief."

"I told her that she had nothing to fear," Elizabeth said.

Mr. Mendum smiled at Elizabeth, the second time he had done so.

"Miss Munn is a protégé of mine," I said. "I have been training her up as a proper infidel."

"She has had the best of teachers. Is this your first time in the city, Miss Munn?"

"It is. I will be sorry to have to depart tomorrow."

"Then perhaps I could show you around—you and Mrs. Rose, of course—for an hour or two. What do you say?"

"If you're not too busy," Elizabeth said.

"Oh, I am busy, but one of the pleasures of owning this paper is that I can take off as I please. Today it makes up for the less pleasurable aspects."

Elizabeth looked toward me, and I nodded. "A walk would be charming."

And indeed it was. As often as I reasonably could, I found an excuse to drop behind my friends, who seemed happy to let me trail a bit at a distance. When Elizabeth and I returned to our hotel, she had a distant, dreamy expression on her face that boded quite well.

All in all, it was a very successful trip to Boston.

~ ~ ~

In the late spring of 1845, I set off on a lecture tour to the West—"West" in those days meaning what is now the middle part of the United States. I went partly to recoup my health, which had been annoyingly feeble, and partly because I had long been curious about seeing this part of the country. From what Madame D'Arusmont, who had settled in Cincinnati, had told me when she passed through New York, it could use some shaking up. So William and I spread railroad and steamboat schedules out upon our table and plotted my journey, which would take me away from him for months. "Are you still planning on visiting one of the slave states?"

I had two from which to choose: Kentucky and Missouri. "I think I should," I said. "I have been invited from time to time to speak against slavery, and although I despise it on principle, I think it is important that I actually see what I am talking about."

"Will you give a speech against slavery in a slave state?"

"I don't know. From what I hear, Southerners love to ask visitors what they think of slavery, but they don't necessarily want to hear the answer."

"That has never stopped you. But you must take care for your own safety."

"I shall. But I think we should discuss something else. How often are you going to write to me? Once a week will not be enough. I will miss you so very, very much."

William sighed, put down his timetable, and took me into his arms. "That is the drawback to trying to change the world."

~ ~ ~

Although I tried to economize on my travels by staying with friends or friends of friends, this was not always possible, and William was insistent that as a woman traveling alone, I not compromise my safety or comfort. So in Louisville, I checked into the Galt House hotel, which came recommended by none other than Mr. Charles Dickens, who had praised the place in his book about his American travels. As he had written, it was a comfortable establishment, and as he had also written, the streets were full of pigs, cheerfully poking their snouts into everything that looked pokable. It reminded me that although I had abandoned most of the tenets of my childhood faith, I had never been tempted to try pork.

That evening, after writing to William to tell him of my safe arrival, I read through the newspaper and found that the next day, a number of slaves were being auctioned, their owners having died or met financial reversals. Watching such an outrage was the last thing I wanted to do, but I felt that I had to see it.

I arrived at the courthouse, where I found a couple I had seen at breakfast at the hotel: a pretty young lady and her much older husband. It soon appeared that the young lady had her heart set on Bessie, whom the ad had described as age twenty-seven and an excellent cook, and had dragged her husband to the city expressly for this purpose. The testator had insisted that Bessie be kept with her children, ages five and three, and this was a sticking point for the husband. "I don't need three slaves," he protested. "I promised you a cook, not an entire family."

"But you can rent them out when they're of age to work, and in the meantime they can pick up around the house. And rock the cradle when I have a child!"

Another lady stifled a giggle. I stared gloomily ahead.

"Well," Older Husband said. "Let's talk to her first. Maybe you'll find she won't do."

As Pretty Young Lady spoke to Bessie, who like the other slaves was standing against a wall to be questioned by prospective buyers, more people packed the room. Finally, the auctioneer appeared, leading Bessie and her children out. Bessie was plain, which seemed to please Pretty Young Lady, and she listened impassively as the auctioneer explained that due to her master's kindness, she and her children had to be sold together and kept in the state.

"It would be kinder if he had freed them."

All eyes turned to glare at me. Having learned to project my voice across a lecture hall, I appeared to have lost the skill of muttering.

With my interruption out of the way, the auctioneer resumed, expounding upon Bessie's skills as a cook and her obedient disposition. There was little he could say about the children, other than that they were "likely" and no doubt would soon be immensely useful around the house. Poor Bessie nodded, as did Pretty Young Lady, who also nudged her husband.

The bidding began. Pretty Young Lady had two competitors, but whether it was due to his young wife's charms or his desire not to be outmanned by the other bidders, Older Husband shook them off handily and emerged triumphant, to be rewarded with a squeal of delight and a kiss on his cheek. It would all have been quite amusing if the objects of the bidding had not been human beings.

Next for auction was a man in his late teens. He was described as a strong young buck who also had to be kept in the state, but who was good-humored and could do any sort of work, be it light or heavy. I half expected Pretty Young Lady to use her wiles again, but the only interest came from two men who managed the impressive feat of making their bids and expectorating at the same time.

A few more young men were sold—it saddens me to see how casually I have written this—but still the room was full. There were several men here who were finely dressed, even aristocratic in appearance, and I could not understand their presence, as none of them appeared to be in need of a cook or a skilled laborer, and they would surely send an agent if they were just looking for a man to work in the fields.

And then the auctioneer led to the platform a pale-skinned young girl, one who had not been standing around with the rest, and I understood why these men were here.

The other unfortunates on the auction block had been dressed simply, the men in clean but rough shirts and pants, the cook in a calico dress. Not this girl. She wore a silk gown, cut in the latest fashion, and a gold hoop dangled from each ear. The poor child—she could not have been more than fifteen— carried her bonnet instead of wearing it, the better to show off her pretty face. Everything about her mien, including her downcast eyes and her unconfined hair, betokened virginity.

I knew from my reading who had fathered this girl: her master, or one of his relations or friends. I also knew what her fate would be: that of a concubine. Tears came to my eyes as I contrasted her plight to my own life at fifteen: a snug little bedroom, a mother to whom I could confide all my petty woes, a father who loved me and truly wished the best for me despite our marked disagreements over what that might be.

What if I bought this young girl? But the bidding, which was fierce, was already well over what William and I could afford, even if William worked day and night. And even if I could afford the purchase, no one would have sold her to me, given my outburst and the revulsion that showed too clearly on my face, judging from the stares that were being directed at me. "Go back to where you came from if you don't like this," someone hissed.

And even if I could take charge of this girl, was she more deserving than the boy who had been sold before her? He was much darker than the girl. Was my especial sympathy for her roused because she was of my sex, because of her destiny, or because she looked more like me than the rest?

Whatever the answer to this question, I could not bear to see the auctioneer's hammer fall. I turned and left the room.

~ ~ ~

I slumped on the bench of the Buffalo railway station, my head resting against a pillar. The Buffalo steamer had not hit any unpleasant weather, but I had not felt this miserable since I had crossed the Atlantic. It would have been wise if I had stayed the night at a hotel, or better yet, stayed with the Howlands, a Quaker couple whom I had stopped with on my previous trips to Buffalo. But in my tired and cranky state I had not wanted to intrude upon them, and besides, the sooner I could get a train to Albany, the sooner I would be headed back to New York and William. So I had gone directly from the steamer to the railway station. Once I got on the train, I could nap on it, an art I had perfected over the last several years. That would surely make me feel better.

"Madam! Aren't you for the Albany train?"

"Yes."

"Well, it's here."

"Oh." I staggered up. How could I have missed the arrival of something as large as a railway train? The stupidity of it made me smile.

"Madam, are you quite sober?"

"Of course I am," I said, and hoisted up my carpetbag huffily. It wasn't as though I was keeping the train waiting; there were still people hurrying toward the station door. With the intention of following them, I took a couple of steps, only to find the railway station suddenly shift beneath my feet. Reaching out to steady myself and striking only empty air, I crumpled to the ground.

"Madam!" Someone put a hand to my forehead. "My God, she's not drunk. She's burning with fever."

"I could have told you that," I muttered. And that is the last thing I remember.

~ ~ ~

Over the next few days, I tossed and turned. I knew vaguely that there were people tending me, but they were not the right people, and I am quite sure I informed them of this over and over, along with other sundry ravings. Then someone pressed my hand and kissed my cheek, and I quietened.

It was still a day or two before I came fully to myself, though. Then I recognized him, the dearest man in the world, looking worn and tired but smiling at me. "William," I croaked.

"Yes, sweetheart."

I tried to tell him about the indignity at the railway station with the man thinking I was intoxicated, but he stopped me, and I was unequal to pressing the point any further. Instead, I let him feed me some soup, then read to me. I could hardly comprehend what he was saying, but the words lulled me to sleep—the first natural sleep I'd had in days. When I awoke, I was as weak as a newborn kitten, but now I recognized the Howlands' guest room, and then the Howlands themselves, standing next to William. In a voice that sounded quite froggy even to me, I said, "Thank you very much for tending to me. I suppose I must ask for form's sake how I got here."

"Fortunately, you had an address book on you, and some visiting cards, so the man went looking for a Buffalo address and found us," Mr. Howland said.

"I cannot thank you enough for your kindness."

"Your husband already has." Mrs. Howland smiled at him. "And now we are going to leave you with him. Poor dear, you begged for him over and over again, and seemed to think there was quite a conspiracy to keep him from you."

She shut the door behind her, and William wrapped his arm around me. "You came very close to dying, I must tell you. The doctor told me when I arrived to prepare myself for the worst, and for several days after that it was not certain that you would recover. You were still out of your head."

"I hope my babbling wasn't very tedious."

"No."

I could not escape noticing the shadow that came over William's face. "What is it, my dear? I have distressed you."

"I don't want to trouble you with it."

"But I will be more troubled not knowing what you are thinking."

"Well, it's just that you talked a great deal about—about your first husband. You had tried so very hard to please him, you said. Do you still love him?"

I winced, wondering how much I had disclosed to the Howlands in my delirium. "No. I never did. I was fond of him, and we shared a child. I sometimes think I dealt badly with him, because I do believe he loved me. But there is only one man I have ever loved, and ever will love, and that is the one who has been listening to me rant for—how many days? Three?"

"Four."

"You poor man. I hope I babbled a little about you."

"As a matter of fact, you did. But it was mostly about our Joseph and your little girl." He hesitated. "I have wondered if you might want to find a child to raise as our own."

This was something I had thought of from time to time. I shook my head. "We have become too set in our ways. I could not travel, because I would not have a child just to hand her over to a nurse. I can do more good in the world as I am."

"I understand and agree." He stroked my hand. "You are all to me, anyway. But you must not think of traveling again until you have recovered."

"I won't." I sighed. "This was a successful trip—my present circumstances excluded—but I wish I could have done more. I spoke against slavery after seeing that dreadful auction I wrote to you about, but I was in front of friendly audiences, so it had very little impact."

"I think that ending slavery will take much more than talk. It's too profitable. But that is only my opinion."

"You may well be right."

"But don't let that discourage you. Just look at the progress women's property rights are making in New York. And think of the cup of tea I am about to make you, after I have made you talk about all of these things when I should have been letting you rest."

I smiled back up at him. "The best medicine."

"The talk or the tea?"

"Both."

~ ~ ~

Having assured himself that I was recovering, William returned to New York, but it was several more weeks before the doctor would allow me to join him. At last, though, I was ensconced in our apartment, bright with autumn flowers. "You mustn't pamper me too much," I said as he settled me on the sofa with a warm blanket and a mug of steaming tea. "I will get spoiled, and then where will you be?"

But what I wanted to do more than anything else was to have William take me into his arms, which he did that night, a little too carefully at first. Once he had assured himself that I would not break, however, we had a fine time of it.

For a couple of weeks after that, I passed my days quietly on the sofa, but this soon became intolerable. Once again I began to trod the streets with my petition, although in deference to William and the doctor I wrapped myself especially snugly and took omnibuses for my longer excursions. Once again I presented my petitions in Albany, once again I spoke before a committee. "I will see you gentlemen next year," I informed the committee as I took my leave. "Unless, of course, you have the wisdom to make it unnecessary."

9

JANUARY 1847 TO APRIL 1848

I began 1847 with another trip to Albany, where I found Mrs. Stanton bewailing the probability that because Boston disagreed with her husband's lungs, the family would be moving to a more rural area. "Seneca Falls," she said. "I am afraid I shall not like it. My sister lives there, and there are some other interesting people as well, but also quite a few ignorant foreigners—that is, the Irish," she added hastily. "Not all immigrants have your cultivation and breeding."

I grimaced but said nothing. In fact, I was eligible to become a citizen. William had already done so, but I had decided to wait until America improved itself to its full potential—or until we women won the vote, which had begun to preoccupy my thoughts. It was irksome to think that the ruffians who frequented the Bowery could vote, and would happily do so for anyone for the price of a dram, but a respectable woman could not. "I daresay you will make the most of it."

"Well, there is a railway station there, so that's something. You must come and visit me in my exile sometime. I assume you will be traveling this winter?"

"Yes. William worries about my health since I fell ill that time, so we decided I would take a look at South Carolina after I do a few lectures. He thought a visit there would do me good."

"Just don't tell my Henry if it does," Mrs. Stanton said glumly. "Seneca Falls is quite healthy enough, in my opinion."

~ ~ ~

It being a fine day, I sat on the veranda of my hotel at Charleston, having just returned from a walk on the Battery. It was a beautiful city, with splendid mansions and exquisite water views, but slavery permeated every facet of its life. Slaves built the fine houses, repaired the roads, shod the horses, and—

"Lemonade, madam?"

"Yes, please."

The hotel waiter, who like all the waiters here was enslaved, set a fresh glass in front of me. He wore a metal badge around his neck, which I had learned meant that he was rented out by his master to perform tasks for others. It had been a slave who had carried my bags to my room, a slave who had been making my bed, and a slave who had served my meals. I was benefitting as much from slavery as any white person in the city. If I had been born into a slave-holding family, would I have had the courage to relinquish such a life? The Grimké sisters, born in Charleston, had done just that, and were still hated here even though it had been years since they had settled in the North. I knew this because, after I mentioned to a lady that I spoke in public, her eyes had widened and she had said, "Like those Grimké women?"

"Yes. I have attended their lectures, as a matter of fact."

I might as well have announced that I had the smallpox, the lady hurried away from me so quickly. Since then, she had made a point of staying as far from me as possible.

Snorting at the memory, I rocked my chair gently with my foot. At least no one had assigned that task to a slave—yet.

As I dawdled on the veranda, a young man approached. He tipped his hat to me, for we had become acquainted a few days before. Mr. Michael Thompson, not to be confused with my friend from New York, was a lawyer who boarded at the hotel. We seldom agreed on anything, but with his excellent manners and pleasant drawl, I found him to be pleasant company. "You are past your time, Mr. Thompson."

"I was listening to the address Senator Calhoun made here yesterday evening after returning from Washington. Do you know who he is, madam?"

"Of course I do. The Great Nullifier." Mr. Calhoun, in case you are too young to remember, held that the states could ignore—that is, nullify—any federal law they deemed unconstitutional or, in my view, simply did not like.

"You know your politics well, for a foreigner and a lady."

"I have lived in this country for over a decade. I make it a point to know the history of wherever I live, but as it happens, I have read about the history of the United States since I was quite a little girl. As soon as I found out what a republic was, I wanted to live in one. But enough of that. What did the senator have to say?"

"He spoke at length of our peculiar institution."

"We are quite safe here, Mr. Thompson. You can call it slavery."

"It's just what we call it here," Mr. Thompson said. "It is an institution, and it is peculiar to the South, so—"

"It is indeed peculiar, in another sense altogether. But I have gotten you off your train of thought."

"He spoke of next year's presidential election, and the pandering of the non-slaveholding states to the abolitionists, and the slaveholding states' duty to resist them. He believes that the Union should be preserved, but if our institution is threatened, we must 'sever all political ties, or sink down into abject submission'—his words, which I wrote down. You are welcome to see my notes."

"I think your summary is quite adequate. But I do not think the South would want to put disunion to the test."

"Why, we could afford to dissolve the Union today."

"To the contrary, you need us. You attended college up north, I suppose? Harvard or Yale?"

"Harvard."

"And I imagine that after your mother taught you your letters, you were educated by a Northern tutor."

"Well, yes."

"The South produces the raw material, but who weaves it? Northerners. Every bit of cloth you are wearing, I wager, came from some Northern mill. Who manufactures most of your goods? Northerners. So I think you would miss us, but in all fairness we would miss you too. It would not be so hard to figure out how to do without slavery, surely?"

We argued back and forth about this for some time, neither convincing the other, until finally we parted on friendly enough terms. The next morning, I left for Columbia. I did not particularly want to go there, or even to remain in South Carolina, but since my bout with brain fever William fretted about my health, as I had told Mrs. Stanton. He and our doctor regularly conspired to make me rest, which I could only do by traveling.

From the ladies' car on the train I could see sumptuous plantations with outlying slave quarters. My various seatmates, unprompted, took care to assure me that the latter were quite comfortable, nicer than anything a factory worker up north enjoyed. (Every Southerner I met professed an intimate knowledge of Northern factories.) We also passed by miserable little farms owned by poor whites. If these people derived any satisfaction in life, I supposed, it was from lording it over their black neighbors.

Between the journey and my observations, I was rather weary and cranky when I arrived in Columbia, and even a good night's sleep did not put me entirely right. So the next morning, I was content, after breakfast, to sit on the veranda and read instead of taking my usual walk.

"You are looking very well today, Mrs. Rose."

A man had materialized at the rocking chair beside me. I had spoken to him briefly at breakfast, and something in his manner had already made me suspect he regarded the gold wedding ring I wore as a challenge. "Thank you," I said coolly, fluttering my left hand so the sun caught the gleam of my ring. I returned my attention to my book.

"What do you think of Columbia?"

"It is a lovely city, from what I have seen." I looked back at the page, trying to find where I had stopped.

"But what do you think of us as a whole, madam?"

Clearly Mr. Dickens's novel and I were not to be left in peace together. "In truth, sir, I believe you—that is, the South—lag far behind the North. Your slaves do most of your work, including the fine work of a craftsman, while their masters stand around idle and useless. It is not good for the slaves, nor is it good for the masters. There is great wealth, and great poverty, just as there is in Russia, as I know firsthand. Such a civilization can only consume itself and die if it is not reformed."

"You have some big opinions, for a little lady. You had better thank your stars you are a woman."

"I always thank my stars that I am a woman. But why in particular should I be thanking them now?"

"Why, here, if an abolitionist spouts off his mouth, we tar and feather him. Unless, of course, the abolitionist is a lady."

"Well, I am an abolitionist, and a proud one at that. And while your refusal to tar and feather a lady might be chivalrous, getting the tar and feathers together might at least give you something to do." I rose as my acquaintance's mouth flopped open and his face reddened. "Now, let me tell you something, sir. I was an abolitionist before I came to the South, but if I had not been, I do believe this visit would have made me one."

I stalked away to my room, not looking back, although I was tempted to do so to see whether he had suffered an attack of apoplexy. Southerners, as other travelers besides me had observed, insisted on asking Northerners for their opinions. Did they assume that they would all be favorable? I would have kept mine to myself had I not been asked.

But I wasn't in the habit of keeping my opinions to myself. Why should it be different here?

I'd had enough of quietly observing. I would rent a hall, and I would give a speech. If I could change one person's mind, perhaps one slave might end up a free man or woman. Surely that was worth the effort.

~ ~ ~

Although I could not find a hall to rent in Columbia—perhaps word had gotten around about my abolitionist views, for I found Columbia rather cool in general to me after that encounter—I secured a good place in Charleston, which suited me anyway because I would be taking the steamer from there to New York. I advertised my lecture as one on "social reform," which certainly could encompass abolitionism.

There was a good-sized crowd, though not, I found as I began my lecture, an enthusiastic one. I'd had this sort of audience before. The people came not so much to listen as to gape at the sight of a woman speaking, in the spirit of Dr. Johnson's rather overrated quip about a woman preaching being akin to a dog walking on its hind legs: it was not done well, but one was surprised to find it done at all. (Boswell would have done well himself not to record that particular sally.) Sometimes I could charm such audiences, sometimes I could shock them, and sometimes I just hoped the roof would collapse so we could be well out of each other's company.

Gradually, I elicited a few nods and chuckles from the assembly. It was time to touch on the Peculiar Institution. "I say what I say now more in sorrow than in anger. Your state, from the little I have seen of it, is a beautiful one. Your people are charming. But there is one thing that is unworthy of you, and that is your slave system. It debases the Declaration of Independence, the noblest document ever written. It debases the slave by robbing him of his own self. And it debases the white man by turning him into an owner and breeder of men. It debases the very institution of marriage. How so? A man takes a wife, and yet he also keeps a concubine among his slaves. Nowhere in the North would a wife and mistress reside under the same roof. Yet here, it is not only tolerated, it is profit—"

To a person, the crowd, which had been silent, rose, their eyes full of what I had never seen before in an audience—sheer hate. At the same time, my friend Mr. Thompson from the hotel hopped on the platform and grabbed my arm. "You need to get out of here. Now."

He dragged me back into an anteroom. "What on earth were you thinking, Mrs. Rose? No one discusses that topic. No one."

"I might have gotten a little carried away." I looked toward the now-bolted door leading to the stage. The crowd had found its voice and was now talking about teaching me a lesson, in none too pleasant terms. "Do you think they'll force their way back here?"

"I honestly don't know. If you were a man, they'd probably tear you to pieces. But as you're a woman—I don't know. No one's been talked to by a woman here like you just did. They could throw you in jail for disturbing the peace, or for being a common scold, or some such. They could find something, I'm sure. All I know is that you shouldn't stay here. Fortunately, I have a horse. I can get her from out front, bring her to the alley, and get you back to the hotel on her."

"But—"

"No buts, Mrs. Rose. Lock the door behind me. I'll tell you when it's time to go outside."

He hastened out, leaving me to listen to the crowd denouncing me as a strumpet and a whore and to contemplate the fact that I had never ridden a horse in my life. The second was somewhat more disconcerting than the first.

"Ready, Mrs. Rose."

I ventured outside to find a suitably gloomy-looking alley and Mr. Thompson with his beast. "Some of them are milling around front, waiting for you to come out. We need to get out before someone thinks of looking for you back here. You're going to have to ride astride, but fortunately the hotel isn't far."

Astride, sidesaddle—it was all the same to me. I surveyed the beast, which took that moment to snort at me. "I think I'll be just fine walking," I said as I jumped back.

Mr. Thompson slapped his thigh. "I do believe that you are afraid of horses, Mrs. Rose."

"I don't ride them. It was never necessary to learn."

"Well, let's remedy that." He chuckled. "Imagine! A lady tells a room of Southerners that they should give up their slaves, but is afraid of a horse!"

With considerable help from Mr. Thompson, and with every bone of my body protesting, I inserted a foot into the stirrup and grimly hauled myself up on the horse. At least I was one of those ladies who had added drawers to her array of garments. With my skirts in utter disorder, my pantalettes were the only thing standing between Mr. Thompson's eyes and what men called "the gates of heaven," and even they did not provide a perfect shield. I could only be grateful that (a) I was not a maiden and (b) I was over forty, the first time and probably the last I had appreciated that unpleasant fact of life.

"Good girl."

"Thank you."

"I meant the horse, Mrs. Rose. She's being quite patient, considering she seldom has a lady's skirts upon her. But you've done well too. Now, hold on to me, and if I bend, you bend too." He clucked at the horse.

We trotted—it felt like a gallop, but Mr. Thompson later insisted it was a mere trot—down the alley and into another. If I had held onto Mr. Thompson any tighter, William would have had grounds for divorce. Fortunately, the crowd had been having so much fun excoriating me that no one had thought to actually look for me, so we reached the hotel with nothing injured except for my dignity and perhaps the horse's pride. I doubted the poor creature had ever carried such a rank amateur as myself.

"Have you arranged for your passage home yet, Mrs. Rose?"

Safely on the ground, I swatted down my skirts as Mr. Thompson looked away politely. "No. I suppose I should."

"I will arrange it for you, and have a word with the mayor. I think you had better stick close to the hotel for the next day or so."

With my bones already aching from my equestrienne exertions, this would be no difficult task. "I suppose you are right. I am sorry to have given you so much trouble."

"No trouble at all."

"I must ask, Mr. Thompson. Just where do Southerners think those half-white children on plantations come from?"

"The stork." Mr. Thompson shrugged. "No one notices the ones on their own plantations, only those on their neighbors'; it's easier for all concerned. I do say, I think you made some very fair points. It is a cruel system."

I decided to count this as a victory.

~ ~ ~

Having left South Carolina unscathed, I returned with considerable relief to New York, which might be grimier than Charleston or Columbia but at least had never required me to mount a horse. Henceforth, I decided, any excursions I took for my health would be in the North or West.

One sultry day in August, William returned from his shop with a handful of mail he had picked up from the post office, including, I found, a letter from my sister Sophie. I eagerly picked it up to read about the latest from Berlin. Then tears began rolling down my face.

"Darling, what is it?"

I thrust the letter at William. "Read it."

"It is in German, my dear."

"Oh, yes." I took back the letter and stared at it stupidly.

"Has something happened to Sophie or her girls?"

"No." I wiped my eyes and made an effort to regain my composure. "It is Marcus Kaufmann. He died in the St. Marylebone workhouse."

An Englishman needed no further explanation; it was a fate dreaded by all. "I hope he was not there long. But how did he get to London?"

I cleared my throat. "Sophie heard it from his brother, who was one of Amalia's godfathers. Marcus continued to travel about after we divorced and found work in London teaching languages—just as I did—and selling books now and then. He was able to live off that, but saved very little. London never agreed with his constitution, but he stayed there because he liked it better than Berlin. A year or so ago he fell ill with consumption and soon became too sick to work. He ran through the little savings he had, but apparently was too proud to tell his brother how poor he was. Finally, though, he wrote to his brother and told him he was ill and wanted to come home to die. His brother traveled to London and found that he was already dead and buried. His landlady had taken care of him for a while, but he became too ill for her to manage, so she had no choice but to send him to the workhouse. He was mere skin and bones at that point." I stared at the letter. "It breaks my heart to think that I could have made his last days comfortable with just a little money."

"He would not tell his brother of his difficulties until it was too late. What makes you think he would have told you, or that a letter would have reached you in time?"

"There you go being logical." I fingered the letter. "But there is more. His brother told Sophie that a few months after we came here, Marcus came himself, looking for me, apparently hoping to win me back. He tracked us down to your shop, saw me sitting on your lap, and realized that it would be hopeless, so he went back."

"That was wise of him."

"I just wish things could have ended differently for him. He was not a bad man; it seems hard that only one of us should find happiness in another person."

"He had his chance." After a moment or two, William said more kindly, "But if he had written to you, I would have been glad for you to offer him what help we could, as long as he kept himself on his side of the Atlantic. It is a cruel disease."

I sighed, thinking of Marcus's Byronic chin and my youthful foolishness. If I had resisted temptation, might he still be selling books in Berlin? Might he have found a more congenial bride, who would have kept him from want? "It is indeed."

That night when I lay with William (who, I must say, was rather insistent that night on enjoying the marital act), I clutched him all the more tightly, knowing how lucky I had been.

~ ~ ~

It was not all gloom during those last months of 1847, though. At the end of October, Elizabeth Munn married Mr.

Mendum; much to our pleasure, they elected to hold the ceremony at our apartment, in the company of a few other infidel friends. I grew rather teary-eyed at the couple's departure, as the new Mrs. Mendum would be moving to Massachusetts with her new husband. "All the more reason for you to give more speeches in Boston," Mr. Mendum said as I gave his bride one more hug goodbye.

The year of 1847 slipped away and ushered in that year of revolution: 1848. Louis-Philippe, whom I had watched accept the French crown eighteen years before, was thrust from the throne in favor of a republic, which I hoped would endure. But my eyes were not on Paris that year so much as they were on a humbler place: Albany. The Married Woman's Property Bill, after years of languishing in committees and often not getting even that far, at last cleared one committee, then another. I followed its progress in the newspapers, expecting daily to hear that it had stalled; it always had in the past. But the bill was passed by one house, then the other, until finally, in April, it was signed into law.

As soon as I heard the news, I hurried to congratulate old Judge Herttell, who was now infirm and growing quite deaf. But he was smiling over a pile of engrossed copies of the new law that a friend had sent him from Albany. "Take a few, my dear Mrs. Rose. You have been invaluable in our effort. I am sure you have a few friends you would like to bestow them upon."

"I do indeed."

I kept one for William's scrapbook, but the other five were designated for the five ladies who had signed my original petition eleven years before. Four had signed my subsequent petitions, so I had no trouble finding them. But I hadn't been back to Mrs. Turner's establishment—not since

I had begun speaking in public. It wouldn't do to be seen entering a brothel, after all.

But without Mrs. Turner, my first signer, perhaps I might have given up on that long-ago day.

Mrs. Turner's place had been spruced up over the years, with freshly painted shutters and new curtains. I knocked, realizing as I did that it was entirely possible that Mrs. Turner had moved, or even died, and then where would I be? But the same maid, with graying hair, came to the door. "Mrs. Rose! Mrs. Turner often sees your name in the papers. Will you come inside? She is free."

"I will."

The parlor had not changed much, and I wondered if there was a certain timelessness to the decor of these places. But Mrs. Turner, who entered moments after I took my seat, was dressed in keeping with the times, although there was a matronliness about her that had not been there previously. "Ah, Mrs. Rose. I wondered if we might see you again someday."

"I thought you might want to have this." I handed her the printed law, rolled up in a silver vase.

Mrs. Turner smiled. "So they passed your law at last, my dear? And what a beautiful vase. Your husband's work?"

"Yes."

"I knew he was a silversmith, you see. I've seen the two of you walking into his shop from time to time. You make a lovely couple. Been putting my hints to work?"

I blushed. "I have."

"It's a good thing you caught me when you did. I'm selling this place and all the furnishings. Marrying my favorite client, as a matter of fact. Don't worry, I'm a better judge of men than I was back when I married my first one.

This man's a good one, a widower with a steady business as a stationer. And a policeman friend of mine checked him out, just in case. But I'm glad to have your bill passed, because you never know, do you?"

"I hope you will be very happy, and I am quite sure you will."

"Well, it's been a good living, but it's not what I want to be doing when I'm sixty or seventy. So might as well settle down. He's got a couple of grandchildren who rather like me, so it won't be half bad. So what's next for you?"

"Working for a bill that gives women even more. Maybe even working for the right of women to vote. This was a start, but we have a long way to go."

"You'll get there. But in the meantime, give yourself a good pat on the back. You did it."

"No, we did it—we women who worked for this and more than a few good men. But you're right. We did it." I patted myself on the back. "And we won't stop there."

10

JULY 1848 TO OCTOBER 1850

One of the charms of being infidels was that William and I could relax on Sunday morning with the *New York Herald* and whatever papers had been unread during the week. We had a friendly competition as to who would get to read the *Herald* first, and on that day, the last Sunday of July, William had won. I was looking through a Saturday paper when William said, "Doesn't Mrs. Stanton live in Seneca Falls?"

"Yes. Has she burned the place down? She was not happy about leaving Boston."

"There was a woman's rights convention held there, it seems. Here."

The paper gave no names, but stated that a group of people had attended a meeting at Seneca Falls on July 19, where they drew up a "Declaration of Sentiments," patterned after the grand language of the Declaration of Independence, a document I have made a point of reading at least yearly ever since my youth. *We hold these truths to be self-evident—that all men and women are created equal—that they are endowed by their Creator with certain inalienable rights . . . The history of mankind is a history of repeated injuries and usurpations on the part of man toward woman, having in direct object the establishment of an absolute tyranny over her.* I nodded in agreement as the Declaration listed example after example. Over a hundred women had signed this document.

"This surely must be Mrs. Stanton's doing. If not, she must certainly have been present."

"No one told you of this? You should have been there."

"No. No one did. I suppose there is some reasonable explanation."

"Perhaps."

But William sounded no more certain of that than I did. We returned to our papers in silence, but I could not forebear from reading the Declaration of Sentiments again, and then again once more. *He has never permitted her to exercise her inalienable right to the elective franchise. . . . He closes against her all the avenues to wealth and distinction which he considers most honorable to himself. As a teacher of theology, medicine or law, she is not known. . . . He has created a false public sentiment by giving to the world a different code of morals for men and women, by which moral delinquencies which exclude woman from society are not only tolerated but deemed of little account in man.*

Mrs. Stanton and I had not been close friends, but we had certainly been friendly, and she knew how hard I had worked to get the property law passed—approaching strangers, not legislators who happened to be friends of my father, I thought sourly. Why, then, had I not been told of this convention on a subject so dear to my heart? I told myself that I would not think of the matter further, that all would become clear eventually. Instead, of course, I brooded all day and all night on the subject, and so, I suspect, did my dear William. When we left for Long Island a few days later (William and the doctor having decided it was best I spend August by the sea), I was still brooding. When I learned from the papers that a follow-up convention had taken place in Rochester, New York, in early August without a word to me, I could take it no longer. I wrote to Mrs. Stanton to inquire why I had been left out.

In due time, a rather mealy-mouthed reply from Mrs. Stanton arrived. The Seneca Falls convention had been called on the spur of the moment by Mrs. Stanton, her friend Mrs. Lucretia Mott, and a few other ladies from Mrs. Mott's Quaker circle. No one had thought to advertise it beyond the area, although Mr. Frederick Douglass, who published the *North Star* in Rochester, had been kind enough to advertise it in his paper. There had scarcely been time to get everything ready for those who came, much less to invite those from outside of western New York. As for the Rochester convention, it had been largely organized by the Quaker ladies, with whom I was not acquainted. Really, Mrs. Stanton concluded, the conventions, though most enjoyable and productive, had been thrown-together affairs. She certainly hoped I would be present at the next convention, wherever that might be.

I snorted at the ocean, which I was facing as I read the letter. Mr. Douglass had spoken at both assemblies. I had met him in the early days of his celebrity, and his fame had only grown since then. No gathering at which he appeared could be deemed a thrown-together or paltry affair.

Had I been excluded because of my foreign birth, my Jewish background, my atheism? Or was it merely an oversight?

It would do no good to investigate the matter further; instead, I would write Mrs. Stanton a cordial reply. And I would make certain that I indeed was not excluded from the next gathering.

~ ~ ~

"I'm afraid I have some good news and bad, my love."

I looked up at William, newly arrived from work on a chilly day in February 1849. He looked more pleased than otherwise, so I said, "Out with it."

"I have a chance to lease a shop on Reade Street, with living quarters above. It's a stone's throw from Stewart's."

Stewart's was the first department store not only in New York City, but in the entire United States. Its four-story marble palace on Broadway had bedazzled shoppers when it first opened and even while it was still being constructed; William and I had often walked over to admire its progress. Now every business in New York that lacked a marble building felt downright deprived. "I presume you can afford it."

"Yes." William could not hide his smile.

"Then you should take it." Fashionable ladies and gentlemen flocked to Stewart's, and William's shop, full of jewelry, silver, and fancy walking sticks, could only benefit from the proximity. "What is the bad part?"

"I can move into the shop next month, but the apartment is occupied until Moving Day."

May 1 was known in New York as Moving Day. By custom, nearly every residential lease in the city ended on May 1, which meant that the streets of New York would be filled with carts and grumpy citizens hauling their goods from one to place to another. William and I had been through our share of Moving Days, and on the years when we were fortunate enough to stay put, we kept inside as much as we could to avoid the general mayhem.

"Well, we are quite good at it by now, aren't we?" We had learned to carry our valuables ourselves—our keepsakes, my jewelry, and some cherished books and paintings—and leave the rest to the carters. One year our carter had collided with another, and we had ended up with two very nice chairs but lost our dresser. It had taken a week to restore everyone's goods to their rightful places, which I had regretted somewhat as far as the chairs were concerned. "At least we can store some things in the new shop, so everything will not have to be left until the last minute. But what counts is that you have come so far. You came here with nothing, you might recall."

"Nothing but the dearest wife a man could ask for."

I pass over the rest that followed.

~ ~ ~

William and I got through Moving Day satisfactorily, other than the fact that we seemed to be accumulating more things each year despite living rather sparingly. We were still marveling over this phenomenon, and our wonderful water closet into which the city's Croton water flowed so freely, when trouble began stirring. By some odd coincidence, the American Shakespearean actor Edwin Forrest and the English Shakespearean actor William Macready were both playing Macbeth in the city. The two actors, who'd had a falling-out and had quite different styles of acting, each had his own set of partisans. (I was neutral, but William was firmly in the Macready camp, as one might expect.) All might have passed with only a few catcalls, however, had not Mr. Forrest's admirers included the b'hoys, as New Yorkers called them. No one could miss them when they left their natural habitat of the Five Points slum to saunter around the city, resplendent in their red shirts, stovepipe hats, and trousers tucked artfully into their boots. Many were not long from Ireland, although others were native New Yorkers. They disliked many things, including Englishmen, black people, abolitionists, the upper classes, and, in the case of the Irishmen and the native New Yorkers, each other. In much of this they were encouraged by Captain Isaiah Rynders, then one of the city's most powerful political bosses. With his backing (so everyone believed, although the captain professed innocence), the b'hoys had purchased most of the tickets to Mr. Macready's performance and brought it to a crashing halt, heckling the actors and pounding the floor with their boots. Unsated, they had returned for Mr. Macready's next performance three nights later. This time, thousands had encircled the theater. The police and militia had turned out, and what had begun in farce turned into tragedy when a riot ensued. Thirty people, perhaps more, lay dead at the end of the evening.

I had this in mind a year later when I prepared to attend a meeting of the Anti-Slavery Society at the Broadway Tabernacle, where I'd had my run-in with the Reverend Mr. Breckenridge years before. The *Herald*, edited by Mr. James Gordon Bennett, a man who had never met a progressive movement he liked, had been working itself into a conniption over the planned meeting. If the abolitionists had their way, it thundered, the slaves would butcher their masters and rape their mistresses. The country (what was left of it after all this rapine and butchery) would be torn asunder. It was the duty of all good New Yorkers to oppose this scheme of carnage by turning up at the Tabernacle. "Mr. Bennett has excelled himself," I said to William. "Is he in the pay of some Southern planter?"

"I don't like his tone. He's all but encouraging another riot. Which means, of course, that you will be all the more determined to go to the meeting."

"You too, my dear."

"True. I'll carry my special cane just in case."

William's special cane, made years ago for a competition, had a beautiful handle that concealed a deadly blade. He seldom carried it and had never had to use it, but I must admit I was not sorry to have its extra protection.

So, hand in hand, we walked the short distance to the Broadway Tabernacle to find the place packed. There were many women, which was encouraging, as our sex was not in the habit of rioting. I saw no obvious b'hoys. "So far, so good," I said.

"Rynders is here."

I peered up at the balcony, the direction toward which William had nudged me. "Are you sure?"

"Quite sure. He's been in my shop." William shrugged. "I can't help if he has good taste in some things."

"You sold something to him?"

"Yes, some candlesticks. I might have slipped a pamphlet or two in when I wrapped them up."

"Abolition?"

"And freethought. Put it this way: he probably won't be referring the Dead Rabbits to me."

This was one of the warring gangs who did Captain Rynders's dirty work for him. "A pity. I'm sure you could make them something appropriate. Something for the dead rabbit they are supposed to carry around?"

All started out quite well. There were the obligatory prayers, which William and I sat smiling through, and then Mr. William Lloyd Garrison, the president of the Anti-Slavery Society, started to deliver his address. It was an excellent one about the hypocrisy of the churches that condoned slavery, but I soon sensed trouble coming when smatterings of applause erupted where Mr. Garrison had said nothing noteworthy. I was not alone; those seated on the platform (Abby Kelley Foster, with whom I had lectured once or twice, was the only woman among them) looked at each other and frowned.

"Do you believe in Jesus?" Mr. Garrison asked the crowd. "If so, it is no test of goodness on the part of the person professing to believe in him. His praises are sung in the South by the men, women, and children."

Even from the orchestra I could hear Mr. Rynders hop up. He leaned over the balcony precariously. "Are you aware that the slaves sing psalms, preach, and pray without hindrance from the whites?"

"Yes, they sing psalms to Jesus, but not to a slaveholding, slave-breeding, and slave-selling Jesus."

The room might have been full of snakes, for all of the hissing that went on.

From there, it went downhill. Mr. Garrison finished his speech, but only on the condition that he allow Mr. Rynders, who by that point was all but on the platform himself, to say a word. That word proved to be a creature named Professor Grant—if he was a professor of anything besides whiskey I would be sorely surprised—who extrapolated for some time on the inferiority of the black race, whom he regarded as only half-human. The Hutchinson family, an abolitionist singing group, also in the gallery, tried to soothe everyone with a song, but was drowned out by the b'hoys. A young man from Philadelphia, an abolitionist, came close to punching Captain Rynders and had to be restrained by his elders on the platform. Finally, those of us who had not been driven out by all of the hissing and hooting and near-fisticuffs called for Frederick Douglass, who took the platform with his usual panache and, responding to the good professor, told the audience, "I offer myself for your examination. Am I a man?" When Captain Rynders pointed out, in language I need not reproduce, that Mr. Douglass was only half-black, Mr. Douglass beamed at him. "Then I am half-brother to Captain Rynders!"

The captain did not stifle himself after that, but he became decidedly more subdued, although he revived somewhat when a second black man, the Reverend Mr. Samuel R. Ward, took the platform. But despite the hooting, the Reverend Mr. Ward gave an excellent speech, and even the atheists in the audience, William and I, had to give him a round of applause.

Because the time the hall had been hired for had expired, the meeting adjourned, to be recommenced that evening at the hall of the New York Society Library at Leonard Street and Broadway.

Nothing boded well from the moment William and I arrived at our destination. The hall was full of men who did not appear to be at all acquainted with libraries, and several of them were carrying bagpipes with the air of intending to use them. Seeing them, and the tin kettles some were carrying (goodness knew how many women in Five Points were looking around for their kettles that night) was enough to tempt the two of us to head back home, but just at that moment Mr. Garrison, looking his usual unperturbed self, came over to us. "Ah, Mr. and Mrs. Rose. I saw you this morning but was unable to say anything with all of the bother going on. I am wondering if you might care to speak tonight, Mrs. Rose? We are down a few speakers, and perhaps a woman might sooth the savage beasts. And they know you here in New York. Perhaps that will improve their manners."

"I fear my soothing powers are quite inadequate, but I will try."

I took my place on the platform, accompanied by William—he insisted upon it, and as he looked quite distinguished and we could use all the men on the platform we could get, no one argued.

At eight o'clock sharp, Mr. Garrison called the meeting to order, which the crowd found hilarious in itself, and Mr. Parker Pillsbury rose to speak. The poor man had barely opened his mouth—to speak on the freedom of speech— when the bagpipes moaned, the tin kettles rattled, boots stomped, and canes thumped. Mr. Pillsbury might as well have been speaking Chinese, for no one could hear a word he was saying in the din. Just then Mr. Charles Burleigh hastened in. With his thatch of bright red hair and his impressive height, he was not a man who could be overlooked, and that was not his only distinction. As a youth, he had vowed not to cut his hair until slavery had been abolished, and as slavery had not obliged, he had a mane of hair and a beard that Father Time himself would have coveted. To keep his hair tidy, he wore it in ringlets—very nice ones, I must say—but that was the only tidy thing about him; his suit looked as if he had worn it for three straight weeks in steerage, then trampled upon it for good measure. To the b'hoys, he was catnip.

"Hullo, mister, what's the price of razors in your district?"

After a period of merriment in this vein, Mr. Pillsbury ceded the platform to Mr. Stephen Foster—the abolitionist, not the composer, in case you were expecting a banjo. Mr. Foster, who farmed for a living and was not averse to barging into churches and denouncing slavery, seemed a fair match for the rowdies at first. "Bennett knows you are here," he said, referring to the b'hoys' favorite newspaper publisher. "You came to disturb the meeting, as my dog goes out to drive away my neighbor's cattle that trespass on my land. I tell him to bark, and he—"

To a man, it seemed, the audience began barking, with some rooster crows thrown in for good (or bad) measure. Beside me, Mr. Foster's wife, Abby Kelley Foster, who had been planning to speak, groaned. "You might as well go next, Mrs. Rose. What a farce."

The menagerie having exhausted itself, I stepped onto the platform that a grumbling Mr. Foster had vacated.

"Woman's rights, boys!"

"Mrs. Caudle's curtain lectures!"

I glared at a contingent of policemen. I supposed they might have intervened had it appeared that any of us would get killed, but that not being the case, they had been content to play the role of spectators, save for one who had let out a commendable "Cock-a-doodle do!" before he remembered himself. Seeing no help would come from that quarter, I began. "You are worthy Americans, either by birth or by adoption. You read the papers—especially the *Herald*."

"Three cheers for the *Herald*!"

"Have you not read of the way in which freedom of speech has been prohibited in Ireland? Why do you want to deny that right to your fellow men—and women?"

"Three cheers for George Washington!"

I have no idea what President Washington had to do with any of this, but he, and nearly every other president the rowdies could think of, had been cheered that evening.

For a few more minutes I persisted, but futility was the theme of the evening. After asking, as politely I could muster, "Are you done?" which occasioned more cheering for absolutely nothing, I gave it up. There being no one else willing to take the platform, we took counsel and declared the meeting adjourned. With the help of the police, who finally remembered they were police, everyone got out in perfect order.

There was a second day of the meeting, just as dismal, but I did not attend. A day or so later, I read the account in the papers. *After the meeting was broken up, one of the policemen gravely told some folks who inquired why order could not be preserved, that it was a political meeting, and, alluding to a Mrs. Rose, who had attempted to speak, that a woman had no right to speak at such a place.* "Scoundrels," I muttered. "William, what are you doing with that paper? I haven't read it yet."

"It's repetitive, my dear."

"Still, I like to see them."

With a sigh, William handed it to me. *Mrs. Rose, a rather modest looking, elderly lady, tastefully dressed, ascended the rostrum . . .*

Elderly! I let out a stream of Yiddish so foul that a fishwife might have had to resort to her smelling salts. (I'd only heard these phrases once as a very little girl, when a carter's load had tipped over, but they had impressed me so much I had repeated them a day or so later when I spilled some soup, resulting in a sound boxing to the ears by Mama.)

"You found that word, I suppose."

"I did." I looked forlornly at William. "They're just being unkind, aren't they?"

"Of course they are. And the light was terrible in there. You're as beautiful as you ever were."

"Flatterer."

"But it's true. May I ask what you just said?"

I shook my head. "You really don't want to know, my dear. It would be corrupting the young."

~ ~ ~

"Allow me, Mrs. Rose."

Fresh from the train, which had just pulled into the depot at Worcester, Massachusetts, I smiled at Mr. Chester Dow of the *New York Herald* as he took my carpetbag. "Thank you. You are here for the woman's convention?"

"What else would bring the New York press to Worcester?" Mr. Dow winked at me. "My colleague from the *Tribune* is here too, but only the *Herald* reporter is gentleman enough to assist a lady. We're eager to hear what you and the other ladies have to say. You will be speaking, won't you?"

"Yes. I trust the bully-boys Mr. Bennett prodded on will not be at this meeting. When one speaks in public, one likes to be allowed to actually speak."

Mr. Dow had the grace to look abashed. "Massachusetts is quite out of their habitat. And there was a great deal of sympathy for the abolitionists after that meeting, you must admit. Not sympathy, perhaps, but there was a consensus that the crowd had been unfair."

"Well, life goes on. But while I am airing my grievances, I do wish you would render my words in proper English for a change instead of 'dis' and 'dat.' Surely after nearly twenty years of speaking your language I have improved somewhat."

"I think your English is excellent, and your accent quite pleasing, but Mr. Bennett insists on reporting your speeches in that manner. Not that he dislikes you—quite to the contrary, I suspect."

"You may well be right." I had met Mr. Bennett when he attended one of our infidel dances years before. I'd seldom encountered a man so utterly pleased with himself, but he had been quite the gentleman. "It is only a shame that he is not more enlightened, but at least you and the rest print my speeches accurately, other than the pronunciation."

"He thinks someday someone will make a Christian out of you."

I snorted. "That has been tried." *If only he knew that little story*, I thought.

"And he knows you are a subscriber, and your husband an advertiser. By the way, you have not admired my cane."

I looked down at Mr. Dow's cane, the silver head of which bore a fine likeness of the singer Miss Jenny Lind. She was touring the United States that autumn of 1850 under the auspices of Mr. P. T. Barnum, and through his exertions a perfect mania had developed for all things Jenny Lind. William, no fool, had spent days crafting a cane head with her likeness and had sent it to Mr. Barnum, who had pronounced it beautiful. With William having published this commendation in the papers, the orders for the canes had come in faster than William could fill them, and he was making a rather unsettling amount of money from them. "My husband is a talented man. And here is my hotel."

"Married to a talented lady." Mr. Dow doffed his hat in case I missed this pretty little compliment. "I shall look forward to hearing you, Mrs. Rose."

I smiled, knowing that we were likely to be pilloried nonetheless. Those of us working for progress and those who reported on it needed each other, but it was a strange relationship.

This gathering, the first national convention for woman's rights, had been born out of an antislavery conference earlier that year in Boston, at which a group of ladies, believing that the question of women was being neglected, agreed to put a call out for a meeting in Worcester. I had not been at the Boston meeting—a much more sedate affair than the one in New York—but since Seneca Falls I had taken more care to make it difficult to forget about me, by lecturing more often with others and in general confining myself less to the freethought movement where I was still most at home. It had worked; this time Mrs. Mott herself had invited me to lecture at Worcester. Mrs. Paulina Wright, who had been widowed and remarried and was now known as Mrs. Davis, would be presiding.

Brinley Hall was packed when I took my place on the platform on that October morning. Many of us had been at the New York anti-slavery meeting just months before, including dear Mr. Burleigh, who was staying at the same hotel as the rest of us but had the look of having slept in a dustbin. I looked for rowdies, but saw none. Perhaps they had not been able to figure out the Worcester trains.

Thus reassured, I sat back and enjoyed the excellence of the speeches and the receptiveness of the audience, although the occasional sound of a hand organ from another part of the building, where a fat girl was being exhibited, distracted us occasionally, as did the cry of "Three hundred pounds of glorious FLESH!" coinciding with the point that Mrs. Davis took the stage.

In the afternoon, it was my time to speak. The fat girl and the hand-organist had left, but the audience had grown to five or six hundred men and women, apparently due to people hearing favorable reports about the morning's speeches. Mrs. Mott, the oldest lady present, had to shush the audience, which she did with the mildest voice and the sternest of looks.

"When a father and a mother have a son born to them, what do they do?" I asked the audience. "They sit down and consult together about his education, how he shall be trained and fitted for the usefulness of life. If they have a daughter, what do they do? Nothing. A girl is educated with one single aim—to catch a husband. She is educated in accordance with man's desires, wishes, and aims, and it is no wonder she has not risen to the true level of her womanhood.

"But she can aspire to that level. She can study any of the professions. Is perseverance necessary? She possesses it. Look at her by the bed of sickness, where toil and sacrifice are needed. Who is it that holds out to the last? Feeble woman. Look at man when he is ready to give up with despair. Who is it that upholds and strengthens him? Feeble woman.

"If the error of the inferiority of woman is at once trampled underfoot, and other necessary reforms instituted— such as the right of universal suffrage—woman will not only have a higher knowledge and estimate of herself, but she will impart her improvement to society at large. Elevate her to the position she should occupy, and charity, morality, and every other humanizing sympathy and principle will flow from her in its essence and purity."

Signifying that I was finished, I inclined my head and stepped back from the platform. And then the applause began.

I would not be left out of any such gatherings in the future, I knew then.

11

SEPTEMBER 1852 TO DECEMBER 1853

Donning a pair of William's trousers that I had pulled from the laundry bag, I rolled up the legs. Then I topped them off with a paletot. The result was not anything that could be worn in public, of course, but it was a fair enough approximation of a Bloomer garment, so-called because Mrs. Amelia Bloomer, after she, Mrs. Stanton, and others took to wearing them, had promoted their adoption in her newspaper. Several ladies intended to wear them to the woman's rights convention in Syracuse. Having studied myself in the bedroom mirror, I strode into the sitting room where William was reading. "What do you think? Bloomers or not?"

William clapped his hand to his mouth, whether in horror or to suppress a laugh I could not tell.

"You don't like them?"

William removed his hand. The twitch of his mouth suggested he had been snickering. "Well, maybe if you had a proper set made—but no, my dear. I don't. They just don't suit you."

"You're probably right." I sat down and crossed one leg over the other. "I thought back in the bedroom that I did look ridiculous. They are comfortable, though." I looked enviously at William in his well-fitted pants.

"You are too elegant for them. But aside from that, I think any gain in comfort will be outweighed by the annoyance you will encounter. I am not certain New York is ready for you in Bloomers."

"Perhaps not." I rose to change back into my accustomed dress. "Well, maybe I'll have a set made for the garden." We had a fine rooftop garden, which yielded us excellent vegetables and beautiful flowers. "The plants won't mind a bit."

~ ~ ~

"Mrs. Rose! How lovely to see you." Mrs. Mott took my hand, then indicated the woman next to her. "This is my friend Miss Susan B. Anthony. She is rather fond of the *B*, so it must stay in. It is her first convention with us, but I do hope it will not be her last. She is here as an agent of the Woman's Temperance Society."

Like Mrs. Mott, Miss Anthony was not wearing the Bloomer dress, but wore a simple gray gown hemmed sensibly around her ankles. As Mrs. Mott hurried off on a matter of business, Miss Anthony smiled at me. "I am delighted to meet you, Mrs. Rose. My friend Mrs. Stanton—we met not long ago, but it feels as if we have known each other for years—tells me that you are quite the queen of the platform."

I blushed. "That is very kind. How is Mrs. Stanton?"

"She is expecting her confinement very soon—I really hope it is her last one—but says she feels quite hearty."

"I understand that she has adopted the Bloomer costume."

"Oh, yes, and she has been trying to make a convert of me. I dare say she will succeed. I see you have not adopted it."

"No, I considered it, but I did not care for how it looked, and my husband cared for it even less. I shall leave it to the younger ladies." I glanced over. "I see Miss Stone has taken it up."

Miss Lucy Stone was headed in our direction. Not only had she donned Bloomers, she had shingled her hair, which she kept tucked behind her ears. I had met her at the first woman's rights convention, when she was not long out of Oberlin College. She was an admirable woman, having struggled to pay her way through college and succeeded, and a fine speaker, but we had not drawn close to each other. She appeared to be on excellent terms with Miss Anthony, however, and soon was chatting away with her about business matters relating to a temperance society as if I were invisible. Miss Anthony tried on occasion to draw me into the conversation, but to no avail, so I finally found a new companion in conversation, soon after which the meeting was called to order.

Miss Stone loomed large. "What is our position politically?" she asked the audience in the afternoon. "Why, the foreigner, who can't speak his mother tongue correctly, the Negro, who to our shame we regard as fit only for a bootblack, and whose dead, even, we bury by themselves, and the drunkard, all are entrusted with the ballot—all placed by men, politically higher than their own mothers, sisters, wives, and daughters."

I squirmed in my seat. Her point was true enough, but to place immigrants on the same level as drunkards irked me, especially since Miss Stone knew perfectly well that I myself was one, having heard me speak in what I knew was still a marked accent.

Miss Stone could not have pleaded ignorance, though, after I was introduced that afternoon as "a Polish lady, and educated in the Jewish faith." There were some murmurs in the crowd as I stepped to the podium; many, I suspected, had assumed I came from a more conventional place, such as Prussia, and was a lapsed Christian rather than a lapsed Jew. (In a sense, I suppose, I was both.) "It is of very little importance in what geographical position a person is born," I said, "but it is important whether his ideas are based upon facts that can stand the test of reason. I am an example of the universality of our claims, for not American woman only, but a daughter of poor, crushed Poland and the downtrodden and persecuted people called the Jews, pleads for the equal rights of her sex. It is a melancholy fact, that woman has worn her chains so long that they have almost become necessary to her nature—like the poor inebriant, whose system is so diseased that he cannot do without the intoxicating draft." As I had anticipated, there was a burst of applause, for many of those present, like Miss Anthony, hailed from the temperance movement. "Or those who are guilty of the pernicious and ungentlemanly practice of using tobacco until they cannot dispense with the injurious stimulant." I wrinkled my nose as the ladies laughed; it was no coincidence that our conferences, though open to men, were bare of spittoons. When I wound up with, "In claiming our rights, we claim the rights of humanity; it is not for the interest of woman only, but for the interest of all," I felt that I had vindicated my right to the ballot, whenever I might be able to exercise it.

The next evening Miss Antoinette Brown, who was also an Oberlin graduate and a bosom friend of Miss Stone, offered a resolution declaring that the Bible recognized woman as a public teacher, that it enjoined upon her no subjection that was not enjoined upon man, and that it recognized neither male nor female in Christ Jesus.

I had no quarrel with Miss Brown, although I course did not share her beliefs; in fact, she planned to seek ordination as a minister, and I could not help but admire her for her pluck. But nor did I wish to see the cause of woman's rights being turned into a religious crusade or to turn upon what could be justified by the Bible. When Miss Brown had finished, I rose. "If the able theologian who has just spoken had been in Indiana when its constitution was revised," I said, "she might have had a chance to give her Bible argument to some effect. At that convention, Robert Dale Owen introduced a clause to give to a married woman the right to her property. The clause had passed, but by the influence of a minister was recalled—"

The audience hissed, not at me but in disapproval of this foolish minister.

"Yes, recalled," I said. "By his appealing to the superstition of the members, and bringing the whole force of Bible argument to bear against the right of woman to her property, it was lost. Had Miss Brown been there, she might have beaten him with his own weapons. For my part, I see no need to appeal to any written authority, particularly when it is so obscure and indefinite as to admit of different interpretations. When the inhabitants of Boston converted their harbor into a teapot rather than submit to unjust taxes, they did not go to the Bible for their authority. On human rights and freedom, on a subject that is as self-evident as that two and two make four, there is no need of any written authority."

I then introduced my own resolution: *That we ask for our rights not as a gift of charity, but as an act of justice. Any difference in political, civil and social rights, on account of sex, is in direct violation of the principles of justice and humanity, and as such ought to be held up to the contempt and derision of every lover of human freedom.* It passed, and, I must say, very handily. Miss Brown's resolution was postponed until the next day, at which time I insisted again, "We have met here for nobler purposes than to discuss theology. It has done mischief enough." Mrs. Mott, the president of the convention, agreed with me, and the resolution was tabled. For that, we got a scolding from the *New York Herald* (which for reasons known to Mr. Bennett alone nonetheless threw me a crumb of praise by crediting me with "much argumentative power," as William pointed out), but we would have gotten one anyway.

A couple of months later, William's errand boy, Peter, knocked at our apartment door. "There's a lady asking if she can stay the night with you and Mr. Rose, ma'am. A Miss Lucy Stone. Mr. Rose said she can stay if it's all right with you." Peter cleared this throat. "Her hair's been chopped, and she's wearing pants of some sort."

"Bloomers," I said. "Some ladies find them more comfortable than long skirts. Yes, she can stay. Send her right up, please."

Peter looked dubious, but nodded. I think he had the notion that Miss Stone had escaped from the lunatic asylum on Blackwell's Island.

Miss Stone, looking natty in her Bloomers, appeared shortly and stretched out her hand. "I do apologize for the intrusion, but you have no idea how foolish the hotels here are about ladies in Bloomers. I was treated like a streetwalker, so I thought I would come here."

"How silly of them. I am glad you found your way here." I led the way to our spare room, which was more of a cubbyhole. "It's tiny, you can see, but I'm sure you've slept in far worse in your travels."

"I certainly have. You too, no doubt." Miss Stone laid down her carpetbag. "It won't be an imposition? Your husband seemed a little cool. Or perhaps he was put off by my Bloomers?"

"No. He thought they looked odd on me, as they do, but he would never presume to tell any woman what she can or cannot wear. He has been a friend to our cause since even before there was one." I hesitated, but decided that if I said nothing, it would be a dismal evening when William came in from his shop. "My husband takes a great interest in our conventions, although his work prevents him from attending. Between the newspapers and what I tell him, he is quite well informed. I believe he is vexed at what you said at the convention about the immigrant who does not know his mother tongue being allowed to vote. Indeed, I know he is."

"That? But of course, Mrs. Rose, I did not have him in mind at all. He is everything the United States could want in a citizen. A perfect gentleman."

"He is very protective of me, and I believe he thought you might have had immigrants like me in mind—those who come from elsewhere in Europe."

"But no! I meant the Irish, of course. They are everywhere, you know. Indeed, here in New York, you must know that as well as anybody."

"They are here because their native land has become intolerable to them, because they cannot survive there. Can there be a better reason to leave a place? In any case, we are quite happy to accept the work they do. They are good enough to clean our houses and pave our roads. Why should they be denied the ballot once they become citizens?" I softened my voice. "You must understand why I grow heated; my country is ruled by a despot, so I treasure the right of every person to vote—even though it is denied to us women at present. Why, even in England my husband could not vote, simply because he did not own sufficient property, even though he was far better informed than some of those fops who couldn't be bothered to read anything more weighty than a racing form."

"Well, I would be better satisfied with all men voting if all women could."

"We can certainly agree on that."

With that we changed the subject. William came in an hour or so later, with some trepidation. Seeing Miss Stone and I talking pleasantly about our travels (like all lecturers who spoke in rustic towns, we had a wealth of stories about some of the out-of-the-way places in which we had been forced to lodge at night), he relaxed, and the evening passed quite nicely. In the morning, William even essayed to escort Miss Stone to the train station to spare her the indignity of being hooted and hollered at by passing boys. Instead, as William told me when he returned from his mission of chivalry, they'd had to content themselves with staring at Miss Stone and at William for being with Miss Stone. "I must thank you, my dear, for sparing me that ordeal on a daily basis. So do you think more highly of Miss Stone now?"

"She is talented and will do great things for our causes. But she clearly has her prejudices—as we all do, I suppose. Perhaps she is simply more honest about hers."

~ ~ ~

Soon after the New Year of 1853 began, I came home from some errand to find our dear friend James Thompson in the parlor with William. Even if we had not been friends, this would have been no surprise, as the annual celebration of Thomas Paine's birthday was approaching, and William and Mr. Thompson generally were among those seeing to the arrangements. "Is there anything new planned for the celebration this year?" I asked after I had removed my cloak and bonnet.

"As a matter of fact, there is," Mr. Thompson said, smiling at William.

"What, the venue?"

"No. The City Assembly Rooms, same as last year."

"That should do well. They are very conducive to dancing, and William and I are due for a waltz. But what is new, then? Why are you two smirking so?"

"There will be a lady presiding this year," Mr. Thompson said.

"Who?"

"Why, you, assuming you are agreeable. Who else?"

I felt tears forming. Years ago, William and I had succeeded in opening the dinners to women, and now this.

"I had nothing to do with the decision," William said. "I learned of it only this afternoon."

"It is true," Mr. Thompson said. "I proposed the idea to the committee of arrangements in your husband's absence, and it was unanimously accepted. It was your speech at last year's dinner that clinched the matter."

I had spoken in response to a toast on foreign affairs. The *Herald* reporter had been present and had rather shocked me by printing the speech in its entirety, without a "dis" or "dat" to be found, and praising it as "eloquent, political, interesting, and sarcastic."

"Well, I am honored, and I hope I will do justice to the memory of Thomas Paine. I suppose I cannot wear myself out dancing, then." I smiled at William, beaming beside me. "But I still plan to waltz just a little."

~ ~ ~

"Mrs. Rose! My favorite infidel."

I smiled at Mr. Garrison, who had endured Mr. Rynders and his b'hoys with me in New York. This fine June day found us at the railway station in Hartford, Connecticut, where a Bible convention was being held, not to venerate the old book but to question its authority. Naturally, as soon as I had read of the conference in *The Liberator*, Mr. Garrison's newspaper, I had hastened to make arrangements to come. "You promised in your paper to be here, and I am glad to see you keep your promises."

"Aside from my disgust at the way in which those responsible for organizing the conference have been traduced by the other papers, I think the subject is well worth examining."

"Ah, we will make a convert of you yet—although I suppose that is not the best word to use."

"I do intend to introduce some resolutions, among them pointing out the hypocrisy of proclaiming the Bible to be divinely inspired while withholding the reading of it from the slaves. Do you plan to speak?"

"I am not on the schedule—as a matter of fact, I am quite worn out from my travels—but I will if I feel called to do so."

"Which means you probably will."

"No doubt."

It soon emerged that Mr. Garrison and I were bound for the same place: the home of Mr. Andrew Jackson Davis, a spiritualist gentleman who was known as the Poughkeepsie Seer after his former residence. (I suppose Poughkeepsie, in need of all the seers it could get, had no desire for him to relinquish the title.) "I could not refuse his offer of hospitality, as it was so gracious," I said. "But I do hope the spirits—or what the man fancies are spirits—keep their distance while we are there."

"So you believe in no form of afterlife, Mrs. Rose?"

"I do not—only that we mingle with the dust. Trust me, I have thought that it would be a comfort to hold such a belief, for like everyone I have lost dear ones. But my reason dictates otherwise."

"You can't be faulted with inconsistency."

Soon afterward, we came to Mr. Davis's house, where we found other guests, including Mr. Joseph Barker, an Englishman who had renounced his ministry. He had been active in the Chartist movement, and had indeed been arrested for his advocacy. Naturally, I gravitated toward him, and as Mr. and Mrs. Davis were excellent hosts, all passed agreeably. As we had to rise early, there was no spirit-rapping, which was just as well, because I knew I could not have refrained from testing my host's abilities.

Aptly enough, Melodeon Hall, where the convention was held, was a former church. It was packed to the rafters. I was pleased to see more than a smattering of women in the crowd, along with some black people. Only a few ordained ministers had turned up to defend the Bible, but the gallery was full of starchy-looking young men, whom I soon divined were divinity students from nearby Trinity College. Seated in front, amply supplied with pen and paper, was a man whom I recognized as a reporter from the *New York Herald*. Mr. Bennett might fulminate against us infidels, but he had to concede that we made excellent press.

For two solid days, freethinking men argued with two ministers, the Reverends Storrs and Turner, over the Bible. It was all very stimulating, and to my surprise the divinity students emitted only the occasional hiss, but each time the topic of women came up, the subject was canvassed by men. By the afternoon of the third day, I could take no more. When the men started squabbling on the afternoon of the third day about who had had the most time to speak, I got to my feet. "If anyone has had reason to find fault with regard to time, it is woman. I think you ought to leave us, out of four days, at least one."

In the balcony, the divinity students rustled. When Mr. Barker, who was presiding, said that woman certainly would be heard, there was a faint hiss.

Woman—that being me—had her turn Saturday night. I was dressed plainly in black silk, which I found practical to wear when speaking out of town, but the divinity students gaped at me as though I were a veritable Jezebel. Presumably I was the first woman they had heard speak in public. I would have to make it a memorable experience for them. "This movement seems to me to be one of the highest and greatest importance that has taken place in our age. It is of more importance even than the one that has so long lain at my heart, the rights of woman, for it is closely connected with it. As woman has not been represented here, I feel it is my duty to raise my voice and protest against the Bible."

The hissing grew louder, followed by sundry boot-thumping and cane rattling. But I pressed on.

"The Bible has been a two-edged sword to men; it has united them in nothing but persecution. To woman it has been like a millstone tied to her neck to keep her down; it has subjected her to the entire control and arbitrary will of man. It is an insult to the supposed Creator to say he created one half of the race for the mere purpose of subjecting it to the other, as well as a libel on the nature and powers of woman to say that there is no other aim nor destiny in her existence except to be a mere plaything or a drudge to man, as the circumstances may require.

"The idea that 'he that believeth shall be saved, and he that believeth not shall be damned' has caused more mischief to man than all the rest of the Bible could ever have benefited him, for it has produced all the persecution and ill-will on account of belief. But there can be no merit in belief, nor demerit in disbelief, for it is not in our power to believe or disbelieve by a mere effort of the will. We can make a child believe error to be truth, and it may die or sacrifice the lives of others in maintenance of it, and yet the error is not truth but err—"

This time, there was a different hiss—the hiss of gas being shut off. The room was plunged into darkness.

"Is this how you defend the Bible?" Mr. Barker shouted.

Mr. Barker and Mr. Garrison—at least, I assume they were Mr. Barker and Mr. Garrison—placed themselves beside me to prevent any attacks, and a lady bounded up on the platform to put her arms around me, but the divinity students contented themselves with making as much noise as possible as the proprietors of the hall wrestled with the peculiarly modern problem of restoring the gaslight without gaslight. When the light blazed again, I returned to my spot and fixed my eye on the clerical rowdies. "When the lights were extinguished," I said sweetly, "it reminded me of one of the true things we find in the Bible: that some there are 'who love darkness better than light.'"

On the platform, Mr. Barker snorted with amusement. A lady called, "Tell the louts, sister!"

A pair of boots appeared over the gallery railing. I thought the entire man would follow, but when no more appeared, I said, "I do not know but exhibiting the boots over the railing may be a part of the defense of the Bible, but whether it is so or not, we live in an enlightened age, in the free United States of America, where everyone may do as he pleases, so long as he does not interfere with the rights of others, even to exhibit his boots or discourse in favor of the Bible.

"The Pope has oppressed and all but destroyed poor Italy with the authority of the Bible. When the tyrant of Russia laid his iron heel on the neck of my own poor, prostrate native land, Poland, he brought the same authority. When with the iron rod, that terrible thing called a scepter, said to have been given from heaven, the usurper sways the liberties and lives of millions, he brings good authority from the Bible."

A hiss, from a new spot, ensued.

"Do you hiss the Bible, or Russia? All this does not disturb me or ruffle my temper; it is only additional evidence to me of the pernicious influence of the Bible. This is a practical illustration of it. It inspires me with no other feeling than pity and commiseration for such irrationality, but it is late, and I had better save my voice. To you, my sisters, I would but say that the defenders of the Bible have given you a most practical evidence of the rights and liberties Christianity has conferred upon you. The Bible has enslaved you, the churches have been built on your subjugated necks; do you wish to be free? Then you must trample the Bible, the church, and the priests under your feet!"

You would not be remiss in thinking that this last sally was received badly by the divinity students, that the session was adjourned immediately afterward, or that a certain amount of police assistance was required for all of us to exit the building.

The next day, the last, I passed in a discussion of the fine points of scripture with the Reverend Mr. Storrs, which caused an equal amount of upset, so that my mere appearance on the platform in the evening session occasioned howls of indignation. There was very little done after that, except that a young man was arrested for drawing a dirk, whether with the intent of using it against me, one of the gentlemen on our side, or the entire lot of us I was never sure. Nor was the *Herald* reporter, who gallantly escorted me out of the building that last evening. "What I do know is this: you never disappoint, Mrs. Rose."

"Well, well," said William when I got off the train a couple of days later. "If it isn't the Scourge of Hartford."

I linked my arm in his. "Really, such an excitable lot of boys. I fear for their future congregations."

~ ~ ~

"Let me say a word about the short dress, which at present causes so much remark," Mr. Henry Blackwell said from the podium at Cleveland, Ohio. "If you would conquer your prejudices, do as I once did when I was a boy. I borrowed my sister's dress and petticoats and tried to walk about in them. I shall never forget the experiment. I can truly say, the sensation was awful."

I suppressed a snicker at the thought of the bearded Mr. Blackwell in a dress, then stole a glance at Miss Stone, dressed becomingly in Bloomers. This speech, and indeed Mr. Blackwell's presence at this national convention, was entirely for her benefit, I suspected, as gossip had informed me that he was enamored of her. Though I was not in a position to know whether Miss Stone returned his affections, I could not help but admire his dedication.

"Really, the man spoke far too long," Miss Anthony hissed to me after we had adjourned for the evening. Mr. Blackwell had proceeded to mention Joan of Arc, Queen Elizabeth, Maria Theresa, Harriet Beecher Stowe, the dangers of early marriage (Miss Stone being safely into her thirties), the nature of the Deity, Mary Wollstonecraft, and Mary Shelley. "It's a woman's convention, for heaven's sake!"

"He seems a well-meaning young man, and he is at least used to women of character." Mr. Blackwell's sister Elizabeth had obtained a medical degree, the first woman in the United States to do so, and a second sister had followed in her footsteps.

"Yes, I do fear Miss Stone will capitulate and marry him sooner or later. He has already talked her into visiting his family in Cincinnati, they say. And then the childbearing will commence." Miss Anthony shook her head. "But enough of that. Did you see the letter the Reverend Channing sent?"

It was the custom of those who could not be present, like the Reverend Mr. William Henry Channing on this occasion, to send a letter in their stead. "His ideas for petitions? Yes. Especially the one about drunkenness being grounds for divorce. That will set—how does that saying go? The cat among the sparrows?"

"Pigeons. Mrs. Stanton—if only she would stop breeding and join us here—is eager to broach the topic of divorce, you know. The Reverend Miss Brown is opposed, and Miss Stone is reluctant to bring up the matter. But I think we must read the letter as it was written."

I nodded. It was indeed a fraught topic. "We must deal with it sooner or later. But this may not be the best time or place." Saying the wrong thing, we all knew, would brand us as "free lovers," an epithet that could be ruinous to any cause and ours in particular. There were at least three divorcées in our movement—me, Mrs. Clarina Nichols, and Mrs. Mathilde Franziska Anneke, a German-born lady for whom I had translated at a New York convention just weeks before—but we had all remarried, and we kept the circumstances of our earlier unions to ourselves and a few others we trusted. Mrs. Anneke's husband had been a drunkard and a vicious man, and Mrs. Nichols's husband had been cruel and improvident. Marcus, except for that unhinged day after our Amalia's death, had been none of those things, so if these two women, with their very unsatisfactory first husbands, felt it advisable to stay silent, there was all the more reason for me to follow suit.

No, it would not do to press the divorce issue too hard. Once we got the ballot, it would be different.

But the next morning, when Miss Brown, at the podium, read out the Reverend Mr. Channing's letter and declared that she would alter it so that habitual drunkenness should be a reason for legal separation, not divorce, I could not but ask, "Should legal separation have the same force as divorce?"

"It would not allow the parties to marry again."

I shook my head. "What constitutes marriage? The violation of that, whatever it is, is a sufficient ground for a legal, social, and entire separation between them, and that is divorce. But I will not enter upon the discussion of that subject at present. We must come to it, we must face it. I know well, and have known for years, that this subject will encounter more prejudice and in consequence more difficulties than any subject hitherto brought before the public, and hence it is all the more necessary to meet it. But here I must leave it."

Mrs. Stanton's Declaration of Sentiments, propagated at Seneca Falls, had been printed for the convention and read to us with the intent that we adopt it. I picked up my copy. "To me, this passage is beautiful, because it is true: *He has created a false public sentiment by giving to the world a different code of morals for men and women.* I acknowledge no different standard of morals for the sexes; there is none in nature, in truth, and should be none in practice. But a different code is recognized in practice in all our society, in all our law, in all our public opinion, that greatest of all tyrants. All those have established a different code of morals for the sexes, and hence comes so much of immorality, so much of crime, so much of suffering.

"It *is* time to consider whether what is wrong in one sex can be right in the other. It is time to consider whether when a woman is drawn down to sin, and has broken the law of society—too often from ignorance, from inexperience, or from poverty—whether such a being should be cast out of the pale of humanity, while her despoiler goes free?"

"No! No! No!"

I leaned over the podium. "And yet he does go free!"

There was a round of applause, which I must say took a while to subside. Although I wished I could have said more about the subject of divorce, I had at least spoken up for a group of my sister women who were too often ignored—the so-called fallen women. I had not forgotten how close I could have come to sharing their fate had not my father and my sister been kind and Marcus honorable.

When we adjourned for the morning, Mr. Blackwell approached me and wrung my hand. "I was moved by your speech, Mrs. Rose. It made mine look quite pitiful, especially as mine was rehearsed, and yours not, I think."

"I think you did quite well, sir—especially if that was your maiden effort, if I may use that phrase."

"It was, at least for woman's rights." Mr. Blackwell brightened, then looked worried. "Do you think Miss Stone liked it?"

"She attended to it very carefully, I thought."

Mr. Blackwell sighed happily.

~ ~ ~

In December, I returned from Rochester, where I had gone to a local woman's rights convention. The city had been quite friendly to us, as one might expect from a place where both Miss Anthony and Mr. Douglass resided. The Reverend Mr. Samuel J. May, who could not have been more different from the mobocrat ministers-in-training at Hartford, had presided. When I had mentioned to him during a break how pleasant it was to find a man of the cloth well disposed to us, he had said that he had four charming nieces in Concord, Massachusetts, whom he hoped would benefit from our efforts.

Because William was quite busy producing beautiful gifts for the holidays, I did not ask him to meet me at the station (as I usually did, not out of necessity, but for the pleasure of seeing his dear self waiting on the platform for me). Instead, I took a streetcar to Reade Street, where William's store sparkled for the holidays. "I'm back, darling," I said. "As you can see."

William kissed me as his workers looked on benignly. "Was it a good conference?"

"Yes, and I hope my last one for the year. I shall tell you about it when you get upstairs."

"Well, there's a pile of mail waiting for you. Mainly invitations for you to speak, a few religious tracts, and the usual crank letters. I threw away the crank letters and the tracts. Oh, and a letter from Poland."

"I wonder if my father has remarried." Liba had died of a fever the year before, much to my father's sorrow and mine as well, for she and I had gotten along quite well by mail. Over the years, I had commiserated with her on the loss of her children—of the many she had borne, only three, all boys, were still living—and had enjoyed the gossip she passed along. In his last letter, Papa had broached the topic of his taking a new wife, perhaps a widow near his own age. I, wiser than I had been when I was a callow girl, had given my approval, not that it was necessary. "Well, we shall soon find out."

As promised, a stack of mail sat on the secretary. The letter from Poland was not in my father's handwriting, but that of my half-brother Isidor. He and the oldest of the boys, Simon, had lately taken to writing me. Simon, having been whisked out of Poland to avoid the compulsory military service that the tyrant Russia had imposed, was grown and studying dentistry in Dublin—goodness knew what type of accent he would pick up—and Isidor, still in his early teens, would no doubt emigrate too when the time came. They were both amusing correspondents, and I broke the seal with cheerful anticipation and began to read.

Then I hung my head over the secretary and cried.

"I'm home, dear—Ernestine! What is wrong?"

"My father. He is dead." I tried to compose myself. "Isidor—poor boy!—said that he died in his sleep. He was not a young man, and I should have anticipated this news. But I think I always hoped that I would see him again."

William led me to the sofa and put his arms around me. "I am so sorry. But you can at least take comfort that you stayed in touch with him."

"Yes, Isidor said he had read my last letter that evening." I settled into the comfort of William's arms. "I know he took some pride in me, but I wish I could have pleased him better. Yet I could take no other path."

"He knew that. You will light a candle for him as you do your others, I suppose."

"I shall." Each anniversary of the deaths of my mother, the children, and—with William's approval—poor Marcus, I lit a candle in their memory. "It is a good custom, and I am not averse to following good customs. And I know he would have wanted it."

12

February 1854 to October 1854

"I can't tell you what a pleasure it is to be here, instead of wiping noses at home," Mrs. Stanton said. "Of course, the noses are at the hotel with their nurse, but still it is a change. I came very close to not coming here at all. Did I tell you that one of my sons shot the baby in the eye? An accident, of course. Fortunately, there was no lasting damage."

I shuddered. Miss Anthony said, "Well, now that the baby is weaned, perhaps you will be able to join us more often. Perhaps even permanently."

"I take your meaning, Susan, but the babies will come when they will. There is only one infallible method to keep them at bay, and that is too unpleasant to contemplate for both myself and my husband." Mrs. Stanton, who had grown a little plumper since I last saw her and who had forsaken Bloomers, gave herself a rather complacent shake. "But let me tell you about my father. He helped me with the legal points in my speech, because he said he didn't want anyone to think that my father and brothers had misled me, but oh, what a fuss he made about me speaking! You would think I was speaking to the legislature here, instead of to our meeting. Mrs. Rose, did your father ever raise such a row about you speaking?"

"No."

"Mrs. Rose has recently lost her father," Miss Anthony said.

"Oh, dear—I am sorry. I had no idea, or I would not have babbled on so. As you are not in mourning—"

"There is no need to apologize. I put on full mourning when our little son died—some years ago—and found the attention it attracted disagreeable, so I kept to plain black silk. Besides, it struck me as unjust that a woman should have to muffle herself in crape when a man could wear an armband or a hatband."

"Very true. Still, I am sorry to have caused you pain."

"In any case, I should not have answered you so shortly. My father never opposed my speaking, although he was hardly in a position to prevent me from doing so. He actually said that he was proud of me, but of course I did not acquaint him with my more infidel speeches." I smiled. "Some things are best kept to oneself when family is concerned."

"Yes, the Hartford speech might have been a bit too much for the rabbi," Mrs. Stanton said dryly. "Goodness knows the papers kicked up enough fuss about it. But he sounds like a very good man, and I am sorry for your loss."

"He was a good man. He stood behind me when he could have cast me—well, he always stood behind me. I do wish he could have come here and heard me speak, because of course anything I could have said in Poland would probably get me thrown into prison. Since the failed revolution there the Russians have been very intolerant of any dissent. But Papa felt that he was needed in Poland, and of course at his age it is no easy matter to leave everything one has known behind." I felt that I had spoken quite enough in this vein. "But enough of that. I have three brothers whom I have never seen, and I hope that they will be coming to our country, as there is no future for them for Poland. One has already left, and he and my sister and I are working on getting the papers for the others, which mainly means bribing the right people."

"Are they grown?" Miss Anthony asked.

"One is. The other two are still youths, but well past the shooting-out-eyes stage."

Mrs. Stanton chuckled. "Thank your stars for that. Now, Susan, I have a question for you. When are you going to give up those Bloomers?"

Mrs. Stanton, Miss Anthony, and I were at Albany, where we were holding a convention to coincide with the legislature meeting in the hope that our numbers would convince the politicians to give our demands more serious attention than had been their wont. Mrs. Stanton would give the opening speech, which we planned to print and distribute to the legislators, while Miss Anthony, who could organize a tempest at sea if she put her mind to it, was in charge of the arrangements. I would be giving my usual speeches and speaking to the legislators in person.

Having talked about Papa, whose absence I still keenly felt, quite as much as I wanted, I was content to sit back and listen to my companions squabble amicably about Miss Anthony's continuance in Bloomers. "They are so comfortable," she protested. "And having been pestered so much about them, I would be admitting defeat to give them up now."

"They are wonderfully practical, but the comfort is nothing compared to the joy of walking down the street in peace. Even Miss Stone is on the verge of capitulating. And Mrs. Rose has been her sensible self all along and never worn the things."

I snorted. "An infidel in Bloomers would have been too much."

~ ~ ~

"Hateful thing," Miss Anthony muttered, extricating her foot from the hem of her long skirt as we walked into the legislature's assembly hall. "I shall never get used to this again."

We were each on the arm of a politician. As our escorts assisted us to our seats, I took a look at my surroundings. Although I had spoken in Albany before, it had always been in a cramped committee room and always before a dozen or so legislators. This hall was crammed, because not only the committee members but other legislators were present, along with a good many women spectators. Even the ubiquitous spittoons scattered about could not detract from the chamber's elegance. I'd not dreamed of this possibility back in 1836 when I was trudging through New York with my petition, pen, and ink.

Miss Anthony read a list of the reforms we sought, including the right of a married woman to keep her own earnings, a revision of the laws relating to divorce, the right of women to serve on juries, the right of women to be employed in all public offices, further property reforms, and, of course, the right to vote. As eyebrows, having been raised to their utmost, assumed their natural positions, I stood and spoke. "These are not the demands of the moment for the few," I said in conclusion. "They are the demands of the age, of the second half of the nineteenth century. The world will endure after us, and future generations may look back to this meeting to acknowledge that a great onward step was here taken in the cause of human progress."

To my surprise, there was a great deal of applause, not the least of it from the ladies. I left Albany—having haunted the legislature into the first week of March—with a certain optimism.

I returned late on Monday night, too tired to do anything but crawl into bed with William and fall into a deep slumber. The next morning, after a pleasant welcome-home interlude and breakfast, William scanned the *Albany Register* I had brought home. "Did you read this?"

"No. I read so many newspapers while I was there, and I had a novel for the train. Miss Brontë's *Villette*. Is there anything of interest?"

"Well, let's put it this way. You seem to have made quite an impression on the editor. Five paragraphs' worth."

I took the paper he handed me. The editor, having ranted for a paragraph about "unsexed women" who scoffed at religion and repudiated the Bible (now, who would that be?), then announced, *It is a melancholy reflection, that among our American women, who have been educated for better things, there should be found any who are willing to follow the lead of such foreign propagandists as the ringleted, glove-handed exotic, Ernestine L. Rose.*

I looked at my hands, which were bare at the moment but admittedly during speeches were always covered in kid. I felt naked in public otherwise.

But the newspaper was just getting started. The Reverend Mr. Channing, who had appeared at the convention and accompanied Miss Anthony and me to some of our committee meetings, was my deluded disciple, as was the Reverend Mr. May. (Although the editor took care to level no explicit accusations, a reader would not be blamed for reaching the conclusion that both reverend gentlemen, said to be devoted both to my doctrines and to me, were my lovers.) Were I in Poland, from which I had been "compelled to fly," or nearly anywhere else, my "infidel propagandism" and my efforts to overthrow social institutions would not be tolerated—a fair enough point—and I would be returned by force to my womanly sphere. Here in the United States, I was free to give my "genius for intrigue full sway," but the creators of our government had never envisioned that "exotic agitators" would have the temerity to actually set foot in the legislature. By now, the editor was wearing out, as I was, but he managed a few more lines before concluding, *The great body of the people regard Mrs. Rose and her followers as making themselves simply ridiculous, and there is some danger that these legislative committees will make themselves so too.*

I looked up at William, who had been following my reading half with amusement, half with trepidation. "Will you answer it? Or shall I issue a challenge? I must warn you that Cockneys aren't noted for their dueling skills."

"No, an oaf with a pen is best handled with a pen. I will write a reply this very day."

And so I did. *Everyone who ever advanced a new idea, no matter how great and noble, has been subjected to criticism, and therefore we too must expect it. . . . It is true that I came from Poland. But I have no desire to claim martyrdom which does not belong to me. I left my country, not flying, but deliberately. I chose to make this country my home, in preference to any other, because if you carried out the theories you profess, it would indeed be the noblest country on earth. And as my countrymen so nobly aided in the physical struggle for freedom and independence, I felt, and still feel it equally my duty to use my humble abilities to the uttermost of my power, to aid in the great moral struggle for human rights and human freedom.*

A few days later, I found my letter in print, accompanied

by the following: *We had intended to have accompanied this communication from our fair correspondent, Mrs. Ernestine L. Rose, with comments; but a certain lady of our acquaintance, to whom we were married about a quarter of a century ago, and with whom we have lived very comfortably ever since, insists that she has acquired certain rights, among which is that of absolute veto power over all correspondence on our part, with the rest of the feminine world. We shall not therefore attempt to answer Mrs. Rose, for fear of trenching upon the rights of our "folks at home."*

"In other words," William said, "he knows you are right, and hides behind her skirts rather than attempt to answer you."

"I am glad you didn't waste a bullet on him, darling."

~ ~ ~

"Take care of my wife, Miss Anthony," William said as he helped us to our seats on the southbound train. "Make sure she rests occasionally."

"I will, Mr. Rose."

Clearly, William did not know Miss Anthony well.

William kissed me and hurried off just before the horn announced our imminent departure. When we had finished waving goodbye, Miss Anthony said, "Your husband is certainly fond of you."

"I am very lucky to call him my husband."

"He doesn't resent you traveling so much?"

"No. He understands it is for a good cause. I do feel sad about leaving him so often, but we write regularly, and he and our friends visit back and forth. Sometimes he leaves the shop on Friday and runs up to Boston for a day or so."

"Well, I am glad he is a friend to progress; so many

husbands only get in the way."

Miss Anthony and I were on our way to Washington, DC. At the national woman's rights convention the previous year, I had suggested that we convene there for our 1854 meeting. I had not prevailed—Philadelphia had been chosen instead—but Miss Anthony had liked the idea well enough to propose that we travel to the federal city ourselves, with me doing most of the speaking and Miss Anthony doing most of the organizing. Having usually traveled alone, or with companions for only short intervals, I was somewhat uneasy about how we would fare in close quarters, but I had found it exceedingly difficult to refuse Miss Anthony. Besides, I had not been to slave territory since South Carolina, and Miss Anthony had not been there at all. It seemed a particularly opportune time to go, as the issue of whether to expand slavery into the territories of Nebraska and Kansas was afoot. Under the Missouri Compromise, it would have been a foregone conclusion that both territories, located above the Mason-Dixon line, would be free of slavery, but Senator Stephen Douglas had proposed that the settlers be allowed to decide the question for themselves.

We reached Washington without incident and made our way to the St. Charles Hotel, where our compatriot Mrs. Paulina Wright Davis and her husband, a member of Congress from Rhode Island, were staying. The day after our arrival, we called on Mrs. Davis, with some trepidation on my part. I knew Miss Anthony disapproved somewhat of Mrs. Davis, not because of anything in the latter's conduct or views, but because of her very stylish clothing, which had not grown less so with her marriage to a wealthy man. At one convention, Miss Anthony had even opposed Mrs. Davis's selection as president due to the flowing and quite impractical dress the lady appeared in, arguing that allowing her to preside would be an affront to the hard-working women of America. I hoped that Mrs. Davis, who had begun her own paper, the *Una*, did not hold a grudge.

Civility reigned, however, as Mrs. Davis, clad in a lovely morning dress, waved us into her suite the day after her arrival. As a hotel servant—I hoped he was not a slave—brought in tea, she said, "I must warn you, the people here prefer to go to Congress to get their fill of speeches. Miss Stone drew a miserable crowd when she was here, although the weather did not help. I haven't even tried to speak; the *Una* keeps me busy enough."

"I still think it worth a try," Miss Anthony said.

"Are you going to speak on slavery, Mrs. Rose?"

"I intend to speak on woman's rights primarily. It is a subject that has been sadly neglected here. But I may touch upon the Kansas question. It would be cowardly to avoid it." I smiled at Miss Anthony, who was looking worried. "But I shall not do so without advertising in advance. I learned my lesson about that in South Carolina."

Armed with letters of introduction from Mr. Davis and Mr. Gerrit Smith, a wealthy abolitionist who was Mrs. Stanton's first cousin, Miss Anthony and I proceeded to hire Carusi's, a popular lecture hall, for me to give my talks. But the weather that had stunted Miss Stone's audience followed me to Washington as well, bringing snow and rain on the day of my lecture. It was a small audience, and a rather too quiet one, especially one gentleman who ambled to a seat in the front row, fell into a peaceful doze, and remained in that condition throughout my lecture until his wife shook him awake at its conclusion. (The *Evening Star*, of course, reported this.)

"Northern audiences have spoiled me," I said that

evening at our hotel as I undressed and climbed into bed next to Susan. (Our several nights of sharing a bed, which listed in the middle so that we often ended up rolling against each other, had been conducive to putting us on a first-name basis.) "At least they hiss occasionally."

"We must get you a better forum," Susan said. "I shall feel dreadful if we have dragged you from Mr. Rose for nothing."

So the day after my second speech—which was considerably better attended than the first, thanks in no small part to Susan handing out tickets to members of Congress—we sallied forth to the Capitol to request the use of it for another talk, under the principle of taking the mountain to Mohammad, I suppose. The Speaker of the House, a Kentuckian, fobbed us off with lightning speed to the House chaplain, the Reverend Mr. Millburn. "I have heard of you, Mrs. Rose. Much as I dislike to refuse a lady, I cannot allow it."

"May I ask why?"

"You recognize no higher power. Is that not true?"

"It is true indeed, but I have no intention of lecturing upon religion. I intend to speak on the rights of women, and perhaps the Kansas question."

To see Mr. Milburn's face, "Kansas" in the mouth of a lady must have been a shocking word indeed. "Even so, madam, we cannot allow it."

"But why? Kansas is the leading topic of the day. Miss Anthony and I have attended some of the debates here in our spare time, as a matter of fact. None of them have assumed a religious aspect that I have noticed. Slavery, not theology, is the issue. And"—I smiled sweetly—"unlike the gentlemen I have seen here, I do not use tobacco, so there would be no need to empty the spittoons afterward."

Mr. Milburn looked at me sourly. "I cannot allow an

infidel to speak here, Mrs. Rose, on any subject."

"Not even infidelity?"

"There is no use in pressing the matter further, madam." Mr. Milburn rose. "I am sorry to be unable to oblige you. You and Miss Anthony seemed well-intentioned, so I will say that I will pray for you, Mrs. Rose, that you will renounce your heretical views someday."

"Sir, I assure you it will be a wasted effort."

Susan and I strode out. The next day, however—Sunday—we decided to hear the Reverend Mr. Millburn preach. He said very little about what was on everyone's mind in Washington, the Kansas question, other than to hope that Congress would act wisely (whatever that meant); otherwise, he devoted his sermon to "home life." It was not, in fairness, a bad sermon; he advised both spouses to treat each other with kindliness and consideration, and urged that children be raised in love rather than fear. But toward the end, he intoned, "It is in the house that most men's and *all* women's chief duties lie," with a mighty emphasis on the "all."

"Do you think he was having a fling at us?" I asked Susan as we left.

"Most certainly."

That afternoon, we called on Mr. and Mrs. Gerrit Smith. After some talk of Mrs. Stanton, Mr. Smith told us of his attempt to establish a black community in the Adirondack region by giving tracts of land to free blacks who wished to take up farming. "It was misguided, I fear. I underestimated the harshness of the terrain, and most of the settlers were city men with no experience of farming. Worst of all, I underestimated the prejudice of the whites in the community. I must count it a failed experiment on the whole, but a few have stayed and prospered. Nor were all the whites in the area unreceptive; some families welcomed the newcomers, and I sold land to a fellow from Ohio who wished to settle there and help them. A John Brown. He did a great deal to encourage those who chose to stay."

"He sounds like a fine man," I said. "Is he an abolitionist?"

"Yes, but he belongs to no organization. He is primarily engaged in raising sheep. Indeed, his business has taken him back to Ohio, I understand. He is quite proud of his flock."

Having exhausted the topic of the unimaginatively named Mr. Brown and his sheep, we listened to Mrs. Smith play and sing for us most beautifully. Presently a few gentlemen stopped in, all of them spiritualists—these being the days when half the population was convinced that every stray rattle in a house might be a restless spirit. As Mrs. Smith was a spiritualist as well, it was inevitable that we would all gather around a table. Politeness and my liking for our hosts demanded that I join them, but I could not suppress a sigh, much to Susan's amusement. As I gamely pulled up my chair to the circular table (a square one would not do), it was decided that because no one in the group could actually claim success in raising spirits, Mrs. Smith would try to entice them forth with music. But either the spirits did not care for Mrs. Smith's choice of music, or it all was bosh, because nothing occurred even after Mrs. Smith sang herself hoarse. It was a pleasant evening, if disappointing from a spiritualist point of view, and Susan and I left twenty dollars to the better, Mr. Smith having insisted that we take that to defray our expenses.

The next day, Susan and I strolled to the Patent Office, where we admired not only the models of various ingenious inventions, but a number of artifacts belonging to George Washington. "I can't tell you how moved I am to see these," I said, peering one last time at the president's belongings, which included the sword, cane, and coat he had carried or worn when he resigned his army commission. "He was my hero when I was a child, and although Thomas Paine has superseded him in my affections, one does not forget one's first hero."

"I am surprised to hear you say that. I have noticed that you think more highly of those that the world has traduced, rather than those it has praised."

"Yes, I suppose so; someone must stick up for them. But a kind man gave me a book about Washington when I was quite a little thing in Poland, and I still have it."

Susan put her arm in mine. "President Washington has had a strange effect on you. I have never heard you talk about yourself so much in our entire acquaintance until just now."

"Who knows what I will say when we see the Declaration of Independence?"

But I was silent as we gazed at the noble document, which along with Washington's commission as commander in chief hung opposite a window that on a sunny day must have poured light onto the parchment. Some of the signatures were barely legible. But for all that, I found that tears welled in my eyes as I read the magnificent words I had memorized as a child.

Having lingered by the Declaration of Independence for a considerable time, Susan and I finally left the Patent Office and braced ourselves against the chill that had pervaded Washington our entire time there. By and by, we arrived at the President's House. "Do you think it worth our while to try to see the president?" I asked.

"Quite probably not. He is a supporter of the Kansas bill, after all. And he is not a temperate man."

"True; goodness only knows what he thinks of woman's

rights." I glanced at the upper windows of the mansion, where Mrs. Pierce was presumably passing her days. The couple's only surviving child had been killed in a railroad accident the year before, in plain sight of his parents, and the poor woman, who had never been one for society to begin with, was now a virtual recluse. "Well, let us at least take the citizen's prerogative and peep inside."

We had no difficulty gaining entry and were soon admiring the East Room. But while it was splendid, it could not compare to the faded Declaration of Independence.

The following night, I spoke for the third and last time at Carusi's. I had about five hundred people, which I was told was a good audience for Washington. As I had taken care to include the word "Kansas" in my advertisements, the audience could not complain when I moved to the topic of slavery. Still, wishing to avoid any further adventures on horseback, I weighed my words more carefully than I had in South Carolina. "The South says to the North, 'Slavery has been handed down to us, from sire to son, and our means of support depend upon it. We can no more relinquish it, than your capitalists can relinquish their grasp upon their ill-gotten gold.' This is a feeble argument, because man's inalienable right to himself and human freedom cannot be placed in the balance with gold. But for all that, I cannot but pity the slaveholder, because he too suffers from the evils of slavery. It degrades his character, it degrades the education of his young, the arts—everything that constitutes civilized society. But I can have no pity or forbearance for those Northern men, like Senator Douglas, who pander to the South by supporting the Kansas bill. Yet I cannot deprecate the bill entirely, because it has awakened so many to the evils of slavery. But if it is passed—mark my words—it will create distrust and discord in every section of the country, even to such an extent as to endanger the safety of the Union itself."

Leaving Washington with this warning, which was being given by others as well and which Congress would heartily ignore, I traveled the next morning with Susan to Mount Vernon, taking the river route. We planned to tarry a few days in Alexandria, Virginia, and had sent our luggage there by stage, with some trepidation because we appeared to be only ones concerned as to whether it actually arrived. Washington had not impressed us with its efficiency.

We disembarked at Mount Vernon, where a young black man, whom I assumed rightly to be a slave, greeted us. He proceeded to show us around the best he could, his master, a great-nephew of the former president, being away. The view from the mansion, which commanded a fine prospect of the Potomac River, was splendid, but it was plain that the present Mr. Washington was hard-pressed to keep up the place. "Are those ship masts?" I asked, pointing to the piazza, where some long wooden objects stood between the peeling columns.

"Yes'm. Roof would fall smack down if they weren't there."

Susan clucked indignantly.

But I had one goal at Mount Vernon, a purely selfish one. The key to the Bastille, given by Lafayette to George Washington, hung in a glass case in the hallway of the mansion. Thomas Paine had taken charge of the key during part of its journey to America, and I itched to touch it myself. Had the master been there, I would have begged for the privilege, but I could not ask such a favor from his slave. Instead, I placed my hand gently on the glass.

"You want to hold it, ma'am?"

"Can I? Really?"

In answer, the guide simply opened the case, which appeared to have a broken lock, and placed the key in my hand. I turned it this way and that before I finally remembered to have the courtesy to pass it to Susan, who with some amusement held it for only a moment or two before passing it back to me. After one last brush of my hand against the object Thomas Paine and so many others had touched, I returned it to our guide, who restored it to its place. "Thank you very much." I brushed a tear from my eye.

"I don't usually do that, ma'am, but there's just you two ladies, and you just looked like you wanted to hold it so bad."

"Yes, well, I suppose a lot of people must make fools of themselves here." I smiled. "Thank you for indulging me." As the man took us down the hall, I hissed to Susan, "Now I am complete. But they really must fix that lock."

We passed through a few open rooms, including the one in which the president had died, although our guide, who could not have been more than thirty, was uncertain what articles had actually belonged to its former master. We found out that he was the butler, but when no one from the family was around—they were visiting Mr. Washington's mother near Charles Town—he showed people around the house. "Master took over this place a few years ago; his mother's still alive, but she agreed to put him in charge. He didn't like so many people coming here at first, but then he realized there was money to be made, so he arranged for the steamer to dock here regularly. He sells little trinkets too, which I'll have to ask if you ladies want to buy."

"Certainly. Were you born here?"

"Yes'm. My wife was born here too. She's the cook."

Susan glanced at me, and I knew we were both hoping that this man and his wife would be able to stay together in the future. There was always the chance that they might be sold apart, especially as the tottering condition of the mansion suggested that the owner might be in need of cash.

But the cook offered us some biscuits, which were so delicious that we could only hope Mr. Washington felt the same and would keep her around. She confirmed our suspicion that the buildings in the rear of the grounds were slave quarters. Some appeared to be as old as the mansion itself, a dispiriting reminder that my old hero had feet of clay in one respect.

Having bought some trinkets and tipped the butler for his pains, we wandered around the grounds until it was time for our steamer to take us to Alexandria. Some of the outbuildings appeared not to have been put to use since the president's time, and even the others bore the same air of decay and dilapidation. Finally, we stood beside Washington's tomb, a humble one that I somehow liked better than his monument in Washington—a half-finished obelisk that seemed to be symbolic of that city's laggardness. "How wonderful it would be to honor the late president's memory by restoring this place to its former grandeur. And by putting free labor here instead," Susan said.

We boarded the steamer and, as the wind was picking up, were glad to huddle by the stove there. Although Susan and I did not know it then, a group of women was already raising funds to buy the place from Mr. Washington and restore it properly, and a few years later, they succeeded in doing so. It is now worthy of the president's memory, I understand.

And all on account of the ladies.

~ ~ ~

"How are our receipts?" I asked Susan as we sat in our Baltimore boardinghouse. Susan had deemed a hotel too expensive.

"Terrible," Susan said. "It's no fault of yours or mine; the people here are simply not interested in the topics of the day. Their phlegmatic temperament won't admit of it. And some assume that anyone from the North is going to lecture them on slavery." She sighed, for our room had just been tidied by the landlady's chambermaid, a slave. "As if we have room to talk."

"What we need is some rapping spirits to bring in the audiences," I said. The night before, an acquaintance had invited us to tea, which turned into a spirit circle, albeit without any spirits making an appearance. Mrs. Needles, our hostess, had thought there might be too many skeptics in the room, although surely any spirit worth the name would not have let that stand in the way. As Susan still looked glum, I patted her hand. "But consider how little has been said in these parts about woman's rights. We are at least laying the groundwork, and attendance at my second lecture here was much better than the first. And you got a good audience at your temperance lecture, which was impressive considering all the beer that is sold here."

"True." Susan put away her ledger book with a sigh. "What will bring them out is a Know-Nothing meeting. They've even infected the city government here."

"They are everywhere," I said. "But the Know-Nothings are not the only ones to profess vile sentiments, sadly. I have heard them even in our movement, as far as immigrants go."

"Us? Surely not."

"I have overheard Miss Stone suggest that immigrants should be denied the franchise unless they can prove their fitness—whatever that entails—and Mr. Wendell Phillips has said similar things. It grieved me to hear it, because I respect them both and thought that such statements were unworthy of them."

"I cannot believe they have that mean prejudice in their souls."

"It is difficult to see fault in our own. But it is there."

"Well," Susan said doubtfully. "I cannot speak for either of them, but I am certain there is some explanation for Lucy's seeming fault."

Perhaps Susan and I had been traveling too long together—I was certainly missing my dear William, and no doubt she was missing her own family. For whatever reason, I snapped, "You are blinded and can see nothing wrong in that abolitionist clique."

"And you can see nothing right."

"There is nothing right about pandering to the prejudices of the public."

"I hope you do not place me on the list of panderers."

"I will tell you when I see you untrue."

Susan began writing something while I, thinking that I had said quite enough, stayed silent. At length, she handed me a sheet of paper containing a verse from a hymn we had heard that morning, having attended the service of a popular Unitarian minister who had advertised a sermon on "woman's sphere" (quite narrow).

> 'Tis man alone who difference sees
> And speaks of high & low
> And worships those, & tramples these
> While the same path they go.

—Susan B. Anthony for her dear friend Ernestine L. Rose

Tears welled in my eyes.

"Mrs. Rose, have I been wicked and hurt you?"

"No, I thought it a lovely gesture. I do not believe you untrue. If I am disappointed in some, it does not carry over to you. I often feel isolated, and this conversation has reminded me of it. But none of this is your fault."

Susan sighed. "You are not wrong in feeling that some are against you. I have been loath to say it, but there are some who would keep you off our platform."

"Miss Stone?"

Susan seemed not to hear my inquiry. "Some give no reason. I suspect in those cases it is because you are a foreigner or because you were raised a Jew. But most object because you are a freethinker. They say, 'Can't she just stay silent on that subject?'"

"I cannot."

"I know."

"Well," I said. "I do not expect to be understood in my lifetime. I have suffered for it." I looked down at my hands. "I left a loving home for my beliefs, and I hurt a good man, which I have regretted."

"I certainly do not want to add a feather's weight to your burden."

I could bear this no more. I had talked about myself to an intolerable degree, and I had hurt Susan's feelings. "I must beg your pardon for my ill grace. I value your friendship, and I cannot think what I would have done without you on this trip. I will say nothing more than this: You must not think I pity myself. I do not. My husband truly understands me, and that is more than many women can say."

Susan gave me a faint smile. "You know, I think you are missing him."

"I am. I think after a talk or two in Philadelphia I shall return to him."

"I will tell you this. As long as I have any say in the matter, you shall never be kept off the platform." This time Susan gave a full smile. "But I must say, you are rather ultra even for us ultras. The difference is that you have no compunction in admitting it."

That evening, I spoke at the Maryland Institute, which Susan had engaged in the hope that it would draw a better audience than the Temple, where I had spoken before. She proved to be more than right. The hall held five hundred people, and I saw not a vacant seat and quite a few standing in the rear. Later, Susan told me that hundreds had been turned away. "We made a profit!" she said that night at the hotel. "The people must have been hearing good reports of you."

"Thanks to you."

"No. Thanks to you."

~ ~ ~

I gave a couple of talks in Philadelphia and then headed home. All was uneventful until one day in mid-June when William came upstairs from work. Usually I would recognize his step by its bounce, but that evening, he plodded. "Ernestine," he choked out. His face was the color of ash.

"William! What on earth has happened?" I then noticed the letter he clutched in his hand, which bore a stamp with Queen Victoria's visage. "Your mother?"

"My sister. Hannah. She is dead." William held up the letter, then let his hand drop to his side as he began to weep. "She killed herself."

I led William to the sofa and let him sob against me until he finally regained his composure. "You remember that her husband died of consumption several years ago. Ma said that she never recovered from the blow. She moped around, would not do anything she used to take pleasure in, like going to the theater. She wouldn't even go to church. A few days before she died, though, she finally seemed to be more her old self. On the day she died, Ma and Mary Ann went out on some errand. When they came back they found her hanging. She used her stocking. A neighbor cut her down, but it was too—too late."

I shuddered and held William even closer. Hannah— who would have thought it? She had always seemed to be the most cheerful of the Rose ladies, especially after she married a nice young printer; in the family letters to William, she always added a line or two for me. I had known that she grieved for her husband, but had trusted that time would moderate her sorrow.

"I should have done something. I should have offered to have her come here. It would have been a change for her."

"She would have missed him as much here as there, my love." But I knew my words came as scant comfort to him.

That night, both of us composed letters to Mrs. Rose (I had never been invited to call her "Mother") and to Mary Ann. The next day, I took them to the post office and carried out several other tasks as well. When William returned from work, looking as weary and sad as the day before, I said, "You are not going to work tomorrow. You are going to the seashore for two weeks."

"I am?"

"Yes—with me, of course. I have arranged everything, and you have trustworthy people who can manage in your absence. When is the last time you were out of the city?"

"Don't you have talks to give?"

"I canceled them. Even if this dreadful thing had not happened, you need a change. I should have seen it before this."

William sighed. "I suppose I do, my dear."

I had picked a quiet, unfashionable beach on Long Island, one where I would not be recognized—as happened often in New York—and where there would be little to intrude on William's peace of mind. We paddled around in the ocean, went for long walks, collected shells, and rocked on the porch that faced the Atlantic. I avoided talking about Hannah, knowing that it was a topic William would broach when he felt up to it. Finally, one night as we sat on the porch watching the stars, William said, "I have been asking myself whether anything would have been different if I had stayed in England."

"And?"

"I don't know. Maybe if I had been there I could have been some comfort to her, but if Ma couldn't, how could I? Hannah was always her pet.

"But had I been there, or even if I had brought her over here, I don't know what I could have done, other than be kind and try to put some eligible men in her path—although Ma made it seem as if she'd had an offer or two but took no interest. The two times I nearly lost you—when you fell ill with the brain fever and when you gave birth to our son—I was terrified. I don't know if I would have had the heart to go on. Perhaps Hannah didn't either."

"The poor girl. All I know is this, William: you are not to blame."

"I know."

"Good." I wrapped my arm around him. "Then these two weeks have not been for naught. Is that even a proper sentence?"

"It is." William squeezed my waist. "I have been thinking I should return to London for a visit. Not now, unless it should become necessary—it would be too painful. I cannot offer Ma and Mary Ann the comfort that a religious person can, and I think they would regard me as an intrusion more than anything. A couple of years from now will be better. I think we will be able to afford it better then, and perhaps we can even see your family—if they are not all over here by then."

"I would like that."

"We can see Mr. Owen again too."

"And eat whitebait. Do they still eat whitebait?"

"They'd better, my love."

~ ~ ~

On a fine day in October, I alighted from my train in Philadelphia and looked around for a hack, only to find Mr. James Mott hurrying toward me. He relieved me of my bag. "Mrs. Rose! Allow me. Miss Anthony thought you would be on this train, and hearing that you had been ill, Mrs. Mott and I thought it best to meet you here."

"That is very kind of you."

"I hope you have quite recovered."

I nodded. "I am ready to rejoin the fray. All of this inactivity has been irritating." We had no sooner gotten William tolerably cheerful again than I developed an inflammation of the lungs. For a while, I had thought I would have to miss this meeting, the annual national woman's rights convention, but the poultices and salves I had applied had finally had their effect, and here I was.

I walked with Mr. Mott toward the Motts' fine carriage, which the good couple kept not so much for their own benefit as for that of their many visitors. Having ridden in the carriage just a few months before and made the acquaintance of the horse that pulled it, I felt sufficiently emboldened to stroke it on the nose and got a nuzzle in return.

"If you have not made other arrangements, Mrs. Mott and I would be delighted to have you stay with us. It will be a little crowded, though, as others have accepted our offer as well."

I accepted gratefully and soon found myself in what the Motts' acquaintances called the elastic house, as it always expanded to host the couple's fellow reformers, relations, and the occasional fugitive slave. Susan was there, as were Miss Stone and a few others, and by and by we congregated in the double parlors. Mrs. Mott, sitting near Susan and me, asked, "Have we a president in mind yet? Miss Stone, perhaps?"

Susan snorted. "Miss Stone could not preside over a dogfight in her present state."

In the opposite parlor, Miss Stone had taken a letter out of her pocket and sat reading it, smiling. Dreamily, she returned it to her pocket, and then promptly took it out for yet another perusal. "Ah," I said. "Your lovesick Pickwick. Mr. Blackwell is making progress, I gather?"

"Indeed he is. He took a slave girl from her master when their train passed through Ohio, and Miss Stone is besotted now. She has been warming to him for some time, but that seems to have been the deciding factor."

I snickered. "It is a pity more men don't take such means of impressing ladies. Think of the happy results that would follow."

Susan did not seem amused. She sighed. "Well, I hope this does not portend more thinning of our ranks. Marriage, and then babies, and then retirement. It never fails."

Mrs. Mott said, "Why not you, then, Mrs. Rose? I should have thought of you before, had it not been for your illness. But you said you were feeling well again."

"Of course it should be Mrs. Rose," Susan said. "Who has fought harder for us over the past year? Who took all the slings and arrows of the New York legislature?"

"I would be honored. But do you think there will be opposition?" I had not forgotten our conversation in Washington. Since then, I had been more sensitive to the coolness with which I was treated by some.

"Possibly, but it can be overcome. Leave it to me," Susan said. "Say nothing—I know that is no easy matter for you—and I will handle it all."

"No easy matter? It is almost impossible." But I remembered that Susan had objected to Mrs. Davis in her flummery being made president some years before, and she'd gotten her way despite being brand-new to our conventions. I did not underestimate her.

Miss Anthony rapped on the table. "It is not the spirits, ladies and gentlemen. I am calling for your attention. I propose to nominate Mrs. Rose for president tomorrow. Are there objections?"

A lady whom I knew only slightly stood. "I mean no disrespect to Mrs. Rose. She is a fine speaker. But she is a nonbeliever. I do not think that serves our cause well."

"Mrs. Rose has been speaking at our conventions for four years. They have only grown more successful."

"But she's an out-and-out atheist," another lady said.

"We want the vote, and no one asks a man's religion when he casts his vote. Mrs. Rose's religious beliefs, or lack thereof, are of no relevance to our cause. Every religion, or none, has a right upon our platform. Has Mrs. Rose ever said anything there to embarrass us? Has she ever compromised the dignity of our meetings? Has she ever jeered at anyone's religion? That is what we must ask ourselves. If anyone can answer that in the affirmative, I will be sorely surprised. So I ask again, does anyone have any objections?"

A silence ensued.

"Then I trust the matter is settled. Mrs. Rose, would you care to speak? I know you are bursting to do so."

"I only wish to thank Miss Anthony for her support," I said. "I am honored by it. I may point out that I have worked with clergymen, and of course the Reverend Miss Brown, for several years without anyone, I think, being worse for the experience." I began coughing.

"Do you have the stamina for this, Mrs. Rose?" Miss Stone asked when I had cleared my throat.

I liked Miss Stone better in her lovesick state. "Certainly. I have only coughed once or twice in the past few days before now."

Still, I applied just a speck of rouge the next morning before we all made our way to Philadelphia's Sansom Hall.

When we assembled on the platform, I was pleased to see a number of black faces in the audience, seated amongst the whites in harmony. The City of Brotherly Love was living up to its reputation.

Having been introduced, I took the podium as president. "If anyone would care to offer a prayer," I said sweetly, "please come forward and do so."

13

AUGUST 1855 TO DECEMBER 1855

"There's really nothing left to dust, my dear. If anything, you're putting dust on the furniture."

"You're right." I sighed and put down my duster. "I hope he isn't lost. New York can be so difficult for a foreigner."

"He's been in London," William said with a certain air of superiority. "If a man can handle London, he can handle New York."

"True. I suppose it is just my being anxious. After all, I haven't met a blood relation of mine in over twenty-five years."

A knock sounded. "Well," William said, rising. "Get ready, my dear."

I blinked as William ushered in our visitor. It was as if my father as a young man stood before me—had my father been a fashionable gentleman of 1855. Simon wore a top hat and carried a cane, which William was eyeing professionally. Like Papa, he had a beard, although his, neatly trimmed, was clearly dictated by fashion rather than religion. He took off his hat and embraced me. "Sister! You're just as I imagined you."

"And you look just like Papa." Foolishly, I blinked back tears.

We sat down and Simon reached into his coat pocket. "Speaking of our father, I brought this for you. He had it taken in Warsaw a few years back. Praszka is too small to support a photographer."

I stared at the daguerreotype. "He aged well. How I wish I had seen him before he died."

"I thought you might like these too."

They were miniatures of my mother and myself, probably painted around Napoleon's time. I could not even remember posing for mine; I hoped for Mama's sake I had been cooperative. "Thank you for these. I had forgotten how beautiful Mama was."

"Father kept them in his favorite desk drawer. They were the first thing I found when I went through his study. On top of his papers."

I was going to be in a puddle of tears. William saved me by asking Simon, "So do you think you will stay in Boston, or settle in New York?"

"For now, I will stay in Boston. There would be no point in getting established here if I were to leave suddenly. I am returning to Berlin next year to marry, you see."

"Marry?" I asked, dabbing at my eyes. "Who?"

"Well . . . Bertha, actually. Sophie's daughter."

"But she's your—"

"Niece," Simon said.

"Half-niece," William said helpfully.

"It is legal under Jewish law, as you know," Simon said. "It is legal in Prussia too, so that is where we shall marry."

"Do you love her?"

"She's a charming woman, and she is very eager to go to America. She's very cultured—all of Sophie's girls are—and plays the piano beautifully. I thought it was time I should marry, so why not?"

I did not want to argue with my little brother upon our first meeting. Instead, I complimented him upon his English, which was indeed excellent. He had been in Dublin and the North of England as well as London, and had traveled through Prussia as well, so he had plenty of travel stories to amuse us with. All passed quite nicely.

After a few hours, Simon rose to go. "You could stay here," I said.

"Perhaps another night. I am engaged to stay with a friend from dental school, you see. He promised to show me some places in town."

"Of course." My hurt must have shown, though, for Simon said, "I will stay tomorrow if it is convenient for you."

We saw Simon to the door. When my brother had walked the length of a few houses down the street—White Street, where we had our latest residence—I said, "I do think he could have stayed the night instead of heading over to his friend's. It was rather impolite."

William grimaced. "He is a young man, and new to the city. I suspect that his friend can show him the town in a way that we could not."

"We could have taken him to the theater."

"I believe he has a different sort of entertainment in mind, my dear."

"But he is engaged!"

"To a woman he does not love, an ocean away."

"True." I sighed. "Well, let us hope he gets that foolishness out of his system before he marries—not that I can talk, I suppose."

"Nor I, my dear. I had a spree or two before I met you."

We smiled at each other. Then I frowned. "But you don't think he will be drugged and robbed, do you? That does happen, you know. Perhaps you should catch up with him and give him a warning."

"No, my dear. He seems quite worldly. I am certain he will manage just fine."

I gazed after my brother. How quickly he made his way down the street! "I must say, having a brother twenty years younger than me makes me feel elderly."

William very kindly did not point out that it was more like twenty-five.

~ ~ ~

Simon did return the next day, unharmed and in excellent spirits. He had his carpetbag with him this time and seemed well disposed to humor the elderly with his presence. I found that he was quite interested in American affairs and had a good grasp of the Kansas situation. Despite all of our hopes, Congress had given in to Senator Douglas's maneuvering, and the settlers of Kansas and Nebraska would be deciding whether these states would be free states or slave states. Nebraska appeared safe from the pro-slavery settlers, but Kansas, on the border of Missouri, was becoming more contentious every day. "I would like to go to the Reverend Mr. Beecher's church and hear him preach on the subject," Simon said. "I have not converted, and will not do so, but I am curious to hear his sermons. They say he is a great speaker."

"He is. We have heard him. Everyone goes to hear him; it is more like a lecture than a church service. But he is not in Brooklyn in August, I understand, but in the Berkshires in Massachusetts." I could not let the subject of Simon's religion pass unnoticed, however. "So you are a believer?"

"Yes, although I would not call myself devout. Still, I attended the Reform synagogue in Berlin on occasion. I suppose I shall do the same here." He smiled at me. "I hope that does not distress you."

"No; I am quite happy to leave everyone to his own religion, as long as I am left to have none at all. I would be sorry if I had heard you were converting to Christianity, because then you would have a whole trinity standing between you and unbelief. With Judaism there is only one, at least." I wondered if Simon knew of my conversion to Christianity, which had taken place before he was born. If he did—and I hoped that Papa, Liba, and Sophie had been kind enough to keep it quiet—he said nothing, though.

"So if I cannot hear Mr. Beecher speak, then when I can hear you speak? Your name was in one of the first newspapers I opened when I came here. I am immensely curious."

"I will be going to Saratoga Springs very shortly. There is a woman's rights convention for the state of New York then. It is a spa town, very fashionable, and we are hoping to reach the society people, who hitherto have been able to avoid us."

"Perhaps I will try to come there, then."

"You can tell your patients you have just come from Saratoga Springs," William said. "They'll be very impressed."

"An excellent thought," Simon said.

~ ~ ~

"Who was the handsome young man you were speaking with?" Susan asked me as she and Antoinette Brown approached me on the veranda of our hotel in Saratoga. "If Mr. Rose were not so enamored of you, he would be quite jealous."

"Not of this young man. He is my half-brother. He came here to hear me speak."

"I never knew you had a brother," Miss Brown said. "I never knew you had any family, other than your father."

"Mrs. Rose says as little about herself as any human being I have met," Susan said, not without affection.

"Well, I had to spring up from somewhere. My brother just arrived in America a couple of months ago. He is a dentist." I tapped my right jaw. "And a good one, I must say. He filled two teeth, and they have not given me any trouble since."

Having stopped by the hotel to see me, Simon had gone off to take the waters, which I wished I could do myself. But Susan had work for us to do, and I had to settle for a bracing glass of mineral water. "Will Mrs. Blackwell—I mean, Mrs. Stone—be joining us?" Mr. Blackwell and Miss Stone had married, but Miss Stone had elected to keep her maiden name. Even I found this hard to get used to.

"Yes, unless she cannot find it in herself to put some distance between herself and her new husband," Susan said. "Mind you, it could be worse. She tells me that he had no objections to her coming here, that indeed he said it was not his place to make objections. So that is encouraging."

"I think it promises to be a successful marriage, then."

Miss Brown said nothing, but stared gloomily at the couples strolling by with parasols aloft and canes swinging. She was so much unlike her usual effervescent self that I could not help but ask, "Are you well, Miss Brown?"

Susan answered for her. "Yet another Blackwell man has set his sights on matrimony. Samuel Blackwell has proposed to Miss Brown."

"I told him we must remain friends," Miss Brown said. "I really don't know if that was wise. He is a very good man, and he has been very helpful to me recently. I have been questioning some of my religious beliefs, and I found that he was a most sympathetic listener—the best, in fact."

"Well," I said. "It is a decision you must make for yourself, but I can tell you this. I never had a thought of marrying my dearest friend in the whole world, the one to whom I could tell everything, until he told me he loved me. I did marry him, and I have never regretted it."

"I will take that into consideration." Miss Brown looked a shade less unhappy. Perhaps, I thought as Susan's cough called us back to order, my revelation, uncharacteristic as it might be, had not gone amiss.

As we gathered on the platform the next evening I saw Simon, natty in a linen suit, sitting near the front. He was surrounded by fashionable ladies and gentlemen, most of whom were looking at us as if we were one of P. T. Barnum's museum exhibits. Anticipating this, we had assigned the Reverend Mr. May to speak first so as to gently ease the audience into witnessing ladies speaking, but the audience, it turned out, was quite eager to see us and started stamping its collective feet and yelling (in the most genteel manner) to that effect. Only when we ladies rose and informed them that we would not say a word of substance until the reverend gentleman had had his say did the crowd hush.

Looking more relieved than otherwise, the Reverend Mr. May retired, and I took the podium. Simon, who appeared to have made the acquaintance of the gentleman next to him, nudged him and whispered something in his ear.

"Man can study the professions, the arts, the sciences, or engage in mercantile pursuits, and if he finds one does not answer his purpose, he can change it for another. How is it with woman? What are the means given to her to enable her to obtain an honorable independence? Why, society has assigned her to the kitchen, to the needle, and to the schoolroom, and even then man stands as her competitor, for the female teacher gets three hundred dollars for the same amount of labor for which the male teacher gets five hundred. In the possession of man, cooking assumes the dignity of a profession; in the hands of a woman it is considered mere drudgery. She may, of course, toil in a mill, or break her back as a laundress, or scrub floors as a scullery maid.

"But if none of these occupations can sustain a woman, who has often been ill-trained even for them, what can she do? Well, in the usual course of things, she will marry, for better or for worse—too often, for worse. But if she cannot marry, she may have only one recourse—the streets.

"We talk of man as woman's natural protector. Well, look at these wretched creatures in our streets, and ask what brought them there! Man's protection brought them there! And yet we are told that woman's virtue will be contaminated by coming into contact with man at the ballot box, or in the halls of the legislature!

"Educate woman, enable her to live a life of intelligence, independence, virtue, and happiness, and she will not be driven to degradation, sin, and wretchedness. She will be happier and better for it—man will be better and happier for it—the human race will be better and happier for it."

I stepped back amid applause, in which Simon joined. As I was the last speaker for the evening, we adjourned until the morning. Simon hurried to the platform and handed me down the steps. "What did you think?" I asked.

"Well, it was shocking."

"Really? I am pleased to be able to shock the younger generation."

"Well, not in a bad way. You spoke beautifully. I think Father would be proud—once he recovered from seeing his daughter on the platform. He knew of it, of course, but seeing is another thing altogether. It is not done in Berlin, and it certainly is not done in Poland. It is barely done in London."

"So I hear, and it is a pity. I am worn out and will be retiring to bed. Will you be attending tomorrow's session? It would be a pity for you to come all this way and hear only your sister."

"I will, without fail."

Simon kept his word. We had a lively day and evening of it. Miss Brown spoke, and she and I tangled in the politest way as to whether women in their present state were superior to their present positions. Mrs. Stone appeared in Bloomers (though I fancied that they were cut more dashingly than they had been in the past, perhaps a result of her recent marriage) and discussed our ultimate goal—suffrage. Miss Anthony passed through the aisles hawking pamphlets, and managed to sell a good many. I noticed that Simon was one of her customers. Again, Simon handed me off the platform at evening's end. This time, we lingered on the veranda for a while. "So that Miss Brown is an ordained minister?"

"She is."

"And what was that one lady wearing—pantaloons? Pantaloons called balloons?"

"Bloomers. They are named after a Mrs. Amelia Bloomer, who had no intention of giving them her name, but it has stuck."

"Lady ministers, ladies in pantaloons, and a Jewish lady atheist daring to talk to the cream of society about prostitution." Simon smiled. "I think I love America."

~ ~ ~

I had my doubts about the site of our national convention that October—Cincinnati. By all accounts, it was a conservative city, influenced by its slaveholding neighbor across the Ohio River, Kentucky. But we would not win our cause by appealing to Easterners alone, so I kissed William goodbye and headed west.

Perhaps because everyone was wary of alienating the crowd and tailored their speeches accordingly, the convention was not as stimulating as those I had previously attended. It was strange, too, not to have Susan with us; she was badly in need of rest and had gone to a water cure. But she had sent her sister Mary, who proved to be nearly as well organized as her sibling. Mrs. Mott was there, along with her sister Mrs. Martha Wright. My friend Joseph Barker, a former minister turned freethinker, joined us. Mrs. Stone, who for now was living with her in-laws in Cincinnati, was naturally present. We did not draw large crowds, but those who came were respectful and attentive, and no one hopped upon the platform to argue with us, as was not uncommon. The conference, therefore, could not be called a failure by any means. Afterward, Mrs. Stone invited a few of us to stay at the Blackwell home for a few days. I enjoyed hearing of the accomplishments of the family's two lady physicians, so all passed quite pleasantly—until the day of my departure.

We had all breakfasted, and Mr. Barker and I decided to walk off our hearty meal in the surrounding neighborhood of Walnut Hill. Upon our return, we heard Mrs. Stone's bell-like voice coming from a fenced-in garden. "I am so glad you came to help, Mary. I thought we would be quite lost without Susan, but you were a marvelous substitute."

"I cannot possibly fill my sister's shoes, but I am glad to have been of some help. Do you think it was a success?"

"Sadly, no. I hoped for more people. I do believe Mrs. Rose's being here was a liability. She is a talented speaker, but her face is so very Jewish, and Cincinnati has some very mean Jews. I think the audiences assumed that she was one of them, and were quite repelled by her, especially when she glitters with her husband's gold jewelry as she does. He pampers her terribly."

Mr. Barker made as if to open the gate. I shook my head.

Miss Mary Anthony said, "She is a lovely woman, and I believe her husband is a jeweler. No doubt it gives him pleasure to make fine things for her."

"No doubt indeed, but between her face and the jewelry and the silk dress she wore, it was really too much. But at least she didn't do as Mrs. Oakes Smith did this spring in Boston. Did Susan tell you about it? She wore a gown that was fit only for the stage and read the most dreadful long poem. I was ready to cry with frustration—"

Mr. Barker and I had heard enough. I knocked on the high wooden gate and called, "Mrs. Stone, may Mr. Barker and I join you in the parlor? We will be leaving Cincinnati soon, and you had mentioned settling up expenses before we left."

There was a long pause before Mrs. Stone said in a shaky voice, "Why, certainly."

I take no pleasure in the memory of what transpired after that. Mr. Barker and I said nothing of what we had overheard. Instead, we quibbled about expenses, grumbled over the management of the convention, and in short, made poor Mrs. Stone twice as miserable as she must have been already. When, to everyone's relief, the carriage that was to take us to the station arrived, we thanked Mrs. Stone and the other Blackwells for their hospitality and said goodbye to Mrs. Mott and Mrs. Wright, who would be leaving on a later train. Mr. Blackwell, who had been elsewhere during Mrs. Stone's conversation with Miss Mary Anthony and was ignorant of all that had transpired, said, "I hope you will stay with us the next time you find yourselves in Cincinnati."

"Yes, I would have liked to stay longer. I have some old friends I did not have a chance to see." I glanced at Mrs. Stone. "Jewish friends."

~ ~ ~

Mr. Barker and I did not go directly to the railroad station. Instead, we stopped by Cincinnati's Spring Grove Cemetery, where Frances Wright D'Arusmont, my predecessor on the platform, was buried. She had fractured her thigh in a fall in early 1852 and had never recovered her health, dying in December of that year. She had not even had her daughter to cheer her, as her marriage had ended and her husband had worked an estrangement between mother and child. I wished I had been able to offer her some comfort—the comfort of human sympathy, as she had not lacked for material resources or for good medical care—but like most other people, I had known nothing of her suffering in her last months until I read her obituary.

"My own children died young," I said as I gazed at the tombstone that Madame D'Arusmont's daughter had had the decency to erect after inheriting her fortune. "If I had to choose between having a child who died and having a child become alienated from me, I would choose death any time."

"I am sorry you had to hear that from Mrs. Stone," Mr. Barker said. "She is a beastly woman."

"I heard worse growing up in Poland." I shrugged. "Still, it did pain me. I have never wished her ill. But it reminded me that we women will never advance as long as we turn upon ourselves."

We contemplated the tomb in silence. Frances Wright D'Arusmont had died without seeing her vision of a just world come to fruition, but at least she had seen the world move forward. It was our job to keep that momentum going. I could not fail her.

~ ~ ~

"You have no idea how much I have missed you," I said, coiling myself against William as we caught our breath after my homecoming. It was November, and I'd been gone since September. "But perhaps you can guess."

"I did."

"If I hadn't agreed to lecture in Bangor, I wouldn't budge from this bed until 1856. Why, what's the matter?"

"It can wait, dearest."

"Well." I kissed William, who was giving indications that he was not nearly as tired from his recent exertions as I had thought. "I believe it can."

The next morning, William handed me the *New York Tribune* from the day before and pointed out a short article— so short that a less conscientious newspaper reader than William might have missed it altogether. It concerned a series of anti-slavery lectures to be held in Maine; I was to speak in December. *One of the Bangor critics lays down this canon for the guidance of Lecture-Committees generally: "The manifest duty of a 'lecture committee' is to secure the best lectures they can pay for, by persons who are not obnoxious to well founded prejudices on the part of any respectable portion of the community.*"

"What on earth are they talking about?" I scanned the article again, but it was a master stroke of vagueness. "Why, do you think—"

"Yes. You."

The other lecturers were all male and included Frederick Douglass, Henry Ward Beecher, Wendell Phillips, and Theodore Parker. None were strangers to controversy, but none were female atheists either. "Well, there is only one way to solve this mystery. I will write to the organizers."

In due time, a pleasant note from the committee arrived. It confirmed that I indeed was the subject of the controversy, which was chiefly being stirred by one cranky reverend gentleman, George Little, in the *Bangor Mercury*, but the committee hoped I would not be dissuaded from lecturing there. The note was accompanied by a batch of newspaper clippings—quite a batch, which suggested to me that I had furnished most of the autumn entertainment in Bangor without ever having set foot there.

With William and Simon, who was visiting, as my audience, I read aloud the last of the clippings, which was from the hand of the *Bangor Mercury's* editor. My speeches at the Thomas Paine celebrations were "ribald blasphemies against the Christian religion" and against Jesus Christ himself. I was the president of an Infidel Club. And—

For ourselves we do not hesitate to confess that we know of no object more deserving of contempt, loathing, and abhorrence than a female atheist. We hold the vilest strumpet from the stews to be by comparison respectable. Such poor creatures may plead the oppressive power of want, but for the conduct of this brazen-faced reviler of the Son of God there are neither excuses nor extenuation.

Simon slammed his fist on the table as I tossed the paper aside. "I'll horsewhip that editor. No one can be allowed to speak of my sister in that manner."

"Or my wife," William said.

"Neither of you will horsewhip anybody." I brushed at my eye irritably.

"I will," Simon said. "Just show me where Bangor, Maine, is, and I'll beat the man senseless. Is it on a railway line?"

"It is on a railway line, and you will not beat anyone!"

William said, "Ernestine, men have been shot dead for milder language toward a lady. Forty years ago, we would have been preparing to challenge him to a duel."

"I know." In fact, I was shaking from the insult. I had been called many names in my life, but comparing me unfavorably to a common prostitute was sinking very low. Even the *Albany Register*'s editorial of the previous year seemed mild in comparison. But my menfolk horsewhipping the editor of the *Bangor Mercury*, though it presented a pleasing mental picture, was not going to help the anti-slavery cause or any other cause with which I was associated. "Both of you must leave this to me, though. Trust me."

"What will you do?" William asked. A resigned note had crept into his voice.

"I don't know." Perhaps my feelings were still raw from the Lucy Stone business, and perhaps the change of life, which had been annoying me lately, was making itself known, but in any event I began to weep. William wrapped his arm around me while Simon hastened out the door, then returned in a few minutes in a state of triumph. "Smelling salts!"

I sniffed them, more for Simon's sake than my own, and wiped my eyes. "I will publish Mr. Little's remarks in the *New*

York Tribune, and perhaps in one of the other Bangor papers, and demand that he publish my Paine speeches to let the public judge for themselves how ribald they are. Mr. Greeley is somewhat of a friend to our cause, and I am certain he will be pleased to expose this man for the ass he is."

"For future reference, do ladies generally use the term 'ass'?" Simon asked.

"Only when merited."

The next day, when Simon had departed for Boston, I sat down and composed my letter. I had an easier time speaking English than writing it, but when I was angry the words flowed. Having given some choice excerpts from the *Mercury*, concluding with "vilest strumpet from the stews," I wrote:

Were it not that I had to give some extracts as specimens of the whole, I would not soil my fingers to copy language evidently dictated by the very spirit of malice, whose pen was dipped in the venom of intolerance. . . .

In conclusion, I will say that, if the writer of these ignoble sentiments is not so utterly debased as to be entirely devoid of justice and honor, I call upon him to publish my Paine speeches, but if he is, alas! How deeply must he have sunk, and how greatly does he need our pity, charity, and help!

Pleased with the result, I left to mail the letter, but came back to find William sitting dejectedly in his favorite chair. "What is wrong?"

"It's hardly worth mentioning."

"To me it is."

"Well, it's just that I feel somewhat unmanned. For once, I'd like to fight your battles for you."

"Darling." I embraced him. "You fight them every day, by understanding me."

~ ~ ~

Mr. Greeley, the editor of the *New York Tribune*—the most progressive of the New York papers—did print my letter, as did a Bangor paper and my dear friends at the *Boston Investigator*. It was in Boston that I stopped to break my journey on my way to Maine. "No William?" Josiah Mendum asked as I took off my bonnet and cloak and accepted the tea he offered me.

"No. He wanted to come, but I did not want it to appear that I was hiding behind him."

"Well, from what I have been told, the man behind the editorials is Rufus Griswold, who is a friend of the editor of the *Bangor Mercury*. His third wife—he tired of the second— is from Bangor."

"Isn't he a literary man?"

"Yes. You probably know his name through his association with Poe. This was his notice of Poe's death: *Edgar Allan Poe is dead. He died in Baltimore the day before yesterday. This announcement will startle many, but few will be grieved by it.*"

I shook my head. "He sounds dreadful."

"No one has any idea why he took up his cudgel against you, except that he loves calumny, and you were a convenient target. So consider yourself in most excellent company."

"I shall. Just don't expect me to take up poetry."

~ ~ ~

As one would expect from its leading industry, Bangor smelled of freshly cut lumber, not an unpleasant scent for someone from New York City. I had very little time to appreciate this, though, because I had no sooner stepped off the train than three lecture committee members appeared before me, having brought a carriage to take me to the Bangor House, the city's most fashionable hotel. That courtesy, and the pleasant manner in which I was greeted by the proprietor, boded well. So did my very comfortable room.

The next morning, I caught up on the Bangor newspapers, which had been laid out upon my writing desk in the hotel for my perusal. The Reverend Mr. Little was banging on about my general dreadfulness, but the Reverend Mr. Battles had joined the fray on my side, or at least the side of free speech. I was touched to find that Wendell Phillips, who had delivered his lecture the week before, had devoted part of it to my defense.

I had breakfasted when a porter arrived with a card bearing the names of several ladies. "Show them up, please."

A rustle of petticoats announced the ladies' arrival. "We are the wives of the committee members," the oldest and best dressed of the group said. "We wanted to apologize for all of the fuss. I think you will have a very good audience tonight."

"There is no need to apologize, and if the kind welcome I have received is any indication, I believe you are correct."

"We also hope you will say something about the attacks upon you, and spare not."

"I have been going back and forth in my mind about whether that is wise. So you think it is?"

"It is indeed. And"—my visitor's eyes twinkled— "everyone will be expecting you to do so anyway. Give them the devil, my dear."

~ ~ ~

The Reverend Mr. Battles, a Universalist minister, turned out to be a lecture committee member, and gave himself the duty of leading me to the podium. "Our hall holds two thousand, we think—it has never held that many until tonight."

Indeed, people were standing against the walls.

As Mr. Battles, having introduced me, stepped back, I indicated my brown silk dress, its plainness relieved only by the gold watch I wore at the waist. "Well, ladies and gentlemen. If you were expecting a scarlet woman, I can only say you will be sadly disappointed."

Laughter and applause rang out.

"I will not dwell on the controversy my being here generated. I only want to thank the committee for staying true to their invitation, the Reverend Mr. Battles for his kind championship of me—all the kinder because he is a man of faith—and the newspapers that permitted my defenders and me to air their views. They embody what is most noble about America—the right to freedom of speech. It is what made me, as a small child, first start to dream of coming here. But most of all, I want to thank all of you for giving me a fair hearing.

"Are my friends from the *Mercury* here? I will not put them on the spot if they are, never fear; indeed, I shall consider them better men for it. They are not? Well, then, I am sorry to hear it, and can only pity them. They must be persons of small minds—or is it better to say *little* minds— who may *rue* the day they raised such a *fuss* over nothing.

"Enough of this, however. I came to this lovely city to speak on the condition of women, and with the air cleared properly, that is precisely what I shall do."

The audience and I sailed happily together through the next hour. Afterward, I was taking the congratulations of the committee, and agreeing to do a talk the next evening, when a man approached us tentatively. I blinked. "Why—this is my husband, Mr. William Rose."

"I was delayed by business but came as soon as I could."

"Your wife speaks wonderfully, sir."

"She does." William squeezed my hand.

At last, William and I arrived in my cozy hotel room. William helped me out of my cloak. "Forgive me, my dear, for following you up here without telling you."

"Were you worried about me?"

"To be honest, no. I felt that the committee and your own good sense would keep you safe. No, I just wanted to hear you give it to those who slandered you—and you did. I wouldn't have missed it for anything. I hope you are not angry."

"Angry?" I kissed him. "I am the luckiest woman in the world."

14

JUNE 1856 TO NOVEMBER 1856

"Welcome to England," the hackney driver at Weymouth said in a voice that was far too buoyant for three in the morning. "Are you stopping at a particular hotel?"

"Any one as far from the sea as possible," I said, stumbling into the carriage. Having never achieved the feat of "sea legs," I now appeared to be lacking land legs as well.

"My wife is not a good sailor," William said. "Any good hotel at a reasonable price will do."

"My husband is an excellent sailor. I was tempted to throw him overboard."

We had been thirty days a-sea on our packet *Northumberland*, having taken a detour (probably not the correct nautical term) to avoid icebergs, which I conceded was sensible but had the irritating effect of keeping us longer on the water. I had spent most of the voyage in the cabin near a basin, listening to the barks, meows, and chirping coming from the adjacent cabin, which was occupied by a family who had taken their menagerie with them. William, on the other hand, had asked intelligent questions of the captain (as we were in the cabins, not steerage, we had seen a great deal of him), chatted with the crew, walked the neighbors' dog, petted the cat, and in short made himself the most popular man on the ship. There had been periods of dead calm, during which I had heaved myself out of my berth and onto the deck to contemplate the sea's tranquility, which though pleasant to the stomach also meant that we were not getting any closer to land. Fine winds had finally blown us into the English Channel, where a pilot boat picked us up, and here we were in Weymouth hours later. "Next time we will travel by steamer," I announced.

"You told the captain that, my dear. I think his feelings were hurt."

"He was an excellent captain. It is not his fault he has a packet instead of a steamer. Or is it? I have no idea how these things work."

Luckily for us, the driver heeded William's command instead of mine, so in no time at all, we were in a pleasant hotel. I threw off my garments and curled up on the big bed, which to my immense gratitude remained perfectly still throughout the evening. When I finally awoke at nine, I was much more disposed to look at humanity, Weymouth, and William kindly, though I still gave the sea a rather sour glance.

Having wandered about Weymouth, a lovely city, we took a carriage to the nearest train station the next morning and were soon heading toward London. We were traveling in the first-class car, which made me feel a little guilty, but the railway clerk had told us that the third class would be miserable and that the second class was nearly as expensive as the first and nearly as uncomfortable as the third. The seat was indeed quite comfortable, and soon I was dozing happily on William's shoulder.

I woke to find us surrounded by verdant beauty. "'England's green and pleasant land,'" I said.

"Not for long," William said cheerfully. "We'll soon be in the outskirts of London."

Sure enough, the air began to assume a foggy quality. "Home sweet home," William said.

"Do you miss it?"

"Once a Cockney, always a Cockney."

But even my Cockney husband found our first few days in London disorienting. The railway had been in its infancy when we left for America; now entire streets had vanished, razed for railway construction, while buildings had sprouted around the handsome new stations. My old lodging, where William and I had consummated our love and held our moral marriage, looked mean and shabby. Ship Yard, where I had visited William's family, had deteriorated from shabbiness to wretchedness; I was not surprised when it and the surrounding streets were torn down in the 1860s to make way for the New Courts of Justice. "Greenwich had better not changed," I said. "I mean to eat whitebait with you there."

But first, duty called us to Hackney, where Mrs. Rose and Mary Ann had moved after Hannah's death. As we rode to Hackney, I told myself that if I could face Captain Rynders, the rowdy divinity students at Hartford, and a room full of slaveholders, I could certainly cope with my in-laws.

Having been brought up to the dressmaking trade, Mrs. Rose and Mary Ann had never had to resort to slopwork— sewing cheap garments at home for wages so low that many had to turn to prostitution to survive—but had always either been employed by respectable shops or worked on their own account, as they were doing now. William, of course, had contributed to their upkeep since coming out of his apprenticeship, growing more generous when he became more prosperous, so I was not surprised to see that their lodgings were in a pleasant street that had not entirely lost an air of rusticity. Mrs. Rose's childhood sampler still hung on the wall, but it now overlooked a sewing machine—a gift from William, who had arranged for its delivery. All was neat, clean, and airy. But a certain gloom hung over the place.

William had made lovely brooches for his mother and his sister, and I had bought them lace shawls at Stewart's, suitable for an English summer. "I see you have surrendered to fashion and got crinolines," I said as I helped pin Mrs. Rose's brooch. "So shall I eventually, I suppose, even though William finds them ridiculous. Most men do, I have found."

"Yes, well, as dressmakers we must keep up. Mustn't we, my dear?"

Mary Ann nodded, then resumed staring at her hands. William had told me that she'd been the first to find poor Hannah, to whom she had been close in her own way.

"William and I also have our pictures for you," I said, handing Mary Ann a daguerreotype case with my husband's likeness on one side and mine on the other. "We would like yours as well. Have you had yours taken?"

"No."

"Then perhaps we should have some taken of you."

"It seems so frivolous," Mrs. Rose said, as Mary Ann had nothing to say on the subject.

"Not at all, Ma. When Ernestine is traveling and I get lonesome for her, I can look at her daguerreotype, and it's almost as if she's in the room next to me."

"If she didn't travel, you wouldn't need a photograph of her. It's a wife's place to stay at home."

I contemplated the sampler in dignified silence.

William shrugged. "It's not what most people do, I know, but it works very well for us. And she does a great deal of good."

"If you say so," Mrs. Rose said.

By and by, though, Mrs. Rose studied the daguerreotype and, having pronounced it a good likeness of William (she did not comment upon mine), condescended to pay a visit to a photographer. It being a Saturday afternoon, we soon found our way to a studio, and in due course a daguerreotype of Mrs. Rose and her children sat on the mantle, and another was in William's waistcoat pocket. "All in all, I think that went well," William said as we left Hackney. "Better than I expected, anyway. And now, my dear, I think we owe it to ourselves to dine at Greenwich."

We soon fell into a routine in London—sightseeing by day, attending the occasional gathering at night, and visiting Mrs. Rose and Mary Ann on Saturday afternoons or Sundays. During my residence in London, I had been too absorbed in learning the language, supporting myself, and going to Owenite meetings to take in the sights; as for William, he'd had but little leisure and like most residents of a city was content to leave the sights to the tourists. So we set to our business with a vengeance. We watched shining gold sovereigns being made in the mint, shuddered at the room in the Tower of London where Edward IV's sons had been made away with, and admired the relics held in the Napoleon Room at Madame Tussaud's. One of the emperor's teeth was on display—how it got there I have no idea—and I rather wished that Simon was with us to give his professional opinion. As I had a certain admiration for Napoleon, I felt it a pity that so many of his relics should have been brought here to delight English gawkers, but that did not stop me from hopping into the carriage he had used at Waterloo. We paid the extra for the Chamber of Horrors and duly shivered at the sight of the blade that had decapitated the king and queen of France. "After this I think a stroll in the Botanical Gardens will do us good," I said, rubbing my neck. And indeed, after the barbarism we had witnessed in the Chamber of Horrors and the Tower, it was lovely to admire the garden's vast expanse of rhododendrons and to get lost amid the forest of rose trees, all blooming in splendor.

Our lack of religion did not prevent us from appreciating England's fine churches. First on my list, at least, was St. Clement Danes, where William had been baptized. "Sir Christopher Wren did an excellent job," I said. "It is quite worthy of you."

"Even if the baptism was a wasted effort?"

"Especially if it was. You got all of the splendor and none of the religion."

Being in a Wrenish mood, our next stop was St. Paul's, where we wandered about until we ascended to the dome's Whispering Gallery, which we had to test. "I love you, William," I said in a low tone on my side of the gallery.

"I love you too, darling," William's voice rang out.

I beamed at a lady standing near us, who was regarding me with amusement. "It works!" I proclaimed.

We continued to the Golden Gallery, from which we could view all of London arrayed beneath us. When we had gazed our fill, I turned to the man standing at the entry to the Golden Ball, beneath the great cross. So far, only a few boys had passed through. "Shall we?" I asked William.

"Madam, very few ladies pass up this way. It's not for the faint of heart."

"Ah," I said. "But my heart is not faint."

Actually, it was, I found when I discovered precisely how one ascended into the Golden Ball. There were only fifty-six steps to mount, the man informed us encouragingly, but they took the form of three steep ladders. With William at the bottom to catch me—what would happen if he missed was something on which I did not dwell—I grimly mounted the first of the ladders, telling myself that (a) it was for womankind that I did this and (b) it was good I had not yet succumbed to the allure of a crinoline.

"You go it, old girl!" a youthful voice cried as I stepped onto the second ladder.

"That's my wife you're speaking of," William said, rather tolerantly.

"You go it, madam!"

With the boys' encouragement, and William standing at the base of the second ladder, I pressed on to the third, which had a rope for one banister. At least now I had the ironwork supporting the ball to clutch onto as well, although I did not like to think about what would happen if it failed at this particular moment. At last, though, I reached the summit. My head was in the Golden Ball, which sounds quite vulgar, especially when the boys called up their congratulations using that very wording. But I could declare victory, even though the next day I was hardly equal to doing more than riding around Kensington Gardens.

Our last ecclesiastical stop in London was at Westminster Abbey. We admired all the chapels, including that of Edward the Confessor, where the coronation chair sat. Whether it is possible for a commoner to sit in it now, I do not know, but in those days there was nothing preventing it, not even a rope, so I seated myself in it, kicking up a cloud of dust as I did so. "Why, it feels quite natural," I said. "I could adjust to being a queen. Pity our ancestors didn't arrange things better."

"You are a queen. What did Miss Anthony call you? The queen of the platform?"

"I believe so."

"Then here is your staff, your majesty." William handed me his cane. "And your crown." He placed his top hat upon my bonneted head. "All hail the queen of the platform!"

~ ~ ~

Soon after William and I arrived in Paris, I made two visits, which I knew were necessary even though I had been dreading them. "This is the place," I said, pointing to the apartment where Marcus and I had wept over our little daughter. Unlike my old lodging in London, time had improved it and the surrounding neighborhood. The bakery had been replaced by a milliner's, evidently a quite stylish one. In a window of our old apartment perched a plump cat, looking so pleased with itself and so very French that I had to smile. "Life goes on," I said. "And quite happily here, it seems."

William put his arm around my waist. I shed a tear and then let him guide me away.

In the practical Continental manner, Amalia's grave had been reused after ten years had expired. But I'd had the presence of mind to write down its location before I left Paris a quarter-century before, so I had little difficulty finding the spot. "I hope the present plot holder doesn't mind," I said as I scattered a few pretty stones in the area. "But I think Marcus would like me to do this, and if truth be told it brings me a little comfort as well. And now, my dear, having revisited the past, we shall enjoy Paris in the present."

And so we did. "The cliché is quite correct," I said as William and I strolled about on our last evening in the City of Light, my crinoline swaying gently under my new silk gown. "Paris is best seen with a lover."

"If I hadn't married you, I might have never seen Paris."

"Oh, some lucky woman would have whisked you off here at some point; I am quite sure of it. I can only thank my stars that you had the sense to speak when you did."

"Me too." We walked in silence for a while. "You do think we'll return on our way to London, don't you?"

I pressed his hand. "Most certainly."

~ ~ ~

"Ernestine!" Sophie drew back from our embrace. "How well you look. I think you are prettier than when I last saw you."

"You look very well yourself," I said. It was true; my widowed sister, though of course no longer young, was dressed more fashionably than she had been when I left Berlin. I noted with interest that she no longer wore a *sheytl*, only a beribboned headdress over her neatly coifed hair.

"And here is the husband you always praise."

"*Guten tag*," said William proudly. "It is my pleasure to meet you."

"I have been teaching William to speak German so we would not bore him to death," I said. "He has become quite proficient. When we went through customs I let him do all of the talking—not that the officials would have listened to a woman anyhow. He managed quite well. In fact, he got us through Koblenz with much more success than did I back in the day."

"I'm sure the authorities were just in a better mood, my dear," William said.

"Well, I am looking forward to introducing you to everyone," Sophie said, leading us into the parlor. "Jeanette will come by with her family later today, and my other girls are out shopping for Bertha's wedding clothes. You just missed Simon; he made a quick call. Dear me, did I forget anyone? Oh, Bertrand. He will be home from school shortly. He is sulky these days, I must say. He wants Simon and Bertha—or the two of you—to take him to America, but I know Papa would want him to get a good German education first. I expect that he will end up there with the rest of you republicans sooner or later, though."

"We will be glad to have him. Have you heard from Isidor?"

"That foolish boy! No, not a word."

My second brother, Isidor, who was seventeen, had turned up in Boston quite unexpectedly in February, having decided to leave Berlin without a word to Sophie, with whom he had been living, or to any of us in America. After some misadventure in New York, which involved a gambling den and a prostitute who had left him what Simon delicately termed "an unpleasant souvenir," he had arrived at Simon's lodging in the lowest of spirits. Simon had taken him in hand and found him a clerk's job, and both Simon and I had deputized our friends in Boston to keep an eye on him while we were abroad. I wondered if they were up to the task, but no ill reports had followed us to Europe.

"He's very bright, but no one can tell him anything," Sophie said. "Don't be offended, but he reminds me of you. Imagine all of the trouble you could have gotten into if you were a boy at that age!"

"Oh, I managed well enough when I was older." I snorted.

"Well, Simon told me that Isidor is considering studying dentistry or medicine, if he can apply himself. But enough of that. Tell me about your travels, William."

William obeyed cheerfully. I had to lend my assistance with German only a couple of times.

The next day, Simon and Bertha offered to show William around Berlin, and I gladly took the opportunity to be alone with Sophie. "Tell me, my dear. Were you upset to hear the news about Marcus?"

"I was grieved, yes. I had hoped things would end better for him. But I would have been miserable had I stayed with him."

"Yes. It is clear that you and William are very happy together, and he is a charming man. Why, he even speaks very acceptable German! Pity he isn't Jewish, but what can you do?"

"Teach him Yiddish?" I giggled. "Do you think Simon and Bertha will get on?"

Sophie sighed. "Neither of them is a romantic; they are much more like me than you. Simon wants a wife because he believes that a professional man should have a wife, and Bertha wants children and a home of her own. I daresay they will do well enough."

"Well, I wish them the best."

"I hope you will come to the wedding. It will be held at the Reform temple on Johannisstrasse. Simon talked me into joining, and I like it. The women are allowed to sit with the men, and no head coverings for the men are required."

"Of course I will come—even if it was not in the Reform temple. I missed Jeanette's wedding, after all. But I must say it will be pleasant not to be relegated to the balcony."

My Berlin wedding had been a hole-and-corner affair—as of course I had wished—and I had fretted much of the time over whether my milk would start leaking through my bodice, even though I wore a shield. Simon's and Bertha's was quite different. Although only family and a few intimate friends had been invited to the wedding, there was to be a grand reception, after which Simon and Bertha would travel a bit in Europe before leaving for the United States. They were to take a steamer, news which I had received with a poke in the rib for William.

Bertha had reluctantly been talked out of having a white wedding dress, like those of Queen Victoria and Empress Elizabeth of Austria, but instead had settled for more practical watered blue silk and a lovely headdress and veil. Having been deputized to assist on the afternoon of the wedding, I was adjusting the aforesaid headdress when William, who had been tending upon the groom, knocked. "I'm sorry," he said in English. "Ernestine, can you help for a moment? Simon needs help with his—with his cravat."

William was perfectly capable of offering any needed help in this regard, but the stricken look on his face spoke for itself. I made some reassuring noises to Bertha and hurried out. "What is it?"

"Cold feet. Very cold feet."

I found Simon in his shirtsleeves, moping in a chair. "I don't think I can go through with this, Ernestine. I don't love her."

"You've known that all along."

"I know. But—I hadn't thought about it as I should have."

I grimaced. "Simon, if you had told this to me months ago—even a couple of weeks ago—I would have advised you to break the engagement. But on your wedding day—I cannot do that. Think of Bertha. She will be humiliated in front of her family, in front of her friends. Every Jew in Berlin will know, and probably a few of the Christians too. There will be speculation and gossip of the crudest, cruelest sort. She will either have to stay here and brave it out, or go alone to the country where she thought you would be bringing her as your bride. And what can she do, here or abroad? She has been trained for no profession and would likely be mortified at having to find one; it is the idiocy of the way girls are reared. You cannot do that to her."

"I know." Simon rose and put on his waistcoat, then his coat, albeit with an air of dressing for his execution.

"She is a sensible woman, very cultured, and quite attractive. She looks lovely in her wedding dress. I am sure you will get along famously." But I realized I was overselling this, so instead I just kissed him on the cheek. "You are a good man, too good to treat her badly. Let me manage your cravat for you."

Simon obeyed, and I brushed at his hair for good measure. "Is it safe to go back to Bertha?"

"Yes."

"If he changes his mind, hit him over the head and drag him to the rabbi," I hissed to William as I left.

"I heard that," Simon called.

Bertha, headdress intact, was pacing about when I returned. "Is something wrong, auntie?"

"No—not now. Simon misplaced the ring, but it is safe and sound." It occurred to me that I would be in for it if Simon actually had misplaced the ring, but it was too late.

But no one could have guessed that the groom had almost ducked out of the wedding. He and Bertha blushed and smiled under the wedding canopy (as far as I could tell under Bertha's lace veil), and when the time came for Simon to smash a glass with his foot for good luck, he did it with panache. At the reception, just before he and Bertha left on their wedding trip, he even unpacked a pair of artificial teeth to clatter for the children in the room. "Families are exhausting," I said to William as we at last settled in bed that night. "After Berlin I will be ready for something peaceful."

"Like Mount Vesuvius?"

~ ~ ~

After leaving Berlin, we traveled through Germany and Italy, tarried at Vienna and Prague, and ascended Mount Vesuvius (I in a litter, William with a sturdy stick). We once again strolled arm in arm through the streets of Paris. Upon our return to London, we braved Hackney. "I thought you might end up staying," Mrs. Rose said at our final visit.

"No, Ma. I have a business in New York, and I need to get back to it. And Ernestine has to get back to her speaking."

Mrs. Rose shook her head. "I'll never get used to a woman doing that," she said, "but you've been good for each other, I suppose. You could have done worse, William."

Our last day in London, before we left to meet our ship at Liverpool (I had prevailed on the steamer question), we received a visit from Mr. Owen, who had helped so many. Now in his eighties, he had come from his lodgings in Seven Oaks just to bid us farewell, which touched me beyond words. He had become a spiritualist, but that made him no less dear to us, even as he happily reported his conversations with the shades of Thomas Jefferson and Benjamin Franklin. "I shall likely never see you two again," he said, not in a maudlin way but as stating a plain fact. "I am not strong enough for another trip to America, and you have your own affairs to keep you there. But I know you will continue to fight for the slave, for the downtrodden, for the rights of women—you, my dear, with your bold words, and you, sir, in your quiet, steadfast manner. Both are worthy. And I hope this sojourn of yours has helped you to gather your strength."

Did William and I shed tears when we parted with our gallant old friend? Of course we did, and I think I saw him wipe a tear too when he waved to us from his carriage.

Our ship, the *Europa*, made good time, and either the seas were benevolent or I was hardened, for I was troubled only slightly by *mal de mer*. Indeed, the cabin passengers were quite a social group, and on what promised to be our last evening aboard we decided to get up a little entertainment. Two of our passengers, Mr. James Anderson and Miss Agnes Ellsworthy, were on the stage, and they favored us with a scene from *Hamlet*. There were, of course, a number of musical young women and ladies who were pleased to sing, strum their guitars, and play their violins. A literary gentleman read a poem.

And I gave a speech. "I am quite out of practice," I warned. "Indeed, I have not spoken in public in months."

But I made no blunders, and my audience was receptive and attentive (granted, they could hardly leap overboard). "It was good to be back on the platform," I said to William as we undressed for the evening. "Much as I have enjoyed our holiday, I have been itching to get back to work."

William grinned. "It's true. I've been waking at night worried that we won't have enough canes on hand for the holidays."

"But I have realized one thing—that your company is more precious to me than it has ever been. I will not go away for months at a time as I have in the past."

"I can't say I mind that."

"Actually, there is another thing I have realized: we have never had relations on a ship."

William pulled me to him. "No time like the present, is there?"

15

JUNE 1858 TO APRIL 1861

Surrounded by the Green Mountains, Rutland, Vermont, was a beautiful place for free speech, though the June sun was stronger than I had hoped. But the shade of the large tent erected for the Free Convention, and the services of the local ice merchants, were keeping us relatively comfortable. On the platform, I sipped cold water and glanced at the clock that someone had cleverly erected on the tent wall. Most of the speakers were cheerfully ignoring it, though I was a fine one to talk.

The Free Convention had been called to discuss all manner of issues, from abolitionism to woman's rights, and spiritualists (of course) were especially well represented. There had been a great deal of chatter about the hereafter and religion on the first day, to which I had urged, "Let us do our duty to humanity here, and when we reach another state of existence, we will attend to the duties of that state." On this, the second day, it was hoped that we might reach the more pressing issues of slavery and woman's rights—and sure enough, that morning an attractive lady of about thirty, Mrs. Julia Branch, arose, announcing that she wished to address a proposed resolution. It stated that the only true and natural marriage was an exclusive conjugal love between one man and one woman, and the only true home was the isolated home, based upon this exclusive love.

"You speak of woman's right to labor, her right to preach, her right to teach, her right to vote, and lastly, though not least, her right to get married, but do you say anything about her right to love when she will, where she will, and how she will?"

The reporters, who were in the front row, suddenly acquired the look of a bunch of tabbies who had wandered into a field of catnip. The young Mrs. Branch—I believe she was a widow—had broached the perilous subject of free love, and while it was certainly more interesting than pondering the afterlife, I knew that trouble lay ahead. But it was, after all, the Free Convention, so I settled back.

"It is the binding marriage ceremony that keeps woman degraded in mental and moral slavery," Mrs. Branch said, having discoursed for some time about the miseries of poor couples, of love turned to indifference. "She must demand her freedom, her right to receive the equal wages of man for her labor, her right to bear children when she will, and by whom she will. I believe in the absolute freedom of the affections, and that it is woman's privilege—aye, her right—to accept or refuse any love that comes to her. She should be the ruling power in all matters of love, and when the love has died out for the man who has taken her to his heart, she is living a lie to herself, her own nature, and to him, if she continues to hold an intimate relation to him. And so is man's relative position to woman; when his love has died out, and he continues to live with his wife on any consideration, he strikes a blow to the morality of his nature and lives a life of deception.

"Love is not dependent on reason, or judgment, or education, or mental acquirements, or society, or control of any kind. It is an inspiration of the soul. It is a holy, sacred emanation from the most vital part of our natures, and to say when or where it shall be limited or restricted is a violation of our individual rights."

No sooner had Mrs. Branch sat down, to muted applause, than three men on the platform got to their feet to set the world right. Mr. Henry Clapp reminded us that Mrs. Branch had a perfect right to speak. Mr. Stephen Foster moved to amend the resolution to include the words "based upon the principle of perfect and entire equality." Mr. Joel Tiffany, having informed us that "free love" was only another name for "free lust" and that to allow those who were dissatisfied to try on all of God's creation was not the remedy for bad marriages, went on to discourse about love as if he were St. Valentine himself. When he paused for a breath, I decided that it was another woman's turn to speak.

"As a woman's rights woman—nay, more, as a human rights woman—I cannot but throw in my mite on this great and important question that has been started here this morning. We have had a glorious and glowing description of true and genuine conjugal love. That description was beautiful; from my whole heart do I agree with it and accept it. But, my friends, facts are stubborn things, and we have not only to look at and investigate what ought to be, but what is. And what is? Just what has been stated here this morning by Mrs. Branch." I glanced at Mrs. Branch, who looked rather cross after Mr. Tiffany's disquisition. "Here I must say that I do not know what her views are about the remedy for these things, and not knowing them, I cannot say whether I agree or disagree. I did not understand, as Mr. Tiffany did, that she meant to let loose the untamed passions either of men or women; if she meant that, I totally and utterly disagree."

"I did not mean it in that light," Mrs. Branch said, taking my life-preserver.

"That is right. I, for one, have never introduced the question of marriage into our woman's rights convention, because I want to combat in them the injustice in the laws. When that injustice is done away with, when woman is recognized by all as the equal of man, she will receive similar education, and have similar rights, and whatever may be found wrong after that in the laws, no fear but that it will be righted.

"We have been told—or the inference to be drawn was—that only vicious persons were dissatisfied. Do you know who is dissatisfied? Those that feel the love of freedom burning within their breasts. They are dissatisfied, and for what? I hardly ever allude to myself, but I will now. I am a married woman: have been married over twenty years; have a husband, and, as far as individual rights are concerned, I have as many as I ought to have. But I do not thank the laws for it. For the good the law is not needed; for the bad it ought to be a good law. A bad law makes bad men worse. Hence we want equality of rights."

A Shaker gentleman, Mr. Frederick Evans, then took up the subject of marriage. I leaned over to whisper to my friend Horace Seaver, "Aren't they celibates?"

"Yes."

"Well, he is a fine one to talk, then." But at least no one could accuse Mr. Evans of free love.

We ladies, of course, were a different matter. *Mrs. Rose and Mrs. Branch both go for free love, on principle*, I read in the *New York Times* the Tuesday after this lively weekend. *They are regarded with a purely platonic affection by the brethren.* "Well, at least they had the decency to add 'on principle,'" I said to Bertha, who had come over, as she often did, for tea.

"How do you bear such slander?"

"Oh, I have had worse said about me. I will write an indignant letter to the editor, it will be printed—by my friends in Boston if no one else—and everyone will ignore it and remember the original remark." I shrugged. "I have ceased to worry much about what the press has to say, for if I did, I would never open my mouth. But I shall answer this, not so much for my sake, but for that of my fellow reformers. A slander against one of us can turn into a slander against all of us."

I did write the letter, but I can hardly judge how efficacious it was, because Mrs. Branch soon made another speech, which had the effect of drawing entirely to her any attention that might have lingered upon me. In the matter of free love, if indeed she professed it, she proved to be most inconsistent, for the next (and last) I heard of her was in 1859, when the newspapers gleefully announced her marriage to a shorthand reporter.

But I get ahead of myself. Late in November 1858, the sad news arrived from England that Robert Owen was dead. This was not unexpected, given our dear friend's great age and delicate health, but William and I both wept like children nonetheless. When we recovered, we called a meeting to plan a suitable tribute for him by his New York friends. I was chosen to give the main speech of the evening. "Let it be engraven on the tablets of fame, that one born in a humble position in life, who by his own energies acquired a princely fortune, mixed with the greatest and noblest of his age, had princes at his table, and sat at those of kings, yet he never swerved nor faltered from his principles nor from his sublime object of ameliorating the conditions of the poor and oppressed. He remained true to himself and to the cause of humanity, and his glorious motto was: *Truth without mystery, mixture of error, or the fear of man. That man was Robert Owen.*"

It was a long speech, and I got through it without tears—but when it was all over, I slipped into an anteroom and sobbed, half from the knowledge that I would never see his like again, half from the pleasure of knowing that I'd had the honor of paying him his final tribute. Aside from his goodness to mankind, he had changed my life when he invited me to speak that long-ago evening in London. It was a debt that I had never been able to repay.

So we slipped into 1859. Isidor, now qualified as a dentist, returned to New York, while Simon and Bertha decided to go to Savannah, Georgia, of all places. "I thought your practice was going well here."

"It is, which is why Isidor will be manning our New York office. We want to see more of the country, and Bertha needs a change of scene." She had borne a short-lived son.

"I would never work in a slave state," Isidor said.

"And with this arrangement, you don't have to, do you?" Simon met Isidor's and my combined glares. "I do not approve of slavery either, but I have met Southerners who are fine people, and I think to understand the South, one has to go there. But I do promise that if the South ends up pulling out of the Union, I will return north."

"Do you think the South might actually secede? There have been threats of disunion for some time. Someone always smooths down their ruffled feathers."

"Something will ruffle them beyond repair."

It was true that the country did seem to be sliding toward something. While William and I were in Europe, the powder keg that was Kansas had exploded. A South Carolina congressman, furious over a speech given by Massachusetts

Senator Charles Sumner on the Kansas question, had cowardly sneaked up on the senator as he sat working at his desk in Congress and had attacked him viciously with his cane. Pro-slavery settlers had crossed into Lawrence, Kansas, looting, pillaging, and burning. John Brown—the very same man Gerrit Smith had mentioned to Susan and me back in 1854—had joined his sons in the territory and with a ragtag army had managed to hold his own against a much larger force at Osawatomie. (He was also rumored to have murdered five pro-slavery men, but I did not believe it.) More recently, he had helped eleven slaves escape from Missouri and had brought them—along with an infant who was born during the ordeal—safely to Canada. With all of this going on, I could not say whether relations between North and South were so close to the breaking point as Simon thought, but I doubted that any improvement was in sight.

Then, in October, I and everyone else woke to the news that John Brown, with a small band of men, white and black, had seized the federal arsenal at Harpers Ferry, Virginia. He had planned to help slaves flee into the surrounding mountains, with the hope of so thoroughly demoralizing the South as to make slavery untenable. But his plan failed. Many of his men were killed; Brown and several others were captured. There was an obscenely quick trial, held by the State of Virginia—the administration of President Buchanan being content to sit back and watch Southern vengeance unfold as each prisoner was tried and sentenced to death. Yet as ill-fated and perhaps ill-conceived as the plan was, I could not help but say when I spoke a week later: "If the Harpers Ferry insurrection is to be regretted, the cause which produced it is even more so. As long as that cause—slavery—

remains, we must expect more such outbreaks, because freedom and slavery can never exist together in peace. One must destroy the other."

After Harpers Ferry, every slaveholder I treat believes that he is about to be murdered in his bed, Simon wrote from Savannah. *They can barely stop talking about John Brown long enough for me to do my work.*

The 1860 presidential election will likely be momentous, Bertha wrote. *Now I begin to understand why you want ladies to be able to vote. I wish I could.*

~ ~ ~

That last year of peace, 1860, did start auspiciously in one respect: the New York legislature passed a bill that vastly expanded the rights of married women beyond those allowed in 1848. We could not rest, of course, until we enjoyed perfect equality of rights, but this was still something to celebrate.

In February, William and I walked to the Cooper Institute, erected the year before and still smelling somewhat fresh and new, to hear Mr. Abraham Lincoln speak. A lawyer from Illinois and a one-term congressman, Mr. Lincoln had run against Stephen Douglas for the Senate in 1858. He had lost, but the rivals' debates on slavery and other topics had attracted multitudes, and Mr. Lincoln had followed up by giving more speeches in the West in 1859. So much was being said about him that the New York Republican Party, mindful of the upcoming presidential election, had invited him here so that the East could take a look at him.

And so, in a packed hall handsomely lit with gas chandeliers, William and I looked at Mr. Lincoln. He was a very tall, ungainly man in an ill-fitting suit that could have used a pressing—I surmised that Mrs. Lincoln, if there was such a person, was not here to superintend him—and his shrill, twangy voice was not appealing. For the first few minutes, I wondered what on earth the party leaders had been thinking. But there is a point where a speaker either loses the audience irrevocably or seizes it, and Mr. Lincoln quickly rallied, adjusted his voice to his surroundings, and captured us. "But you will not abide the election of a Republican president!" he said, referring to the South's threat to secede if that occurred. "In that supposed event, you say, you will destroy the Union; and then, you say, the great crime of having destroyed it will be upon us! That is cool. A highwayman holds a pistol to my ear, and mutters through his teeth, 'Stand and deliver, or I shall kill you, and then you will be a murderer!'"

"Nicely thrust," I whispered to William during the applause that ensued.

"Wrong as we think slavery is, we can yet afford to let it alone where it is, because that much is due to the necessity arising from its actual presence in the nation; but can we, while our votes will prevent it, allow it to spread into the national territories, and to overrun us here in these free states? If our sense of duty forbids this, then let us stand by our duty, fearlessly and effectively.

"Neither let us be slandered from our duty by false accusations against us, nor frightened from it by menaces of destruction to the government nor of dungeons to ourselves. Let us have faith that right makes might, and in that faith, let us, to the end, dare to do our duty as we understand it."

I did not agree with Mr. Lincoln that slavery should be left alone where it existed. But it was a noble speech, and I did not think that Mr. Lincoln as president would be inclined to coddle the South. Alongside William, I leapt to my feet and joined in the applause, handkerchief-waving, foot-stomping, and hat-throwing. Horace Greeley, sitting on the platform as one of the honored guests, was beaming.

"Well?" I asked William as we trudged home, picking our way over the slushy pavement. "Do you think Mr. Lincoln will be the Republican nominee? Mr. Greeley seems besotted with him after that speech."

"I think he'll be the president."

Besides Mr. Lincoln, divorce was in the air in those first few months of 1860. Horace Greeley and Robert Dale Owen of Indiana had been debating the subject in the pages of the *Tribune*, with the latter defending the liberal Indiana divorce law. Not surprisingly, I felt that Mr. Owen had the better side of the question, although both men spent too much time on what Jesus Christ said about the matter, as if that should be a consideration in 1860. "To hear Mr. Greeley tell it, Jesus Christ is a member of the New York legislature."

"Complete with spittoon?" William asked.

"Complete with spittoon and cigar." I snickered at the pleasing picture that raised. "Mrs. Stanton is bursting to raise the divorce question at our convention, Susan tells me. She and I have similar views on the matter, so I shall be interested in hearing what she has to say."

In May, we gathered at the great hall of the Cooper Institute, which still basked in the fame of Mr. Lincoln's triumph. Having not seen Mrs. Stanton in some time, I congratulated her upon the birth of her seventh child. "Thank you," she said. "I do believe that Robert shall be my last effort. After all, I am forty."

"Forty-four," Susan said. "We are among friends."

"Oh, dear, how literal you are." Mrs. Stanton tapped Susan with her fan.

"It is quite all right," I said. "Ladies never grow old." In 1856, a lovely Frenchwoman, Jenny d'Héricourt, had written a piece about me, and without thinking much about it I had given my birth year as 1810. It was, I observed to William, a nice round number, much easier to deal with than 1806.

"Well, forty or forty-four, I do agree that seven children are quite enough. Now that Lucy is in semi-retirement, we need more hands on deck."

"I shall try to get Mother Nature to oblige," Mrs. Stanton said. "So no Lucy? She said she might come." Mrs. Stone was the mother of a healthy little girl, Alice, but the year before, she had given birth to a premature boy, who'd lived only long enough to draw a few shaky breaths. I had written her a letter of condolence, and she in turn had been quite gracious when I attended a lecture of hers in New York a few months later.

"No, she decided she would rather stay home." Susan heaved a sigh.

"Well, I have her blessing to speak on the divorce question. And yours, Susan, I know. Mrs. Rose?"

"Of course. I believe couples should be free to divorce." *It would be rather hypocritical if I did not*, I would have added if Susan, who knew my history, had been the only person present.

"Well, then!" Mrs. Stanton all but clapped her hands. "Let the merriment begin."

Mrs. Stanton chose the second day of the convention to throw her bomb, as she put it. Most eloquently, she told of mismatched couples yoked together, of cruel and deceptive husbands, of lovely young creatures at the mercy of their drunken husbands. I had tears in my eyes, but the Reverend Mrs. Antoinette Brown Blackwell was frowning. When Mrs. Stanton finished, to somewhat startled applause, Mrs. Blackwell arose. "Marriage must be as permanent and indissoluble as the relation of parent and child," she declared. "Let a young woman wait, as a young man does, until she is twenty-five or thirty to marry. She will then know how to choose properly. The cure for the evils that now exist is not in dissolving marriage, but it is giving to the married woman her own natural independence and self-sovereignty."

As if age inevitably brought wisdom. As if a person's character could not deteriorate, or a person could not hide his (or her) flaws while working to draw another into marriage. And what of the case of two people, both essentially good, decent, and responsible, who nonetheless found themselves an ill-assorted match?

I rose when Mrs. Blackwell had taken her seat, to applause that sounded like a collective sigh of relief. If the audience was expecting more in this namby-pamby vein, it was to be disappointed. "The question of a divorce law seems to me one of the greatest importance to all parties, but I presume that the very advocacy of divorce will be called 'free love,'" I said. "For my part, I do not know what others understand by that term; to me, in its truest significance, love must be free, or it ceases to be love. In its low and degrading sense, it is not love at all, and I have as little to do with its name as its reality.

"It would indeed be well if woman could be what she ought to be, man what he ought to be, and marriage what it ought to be; and it is to be hoped that through the woman's rights movement—the equalizing of the laws, making them more just, and making woman more independent—we will hasten the coming of the millennium, when marriage shall indeed be a bond of union and affection. But alas! It is not yet.

"But what is marriage? A human institution, called out by the needs of social, affectional human nature, for human purposes, its objects are, first, the happiness of the parties immediately concerned, and secondly, the welfare of society. Define it as you please, these are only its objects; and therefore if, from well-ascertained facts, it is demonstrated that the real objects are frustrated, that instead of union and happiness, there are only discord and misery to themselves, and vice and crime to society, I ask, in the name of individual happiness and social morality and well-being, why such a marriage should be binding for life, why one human being should be chained for life to the dead body of another?

"*But they may separate and still remain married*, we are told. What a perversion of the very term! Is that the union which 'death only should part'? It may be according to the definition of the Reverend Mrs. Blackwell's theology and Mr. Greeley's dictionary, but it certainly is not according to common sense or the dictates of morality. No, no! It is not well for man to be alone—before nor after marriage.

"I therefore ask for a divorce law. Divorce is now granted for some crimes; I ask it for others also. It is granted for a state's prison offense. I ask that personal cruelty to a wife, whom he swore to love, cherish, and protect, may be made a heinous crime—a perjury and a state's prison offense, for which divorce shall be granted. Willful desertion for one year should be a sufficient cause for divorce, for the willful deserter forfeits the sacred title of husband or wife. Habitual intemperance, or any other vice which makes the husband or wife intolerable and abhorrent to the other, ought to be sufficient cause for divorce. I ask for a law of divorce, so as to secure the real objects and blessings of married life, to prevent the crimes and immoralities now practiced, to prevent 'free love,' in its most hideous form, such as is now carried on but too often under the very name of marriage, where hypocrisy is added to the crime of legalized prostitution. 'Free love,' in its degraded sense, asks for no divorce law. It acknowledges no marriage, and therefore requires no divorce. I believe in true marriages, and therefore I ask for a law to free men and women from false ones."

Mrs. Stanton beamed at me as I vacated the podium. Then Mr. Wendell Phillips, looking as if his meal had not sat well with him, took his place there. Referring to the resolutions in favor of liberalized divorce laws that Mrs. Stanton had introduced immediately before her speech, he asked that they be stricken from the record of the convention. "Every person must be interested in the questions of marriage and divorce, and no one could deny that we have been favored with an exceedingly able discussion of those questions. But here we have nothing to do with them. This convention is not a marriage convention. It is to discuss the laws that rest unequally upon women, not those that rest equally upon men and women."

Susan, Mrs. Stanton, and I stared at each other. "I thought he would support us!" Susan hissed.

"Put not your trust in princes," I whispered. And was not Mr. Phillips a prince of the abolitionist movement?

Mrs. Abby Hopper Gibbons, a Quaker lady from New York, seconded Mr. Phillips's motion to sweep the question of marriage and divorce from the record. "That is, under the rug," I muttered.

In any event, Mr. Phillips was not to have his way with tidying up the record. The Reverend Mrs. Blackwell, Susan, and even Mr. Phillips's dear friend Mr. William Lloyd Garrison all spoke against Mr. Phillips's motion, and when it was put to a vote, a vast majority agreed that the divorce resolutions, though never themselves put to a vote, should be kept on the record. And so when the convention proceedings were printed a few months later, all was there, resolutions, speeches, and all. (I checked. So did Mrs. Stanton. She probably still checks, as a matter of fact.)

But Mr. Phillips's pompous intervention had made it clear to me: the Boston abolitionist clique might support woman's rights, but its support had limits. We had bumped into them that day. Time would tell whether this was an anomaly.

~ ~ ~

Abraham Lincoln was indeed the Republican nominee for president. It was a four-way race, though in New York Mr. Lincoln's three opponents had combined themselves into what was called a fusion ticket. While the Republicans in New York organized "Wide Awake" parades, the opposition press predicted that the direst consequences would flow from Mr. Lincoln's election: working men would lose their jobs and their wives to black men, wages would sink to starvation level, and free love would reign. I never did understand what Mr. Lincoln had to do with free love, but since even John Brown's ill-fated men had been accused of being free lovers, I supposed that no one else did either.

Despite my distaste for monarchies, I was grateful, as I am sure many others were, when the Prince of Wales visited in October, giving us a respite from all of the name-calling and accusations as New York scrambled to impress the young man. The cream of society held a ball in his honor, and to William's delight, quite a few of its members required new canes and jewelry for the occasion.

Election Day, November 6, dawned gloomy and rainy. I knew it was a historic day, so I walked with William to the polls. "I am disappointed," I said as William took his place in line. "They are always telling us women that the polls would be simply too much for our delicate sensibilities, and this looks quite sedate."

"That's just the line, my dear. Inside is where the cigars and opium are smoked, the alcohol guzzled, the fights held, and where . . . unspeakable things take place."

"What sort of things, sir?" the man behind us asked.

"Things that can't be spoken of before a lady, sir. But we men know what they are, don't we?"

"Oh, yes. Dreadful things."

"No man comes out the same from the polls," William said. "It is why my wife, dear as she is, can never be allowed to vote."

"Well, I don't know," the man said. "Some ladies are certainly intelligent enough to vote. I don't agree with much of what the woman's rights ladies say, but I think they do have a point there at least."

"Do you, now?" I said. "I often tell my husband that."

I was rather sorry when, just a moment later, William and his new acquaintance were waved into the polling area.

~ ~ ~

Just over a month after Mr. Lincoln's election, South Carolina seceded from the Union, to which I could only say, "Good riddance." Simon, who had been practicing in

Columbia, seceded from South Carolina. "I took an oath when I became a United States citizen, and I plan to stand by it," he said as I hugged him upon his arrival in New York.

By this point, it was merely a matter of waiting for war. The mood was ugly; when the Anti-Slavery Society convened in Albany, the mob was so vehement that police had to be called to keep order—and they actually did keep order, down to escorting us speakers to our hotel. In February, President-Elect Lincoln boarded a train for Washington, while Jefferson Davis, selected to lead the confabulation of traitors called the Confederacy, boarded a train that would take him to Montgomery, Alabama.

Amid all this, I kept an engagement to speak in Boston in defense of atheism on April 10. "Morality does not depend on the belief in any religion," I said. "We need not go back to ancient times to see the crimes and atrocities perpetrated under its sanction. We have enough in our own times. Look at the present crisis—at the South with four million human beings in slavery, bought and sold like brute chattels under the sanction of religion."

I had a good audience, and made a good speech (if I may be permitted to say so myself), but it was scarcely reported. That was no surprise, because there was but one thing on everyone's mind: Fort Sumter, under siege by the rebels. Indeed, I was barely through my talk when I heard people asking each other, "Is there any news?" I too made that inquiry as soon as I left the hall, and kept a close eye on the papers as I lingered in Boston, having agreed to give a lecture in New Bedford on April 14.

Rumors flew on the evening of April 12 that there had been a rebel attack on the fort, but I mistrusted them. By the next morning, however, there could be no doubt, for the

Boston papers had learned what the New York papers had printed the night before: the fort had indeed been bombarded. This was war now.

For a believer, this would be a time to pray, but all I could do was hope that President Lincoln and his government would manage the war wisely, and that the South and its pernicious institution of slavery would soon go down in defeat. Indeed, people around me were already predicting that the rebels would capitulate in weeks, but I bore in mind what Simon had told me. "They've been wanting a fight for years, and they're going to give it their all. Even if it destroys them."

Would right make might? How much blood would have to be shed? Time would tell. Sighing, I stuffed as many newspapers in my carpetbag as I could and boarded the train.

16

FEBRUARY 1863 TO NOVEMBER 1863

"If there's one thing I can thank this war for, it's getting me out of Seneca Falls," Mrs. Stanton said as I settled into an armchair in her handsome house on New York's Forty-Fifth Street. "Mind you, some less drastic means would have been preferable."

With the war and the new presidential administration had come a flurry of patronage appointments, and Mr. Henry Stanton, an abolitionist and a stalwart Republican, had been one of the beneficiaries, securing a job at New York's customs house. Judging from the comfort of Mrs. Stanton's parlor, the customs house job included plenty of perquisites. "I am glad to see you in your natural habitat," I said.

"Indeed, I shall not be easy to dislodge from a city this time. How are your husband and brothers faring? It is so long since we have seen each other."

"William's mother died last December. William has asked his sister to come visit us, and perhaps to stay for good if it goes well. I cannot say I am looking forward to it, but she is of a nervous temperament and has not been doing well without her mother. Simon is practicing dentistry in Washington. He likes to tell me that he keeps the place running, for where would it be full of men with toothaches?

Isidor served his time in the army and decided not to reenlist. He does not like being told what to do, so I am surprised he lasted that long. He is traveling in Europe. My youngest brother, Bertrand, is in London, and I hope he stays there until the war is over—whenever that shall be."

"I could go to Washington and be as much use as any of the men there are," Susan said, entering the room while untying her bonnet. "I beg your pardon, Ernestine, for being late. I agreed to take Elizabeth's youngest to Central Park, and he balked at leaving."

"You must be firm with him," Mrs. Stanton said. "But don't fear, Mrs. Rose, I am not turning dear Susan into my unpaid nanny. She is staying here for a higher purpose, and we called you here to discuss that very topic. As it is Susan's scheme—is not everything clever Susan's scheme?—I shall give way to her."

"My thought is to organize a women's loyalty group," Susan said. "We can press for the emancipation of all the slaves, not just the few the president has freed, and perhaps in the course of things we can press for our emancipation as well. You know I have been chafing since we women decided to put our cause aside for the sake of the war effort—"

"Can anything this government is doing be called an effort?" I asked. "But I apologize. Do go on."

"And I know you have been chafing as well. This will be good for all concerned—for the soldiers, for the slaves, for us women. Can the government keep putting off its loyal citizens? Look at all the contributions women are making already—in the offices, in the munitions factories, in caring for farms while men are at war. Now is our chance to show our value, and the cynic in me hopes that it will be rewarded with the vote."

"It seems a good plan to me." Soon after Fort Sumter fell, we women had canceled our upcoming national convention, thinking that it would distract from the war, which many had assumed would end shortly and satisfactorily with the humiliation of the South. But the South had yet to be humiliated, and General McClellan seemed to regard his troops like a piece of exquisite china, to be used only on special occasions. He'd gained something close to a victory at Antietam the previous September, but had refused to pursue General Lee, so that President Lincoln, who in my view had been far too patient with the man, had finally fired him the previous November. "I have been missing our conventions. Even the freethought conventions are not as they were. The war is driving people toward religion."

"Yes, well, that can happen," Susan said drily. "In any case, we have had this in our thoughts for some time and will be sending a call for a meeting. I hope you will honor us with a speech there."

"Of course." I rather wished that I had been included in the planning of all this, but it was becoming apparent that the process that would cement Susan and Mrs. Stanton together in the public mind had begun, and that these two ladies together had the force of a locomotive. Only a fool would fail to clear the track.

So over the next few weeks I helped Susan with her organizing as much as she would allow, which was not much, because aside from her personal inclination to take charge, Susan was mourning her father, who had died the previous autumn. She had loved him dearly, and he had repaid her affection by supporting her in her endeavors, so she sorely needed the distraction of the Women's Loyal National League.

When not assisting Susan, I knitted—never my forte—for the soldiers and prepared for the arrival of Mary Ann, William's sister. As I had told my friends, it was not a visit I anticipated with pleasure, but Mary Ann, never in high spirits, had been so low after her mother's death that William and his uncle John in London thought a change might be the only thing that could help her. So the invitation had been sent, we had supplied the funds for her passage, and in early May, just before the Loyal League convened, Mary Ann stood in our spare room on Prince Street. William had rented the entire building, and for the time being, we were living on one floor, with William's shop on the ground floor and the rest let out to lodgers. "It's noisy."

"Yes, well, we are, after all, just off Broadway. One gets used to it, though." I led Mary Ann down the hall. "But look! This is the most pleasant thing. A water closet!" As I flung open the door and gestured, I wondered if I had a future as a house agent.

Evidently I did not. Mary Ann merely frowned. I might as well have been giving a speech on abolitionism to Jefferson Davis.

Sighing, I headed back to the spare room. "I will give you some time to get yourself settled—everything you need should be here—and then we shall have tea together. Won't that be lovely?"

Without waiting for an answer, I practically fled the room.

~ ~ ~

"Would you like to come to our meeting tomorrow?" I asked Mary Ann a few days later as we sat in the parlor.

"No. A woman speaking in public is an abomination in the eyes of the Lord."

"Well, we are the Women's Loyal National League," I said. "We could hardly hold a conference with no ladies speaking. It would be most awkward if we had to speak through men, don't you think? But you are welcome to join us if you change your mind. There are excellent women in the movement, and many are religious, so you would not be made to feel ill at ease."

"You are going to hell, you know."

Almost since the day of her arrival, Mary Ann had been informing me of this. I put down my tea. "William and I are quite happy to have you here. We know that you have suffered a grievous loss. But I will not permit you to tell me every day that I am going to hell. It is tedious."

"But it is true."

I could hardly send Mary Ann to her own room. Instead, grumbling, I went to mine.

It was quite a relief, then, to be able to escape to our meeting, held at the Church of the Puritans in Union Square. Inside the crowded church I saw a mix of familiar faces—Susan, Mrs. Stanton, Lucy Stone—and complete strangers. Susan had done a superb job of bringing all of us together, but I worried that we might be an ill-assorted bunch.

My concerns grew when Susan read to the assembly the resolutions to be voted upon. Some were utterly uncontroversial, but there was a stir when Susan read the fifth. *The property, the liberty, and the lives of all slaves, and all women, are placed at the mercy of a legislature in which they are not represented. There never can be a true peace in this Republic until the civil and political equality of every subject of the government shall be practically established.* Even the

Hutchinson Family Singers, who took the stage after the reading of the resolutions, could not stem the whispering.

Sure enough, a lady named Mrs. Elizabeth Hoyt rose. "I object to the passage of the fifth resolution," she said. "We are assembled here to devise the best ways and means by which women may properly assist the government in its struggle against treason. We all know that woman's rights have not been received with entire favor by the women of the country, and I know that there are thousands of earnest, loyal, and able women who will not go into any movement if this idea is made prominent."

I rose. "I, for one, object to throwing women out of the race for freedom. And do you know why? Because she needs freedom for the freedom of man. It is true that the Negro at present suffers more than woman, but it can do him no injury to place woman in the same category. That resolution simply states a fact: that in a republic based upon freedom, woman, as well as the Negro, should be recognized as an equal with the whole human race."

I resumed my seat and listened to Mrs. Hoyt and several others speak for and against the resolution. Mrs. Hoyt was outnumbered, and although I could not help but admire her courage in taking her lonely stand, I could not countenance it either. Once again, I bobbed up to my feet. "It is exceedingly amusing to hear persons talk about throwing out woman's rights, when, if it had not been for woman's rights, that lady would not have had the courage to stand here and say what she did. It will be exceedingly inconsistent if, because some women out in the West are opposed to the woman's rights movement—though at the same time they take advantage of it—that therefore we shall throw it out of this resolution."

The resolution passed, but not unanimously. I could

only smile at the irony that the equality of the black man should be less controversial than equality of women. The papers alternated between praising us for our loyalty and grumbling that we had dragged woman's rights into the picture.

With the conference over, summer soon encircled New York in its hot, muggy grip. Despite that, Mary Ann seemed to improve slightly; she went for days at a time without telling me that I was going to hell, and she began to take an interest in the war news, having hitherto been nearly the only person in New York who did not. Everyone was an armchair general in those fraught days, and she, William, and I passed our evenings pleasantly enough telling each other what we could do if only Mr. Lincoln would put us in charge.

There were rumors in early July of a Union victory in Gettysburg, Pennsylvania, and of yet another one in Vicksburg, Mississippi. After intently studying our maps, which lay perpetually in readiness spread out upon a table, we took an omnibus to Central Park and spent the Fourth of July—still my favorite holiday despite the noise—lounging about sipping lemonade and listening to the band play patriotic songs. In days, the happy rumors were confirmed: General Robert E. Lee was beating a retreat into Virginia, and General Ulysses S Grant was the master of Vicksburg. "I still bear a grudge against Grant for expelling the Jews from his area of command," I said to William as we settled into bed one evening. It had been a most vile and foolish order, and Mr. Lincoln had had the good sense to rescind it when a delegation of Jews from the West protested. "But I think he may be our man."

"Shall I telegraph the president?"

"We shall see if General Meade follows up his victory

over Lee before I make a decision."

William sighed. "I think we should see how the draft goes first."

"True." The first batch of names in New York were supposed to be drawn on July 11, a Saturday. Many had a sense that it might not go well. There had been enthusiasm for marching off to war in the days after Fort Sumter, but it had passed as poor men contemplated the difference between doing back-breaking work in a factory and having their guts blown out in some field in Virginia. Most chose the former.

But the Saturday draft, conducted on Forty-Sixth Street not far from Mrs. Stanton's handsome house, passed peacefully enough. When the last name for the day had been drawn and the office was locked up to await the next round on Monday, it really seemed that we were a city of Cassandras.

Then—if you will pardon the indelicacy—all hell broke loose.

~ ~ ~

Living where we did, William and I were well accustomed to noise. The Metropolitan Hotel, one of the finest in the city, occupied a block of Broadway and part of Prince Street, and people came and went from it all night. Even in the small hours, carriages and omnibuses rattled back and forth on Broadway. But I had never heard anything like the sound that awoke me around five in the morning on Monday.

Actually, I *had* heard such a sound, thirty-three years before in Paris. I blinked and looked at the man sleeping beside me, halfway expecting to see Marcus's head on the pillow. But it was William. "Wake up!"

"Mmmh?"

"Something's going on outside. Wake up."

William, still half asleep, fumbled with his pants and shirt while I donned a wrapper, not bothering with a corset.

Emerging onto Prince Street, we drew a breath of crisp morning air, probably the best we were likely to get before the humidity drew up, and looked around us. The houses and shops on our street were silent, but we could hear plainly now what had awoken me: the sound of a mass of people moving. It could come from no place but Broadway.

We hastened to the corner to see what appeared to be an entire slum on the move uptown. Men, women, and even children, some dressed in working clothes, some barely dressed at all, strode by silently. One might have thought that they were on their way to some excursion arranged for the city's poor were it not for one thing: no one looked the least bit festive, and almost everyone who was old enough to carry something brandished either a weapon or something that could be used as one.

By now, William and I had been joined by other spectators. Seeing themselves with a respectably sized audience, the group began to chant, "No draft!"

"Come join us," someone called in the direction of the pavement. "Stand up for working men! Anyone can come— unless you're a three-hundred-dollar man." That was the price at which a man could avoid the draft by paying a substitute.

"Or a damned abolitionist."

William's arm tightened around my waist.

"Where are you headed?" someone called.

"To the draft office at Forty-Sixth and Third, where else?"

I gasped, thinking how close that was to Mrs. Stanton's house. William hissed, "Let's go home."

We walked the short way back in silence. When the door

was closed, William said, "I have never ordered you to do anything in my life, and I will not start now. But I beg you, stay here until this passes. You heard what they said about the abolitionists. Perhaps it was just talk, but I don't think so."

"I am so worried about Susan and Mrs. Stanton."

"If there is to be trouble where they are, I hope the authorities will deal with it. But if they are truly in danger, so are you."

Catherine, our maid who tended to us and the lodgers, came in with a duster in hand. She had Sundays off, and usually she returned full of chatter about her family and her "fellow," but the evening before, I recalled, she had been uncharacteristically quiet. "Catherine, did you hear any talk about this yesterday when you were off?"

She looked at the floor. "Yes, ma'am, all over—but I thought it was big talk, nothing more."

"Who were they talking against?"

"Rich people, ma'am. Big bugs of all sorts. Colored people. A lot about the colored people and folks who stick up for them. Should I have told you, ma'am?"

"Perhaps, but I doubt it would have made a difference." I sighed as Catherine turned her utmost attention to a bookshelf. "I will stay here, William."

"Thank you."

"But you are as much as an abolitionist as I am, albeit not as noisy, and you have a store."

"Yes. I intend to shut it up for the morning."

So William sent most of his workers home—some had not turned up—and along with the help of the others, we closed his shutters and stowed everything that might tempt a looter. But few were lingering, much less looting, in the immediate neighborhood. From Prince Street I watched as guests ventured out of the Metropolitan Hotel and, depending on their temperament, scurried back inside after grabbing a newspaper or strode off in the direction of uptown with the air of having stumbled into a most excellent diversion.

It was not quiet, however. As the morning wore on, we began to hear the clangs of fire bells, each from a different station, and there was a perpetual hum of shouts from a distance. Rumors began to float downtown, tales of unchecked mobs running rampant through the upper part of the city, pillaging and burning. William was unwilling to leave Mary Ann and me alone, but a couple of our bachelor lodgers set out for uptown to investigate for themselves. Methodically, each of us packed a carpetbag with a few necessities in case we were obliged to flee the house. William broached the subject of us women taking a ferry out of town, but I would not leave him, and that was that.

Barring the doors and leaving Catherine to her housework (at which she had been uncommonly assiduous), we climbed to the roof, where I had a little garden and had made a pleasant place to sit. But today it held no charms. In every direction we looked, we could see flames in the distance and clumps of people filling the streets. "I've never felt so useless in my life," I said.

"Well, at least we're not out there making things any worse."

It was late in the endless afternoon when we saw a mob reappear on Broadway and advance toward Bleecker Street, just two blocks north of Prince Street. Unlike the grimly businesslike group of that morning—a lifetime ago—this crowd was raging, and I knew that if it reached our block, our house, we would be at its mercy. We were calculating whether to stay on the roof or flee into the street when we saw them: police, advancing from the side streets and up Broadway. They were armed with clubs, and the sounds of rioters' heads being cracked filled the air. At last the mob fled down the side streets, leaving their fallen scattered up and down Broadway.

But this victory for the police was deceptive, as we found when our lodgers returned from their reconnaissance mission. "It's nightmarish out there. The wretches are doing what they like, and there is hardly anyone to stop them, with most of our fighting men in Pennsylvania and there being so many disturbances around the city at one time. The rioters even set the Colored Orphan Asylum on fire. They barely had the decency to let the orphans' minders take them out first."

"Orphans? What do orphans have do with the draft?" But I knew the answer: they were black, and their only home was an easy target for mindless destruction. I wept, thinking of the poor, frightened creatures.

But the orphans had been left alive. Not so for others of their race. Over the next several days, black people doing the most innocent things—such as heading to buy provisions—were lynched and their dead bodies mutilated. The luckier ones fled the city, many never to return to New York.

I do not mean to recapitulate all of the horrors of those days in July, only the ones that angered me the most—aside from the murder of innocents, of course. Abby Hopper Gibbons, the Quaker lady who had spoken against divorce at our 1860 woman's rights convention, had been serving the poor and imprisoned of New York for years and was off nursing soldiers at the front, but no matter: her fine house was looted, with everything that could not be carried away destroyed for the joy of destroying it. Her family's crime, I discovered, was to have illuminated their house in celebration of the Emancipation Proclamation on New Year's Day and to be suspected of harboring Horace Greeley, whose paper's support of the Lincoln administration had made him a special target of the mob's wrath. The rioters had not even noticed Mrs. Gibbons's husband wandering through his own house, so intent had they been on their foul work. The *Tribune* building was attacked, and even a reporter for the *Herald* was roughed up as he went about his duties. Jewish storekeepers were robbed simply because the mob assumed that they were Republicans and, of course, rich men.

All this time, William and I were almost indecently safe from harm. The mayor and the governor took up their headquarters at the St. Nicholas Hotel, just a few blocks from the Metropolitan Hotel. As a result, our stretch of Broadway and the side streets were exceptionally well guarded, both by police and by a force of volunteers whose vigilance extended even to the carpeted halls of the hotels. We vowed to open our house to all who might need shelter, particularly black people, but after the killings those who remained in the city shut themselves up tight.

Despite this, William and I slept in our clothes, and along with our lodgers ensured that at least two people were awake at night. I was sleeping on Wednesday when William nudged me awake. "Good news, my darling. Troops!"

We ran outside, where we saw rows of Union soldiers assembling in front of the St. Nicholas Hotel as hotel residents leaned out their windows and cheered. William and I cheered too, through our anger that these men had had to deal both with Robert E. Lee at Gettysburg and with mobs in New York. Could we not have done better by them?

The troops' arrival did not deter the rioters at first, but

at last the mob was subdued. That Thursday night, William and I felt safe enough to sleep in our nightclothes.

With the city under military guard and the omnibuses running again, William and I rode uptown. It was a dreadful sight. Every block stank of smoke, and shells of brick stood in the place of fine houses and flourishing businesses. But the Stanton house on Forty-Fifth Street bore no signs of disturbance other than being shuttered tight. It was occupied by a lone servant, who informed us that the family and Susan were safe in the country. "Mrs. Stanton had a grand speech planned for the mob," the servant said, "but the coppers ran the rioters off before they got to this house. It's just as well. She talks good—but I don't think they would have listened even to her."

Our next stop was at the orphanage, burned to bare walls. "Those poor mites," William said. "At least they are safe."

I shook my head. "Sometimes I wonder why I—and others—bother talking at all. Will people never listen to reason?"

"Some will. Others—well, it takes more time."

"And the Union army."

~ ~ ~

But there was one casualty of the draft riots that was never recorded: Mary Ann. I'd had some hope for her before; she had appeared to be settling in, as I said, and had even spoken of doing some piecework for the mourning warehouse nearby. (Meanly, I thought that this would be an excellent fit for her.) But as the riots progressed, her religious rants became more frequent and more unhinged—all the violence being God's judgment—and they did not cease once order was restored. I did not try to reason with her, for I knew that she was not a well woman. But what I could not ignore was the fact that she had somehow come to hate me, and I do not use the word ill-advisedly. I would be knitting or reading a newspaper and look up to find her glare fixed upon me. "Is there anything I can get for you?" I asked about the second or third time this happened.

"Yes. Gone." Her voice, which usually had a pleasant enough Cockney lilt, dropped as deep as a man's. "You are bringing my brother to perdition. He will go to hell because of you. I rue the day that he met you. You lured him away from God, and from England."

Another time, I was making bandages when Mary Ann came into the room and asked, almost conversationally, "Do you know why your little boy died?"

Mary Ann did not know about Amalia, and any inclination I might have ever had to tell her had long since passed. "Scarlet fever."

"He died because God could not bear to see a child raised to hate him by an unnatural mother. He took the babe home to save him from the perdition into which you would have led him. I am glad he is dead. Glad!"

Up until that point, I had said nothing to William about Mary Ann's recent behavior. He had enough to concern him; like so many others in New York, he was trying to recoup his lost income from the days when the riots had brought businesses to a halt. But this was too much. I walked down to William's shop and said, "Either she goes or I go," and then I told him why.

William took me into his arms. Then he accompanied me into the parlor. "Mary Ann, my wife told me what you said just now."

"It is God's truth!"

"It is not truth. It is cruel and mean. You have no idea of what it is to lose a child, and no idea how much we loved our boy. My wife has been nothing but kind to you. I will give you three choices. First, you can treat my wife with civility. Second, you can go back to England, and take up your old lodgings or something suitable. I will pay, of course. Third, you can go to a lunatic asylum—a private one if I can find one, or a public one if I cannot. The choice is yours."

The look of hatred Mary Ann shot at me surpassed her previous efforts. "I'll go back to England."

"I will make the arrangements."

William led me to our room. "William—"

"It is necessary, my love. I think you should visit one of our friends for a few days. When you come back, she will be gone."

I decided to visit the Mendums in Massachusetts. (Boston, I should add, had had its own draft riot, but it had been quickly contained, which rather added to the Bostonian sense of superiority.) When I returned, William met me at the station. "Mary Ann is on her way back."

"I am sorry things reached that point."

"We tried. I did not like threatening her with the asylum, but I cannot have you wretched in your own home. I believe that the people she lived with before will treat her kindly—she trusts them, and they were fond of Ma—but if that arrangement does not work we must find another one."

At home, I could not help but look with gratitude at my parlor and reflect that no one would be sitting there accusing me of being a limb of Satan (Mary Ann would never dream of saying "leg"). Proceeding to the bedroom, I opened my wardrobe to put away my things.

Every garment inside had been slashed.

I said nothing to William, but mended what could be mended and replaced what could not. We ladies were being encouraged to give up silk for the duration of the war anyway, so I had some woolen dresses made, thus making a virtue out of necessity. In time, word arrived that Mary Ann had reached London safely and was back in her old lodgings in Hackney. William's uncle John saw her and reported that she was in low spirits, but no worse than she had been, and was doing a little work.

Then, in November, we had another letter, this one from the Colney Hatch Lunatic Asylum. Mary Ann was now an inmate there. Letters from John Rose and from Mary Ann's landlords told the rest of the story: in early October, Mary Ann had become completely irrational, accusing everyone of wanting to kill her, threatening to kill others, threatening to kill herself, talking of some unspecified wrong she had done, pacing her rooms completely unclothed, and on one memorable occasion in Hackney, rushing out into the street in that condition.

"I think we always knew she was heading in that direction once Ma died," William said, folding the last of the letters. "I have been wondering whether it would have been different if she had stayed here, but I think it would have been Blackwell's Island instead of Colney Hatch."

"Probably. I am so sorry, my love. Perhaps she will get better there. Sometimes people do."

"Perhaps. I am also wondering what she might have done to you if she stayed here."

"I can tell you what she did to my clothes." I went to our room, fished in my ragbag, and returned with the remains of my gray silk dress. "This was what she did while I was in Massachusetts."

William sighed as he studied the dress. "Now I know I was right to send her away. One sister dead by suicide, another in a lunatic asylum. It makes a man wonder about his own sanity."

"You?" I wrapped my arms around William. "You, my dear, are the sanest person I have ever known."

17

February 1864 to April 1865

The best that could be said on the subject of circumcision is, it is ridiculous. As to the "barbarity" which "shocks" the nerves of some weak brothers, I don't know that it is more barbarous, if as much, than piercing the ears of girls.

"I don't know about that," William said, reading the *Boston Investigator* over my shoulder. "I mean, I think it preferable that a man's member keep its natural form. With ears, it is a mere hole, and think of the nice earrings you are wearing." He poked one.

"You have a lovely member, and I would not change a thing about it. But circumcision is hardly castration."

"No. And with that, my darling, I think I shall go back to work."

~ ~ ~

The previous October, my dear friend Horace Seaver of the *Boston Investigator* had taken it upon himself to write upon the subject of "The Jews, Ancient and Modern." He was not at his best. He grumbled about being denied entrance to a Boston synagogue because he did not have a ticket, and having noted that the synagogue had once housed a Universalist Society, he added, *Although Universalism is not wholly to our taste, yet it is far better than Judaism. One is liberal, democratic, equal, and saves the entire human race; the other is bigoted, narrow, exclusive, and totally unfit for a progressive people like the Americans.*

A gentleman named Morris Einstein from Titusville, Pennsylvania, entered the lists on behalf of the Jews, but Mr. Seaver grew only more entrenched, complaining that the Boston Jews were strict in observing rituals, down to the "barbarity of circumcision." Then a John W. Cole, who I will not dignify with the name of "gentleman," wrote to snipe at Mr. Einstein and to add that he knew several Jewish families on his street, all of whom also practiced circumcision and could not possibly be equal to the Universalists.

(Evidently these men were very attached to their foreskins. Even William, as you have seen, seemed a little queasy on the subject.)

I could not stay silent, of course. In January, I responded to Mr. Seaver, while at the same time taking a hit at Mr. Cole. *Let us, as infidels, while promoting liberty and spreading useful knowledge, to prevent any sect from getting power, not add to the prejudice already existing towards the Jews, or any other sect.*

Sensible people would have let the matter rest there, but Mr. Seaver, Mr. Cole, Mr. Einstein, and I continued in this vein for weeks. Mr. Seaver continued to favor the Universalists; Mr. Einstein insisted upon the liberality of the Jews, particularly those in Titusville; Mr. Cole insulted Mr. Einstein; and I lectured Mr. Seaver, who accused me of losing my good temper. Because Mr. Seaver published the *Investigator*, he of course contrived to give himself the last word, and in April he finally got it, at least as far as I was concerned. (Mr. Einstein held out for several more issues.) I wrote: *Unless forced by further quibbles, insinuations, new issues, and prevarications, I am quite content to let the subject rest, satisfied in having done my duty in defense of justice.*

Simon and Bertha visited during this time and looked over the clippings from the *Investigator* that William had assembled. "Nicely done, sister," Simon said. He chuckled. "One of the Jewish papers is praising your 'Jewish spirit.' Careful, my dear, or we may lure you back."

Mr. Seaver and I remained friends, and I continued to take the *Investigator*—indeed, I still take it to this day, although dear Mr. Seaver and Mr. Mendum now lie in their graves. I say only one more thing on the subject: In 1867, Mr. Seaver finally gained admission to a meeting of the Warren Street Synagogue in Boston. Though he concluded that modern Jews were better than their ancient brethren, as he put it, he was justly offended that the rabbi spoke against infidels. Nothing, however, seemed to discomfit my old friend so much as being required to keep his hat on during the service. "Should I console Mr. Seaver with the fact that at least no one tried to circumcise him?"

"Better not, my dear."

~ ~ ~

In the meantime, the efforts of our Loyal League were bearing fruit: we gathered hundreds of thousands of signatures on petitions to Congress to abolish slavery throughout the nation. Senator Charles Sumner regularly hauled cartloads of petitions into the Senate, many of our own circulating. In January 1865, Congress at last passed the Thirteenth Amendment; it only had to be ratified by the states. No one was more responsible for the league's success than Susan, of course, but between the league and the war work so many ladies had been performing, we as a sex had shown the nation what women could do when we put our minds to it. Could the vote be far behind? With the South crumbling at last underneath General Grant's assault, anything seemed possible.

I was reading in our parlor on Ninth Street on April 3 (with William having moved his shop to Broadway the previous year, we had relocated to quieter quarters) when I heard shouts coming from outside. I flung open a window to see a crowd heading toward Broadway. I didn't even have to open my mouth before someone yelled in my direction, "Richmond has fallen!"

Everyone who had been following the war news—that is, everyone—had known that Richmond was bound to fall soon. But anticipating the news was a very different thing than hearing it. "Hurrah!" I cried, and ran outside.

Broadway was already exploding in flags and bunting, and lines were forming outside of taverns. Two pretty ladies rushed up to a man in blue and kissed him, while a gentleman wrung his hand. Outside of the St. Nicholas Hotel, a group of young men began singing "John Brown's Body" while a rival group countered with Mrs. Howe's "Battle Hymn of the Republic," which shared the same tune. One after another, church bells began to peal.

When I finally made it to William's shop, we embraced—we had the place to ourselves, as William had sent everyone home. "No one wants to work today, including me. I'll put up a little bunting—there's some left from the Union Jubilee—and then I'll lock up for the day."

With my help, William decked his windows with red, white, and blue. "How will we ever make it home through this crowd?" I asked once we had the place looking properly festive.

"Maybe we should stay here until things calm down, my

dear." William put his arms around me as we stared down at Broadway, which was indeed awash with humanity. "My back office is quite comfortable, you know. Perfect for a private celebration with very select company."

"Is it, now?" I leaned into his embrace. "Why, you rogue, you."

William nuzzled my neck. "Richmond doesn't fall every day, madam."

~ ~ ~

My brother Isidor was back in town—temporarily, as he was contemplating returning to England. The boy could not stay in one place. He had the unfortunate habit of gambling— Simon had often told him that if he had to gamble, he could at least do so in the stock market, where it was respectable— and he was always in some romantic entanglement with some completely unsuitable woman. So on Saturday, April 15, when he woke us out of a sound sleep by beating on the door, my first thought when I saw him weeping was censorious. "Isidor! What trouble are you in now? This must—"

"The president is dead. A villain shot him at the theater last night."

I lowered my hand, raised to chastise Isidor, and began crying too. William took the newspaper Isidor held and sank upon the sofa, his head in his hands.

Of course, I'd had my disagreements with Mr. Lincoln's policies. But he had brought us through this horrid war and shepherded the Thirteenth Amendment, and he was a good man.

New Yorkers spent the day wandering in a daze, rousing themselves only to drape their residences and businesses in mourning cloth, and Simon wrote to me that Washington was no different. Eventually, it was decided that Mr. Lincoln's body would be taken by special train to Springfield, Illinois, with stops in major cities for the public to pay its respects as the late president's body lay in state. New York, of course, was included, and after the days of desponding, it was refreshing to hear the city's leaders bicker about the arrangements. One thing was imperative: New York must not be outdone by any other city on the route.

The president's body, ferried from New Jersey, was taken to City Hall on April 24. I did not join the throngs that came to pay tribute to the fallen leader; I did not think I could stand in the queue that long, and on the whole I preferred to remember Mr. Lincoln as I had seen him at his Cooper Institute speech, especially as it was said that the embalmer was struggling to keep the corpse presentable for viewing. But on April 25, William and I, along with Isidor and a number of our friends, stood at the windows of William's business on Broadway, watching the funeral procession that would take place before the train proceeded to Albany. The men all wore black armbands; we women were garbed in black dresses; and most of us wore a mourning badge of some sort. Draped on the building was a banner with the president's likeness, and bearing the words:

Memento Mori
Born Feb. 12, 1809
Died April 15, 1865
Most strict in his observance of what was right
Most rigid in his adherence to justice

The newspapers estimated that seventy-five thousand people marched in the procession, and I believe it. But it was not the sheer numbers that impressed me as I watched the solemn procession file by. "This is what America looks like," I said. "Blacks and whites, military men and civilians, wealthy men and working men, immigrants and native-born Americans, Christians and Jews—and, I hope, infidels—marching as one. Two years ago, our city turned against its own; today, it is setting an example for the nation. But excuse me, I didn't mean to give a speech."

"You should make a habit of it," William said. "But one thing is missing in this procession—women."

"True." All around me, on the balconies, behind windows, atop roofs, and on the pavement, I could see women watching the procession, but none were included in it. "Well, we must leave that for another day, I suppose."

We watched the procession in silence, and not without tears, until the last row of men's footfalls died away. Then we embraced and went our separate ways, wondering what was to come.

18

MAY 1867 TO JUNE 1869

"You should consider going abroad, Mrs. Rose. I fear the climate here simply does not agree with you anymore. Taking the waters in a more congenial location would help you immensely, I believe."

"You are the third physician who has told my wife that," William said. "Isn't the third time the charm, my dear?"

The year after the war ended, we had held another woman's rights convention. I had been scheduled to speak, but as one gentleman speaker after another explained what was best for us ladies, I became more faint and more tired, and had elected not to take my turn on the platform. Word had gotten round to William, and since then no sign of ill health on my part had escaped him.

"Please, Ernestine," William said when we were alone. "I can arrange my business so that we can go abroad as long as we need to. It is important that you stay with us for years to come."

"I will consider it." I rubbed my aching back before I remembered and pulled my hand away. "But first, let me get through the convention." At the 1866 woman's rights convention, those in attendance, spurred by the success of the Loyal League, had formed an organization called the

American Equal Rights Association; this May would be the first anniversary of its founding. I saw William's hurt face. "I do not mean to put you off, my dear. I know you are worried. But I would like to do what I can before I am of no use to the world."

William sighed. "Save a little of yourself for me, my love."

~ ~ ~

"America has proclaimed to the world universal suffrage; but it is universal suffrage excluding the Negro and the woman, who are by far the largest number in this country. It is not the majority that rules here, but the minority. White men are in the minority in this nation. White women, black men, and black women compose the large majority of the nation. Yet in spite of this fact, in spite of common sense, in spite of justice, while our members of Congress can prate so long about justice, and human rights, and the rights of the Negro, they have not the moral courage to say anything for the rights of woman.

"Let woman have the franchise; let all the avenues of society be thrown open before her, according to her powers and her capacities."

Amid applause, I returned to my seat at the Church of the Puritans. (For an atheist, I reflected, I had spent a great deal of my life in churches.) My legs ached; I knew I would be confined to bed the next day. But at least I'd made a speech, which was a decided improvement over the past year.

Not only my health had been a disappointment to me, but Congress was annoying as well. We had sent a petition for universal suffrage, to include not only black men but we women as well, but it appeared to be going nowhere. It seemed that the energy and patriotism we had exhibited during the war had counted for very little.

Still, there was an encouraging sign: the state of Kansas had amendments pending that would give both blacks and women the right to vote. Lucy Stone and her faithful husband were campaigning there now, and Susan and Mrs. Stanton would be traveling there shortly. I had thought of going, but as William was already worried about me, I had not raised the possibility, and he had certainly not offered any encouragement. It was probably wise; Susan, whose brother had been there with John Brown for a time, and who had gone there herself for a visit during the war, had been full of stories about the peculiar illnesses that seemed to flourish in that young state.

So I stayed home, having put off the topic of Europe for a while, and watched from afar as poor Susan and Mrs. Stanton made utter fools of themselves in Kansas. There is no kinder way to put it.

The pair were seduced (I use the word figuratively, of course) by a man named George Francis Train, a wealthy adventurer who had become interested—I know not how—in woman's rights. He had aspirations of becoming president, despite having never held an office or won a war, and he quite often referred to blacks in the crudest terms. That alone should have alienated Susan and Mrs. Stanton, especially Susan, who had worked so hard for the abolitionist cause, but he charmed them—it helped that he kept clear of liquor and tobacco— and more importantly, he drew crowds when he appeared with them. But the crowds, despite agreeing that Mr. Train (who really should have taken to vaudeville) put on a fine show, did not vote for woman's suffrage, or for black suffrage. They voted against it, and both amendments went down in defeat that November. Still, my friends remained loyal to Mr. Train, especially after he offered them the funds to start a newspaper, the *Revolution*. There is no surer way to win a woman's heart than setting her up with her own newspaper.

I contributed to the *Revolution*, and I remained friends with both ladies, so I am in no position to be censorious. But the Kansas debacle strained relations between Susan and Mrs. Stanton and their fellow abolitionists, never to be entirely repaired.

At the 1868 convention, Lucy Stone, her husband Mr. Blackwell, and Stephen Foster sniped at Susan about wasting money on posters advertising Mr. Train, and about Mr. Train's unfortunate habit of spelling "Negro" with two *g*'s, as they put it. Susan defended herself nobly against the charge of excessive spending—she had no treasury, she pointed out, but was obliged to spend money first and collect it afterward, a task that she had always had to perform on her own—but the best she could say about Mr. Train was that he was a good card and was in favor of woman suffrage. Even the Hutchinson Family Singers, who were called to the stage frequently, could not bring any goodwill to the proceedings. I myself tried to calm the waters. "It is not for women alone that we have battled, but for the rights of all. But I have changed my mind as to suffrage. The ballot ought to be restricted to those who are characterized by honesty, rectitude, and honor. I would not allow the milkman who waters his milk to vote, nor the baker who gave us dyspnea. I will have nothing to do with the butcher. And when editors misrepresent a good cause and abuse each other, I will take the ballot away from them."

There was laughter throughout my little speech, which was all I could manage. But everyone went back to sniping afterward.

That evening, I told William that I was ready to seriously consider a trip abroad.

~ ~ ~

By May 1869, our passage from New York to Cherbourg was secured; our belongings were making their way to storage. Each day our flat in University Place got a little emptier. I could not be sad at the prospect of seeing France again, but I could not help but feel melancholy as I settled into my place at the annual meeting of the American Equal Rights Association. It was the last platform on which I would appear before we left New York; it was possible that I might never stand upon another platform in America.

But I was far from being the only discontented person who sat upon that platform. Congress had passed the Fifteenth Amendment, giving black men the vote, and although that was certainly a good thing, we women had been left out altogether. While the Fifteenth Amendment awaited ratification by the states, our dashed hopes now lay in working for a Sixteenth Amendment—unless Congress found some other cause to enshrine in an amendment of that number instead. Then there was the ongoing problem of Mr. Train—a stall upon the tracks, if I may be allowed. Being a supporter of many causes, he had gotten arrested by British authorities during a trip abroad for his support of the Fenian movement, which had made it impossible for him to give the *Revolution* all the support he had promised. Aware of the damage he had done to Susan and Mrs. Stanton, of whom he was said to be genuinely fond, he had stepped back from their cause. And then there was Mrs. Stanton, who had grumbled a few months ago, "Think of Patrick and Sambo and Hans and Yung Tung, who do not know the difference between a monarchy and a republic, who cannot read the Declaration of Independence or Webster's spelling book, making laws for Lucretia Mott or Ernestine L. Rose!"

"Sambo," I am afraid, was a phrase uttered by Mrs. Stanton far too often those days.

And so it was no surprise when, for two days in May, we engaged in our own little civil war. Mr. Foster told Susan and Mrs. Stanton they should resign their offices because of Mr. Train. Frederick Douglass and Susan argued over whether the black man should be given the vote before women. A woman mounted the platform to inform us that our problems could be solved with a celestial kite. A lady from Chicago wanted us to denounce free love, which to me would only be taken in the spirit of "The lady doth protest too much." I argued with a reverend gentleman over whether Massachusetts (his position) or New York (mine) could claim to be the birthplace of the woman's rights movement, and with a Western lady over which city's newspaper reporters could be trusted more, those of Chicago (her position) or New York (mine). Mr. Burleigh made repeated attempts to speak, and then, when Susan demanded that he be allowed to do so, refused to say anything. Women hissed at men, and men hissed at women. Mr. Douglass grumbled that this had turned into a woman's rights meeting. The only respite was when Madame Anneke gave a speech in German and Madame d'Héricourt in French, and this was mainly because most did not understand what they were saying. I remembered the days when Captain Rynders and his b'hoys had thrown reform meetings into chaos; now we were doing this quite nicely all by ourselves.

When not arguing about free love, newspaper reporters, or birthplaces, I listened to the proceedings and came out with two convictions: we could no longer afford to subsume the issue of woman suffrage beneath other issues, and we could no longer trust to men to support us. These were not bad men; to the contrary, Mr. Douglass, Mr. Phillips, Mr. Garrison, Mr. Burleigh, and their fellows were some of the best men the nation could offer. But our cause was not theirs, and it was time to stop telling ourselves otherwise.

What were the wise Rabbi Hillel's words, after all? *If I am not for myself, who will be for me? If I am only for myself, what am I? And if not now, when?*

Cooper Institute was packed the evening I gave my speech; our dissensions had only increased attendance. "Congress has enacted resolutions for the suffrage of men and brothers. They don't speak of the women and sisters. They have begun to change their tactics, and call it manhood suffrage. I propose to call it woman suffrage; then we shall know what we mean. We might commence by calling the Chinaman a man and a brother, or the Hottentot, or the Calmuck, or the Indian, the idiot or the criminal, but where shall we stop? They will bring all these in before us, and then they will bring in the babies—the *male* babies."

The crowd laughed at my words about the Chinaman and the Hottentot as I inwardly wished I could take them back. The product of my frustration, they were unworthy, and too reminiscent of the Sambo-ing that had justly offended Mr. Douglass.

"I am a foreigner. I had great difficulty in acquiring the English language, and I never shall acquire it. But I am afraid that in the meaning of language Congress is a great deal worse off than I have ever been. I will not be construed into a man and a brother. I ask the same rights for women that are extended to men—the right to life, liberty, and the pursuit of happiness; and every pursuit in life must be as free and open to me as any man in the land. But they will never be thrown open to me or to any of you, until we have the power of the ballot in our own hands. That little paper is a great talisman. We have often been told that the golden key can unlock all the doors. That little piece of paper can unlock doors where golden keys fail."

That was more like it. "Wherever men are—whether in the workshop, in the store, in the laboratory, or in the legislative halls—I want to see women. Wherever man is, there she is needed; wherever man has work to do—work for the benefit of humanity—there should men and women unite and cooperate together. It is not well for man to be alone or work alone, but he cannot work for woman as well as woman can work for herself."

I took a final breath, to make sure what I said next was perfectly audible. "I move that the name of this society be changed from the Equal Rights Association to the Woman Suffrage Association."

Hisses, gasps, and applause filled the room. Mrs. Stone arose. "I cannot support such a change until the colored man has gained the right to vote."

"I by no means want to have the black man thrown overboard," I said. "I merely want the association to have a name—and a purpose—that cannot be misunderstood. We women have given others precedence for too long."

There was a great deal more talk, brought to a halt when Mrs. Stanton decided that the organization's constitution prevented a name change on short notice. But Susan nudged me. "Just you wait, Mrs. Rose," she whispered.

On Saturday evening, I attended a reception for convention attendees at the *Revolution*'s headquarters on East Twenty-Third Street, in a fine house known as the Woman's Bureau because its owner had made it available for women's causes. I went somewhat reluctantly, as I was tired from the convention itself, but I knew this was my last chance to see some of these people, so I put myself in order and proceeded uptown. The place was packed, with ladies even congregating on the stairs, but I noticed that neither Mrs. Stone nor her husband were present.

After allowing us some time to chat, Susan herded us into a double parlor. When we had squeezed ourselves into the space as best we could—I was both grateful and humiliated when a younger woman offered her chair to me— Susan said, "I realize that we are fresh from a meeting, but necessity has determined that we hold yet another one. Many of you, I know, are unhappy with our recent meeting—"

"Most of us," Mrs. Stanton said. She was looking particularly jolly.

"Most of you. Mrs. Rose suggested a change of name, and with it a change of purpose, but I think we must make an even greater change than that. There is a faction in the association who will never consent to woman suffrage taking the lead, and who will be a millstone around our necks. Rather, I propose that we form a new organization. Mrs. Rose has already named it for us, save for one word—the National Woman Suffrage Association. Our goal, to which all will be subsumed, will be to work for a Sixteenth Amendment, securing the vote for women."

The cheers made East Twenty-Third Street shake.

It was late when I returned home; William was already in bed. "What have you ladies been up to?" he mumbled.

I curled up next to him. "Not much. We started a new organization that will be working for a Sixteenth Amendment, drew up its constitution, and appointed officers."

"Just ladies' frivolities, then."

"Just ladies' frivolities. Oh, and some ladies wanted men banned from the organization, but I told them I would not join an association where my husband was not welcome. So with that silliness out of the way, all is well." I kissed William on the cheek. "Good night, darling."

There has been talk, over the years, that Susan and Mrs. Stanton shut Mrs. Stone out of the formation of the National Woman Suffrage Association (a pleasant-sounding name, if I must say so myself), and I cannot say for certain that it is false. But Mrs. Stone would not have been in sympathy, I am quite sure, for she was willing to postpone agitating for woman suffrage until the Fifteenth Amendment was safely ratified, and we were not. In any event, she soon started *her* own suffrage organization and *her* own newspaper, which Mr. Blackwell knew how to place on a sound financial footing. Unlike the *Revolution*, which would became insolvent, Mrs. Stone's *Women's Journal* still thrives, and no doubt will publish my obituary in due course.

But I get ahead of myself. Susan had named me as chairman of the NWSA's executive committee, which meant that I could no longer keep quiet about my departure to Europe.

At the Woman's Bureau, I found Susan seated at a desk already heaped with NWSA material. "I am here on a rather foolish mission. Susan, I am honored to be named to chair the executive committee, but I cannot fulfill my duties.

William and I are leaving for Europe in just a few weeks, for my health. We will be there indefinitely."

"This cannot have been a sudden decision."

"No. William and I have been planning this for some time."

"You are the most contrary, closed-mouthed, oddest creature I have met in my life. Did you tell no one you are leaving?"

"No—only those who had to know for business reasons. You are the first of my friends to know."

"Well, I consider myself honored. What were you planning on doing? Disappearing from New York and then sending us a note from Europe?"

"No, I am not quite that bad. I did plan on bidding everyone goodbye properly." I gazed out of the window onto East Twenty-Third Street. "The truth is, I hate to leave, and talking of it only makes it worse. America is my home, for all of its faults. I feel that it and I have matured together. But my health is getting no better, and William wants me to go. I cannot continue to make him uneasy about me."

"He is a good man. You are right to want to please him. But we shall miss you so, so much."

I suspected both of us were going to cry if we continued in this vein. "Perhaps you could travel there yourself one day. More than any of us, you could stand a holiday."

Susan was as grateful to be diverted from the melting mood as I was. "After the Sixteenth Amendment passes."

~ ~ ~

William and I stood on the deck of the steamer *Holsatia*, watching New York slip from view.

We were surrounded by flowers, brought to us by our friends in the days before our departure. Mr. Mendum had organized the effort among our infidel friends, and Susan, of course, among our woman's rights friends. Each had collected a monetary testimonial as well. "How on earth did you find time for this?" I had asked both of them.

"Why, you know what busy bees we infidels are," Mr. Mendum said.

"Well, you certainly didn't make it easy," said Susan.

I hadn't bothered to conceal my tears at our partings. Neither had William and our friends.

Our last days in New York had been hectic, but I had made time for one task, even though it had required a visit to the courthouse. I fingered the precious paper, folded carefully in my pocket, as the cityscape faded out of view.

Henceforth, no matter where I might find myself, I would be a citizen of the United States.

19

January 1871 to February 1871

"According to our landlady, Jane Austen visited an aunt on this street," I said, gesturing out of our window. "If only she could see Bath now."

Having taken the waters in a number of pleasant places on the Continent until the outbreak of war between France and Prussia in July 1870 made it prudent to travel to England, we had found our way to Bath in December and decided to stay there for the winter. We could live there economically, and it was an attractive place, with baths to soak in and handsome parks in which to amble. But its Regency gaiety and dash had fled, and the pall of religion hung over the town. Save for those who went to church, no one ventured out on Sundays; even the dogs stayed inside. I had a dismal picture in my mind of them lying in front of fires, their heads dutifully tucked between their paws as their masters read the Bible aloud.

But today was a Thursday, and the Paragon, where we lodged in a crescent of Georgian rowhouses, was bustling with people and dogs alike.

"Shall we go out on our walk, my dear? It's a fine afternoon."

"Yes. I promise not to complain about religion anymore. For the moment, anyway."

"That is quite a sacrifice."

I took William's arm—how dapper he looked!—and we sallied forth.

As we neared Bath's Guildhall, we saw a placard inviting the public to a meeting to support two lady candidates for the local school board. I confess that I had not kept up with the local papers, rather snobbishly reading the London papers instead. I did know, however, that Parliament, in a paroxysm of liberality, had extended the vote to women— but only for municipal issues, such as school board elections, and only to unmarried women who met certain property qualifications. And now Bath had not one but two women seeking election to the school board? Perhaps I had underestimated this old city. "Lady candidates? Shall we go to this meeting?"

"By all means," William said.

We went inside the Guildhall to find a crowd assembled, including an encouraging number of ladies. Aside from the lady aspect, the school board served a noble purpose— educating the poor—so William and I listened attentively. The chairman of the committee that had nominated the ladies, a Unitarian clergyman known as Mr. Murch, gave a rather long speech in praise of the ladies in question—it evidently being considered improper that they speak for themselves.

Then a lady got to her feet. "I feel obliged to present to you this letter by Miss Burdett-Coutts, regarding the propriety of ladies serving on school boards."

Miss Burdett-Coutts, a banking heiress, was immensely rich. She was a friend to education and the poor, and no fool by any means; yet when someone had suggested that she might serve on a London school board, she had declined. *I entertain a strong opinion that the presence of a lady could only be an embarrassment to the discussions which must take place at the board. . . . My early and long experience of electioneering life during my late father's lifetime has deeply impressed me with the feeling that it is best for the advantage of us all that ladies should not enter into its toilsome and difficult arena.*

There had been a palpable enthusiasm for the ladies before, which Miss Burdett-Coutts's letter instantly squelched. Many applauded, while some ladies looked at each other in alarm. Mr. Murch, looking much discomposed, asked, "Does anyone wish to be heard as to Miss Burdett-Coutts's letter?"

"Yes." I rose. "I would like to say a few words."

Mr. Murch assented, and I made my way to the platform as the audience murmured. Had not the people of Bath heard a woman speak before? Having introduced myself, and found that my voice carried across the room, I said, "Ladies and gentlemen, I ought to apologize for the liberty I have taken in appealing to the chair to allow me to make a few remarks, but I have all my lifetime been interested in the education of all parties, particularly in the education of my own sex. Had I not heard that little paragraph coming from a lady who presumes to oppose the nomination of ladies on the school board, I should not have ventured to ask permission to say anything—first, because there are enough present to say all that need be said on the subject, and secondly, as I am here only for my health, I am hardly strong enough to be heard or to say what I ought to say on this all-important and interesting question. But if I ever had been in doubt that the world moves, that doubt has been removed by what I have heard today. Yes, the world moves. Woman is actually beginning to be considered as a human being—as a human being who has influences beyond the boudoir, the ballroom, and the theater, for those, until very recently, have been the only places assigned to her except the kitchen and the cradle."

Someone timidly applauded, while others nervously laughed.

"Now, in all these places it is very desirable that the influence of woman for good should be felt, particularly so in the kitchen and at the cradle; but woman can have influences beyond all these—above all things, where the education of the young is concerned. Why, woman, in her capacity as nurse and as mother, is the educator of society. She lays the first fundamental principles in the mind of the child, which are hardly ever eradicated.

"I am a resident, if not a native (which I presume by my foreign accent you may probably discover) of the United States of America. There it is almost a settled fact that woman is a human being; that she has a mind, and that that mind requires cultivation; that she has wants and needs, which wants and needs require assistance. Hence, we are over there—don't be frightened at the name—a 'woman's rights' people. 'Woman's rights' simply means 'human rights,' and no woman earnest enough to claim those rights would for one moment have them based upon the wrongs of any human being. When we claim the right of woman to life, liberty, and the pursuit of happiness, we claim that she shall be able to bring up our children, to lead our youth, to assist our manhood, and to aid the great family of man to become healthy, intelligent, and happy members of society.

"I thank you, my friends, for the privilege you have given me to address you, and will not further abuse it."

This time, there was no hesitation about the applause.

William smiled at me as I resumed my seat. "There you go again," he whispered.

Mr. Murch was smiling too. "In the name of the meeting, Mrs. Rose, I would like to thank you. It is uncommon for us to be addressed by a lady—but I must say, I would like to see more of this."

I had, in effect, robbed the banking heiress (or at least her proxy) of a victory. First one and then the other lady candidate was nominated, and both were carried by a large margin.

Mr. Murch waylaid me as I was preparing to leave and asked if I would meet with the ladies and advise them on their course of action. Having helped carry their nomination, I could hardly refuse. I could prevail on only one of the two ladies to speak in front of the crowd the following week, but the one I did persuade did a noble job of it, and I agreed to say a word myself. "No great undertaking can ever succeed without the combined elements of man and woman. I have heard that man is the head, and woman the heart, but what is man without heart, and woman without head? I ask you to vote for these candidates, not because they are ladies, but so that you might assist those ladies to do their duty to help educate the boys and girls of your city."

On Tuesday, Bath elected both ladies to the school board. "Staid old Bath," I said as we sat reading the city's papers in our lodgings on the Paragon. "It will never be quite the same, will it?"

William smiled at me. "All it took was just a little help from the New World."

20

JANUARY 1882 TO JULY 1892

More than two decades have passed since our sojourn at Bath. Now, I am preparing to leave for Brighton and, as you have probably deduced, am not at all dead. But my supply of paper is nearly exhausted, and so, in truth, am I. Yet I must tell the one thing I most dread telling.

William and I did return to America in 1873, but it proved to be only a temporary stay. I fell seriously ill soon after arriving, as if to prove all the doctors right, and we decided to sell William's business and return to England. There, we settled in London, with me giving the occasional lecture until my health would no longer permit me to do so. Even then, we lived contentedly, and had a small circle of friends. Then, on January 26, 1882, my dear William, going to the City to see our solicitor, kissed me goodbye and promised to be home in time for tea, as he had on so many days.

Teatime came, and no William.

Someone knocked, and I caned my way to the door to find our solicitor, Mr. Philip Justice, there. As he took off his hat and looked mournfully at me, I knew. "I have very bad news for you, Mrs. Rose. The worst, in fact."

"Is it William?"

"Yes."

"He is ill?" Silence. "He is dead?"

"Yes. A heart attack, it seems."

I swayed, and Mr. Justice steered me to a chair. As I sat there, speechless, he said, "Mr. Rose came to my office, as you likely know, to discuss your investments. He appeared to be in perfectly good health and spirits, and the suggestions he made were quite sound. His one concern appeared to be about your health. He said that the winter was hard on you and he was thinking it might be good to give you a change of scene for a few weeks. We talked a little about the places where the two of you might go. He gave no sign of being in any sort of pain. Soon after he left, my clerk heard a commotion outside. Mr. Rose had collapsed on the pavement and was insensible. Every attempt was made to revive him, but from the moment he fell he appears to have been entirely unconscious. He was carried to St. Bartholomew Hospital as soon as could be done, but died on the way. There will have to be an inquest, but everyone agreed that it appeared to be his heart."

I seemed to have lost the capacity for speaking English.

Somehow I had always assumed that it was I who would go first, with my last sight in the world being William's loving face. I had never thought that our last encounter would consist of a quick kiss and a few inconsequential remarks.

In the days after my dear one's death—William was sixty-nine, but in my eyes had never grown old at all—I could not have been more useless. My friends arranged the funeral, which was largely attended. Our friend and fellow freethinker Mr. Charles Bradlaugh spoke at the graveside at Highgate Cemetery, but I do not remember a thing he said, only his supporting me away when all was done.

On those lonely days—every day—when I wake up without my William, and have nothing but his letters, his photographs, and his portrait to comfort me, I tell myself that I was very lucky, that not every woman can say that she met with the one person who humored her, who put up with her foibles, who understood her utterly. That sort of happiness cannot last forever.

I know all that, and yet I can only say this: I miss him more than words can describe.

Susan and Mrs. Stanton visited London not long after William died (Susan having decided that the lack of a Sixteenth Amendment, or any amendment, should not deprive her of a well-needed holiday) and tried to talk me into returning to America. I was tempted, but it would mean leaving my dear one behind, and I intend to be buried with him, our dust mingling together. It is a subject on which I am inflexible and adamant. On fair days when I am feeling up to it (two occurrences that coincide less and less as time plods on), I visit his grave and tend the flowers I have planted there. Although they will no doubt have to be pulled up when my time comes, I like the notion of some life springing up around him, and I like to know that someday I will be brought there, never to be parted from him again.

I have not spoken in public since William's death. For the first few years, well-meaning people asked me to do so, more as a kindness than anything, but I knew it would be farcical. My voice barely carries across a room, much less a hall; I cannot stand for more than a few minutes without assistance; and—yes—my mind wanders now and then. It would be a pitiful sight. And in any case, there are younger, stronger ladies to carry on in my stead, with their own ways of doing things, so it is best to give them their turn. There is much to be said in knowing when one's day is done.

As I pass my time in London, my family has grown smaller and more scattered. William, kind soul that he was, had weighed the possibility of taking Mary Ann from the asylum and placing her in the care of a paid companion, but her doctors advised against that, as she still at times threatened violence to herself or others—those others being William and me. She died in Colney Hatch in 1874, having spent her last couple of years there placidly enough. Bertha divorced Simon for adultery, after which Simon married a pert young lady less than two weeks later. (By all accounts, they are quite happy together.) Isidor, having made an ill-advised marriage after the war, divorced his wife for adultery and resumed wandering the world—the last I heard, he was in Australia. My brother Bertrand, having in due course come to America, married a sweet young Jewish girl, but succumbed to liver disease. Sophie died a couple of years after William, and two of her daughters are gone as well. Yet I hang on.

Sometimes I have thought of helping myself to my end. With a little planning I could probably procure enough opium to kill a horse, let alone an old lady weighing a hundred pounds. But it would dismay my friends, who no doubt would reproach themselves as to how they could have made my life easier, expose the kind and conscientious Miss Byrne to charges of neglect or perhaps even worse, and mortify the little family I have left. Besides, there is always the possibility that I might bungle the dose and only make a fool of myself instead of a corpse. So none too graciously, I have consented to let time and nature take me when they choose, and have even submitted to the entirely unwanted advice of my physician, Dr. Washington Epps, as to how I can prolong my existence. Hence, I eat my meals, take my tonics, and, each summer, depart for the healthful air of Brighton. I allow Miss Byrne to ring Dr. Epps every week from the nearest call office, not so much because there is anything new to report but because Miss Byrne loves ringing people.

(Miss Byrne, by the way, came to me at the insistence of Mr. Justice after an annoying incident when I burned my finger while making tea—a mere accident that could happen to anyone, surely. He told me that I could afford to pay for help, and that William would want to make certain I was well looked after. Mr. Justice knew William's memory had this power over me, and I knew he knew, but its invocation nevertheless always had its desired effect. I submitted, and Miss Byrne came to stay. He is a clever man, Mr. Justice.)

The day before yesterday, Miss Byrne rang my great-niece Anna Allinson, who lives in London and is one of Sophie's granddaughters, to tell her that I would be departing soon (for Brighton, that is), and Anna told her that she would pay a call the very next day.

"Just Mrs. Allinson is coming," Miss Byrne said. "Not her rascal of a husband."

"You still don't care for Dr. Allinson?"

"No, ma'am. Not after he suggested that you give up wearing a corset. That was indecent. And as for him telling you that you should give up meat—well, that was just plain cruel. I told him then and I'll tell him now: Mrs. Rose likes her mutton, and anyone takes it away from her over my dead body."

"Quite right. But I think we need not serve any meat to Mrs. Allinson when she comes."

"If you say so, ma'am. But if she brings it up, I'll tell her that Dr. Epps wants you to have meat, and that is that."

"Yes. One physician telling me what to do is quite enough."

Yesterday, Anna came, bearing a loaf of whole meal bread, which Miss Byrne took from her politely enough, although I suspected some mishap would occur to the bread before we left for Brighton. Anna was a tiny woman, trim in spite of having borne her second child the year before, and had forsworn corsets as well as meat. We were chatting about a variety of things, when I said, "You will vote someday."

Anna blinked, and I realized that my mind had taken a detour. "I beg your pardon. We were talking about—"

"Brighton, but I do hope I will vote someday, and I will thank you when I do."

"Many others will deserve your thanks as well. Sometimes I feel that our cause is hopeless, but then I remember that it is a young one, and the world is very old. We go forward, and we go backward, but on the whole I think we are going more forward than backward."

I must have been looking tired—as indeed I was— because Anna rose to go. "I doubt I will be able to visit you in Brighton, as it is such a nuisance to travel with my boys, but I will come see you when you return to London."

"You will not take offense if I say I hope I never do return to London—alive, that is. I am hoping the journey to Brighton will wear me out for good this time."

"If I may ask, do you have any fear of death?"

I shook my head. "I have always believed that we should worry about this life, and let the next—if there is one, which I still doubt—take care of itself. As I can do nothing now, it is no longer necessary for me to live. It is high time nature understood that."

Anna embraced me. "Then I will say goodbye, and hope it is our last one."

With Anna gone, I watched Miss Byrne pack for our departure to Brighton. Then after a light supper (Anna's bread did not make an appearance), it was time to retire. "You remember your duty, Miss Byrne, in case I should fall ill during the night?" I asked as she helped me into my nightclothes and into bed.

"Yes. I am to keep away anyone who might try to bring you around to religion while you're poorly. Though I'd like to see the fool that would try. If you've got a breath in you, you won't put up with it. But didn't I promise that just the other day, Mrs. Rose? Haven't all your friends promised you that?"

"Yes, well, I worry. But I know I can count on you."

With my mind at ease that Miss Byrne knew her duty, I let my memories lull me to sleep. Papa and Mama and Sophie. Marcus and Amalia. Our darling Joseph. My friends, my colleagues on the platform. William, always William. Pulling out a chair for me at Robert Owen's meeting. Applauding after I gave my first speech in halting English. Kissing me on the steamer after our marvelous day at Greenwich.

It is true, as I told Anna, I can do nothing now. But I did what I could, and no matter what is spoken over my grave when I am brought there to lie with dear William, I am certain it will include this: that I have lived.

EPILOGUE

AUGUST 1892

*Our great pioneer & leader in suffrage Ernestine L. Rose died in
Brighton Eng. this day.*

—Susan B. Anthony, diary entry for August 4, 1892

Author's Note

Ernestine Rose suffered a stroke on August 1, 1892, and died three days later, having been unconscious most of the time. A friend and fellow freethinker, Hypatia Bradlaugh Bonner, noted that "her last hours passed away peacefully and were quite untroubled by any thoughts of religion." Ernestine was buried in the same grave as William Ella Rose, as she had wished. The news of her death was widely reported, both in England and in the United States.

Much of what is known of Ernestine Rose's early life originates in a biographical article published in 1856 by her fellow reformer Jenny P. d'Héricourt in a French journal. There, d'Héricourt wrote that Ernestine had two children whom she "cherished, nurtured with her milk, and whom she tragically lost at a very early age." She also told the stories of Ernestine's youthful rejection of religion, her defending her inheritance in court after refusing an arranged marriage, her father's remarriage to a considerably younger woman, her departure for Berlin, her meeting with the king, her supporting herself through selling perfumed papers and teaching Hebrew and German, her involvement with Robert Owen's movement, and her eventual emigration for America with William. But there is one significant episode in Ernestine's life not found in d'Héricourt's account, or in any contemporary or modern biography of Ernestine. If you have gone a-Googling while reading this novel—as I like to do while reading historical fiction—you may have concluded that Ernestine's relationship with Marcus Kaufmann is entirely fictional, a case of literary license run amok. It is not.

Quite accidentally, I discovered Ernestine's first marriage when researching her family background and have presented my findings in a 2023 article, "The Early Life and Family of Feminist Ernestine Rose: New Findings and an Old Secret," in a peer-reviewed publication, *The Journal of Genealogy and Family History*. (It is available online and can be viewed by the public at no charge; there is a link on my website.) To recite all the evidence here would be repetitive, so suffice it to say that German records show that an Ernestine Luisa Süssmund, the daughter of a rabbi named Nathan Süssmund from the small city of Praszka, Poland, was baptized alongside a bookseller named Marcus Simon Kaufmann, bore his child, and married him, in that order. An obituary of Ernestine, and records pertaining to her sister Sophie, her nieces, and her half-siblings, make it clear that her father was Nathan Sigismund, Süssmund, Züssmund, or some variation thereof (the surname is rendered in what seems an endless variety of ways in the records, and each of Ernestine's siblings spelled it differently) and that he died in Praszka after having fathered a number of children there by his second wife, Liba. Further evidence that "our" Ernestine was the woman who married Marcus Kaufmann can be found in an 1835 issue of Robert Owen's newspaper *The New Moral World*, which mentions a speech by "Mrs. Kaufmann (an intelligent Polish lady)," and by the ship manifest of the *Napier* for May 14, 1836, which shows that William Ella Rose (rendered as William "Miller" Rose) traveled to America alongside not Ernestine "Rose" but

Ernestine "Houffman," the only Polish passenger aboard. (Passenger lists were compiled from information given by ticketing agents; presumably the Roses had not yet married when their passage was booked.)

Although in my research I did discover a number of facts about Ernestine's family, including the names of her parents and her half-siblings, many questions remain to be answered. It is unknown when and how Ernestine's marriage to Marcus Kaufmann ended, but records suggest that he was living in London after Ernestine had married William, which leads me to believe that Ernestine's first marriage ended in divorce (Prussian divorce law being surprisingly liberal at the time). It seems likely to me that the Marcus Kauffman who died in the St. Marylebone Workhouse infirmary in 1847 was Ernestine's former husband (despite the spelling difference), but I cannot be certain of this. While Amalia Kaufmann must be the first of Ernestine's two children mentioned by d'Héricourt as dying young, I do not know where, when, or how she died. Nothing at all is known about Ernestine's second child—not even whether he or she was fathered by Marcus Kaufmann or by William Rose. If Ernestine and William did have a child together, it may have been in the early 1840s, a period where newspapers show a gap in Ernestine's lecturing activity. No child came to America with them in 1836, and no child appears in their household in the 1840 census. We also know nothing of Ernestine and William's courtship—but contemporaries commented on William's devotion to his wife and on Ernestine's intense grief after William's heart attack in 1882.

While the unknowns in Ernestine's story necessitated some imaginative filling in of the gaps, I have stayed as close to known fact as possible. Most of the characters in this novel actually lived, although I had to invent the name of Ernestine's would-be husband, Saul Levinsky. Mrs. Turner, the first person to sign Ernestine's petition, is fictitious, as are some minor characters such as the bookseller who rescues young Ernestine from a group of bullies, Ernestine's Parisian friends from 1830, Amalia's nursemaid, Ernestine and William's Irish servant, the ladies Ernestine meets at Niagara Falls, the reporter Chester Dow, Ernestine's infant brothers Jacob and David, and Ernestine's aunt Rachel.

Ernestine would have been given a Yiddish or Hebrew name at birth, as were her half-brothers, but no one knows what that name is, so I bestowed the unimaginative "Esther" upon her.

The visit the Roses pay to the Cataract House in Niagara Falls is fictitious, but the waiters at the hotel were indeed active in the Underground Railroad.

An oil painting depicting a supposed ritual murder of a Christian child was removed from the outer wall of the Bernardine Church in Piotrków Trybunalski in 1794, but was eventually returned and remained in place until 1825.

William's sister Hannah did indeed kill herself, and the unfortunate Mary Ann died in the Colney Hatch Lunatic Asylum, to which she was admitted in October 1863 after having returned from America. (In a rare moment of consideration for future researchers, someone at the asylum noted William's name and address, thus linking this Mary Ann to William with certainty.) Nothing is known of the personalities of William's mother and sisters, so it is quite possible that I was rather unfair to them here. William's parents certainly deserve credit for bestowing the middle name "Ella" upon their son; it made searching for William's family amongst the huge bouquet of Roses in London a much easier task.

In a couple of her few recorded statements about her past, Ernestine alluded to being present in Paris during the July 1830 revolution. It is unclear whether the Roses witnessed the Draft Riots of 1863 (it is possible that they had left the city for the summer, as they did the following year), but having them on the scene was too tempting an opportunity to resist. Likewise, there is no evidence that the couple went to Abraham Lincoln's famous Cooper Union speech or that they witnessed the massive funeral procession for the late president. William's office, on Broadway in what is now SoHo, was ideally situated for viewing the procession, however.

Lucy Stone complained in an 1855 letter to Susan B. Anthony that she believed that Ernestine's "so essentially Jewish" face had repelled audiences in Cincinnati, but there is no indication that Ernestine knew of this remark. Ernestine did regard Lucy as hostile to foreigners, as Susan B. Anthony recorded in her diary in 1854. Lucy Stone, of course, was hardly alone among reformers in using bigoted rhetoric; even Ernestine stooped to it in her 1869 speech to the American Equal Rights Association.

Ernestine's speeches in the novel are taken, whenever possible, from newspapers and other sources of the period, although they have been shortened considerably and altered slightly for clarity or continuity. In some cases where her speech was not recorded, I have borrowed from earlier or later speeches of hers.

Those who wish to learn more about Ernestine Rose may want to read the biographies by Yuri Suhl, Carol A. Kolmerten, and Joyce B. Lazarus, supplemented by my findings in the article mentioned above. Paula Doress-Worters has collected a number of Ernestine's speeches and writings in a book entitled *Mistress of Herself: Speeches and Letters of Ernestine L. Rose, Early Women's Rights Leader*.

Ernestine Louise Rose did not live to see the passage of the Nineteenth Amendment, granting women the right to vote, and neither did stalwarts such as Susan B. Anthony, Elizabeth Cady Stanton, Lucretia Mott, and Lucy Stone. One woman mentioned in these pages, however, did survive long enough to vote in a presidential election: On November 2, 1920, ninety-five-year-old Antoinette Brown Blackwell, blind and frail, was driven by her daughter to her local polling place, to which she brought a camp stool in case she had to wait. After being waved to the front of the line, she cast her vote for Warren G. Harding.

ACKNOWLEDGMENTS

In researching *The Queen of the Platform*, I received assistance from the staff of a number of research institutions, including, in no order whatsoever, the Columbia University Rare Book and Manuscript Library, Harvard University's Houghton Library, Radcliffe's Schlesinger Library, the Huntington Library, the Library of Congress, Smith College Special Collections, Boston University's Howard Gotlieb Archival Research Center, the Chicago History Museum, the Maine Historical Society, the Massachusetts Historical Society, the American Antiquarian Society, the Wisconsin Historical Society, the Co-operative Heritage Trust Archive, the Bangor Public Library, the London Metropolitan Archives, the Historic New Orleans Collection, the Boston Public Library, the Vassar College Library, the University of Tulsa's McFarlin Library, the University of North Carolina at Chapel Hill's Wilson Library, Brown University, Green-Wood Cemetery, and the Bishopgate Institute's Special Collections and Archives. I have purposely avoided naming individual staff members, as I would most certainly leave out someone inadvertently. All of these institutions and their staff deserve our gratitude for keeping history alive and accessible.

Theresa Berns professionally translated a number of German records for me, and Saskia Albert kindly helped as well. Dr. Przemysław Jędrzejewski assisted me in tracking down Polish records.

Dee Dee Book Covers designed my cover, and Aaron Redfern at Historical Editorial helped me bring this project to fruition with his copy editing services. Working with them was a pleasure.

I have no doubt I have left out someone deserving of thanks. My apologies and appreciation.

Naturally, I would like to thank my husband, Don Coomes, and my children, Thad and Bethany Coomes, for their forbearance and encouragement. Sadly, we had to say goodbye to our sweet friend Dudley during the writing of this novel, but Emmy remains on guard duty, and Annie has brought new feline felicity to our lives.

Most of all, however, I would like to thank my readers. You give me—and other authors—a reason to sit down at the keyboard and to sometimes even write something.

About the Author

Susan Higginbotham is the author of a number of historical novels set in medieval and Tudor England and, more recently, nineteenth-century America, including *The Traitor's Wife*, *The Stolen Crown*, *Hanging Mary*, *The First Lady and the Rebel*, and *John Brown's Women*. She and her family, human and four-footed, live in Maryland. When not writing or procrastinating, Susan enjoys traveling and collecting old photographs. Visit her website, *History Refreshed*, at www.susanhigginbotham.com, and look for her on Facebook as "Susan Higginbotham, Author."